STORIES FROM THE EDGE OF POSSIBILITY

"Storming the Cosmos," written in collaboration with Rudy Rucker, shows how America won the race to the moon . . . with some help from Soviet bureaucracy and a sentient machine from beyond the stars.

Ghettos of civilization are surrounded by a world gone back to the wild in "The Shores of Bohemia."

An ensouled artificial intelligence becomes the first dimensionaut for the glory of Allah, "The Compassionate, the Digital."

In a chaotic American city patrolled by ragtag militias like the Chamber of Commerce and the Library Defense League, a conscienceless scientist must face the hellish landscape he has created, in "The Moral Bullet," a collaboration with John Kessel.

A mysterious smuggler makes the most of chaos in the crumbling former Soviet Union in "Hollywood Kremlin."

ALSO BY BRUCE STERLING

novels

The Artificial Kid

The Difference Engine (with William
Gibson)

Heavy Weather

Involution Ocean

Islands in the Net

Schismatrix

stories

Crystal Express

nonfiction

The Hacker Crackdown: Law and Disorder
on the Electronic Frontier

editor

Mirrorshades: the Cyberpunk Anthology

GLOBALHEAD

STORIES BY
BRUCE STERLING

BANTAM BOOKS
NEW YORK • TORONTO • LONDON • SYDNEY • AUCKLAND

This edition contains the complete text of the original hardcover edition.
NOT ONE WORD HAS BEEN OMITTED.

GLOBALHEAD

A Bantam Spectra Book/published by arrangement with the author

PUBLISHING HISTORY
Mark V. Ziesing hardcover edition/1992
Bantam paperback edition/November 1994

Our Neural Chernobyl—First published in The Magazine of Fantasy and Science Fiction, June 1988. © 1988 by Mercury Press, Inc. *Storming the Cosmos*—by Bruce Sterling and Rudy Rucker—First published in Isaac Asimov's Science Fiction Magazine, Mid-December 1985. © 1985 by Davis Publications, Inc. *The Compassionate, the Digital*—First published in Interzone #14, Winter 1985. © 1985 by Bruce Sterling. *Jim and Irene*—First published in WHEN THE MUSIC'S OVER, edited by Lewis Shiner. Bantam Spectra 1991. © 1991 by Bruce Sterling. *The Sword of Damocles*—First published in Isaac Asimov's Science Fiction Magazine, February 1990. © 1990 by Davis Publications, Inc. *The Gulf Wars*—First published in OMNI, February 1988. © 1987 by Omni Publications International Limited. *The Shores of Bohemia*—First published in UNIVERSE 1, edited by Robert Silverberg and Karen Haber. © 1990 by Robert Silverberg and Karen Haber. *The Moral Bullet*—by Bruce Sterling and John Kessel—First published in Isaac Asimov's Science Fiction Magazine, July 1991. © 1991 by Davis Publications, Inc. *The Unthinkable*—First published in The Magazine of Fantasy and Science Fiction, August 1991. © 1991 by Mercury Press, Inc. *We See Things Differently*—First published in SEMIOTEXT(E) SF, edited by Rudy Rucker, Peter Lamborn Wilson, and Robert Anton Wilson. © 1989 by Autonomedia. *Hollywood Kremlin*—First published in The Magazine of Fantasy and Science Fiction, October 1990. © 1990 by Mercury Press, Inc. *Are You For 86?*—An original publication in this volume. © 1992 by Bruce Sterling. *Dori Bangs*—First published in Isaac Asimov's Science Fiction Magazine, September 1989. © 1989 by Davis Publications, Inc.

ISBN 0-553-56281-9

Published simultaneously in the United States and Canada

Bantam Books are published by Bantam Books, a division of Bantam Doubleday Dell Publishing Group, Inc. Its trademark, consisting of the words "Bantam Books" and the portrayal of a rooster, is Registered in U.S. Patent and Trademark Office and in other countries. Marca Registrada. Bantam Books, 1540 Broadway, New York, New York 10036.

PRINTED IN THE UNITED STATES OF AMERICA

RAD 0 9 8 7 6 5 4 3 2 1

CONTENTS

GLOBALHEAD

OUR NEURAL
CHERNOBYL

The late twentieth century, and the early years of our own millennium, form, in retrospect, a single era. This was the Age of the Normal Accident, in which people cheerfully accepted technological risks that today would seem quite insane.

Chernobyls were astonishingly frequent during this footloose, not to say criminally negligent, period. The nineties, with their rapid spread of powerful industrial technologies to the developing world, were a decade of frightening enormities, including the Djakarta super-tanker spill, the Lahore meltdown, and the gradual but devastating mass poisonings from tainted Kenyan contraceptives.

Yet none of these prepared humankind for the astonishing global effects of biotechnology's worst disaster: the event that has come to be known as the "neural chernobyl."

We should be grateful, then, that such an authority as the Novel Prize-winning systems neurochemist Dr. Felix Hotton should have turned his able pen to the history of *Our Neural Chernobyl* (Bessemer, December 2056, $499.95). Dr. Hotton is uniquely qualified to give us this devastating reassessment of the past's wrongheaded practices. For Dr. Hotton is a shining exemplar of the new "Open-Tower Science," that social movement within the scientific community that arose in response to the New Luddism of the teens and twenties.

Such pioneering Hotton papers as "The Locus Coeruleus Efferent Network: What in Heck Is It There For?" and "My Grand Fun Tracing Neural Connections With Tetramethylbenzidine" established this new, relaxed, and triumphantly subjective school of scientific exploration.

Today's scientist is a far cry from the white-coated sociopath of the past. Scientists today are democratized, media-conscious, fully integrated into the mainstream of modern culture. Today's young people, who admire scientists with a devotion once reserved for pop stars, can scarcely imagine the situation otherwise.

But in Chapter 1, "The Social Roots of Gene-Hacking," Dr. Hotton brings turn-of-the-century attitudes into startling relief. This was the golden age of applied biotech. Anxious attitudes toward "genetic tampering" changed rapidly when the terrifying AIDS pandemic was finally broken by recombinant DNA research.

It was during this period that the world first became aware that the AIDS retrovirus was a fantastic blessing in a particularly hideous disguise. This disease, which dug itself with horrible, virulent cunning into the very genetic structure of its victims, proved a medical marvel when finally broken to harness. The AIDS virus's RNA transcriptase system proved an able workhorse, successfully carrying healing segments of recombinant DNA into sufferers from a myriad of genetic defects. Suddenly one ailment after another fell to the miracle of RNA transcriptase techniques: sickle-cell anemia, cystic fibrosis, Tay-Sachs disease—literally hundreds of syndromes now only an unpleasant memory.

As billions poured into the biotech industry, and the instruments of research were simplified, an unexpected dynamic emerged: the rise of "gene-hacking." As Dr. Hotton points out, the situation had a perfect parallel in the 1970s and 1980s in the subculture of computer hacking. Here again was an enormously powerful technology suddenly within the reach of the individual.

As biotech companies multiplied, becoming ever smaller and more advanced, a hacker subculture rose around this "hot technology" like a cloud of steam. These ingenious, anomic individuals, often led into a state of manic self-absorption by their ability to dice with genetic destiny, felt no loyalty to social interests higher than their own curiosity. As early as the 1980s, devices such as high-performance liquid chromatographs, cell-culture systems, and DNA sequencers were small enough to fit into a closet or attic. If not bought from junkyards, diverted, or stolen outright, they could be reconstructed from off-the-shelf parts by any bright and determined teenager.

Dr. Hotton's second chapter explores the background of one such individual: Andrew ("Bugs") Berenbaum, now generally accepted as the perpetrator of the neural chernobyl.

Bugs Berenbaum, as Dr. Hotton convincingly shows, was not much different from a small horde of similar bright young misfits surrounding the genetic establishments of North Carolina's Research Triangle. His father was a semi-successful free-lance programmer, his mother a heavy marijuana user whose life centered around her role as "Lady Anne of Greengables" in Raleigh's Society for Creative Anachronism.

Both parents maintained a flimsy pretense of intellectual superiority, impressing upon Andrew the belief that the family's sufferings derived from the general stupidity and limited imagination of the average citizen. And Berenbaum, who showed an early interest in such subjects as math and engineering (then considered markedly unglamorous), did suffer some persecution from peers and schoolmates. At fifteen he had already drifted into the gene-hacker subculture, accessing gossip and learning "the scene" through computer bulletin boards and all-night beer-and-pizza sessions with other would-be pros.

At twenty-one, Berenbaum was working a summer internship with the small Raleigh firm of CoCoGenCo, a producer of specialized biochemicals. CoCoGenCo, as later congressional investigations proved, was actually a front for the California "designer drug" manufacturer and smuggler, Jimmy "Screech" McCarley. McCarley's agents within CoCoGenCo ran innumerable late-night "research projects" in conditions of heavy secrecy. In reality, these "secret projects" were straight production runs of synthetic cocaine, beta-phenethylamine, and sundry tailored variants of endorphin, a natural antipain chemical ten thousand times more potent than morphine.

One of McCarley's "black hackers," possibly Berenbaum himself, conceived the sinister notion of "implanted dope factories." By attaching the drug-producing genetics directly into the human genome, it was argued, abusers could be "wet-wired" into permanent states of intoxication. The agent of fixation would be the AIDS retrovirus, whose RNA sequence was a matter of common knowledge and available on dozens of open scientific databases. The one drawback to the scheme, of course, was that the abuser would "burn out like a shitpaper moth in a klieg light," to use Dr. Hotton's memorable phrase.

Chapter 3 is rather technical. Given Dr. Hotton's light and popular style, it makes splendid reading. Dr. Hotton attempts to reconstruct Berenbaum's crude attempts to rectify the situation through gross manipulation of the AIDS RNA transcriptase. What Berenbaum sought, of course, was a way to shut-off and start-up the transcriptase carrier, so that the internal drug factory could be activated at will. Berenbaum's custom transcriptase was designed to react to a simple user-induced trigger—probably $D,1,2,5$-phospholytic gluteinase, a fractionated component of "Dr. Brown's Celery

Soda," as Hotton suggests. This harmless beverage was a favorite quaff of gene-hacker circles.

Finding the genomes for cocaine-production too complex, Berenbaum (or perhaps a close associate, one Richard "Sticky" Ravetch) switched to a simpler payload: the just-discovered genome for mammalian dendritic growth factor. Dendrites are the treelike branches of brain cells, familiar to every modern schoolchild, which provide the mammalian brain with its staggering webbed complexity. It was theorized at the time that DG factor might be the key to vastly higher states of human intelligence. It is to be presumed that both Berenbaum and Ravetch had dosed themselves with it. As many modern victims of the neural chernobyl can testify, it does have an effect. Not precisely the one that the CoCoGenCo zealots envisioned, however.

While under the temporary maddening elation of dendritic "branch-effect," Berenbaum made his unfortunate breakthrough. He succeeded in providing his model RNA transcriptase with a trigger, but a trigger that made the transcriptase itself far more virulent than the original AIDS virus itself. The stage was set for disaster.

It was at this point that one must remember the social attitudes that bred the soul-threatening isolation of the period's scientific workers. Dr. Hotton is quite pitiless in his psychoanalysis of the mental mind-set of his predecessors. The supposedly "objective worldview" of the sciences is now quite properly seen as a form of mental brainwashing, deliberately stripping the victim of the full spectrum of human emotional response. Under such conditions, Berenbaum's reckless act becomes almost pitiable; it was a convulsive overcompensation for years of emotional starvation. Without consulting his superiors, who might have shown more discretion, Berenbaum began offering free samples of his new wetwares to anyone willing to inject them.

There was a sudden brief plague of eccentric genius in Raleigh, before the now-well-known symptoms of "dendritic crash" took over, and plunged the experimenters into vision-riddled, poetic insanity. Berenbaum himself committed suicide well before the full effects were known. And the full effects, of course, were to go far beyond even this lamentable human tragedy.

Chapter 4 becomes an enthralling detective story as the evidence slowly mounts.

Even today the term "Raleigh collie" has a special ring for dog fanciers, many of whom have forgotten its original derivation. These likable, companionable, and disquietingly intelligent pets were soon transported all over the nation by eager buyers and breeders. Once it had made the jump from human host to canine, Berenbaum's transcriptase derivative, like the AIDS virus itself, was passed on through the canine maternal womb. It was also transmitted through canine sexual intercourse and, via saliva, through biting and licking.

No dendritically enriched "Raleigh collie" would think of biting a human being. On the contrary, these loyal and well-behaved pets have even been known to right spilled garbage cans and replace their trash. Neural chernobyl infections remain rare in humans. But they spread through North America's canine population like wildfire, as Dr. Hotton shows in a series of cleverly designed maps and charts.

Chapter 5 offers us the benefit of hindsight. We are now accustomed to the idea of many different modes of "intelligence." There are, for instance, the various types of computer Artificial Intelligence, which bear no real relation to human "thinking." This was not unexpected—but the diverse forms of animal intelligence can still astonish in their variety.

The variance between *Canis familiaris* and his wild cousin, the coyote, remains unexplained. Dr. Hotton makes a good effort, basing his explication on the coyote neural mapping of his colleague, Dr. Reyna Sanchez of Los Alamos National Laboratory. It does seem likely that the coyote's more fully reticulated basal commissure plays a role. At any rate, it is now clear that a startling advanced form of social organization has taken root among the nation's feral coyote organization, with the use of elaborate coded barks, "scent-dumps," and specialized roles in hunting and food storage. Many of the nation's ranchers have now taken to the "protection system," in which coyote packs are "bought off" with slaughtered, barbecued livestock and sacks of dog treats. Persistent reports in Montana, Idaho, and Saskatchewan insist that coyotes have been spotted wearing cast-off clothing during the worst cold of winter.

It is possible that the common household cat was infected even earlier than the dog. Yet the effects of heightened cat intelligence are subtle and difficult to specify. Notoriously reluctant lab subjects, cats in their infected states are even sulkier about running mazes, solving trick boxes, and so on, preferring to wait out their interlocutors with inscrutable feline patience.

It has been suggested that some domestic cats show a heightened interest in television programs. Dr. Hotton casts a skeptical light on this, pointing out (rightly, as this reviewer thinks) that cats spend most of their waking hours sitting and staring into space. Staring at the flickering of a television is not much more remarkable than the hearthside cat's fondness for the flickering fire. It certainly does not imply "understanding" of a program's content. There are, however, many cases where cats have learned to paw-push the buttons of remote-control units. Those who keep cats as mousers have claimed that some cats now torture birds and rodents for longer periods, with greater ingenuity, and in some cases with improvised tools.

There remains, however, the previously unsuspected connection between advanced dendritic branching and manual dexterity, which Dr. Hotton tackles in his sixth chapter. This concept has caused a revolution in paleoanthropology. We are now forced into the uncomfortable realization that *Pithecanthropus robustus*, formerly dismissed as a large-jawed, vegetable-chewing ape, was probably far more intelligent than *Homo sapiens*. CAT-scans of the recently discovered Tanzanian fossil skeleton, nicknamed "Leonardo," reveal a *Pithecanthropus* skull-ridge obviously rich with dendritic branching. It has been suggested that the pithecanthropoids suffered from a heightened "life of the mind" similar to the life-threatening, absent-minded genius of terminal neural chernobyl sufferers. This yields the uncomfortable theory that nature, through evolution, has imposed a "primate stupidity barrier" that allows humans, unlike *Pithecanthropus*, to get on successfully with the dumb animal business of living and reproducing.

But the synergetic effects of dendritic branching and manual dexterity are clear in a certain nonprimate species. I refer, of course, to the well-known "chernobyl jump" of *Procyon lotor*, the American raccoon. The astonishing advances of the raccoon, and its Chinese cousin the panda, occupy the entirety of Chapter 8.

Here Dr. Hotton takes the so-called "modern view," from which I must dissociate myself. I, for one, find it intolerable that large sections of the American wilderness should be made into "no-go areas" by the vandalistic activities of our so-called "stripe-tailed cousins." Admittedly, excesses may have been committed in early attempts to exterminate the verminous, booming population of these masked bandits. But the damage to agriculture has been severe, and the history of kamikaze attacks by self-infected rabid raccoons is a terrifying one.

Dr. Hotton holds that we must now "share the planet with a fellow civilized species." He bolsters his argument with hearsay evidence of "raccoon culture" that to me seems rather flimsy. The woven strips of bark known as "raccoon wampum" are impressive examples of animal dexterity, but to my mind it remains to be proven that they are actually "money." And their so-called "pictographs" seem little more than random daubings. The fact remains that the raccoon population continues to rise exponentially, with raccoon bitches whelping massive litters every spring. Dr. Hotton, in a footnote, suggests that we can relieve crowding pressure by increasing the human presence in outer space. This seems a farfetched and unsatisfactory scheme.

The last chapter is speculative in tone. The prospect of intelligent rats is grossly repugnant; so far, thank God, the tough immune system of the rat, inured to bacteria and filth, has rejected retroviral invasion. Indeed, the feral cat population seems to be driving these vermin toward extinction. Nor have opossums succumbed; indeed, marsupials of all kinds seem immune, making Australia a haven of a now-lost natural world. Whales and dolphins are endangered species; they seem unlikely to make a comeback even with the (as-yet-unknown) cetacean effects of chernobyling. And monkeys, which might pose a very considerable threat, are restricted to the few remaining patches of tropical forest and, like humans, seem resistant to the disease.

Our neural chernobyl has bred a folklore all its own. Modern urban folklore speaks of "ascended masters," a group of chernobyl victims able to survive the virus. Supposedly, they "pass for human," forming a hidden counterculture among the normals, or "sheep." This is a throwback to the dark tradition of Luddism, and the popular fears once projected onto the dangerous and reckless "priesthood of science" are now transferred to these fairy tales of supermen. This psychological transference becomes clear when one hears that these "ascended masters" specialize in advanced scientific research of a kind now frowned upon. The notion that some fraction of the population has achieved physical immortality, and hidden it from the rest of us, is utterly absurd.

Dr. Hotton, quite rightly, treats this paranoid myth with the contempt it deserves.

Despite my occasional reservations, this is a splendid book, likely to be the definitive work on this central phenomenon of modern times. Dr. Hotton may well hope to add another Pulitzer to his list of honors. At ninety-five, this grand old man of modern science has produced yet another stellar work in his rapidly increasing oeuvre. His many readers, like myself, can only marvel at his vigor and clamor for more.

—*for Greg Bear*

STORMING
THE COSMOS

By Rudy Rucker and Bruce Sterling

I first met Vlad Zipkin at a Moscow beatnik party in the
glorious winter of 1957. I went there as a KGB informer.
Because of my report on that first meeting, poor Vlad had
to spend six months in a mental hospital—not that he
wasn't crazy.

As a boy I often tattled on wrongdoers, but I certainly didn't plan to grow up to be a professional informer. It just worked out that way. The turning point
was the spring of 1953, when I failed my completion
exams at the All-Union Metallurgical Institute. I'd been
working toward those exams for years; I wanted to help
build the rockets that would launch us into the Infinite.

And then, suddenly, one day in April, it was all over.
Our examination grades were posted, and I was one of
the three in seventeen who'd failed. To take the exam
again, I'd have to wait a whole year. First I was depressed, then angry. I knew for a fact that four of the students with good grades had cheated. I, who was honest,
had failed; and they, who had cheated, had passed. It

wasn't fair, it wasn't communist—I went and told the head of the Institute.

The upshot was that I passed after all, and became an assistant metallurgical engineer at the Kaliningrad space center. But, in reality, my main duty was to make weekly reports to the KGB on what my co-workers thought and said and did. I was, frankly, grateful to have my KGB work to do, as most of the metallurgical work was a bit beyond me.

There is an ugly Russian word for informer: *stukach*, snitch. The criminals, the psychotics, the parasites, and the beatniks—to them I was a *stukach*. But without *stukachi*, our communist society would explode into anarchy or grind to a decadent halt. Vlad Zipkin might be a genius, and I might be a *stukach*—but society needed us both.

I first met Vlad at a party thrown by a girl called Lyuda. Lyuda had her own Moscow apartment; her father was a Red Army colonel-general in Kaliningrad. She was a nice, sexy girl who looked a little like Doris Day.

Lyuda and her friends were all beatniks. They drank a lot, they used English slang, they listened to jazz; and the men hung around with prostitutes. One of the guys got Lyuda pregnant and she went for an abortion. She had VD as well. We heard of this, of course. Word spreads about these matters. Someone in Higher Circles decided to eliminate the anti-social sex gangster responsible for this. It was my job to find out who he was.

It was a matter for space-center KGB because several rocket-scientists were known to be in Lyuda's orbit. My approach was cagey. I made contact with a prostitute called Trina who hung around the Metropol, the Moskva, and other foreign hotels. Trina had chic Western clothes from her customers, and she was friends with many of the Moscow beatniks. I'm certainly not dashing enough to charm a girl like Trina—instead, I simply told her that I was KGB, and that if she didn't get me into one of Lyuda's bashes I'd have her arrested.

Lyuda's pad was jammed when we got there. I was proud to show up with a cool chick like Trina on my arm. I looked very sharp, too, with the leather jacket, and the black stove-pipe pants with no cuffs that all the beatniks were wearing that season. Trina stuck right with me—as we'd planned—and lots of men came up to talk to us. Trina would get them to talking dirty, and then I'd make some remark about Lyuda, ending with "but I guess she has a boyfriend?" The problem was that she had *lots* of them. I kept having to sneak into the bathroom to write down more names. Somehow I had to decide on one particular guy.

Time went on, and I got tenser. Cigarette smoke filled the room. The bathroom was jammed and I had to wait. When I came back I saw Trina with a hardcore beatnik named Starsky—he got her attention with some garbled Americanisms: "Hey baby, let's jive down to Hollywood and drink cool Scotch. I love making it with gone broads like you and Lyuda." He showed her a wad of hard currency—dollars he had illegally bought from tourists. I decided on the spot that Starsky was my man, and told Trina to leave with him and find out where he lived.

Now that I'd finished my investigation, I could relax and enjoy myself. I got a bottle of vodka and sat down by Lyuda's Steinway piano. Some guy in sunglasses was playing a slow boogie-woogie. It was lovely, lovely enough to move me to tears—tears for Lyuda's corrupted beauty, tears for my lost childhood, tears for my mother's grave.

A sharp poke in the thigh interrupted my reverie.

"Quit bawling, fatso, this isn't the Ukraine."

The voice came from beneath the piano. Leaning

down, I saw a man sitting cross-legged there, a thin, blond man with pale eyes. He smiled and showed his bad teeth. "Cheer up, pal, I mean it. And pass me that vodka bottle you're sucking. My name's Vlad Zipkin."

I passed him my bottle. "I'm Nikita Iosifovich Globov."

"Nice shoes," Vlad said admiringly. "Cool jacket, too. You're a snappy dresser, for a rocket-type."

"What makes you think I'm from the space center?" I said.

Vlad lowered his voice. "The shoes. You got those from Nokidze the Kazakh, the black-market guy. He's been selling 'em all over Kaliningrad."

I climbed under the piano with Zipkin. The air was a little clearer down there. "You're one of us, Comrade Zipkin?"

"I do information theory," Zipkin whispered, drunkenly touching one finger to his lips. "We're designing error-proof codes for communicating with the . . . you know." He made a little orbiting movement with his forefinger and looked upward at the shiny dark bottom of the piano. The Sputnik had only been up since October. We space workers were still not used to talking about it in public.

"Come on, don't be shy," I said, smiling. "We can say 'Sputnik,' can't we? Everyone in the world has talked of nothing else for months!"

It was easy to draw Vlad out. "My group's hush-hush," he bragged criminally. "The top brass think 'information theory' has to be classified and censored. But the theory's not information itself, it's an abstract meta-information . . ." He burbled on a while in the weird jargon of his profession. I grew bored and opened a pack of Kent cigarettes.

Vlad bummed one instantly. He was impressed that I had American cigarettes. Only cool black-market operators had classy cigs like that. Vlad felt the need to impress me in return. "Khrushchev wants the next sputnik to broadcast propaganda," he confided, blowing smoke. "The *Internationale* in outer space—what foolishness!" Vlad shook his head. "As if countries matter any more outside our atmosphere. To any real Russian, it is already clear that we have surpassed the Americans. Why should we copy their fascist nationalism? We have soared into the void and left them in the dirt!" He grinned. "Damn, these are good smokes. Can you get me a connection?"

"What are you offering?" I said.

He nodded at Lyuda. "See our hostess? See those earrings she has? They're gold-plated transistors I stole from the Center! All property is theft, hey Nikita?"

I liked Vlad well enough, but I felt duty-bound to report his questionable attitudes along with my information about Starsky. Political deviance such as Vlad's is a type of mental illness. I liked Vlad enough to truly want to see him get better.

Having made my report, I returned to Kaliningrad, and forgot about Vlad. I didn't hear about him for a month.

Since the early '50s, Kaliningrad had been the home of the Soviet space effort. Kaliningrad was thirty kilometers north of Moscow and had once been a summer resort. There we worked heroically at rocket research and construction—though the actual launches took place at the famous Baikonur Cosmodrome, far to the south. I enjoyed life in Kaliningrad. The stores were crammed with Polish hams and fresh lamb chops, and the landscape of forests and lakes was romantic and pleasant. Security was excellent.

Outside the research complex and block apartments were *dachas*, resort homes for space scientists, engineers, and party officials, including our top boss, the Chief Designer himself. The entire compound was surrounded by a high wood-and-concrete fence manned around the clock by armed guards. It was very peaceful. The compound held almost fifty *dachas*. I owned a small one—a kitchen and two rooms—with a large garden filled with fruit trees and berry bushes, now covered by winter snow.

A month after Lyuda's party, I was enjoying myself in my *dacha*, quietly pressing a new suit I had bought from Nokidze the Kazakh, when I heard a black ZIL sedan splash up through the mud outside. I peeked through the curtains. A woman stamped up the path and knocked. I opened the door slightly.

"Nikita Iosifovich Globov?"

"Yes?"

"Let me in, you fat sneak!" she said.

I gaped at her. She addressed me with filthy words. Shocked, I let her in. She was a dusky, strong-featured Tartar woman dressed in a cheap black two-piece suit from the Moscow G.U.M. store. No woman in Kaliningrad wore clothes or shoes that ugly, unless she was a real hard-liner. So I got worried. She kicked the door shut and glared at me.

"You turned in Vladimir Zipkin!"

"What?"

"Listen, you meddling idiot, I'm Captain Nina Bogulyubova from Information Mechanics. You've put my best worker into the mental hospital! What were you thinking? Do you realize what this will do to my production schedules?"

I was caught off guard. I babbled something about proper ideology coming first.

"You louse!" she snarled. "It's my department and I handle Security there! How dare you report one of my people without coming to me first? Do you see me turning in metallurgists?"

"Well, you can't have him babbling state secrets to every beatnik in Moscow!" I said defensively.

"You forget yourself," said Captain Bogulyubova with a taut smile. "I have a rank in KGB and you are a common *stukach*. I can make a great deal of trouble for you. A very great deal."

I began to sweat. "I was doing my duty. No one can deny that. Besides, I didn't know he was in the hospital! All he needed was a few counselling sessions!"

"You fouled up everything," she said, staring at me through slitted eyes like a Cossack sizing up a captured hog. She crossed her arms over her hefty chest and looked around my *dacha*. "This little place of yours will be nice for Vlad. He'll need some rest. *Poor* Vlad. No one else from my section will want to work with him after he gets out. They'll be afraid to be seen with him! But we need him, and you're going to help me. Vlad will work here, and you'll keep an eye on him. It can be a kind of house arrest."

"But what about my work in metallurgy?"

She glared at me. "Your new work will be Comrade Zipkin's rehabilitation. You'll volunteer to do it, and you'll tell the Higher Circles that he's become a splendid example of communist dedication! He'd better get the Order of Lenin, understand?"

"This isn't fair, Comrade Captain. Be reasonable!"

"Listen, you hypocrite swine, I know all about you and your black-market dealings. Those shoes cost more than you make in a month!" She snatched the iron off the end of my board and slammed it flat against my brand new suit. Steam curled up.

"All right!" I cried, wringing my hands. "I'll help him." I yanked the suit away and splashed water on the scorched fabric.

Nina laughed and stormed out of the house. I felt terrible. A man can't help it if he needs to dress well. It's unfair to hold a thing like that over someone.

Months passed. The spring of 1958 arrived. The dog Laika had been shot into the cosmic void. A good dog, a

Russian, an Earthling. The Americans' first launches had
failed, and then in February they shot up a laughable
sputnik no bigger than a grapefruit. Meanwhile we metallurgists forged ahead on the mighty RD-108 Supercluster
paraffin-fueled engine, which would lift our first cosmonaut into the Infinite. There were technical snags, and
gross lapses in space-worker ideology, but much progress
was made.

Captain Nina dropped by several times to bluster and
grumble about Vlad. She blamed me for everything, but it
was Vlad's problem. All one has to do, really, is tell the
mental health workers what they want to hear. But
Zipkin couldn't seem to master this.

A third sputnik was launched in May 1958, with
much instrumentation on board. Yet it failed to broadcast
a coherent propaganda statement, much less sing the *Internationale*. Vlad was missed, and missed badly. I
awaited Vlad's return with some trepidation. Would he
resent me? Fear me? Despise me?

For my part, I simply wanted Vlad to like me. In going over his dossier I had come to see that, despite his ec-
centricities, the man was indeed a genius. I resolved to
take care of Vlad Zipkin, to protect him from his irrational sociopathic impulses.

A KGB ambulance brought Vlad and his belongings
to my *dacha* early one Sunday morning in July. He
looked pale and disoriented. I greeted him with false
heartiness.

"Greetings Vladimir Eduardovich! It's an honor and
a joy to have you share my *dacha*. Come in, come in. I
have yogurt and fresh gooseberries. Let me help you carry
all that stuff inside!"

"So it was you." Vlad was silent while we carried his
suitcase and three boxes of belongings into the *dacha*.
When I urged him to eat with me, his face took on a desperate cast. "Please, Globov, leave me alone now. Those
months in the hospital—you can't imagine what it's been
like."

"Vladimir, don't worry, this *dacha* is your home, and I'm your friend."

Vlad grimaced. "Just let me spend the day alone in your garden, and don't tell the KGB I'm antisocial. I want to conform, I do want to fit in, but for God's sake, not to-day."

"Vlad, believe me, I want only the best for you. Go out and lie in the hammock; eat the berries, enjoy the sun."

Vlad's pale eyes bulged as they fell on my framed official photograph of Laika, the cosmonaut dog. The dog had a weird, frog-like, rubber oxygen mask on her face. Just before launch, she had been laced up within a heavy, stiff space-suit—a kind of canine straitjacket, actually. Vlad frowned and shuddered. I guess it reminded him of his recent unpleasantness.

Vlad yanked my vodka bottle off the kitchen counter, and headed outside without another word. I watched him through the window—he looked well enough, sipping vodka, picking blackberries, and finally falling asleep in the hammock. His suitcase contained very little of inter-est, and his boxes were mostly filled with books. Most were technical, but many were scientific romances: the so-cialist H.G. Wells, Capek, Yefremov, Kazantsev, and the like.

When Vlad awoke he was in much better spirits. I showed him around the property. The garden stretched back thirty meters, where there was a snug outhouse. We strolled together out into the muddy streets. At Vlad's urging, I got the guards to open the gate for us, and we walked out into the peaceful birch and pine woods around the Klyazma Reservoir. It had rained heavily dur-ing the preceding week, and mushrooms were every-where. We amused ourselves by gathering the edible ones—every Russian knows mushrooms.

Vlad knew an "instant pickling" technique based on lightly boiling the mushrooms in brine, then packing them in ice and vinegar. It worked well back in our kitchen, and I congratulated him. He was as pleased as a child.

In the days that followed, I realized that Vlad was not anti-Party. He was simply very unworldly. He was one of those gifted unfortunates who can't manage life without a protector.

Still, his opinion carried a lot of weight around the Center, and he worked on important problems. I escorted him everywhere—except the labs I wasn't cleared for—reminding him not to blurt out anything stupid.

Of course my own work suffered. I told my co-workers that Vlad was a sick relative of mine, which explained my common absence from the job. Rather than being disappointed by my absence, though, the other engineers praised my dedication to Vlad and encouraged me to spend plenty of time with him.

I liked Vlad, but soon grew tired of the constant shepherding. He did most of his work in our *dacha*, which kept me cooped up there when I could have been out cutting deals with Nokidze or reporting on the beatnik scene.

It was too bad that Captain Nina Bogulyubova had fallen down on her job. She should have been watching over Vlad from the first. Now I had to tidy up after her bungling, so I felt she owed me some free time. I hinted tactfully at this when she arrived with a sealed briefcase containing some of Vlad's work. My reward was another furious tongue lashing.

"You parasite, how dare you suggest that I failed Vladimir Eduardovich? I have always been aware of his value as a theorist, and as a man! He's worth any ten of you *stukach* vermin! The Chief Designer himself has asked after Vladimir's health. The Chief Designer spent years in a labor camp under Stalin. He knows it's no disgrace to be shut away by some lickspittle sneak . . ." There was more, and worse. I began to feel that Captain

Bogulyubova, in her violent Tartar way, had personal feelings for Vlad.

Also I had not known that our Chief Designer had been in camp. This was not good news, because people who have spent time in detention sometimes become embittered and lose proper perspective. Many people were being released from labor camps now that Nikita Khrushchev had become the Leader of Progressive Mankind. Also, amazing and almost insolent things were being published in the *Literary Gazette*.

Like most Ukrainians, I liked Khrushchev, but he had a funny peasant accent and everyone made fun of the way he talked on the radio. We never had such problems in Stalin's day.

We Soviets had achieved a magnificent triumph in space, but I feared we were becoming lax. It saddened me to see how many space engineers, technicians, and designers avoided Party discipline. They claimed that their eighty-hour work weeks excused them from indoctrination meetings. Many read foreign technical documents without proper clearance. Proper censorship was evaded. Technicians from different departments sometimes gathered to discuss their work, privately, simply between themselves, without an actual need-to-know.

Vlad's behavior was especially scandalous. He left top-secret documents scattered about the *dacha*, where one's eye could not help but fall on them. He often drank to excess. He invited engineers from other departments to come visit us, and some of them, not knowing his dangerous past, accepted. It embarrassed me, because when they saw Vlad and me together they soon guessed the truth.

Still, I did my best to cover Vlad's tracks and minimize his indiscretions. In this I failed miserably.

One evening, to my astonishment, I found him mulling over working papers for the RD-108 Supercluster engine. He had built a cardboard model of the rocket out of roller tubes from my private stock of toilet paper. "Where did you get those?" I demanded.

"Found 'em in a box in the outhouse."

"No, the documents!" I shouted. "That's not your department! Those are state secrets!"

Vlad shrugged. "It's all wrong," he said thickly. He had been drinking again.

"What?"

"Our original rocket, the 107, had four nozzles. But this 108 Supercluster has twenty! Look, the extra engines are just bundled up like bananas and attached to the main rocket. They're held on with hoops! The Americans will laugh when they see this."

"But they won't." I snatched the blueprints out of his hands. "Who gave you these?"

"Korolyov did," Vlad muttered. "Sergei Pavlovich."

"The Chief Designer?" I said, stunned.

"Yeah, we were talking it over in the sauna this morning," Vlad said. "Your old pal Nokidze came by while you were at work this morning, and he and I had a few. So I walked down to the bathhouse to sweat it off. Turned out the Chief was in the sauna, too—he'd been up all night working. He and I did some time together, years ago. We used to look up at the stars, talk rockets together . . . So anyway, he turns to me and says, 'You know how much thrust Von Braun is getting from a single engine?' And I said, 'Oh, must be eighty, ninety tons, right?' 'Right,' he said, 'and we're getting twenty-five. We'll have to strap twenty together to launch one man. We need a miracle, Vladimir. I'm ready to try anything.' So then I told him about this book I've been reading."

I said, "You were drunk on working-hours? And the Chief Designer saw you in the sauna?"

"He sweats like anyone else," Vlad said. "I told him about this new fiction writer. Aleksander Kazantsev. He's a thinker, that boy." Vlad tapped the side of his head meaningfully, then scratched his ribs inside his filthy houserobe and lit a cigarette. I felt like killing him. "Kazantsev says we're not the first explorers in space. There've been others, beings from the void. It's no surprise. The great space-prophet Tsiolkovsky said there are an infinite number of inhabited worlds. You know how much the Chief Designer admired Tsiolkovsky. And when you look at the evidence—I mean this Tunguska thing—it begins to add up nicely."

"Tunguska," I said, fighting back a growing sense of horror. "That's in *Siberia*, isn't it?"

"Sure. So anyway, I said, 'Chief, why are you wasting our time on these firecrackers when we have a shot at true star flight? Send out a crew of trained investigators to the impact-site of this so-called Tunguska meteor! Run an information-theoretic analysis! If it really was an atomic-powered spacecraft like Kazantsev says, maybe there's something left that could help us!"

I winced, imagining Vlad in the sauna, drunk, first bringing up disgusting prison memories, then babbling on about space fiction to the premier genius of Soviet rocketry. It was horrible. "What did the Chief say to you?"

"He said it sounded promising," Vlad said airily. "Said he'd get things rolling right away. You got any more of those Kents?"

I slumped into my chair, dazed. "Look inside my boots," I said numbly. "The Italian ones."

"Oh," Vlad said in a small voice. "I sort of found those last week."

I roused myself. "The Chief let you see the Super-cluster plans? And said you ought to go to Siberia?"

"Oh, not just you and me," Vlad said, amused. "He needs a really thorough investigation! We'll commandeer a whole train, get all the personnel and equipment we need!" Vlad grinned. "Excited, Nikita?"

My head spun. The man was a demon. I knew in my soul that he was goading me. Deliberately. Sadistically.

Suddenly I realized how sick I was of Vlad, of constantly watchdogging this visionary moron. Words tumbled out of me.

"I hate you, Zipkin! So this is your revenge at last, eh? Sending me to Siberia! You beatnik scum! You think you're smart, blondie? You're weak, you're sick, that's what! I wish the KGB had shot you, you stupid, selfish, crazy ..." My eyes flooded with sudden tears.

Vlad patted my shoulder, surprised. "Now don't get all worked up."

"You're nuts!" I sobbed. "You rocketship types are all crazy, every one of you! Storming the cosmos ... well, you can storm my sacred ass! I'm not boarding any secret train to nowhere—"

"Now, now," Vlad soothed. "My imagination, your thoroughness—we make a great team! Just think of them pinning awards on us."

"If it's such a great idea, then *you* do it! I'm not slogging through some stinking wilderness ..."

"Be logical!" Vlad said, rolling his eyes in derision. "You know I'm not well trusted. Your Higher Circles don't understand me the way you do. I need you along to smooth things, that's all. Relax, Nikita! I promise, I'll split the fame and glory with you, fair and square!"

Of course, I did my best to defuse, or at least avoid, this lunatic scheme. I protested to Higher Circles. My usual contact, a balding jazz fanatic named Colonel Popov, watched me blankly, with the empty stare of a professional interrogator. I hinted broadly that Vlad had been misbehaving with classified documents. Popov ignored this, absently tapping a pencil on his "special" phone in catchy 5/4 rhythm.

Hesitantly, I mentioned Vlad's insane mission. Popov still gave no response. One of the phones, not the "special" one, rang loudly. Popov answered, said, "Yes," three times, and left the room.

I waited a long hour, careful not to look at or touch anything on his desk. Finally Popov returned.

I began at once to babble. I knew his silent treatment was an old trick, but I couldn't help it. Popov cut me off.

"Marx's laws of historical development apply universally to all societies," he said, sitting in his squeaking chair. "That, of course, includes possible star-dwelling societies." He steepled his fingers. "It follows logically that progressive Interstellar Void-ites would look kindly on us progressive peoples."

"But the Tunguska meteor fell in 1908!" I said.

"Interesting," Popov mused. "Historical-determinist Cosmic-oids could have calculated through Marxist science that Russia would be the first to achieve communism. They might well have left us some message or legacy."

"But Comrade Colonel . . ."

Popov rustled open a desk drawer. "Have you read this book?" It was Kazantsev's space romance. "It's all the rage at the space center these days. I got my copy from your friend Nina Bogulyubova."

"Well . . ." I said.

"Then why do you presume to debate me without even reading the facts?" Popov folded his arms. "We find it significant that the Tunguska event took place on June 30, 1908. Today is June 15, 1958. If heroic measures are taken, you may reach the Tunguska valley on the very day of the fiftieth anniversary!"

That Tartar cow Bogulyubova had gotten to the Higher Circles first. Actually, it didn't surprise me that our KGB would support Vlad's scheme. They controlled our security, but our complex engineering and technical developments much exceeded their mental grasp. Space aliens, however, were a concept anyone could understand.

Any skepticism on their part was crushed by the Chief Designer's personal support for the scheme. The Chief had been getting a lot of play in Khrushchev's speeches lately, and was known as a miracle worker. If he said it was possible, that was good enough for Security.

I was helpless. An expedition was organized in frantic haste.

Naturally it was vital to have KGB along. Me, of course, since I was guarding Vlad. And Nina Bogulyubova, as she was Vlad's superior. But then the KGB of other departments grew jealous of Metallurgy and Information Mechanics. They suspected that we were pulling a fast one. Suppose an artifact really were discovered? It would make all our other work obsolete overnight. Would it not be best that each department have a KGB observer present? Soon we found no end of applicants for the expedition.

We were lavishly equipped. We had ten railway cars. Four held our Red Army escort and their tracked all-terrain vehicles. We also had three sleepers, a galley car, and two flatcars piled high with rations, tents, excavators, Geiger counters, radios, and surveying instruments. Vlad brought a bulky calculating device, Captain Nina supplied her own mysterious crates, and I had a box of metallurgical analysis equipment, in case we found a piece of the UFO.

We were towed through Moscow under tight security, then our cars were shackled to the green-and-yellow Trans-Siberian Express.

Soon the expedition was chugging across the endless, featureless steppes of Central Asia. I grew so bored that I was forced to read Kazantsev's book.

On June 30, 1908, a huge, mysterious fireball had

smashed into the Tunguska River valley of the central Siberian uplands. This place was impossibly remote. Kazantsev suggested that the crash point had been chosen deliberately to avoid injuring Earthlings.

It was not until 1927 that the first expedition reached the crash site, revealing terrific devastation, but—no sign whatsoever of a meteorite! They found no impact crater, either; only the swampy Tunguska valley, surrounded by an elliptical blast pattern: sixty kilometers of dead, smashed trees.

Kazantsev pointed out that the facts suggested a nuclear airburst. Perhaps it was a deliberate detonation by aliens, to demonstrate atomic power to Earthlings. Or it might have been the accidental explosion of a nuclear starship drive. In an accidental crash, a socially advanced alien pilot would naturally guide his stricken craft to one of the planet's "poles of uninhabitedness." And eyewitness reports made it clear that the Tunguska body had definitely changed course in flight!

Once I had read this excellent work, my natural optimism surfaced again. Perhaps we would find something grand in Tunguska after all, something miraculous that the 1927 expedition had overlooked. Kulik's expedition had missed it, but now we were in the atomic age. Or so we told ourselves. It seemed much more plausible on a train with two dozen other explorers, all eager for the great adventure.

It was an unsought vacation for us hardworking *stukachi*. Work had been savage throughout our departments, and we KGB had had a tough time keeping track of our comrades' correctness. Meanwhile, back in Kaliningrad, they were still laboring away, while we relaxed in the dining saloon with pegged chessboards and tall brass samovars of steaming tea.

Vlad and I shared our own sleeping car. I forgave him for having involved me in this mess. We became friends again. This would be real man's work, we told each other.

Tramping through savage taiga with bears, wolves, and Siberian tigers! Hunting strange, possibly dangerous relics—relics that might change the very course of cosmic history! No more of this poring over blueprints and formulae like clerks! Neither of us had fought in the Great Patriotic War—I'd been too young, and Vlad had been in some camp or something. Other guys were always bragging about how they'd stormed this or shelled that or eaten shoe leather in Stalingrad—well, we'd soon be making them feel pretty small!

Day after day, the countryside rolled past. First, the endless, grassy steppes, then a dark wall of pine forest, broken by white-barked birches. Khrushchev's Virgin Lands campaign was in full swing, and the radio was full of patriotic stuff about settling the wilderness. Every few hundred kilometers, especially by rivers, raw and ugly new towns had sprung up along the Trans-Sib line. Prefab apartment blocks, mud streets, cement trucks, and giant sooty power plants. Trains unloaded huge spools of black wire. "Electrification" was another big propaganda theme of 1958.

Our Trans-Sib train stopped often to take on passengers, but our long section was sealed under orders from Higher Circles. We had no chance to stretch our legs, and slowly all our carriages filled up with the reek of dirty clothes and endless cigarettes.

I was doing my best to keep Vlad's spirits up when Nina Bogulyubova entered our carriage, ducking under a line of wet laundry. "Ah, Nina Igorovna," I said, trying to keep things friendly. "Vlad and I were just discussing something. Exactly what *does* it take to merit burial in the Kremlin?"

"Oh, put a cork in it," Bogulyubova said testily. "My money says your so-called spacecraft was just a chunk of ice and gas. Probably a piece of a comet which vaporized on impact. Maybe it's worth a look, but that doesn't mean I have to swallow crackpot pseudo-science!"

She sat on the bunk facing Vlad's, where he sprawled out, stunned with boredom and strong cigarettes. Nina opened her briefcase. "Vladimir, I've developed those pictures I took of you."

"Yeah?"

She produced a Kirlian photograph of his hand. "Look at these spiky flares of suppressed energy from your fingertips. Your aura has changed since we boarded the train."

Vlad frowned. "I could do with a few deciliters of vodka, that's all."

She shook her head quickly, then smiled and blinked at him flirtatiously. "Vladimir Eduardovich, you're a man of genius. You have strong, passionate drives . . ."

Vlad studied her for a moment, obviously weighing her dubious attractions against his extreme boredom. An affair with a woman who was his superior, and also KGB, would be grossly improper and risky. Vlad, naturally, caught my eye and winked. "Look, Nikita, take a hike for a while, okay?"

He was putty in her hands. I was disgusted by the way she exploited Vlad's weaknesses. I left him in her carnal clutches, though I felt really sorry for Vlad. Maybe I could scare him up something to drink.

The closest train-stop to Tunguska is near a place called Ust-Ilimsk, two hundred kilometers north of Bratsk, and three thousand long kilometers from Moscow. Even London, England is twice as close to Moscow as Tunguska.

A secondary line-engine hauled our string of cars to a tiny railway junction in the absolute middle of nowhere. Then it chugged away. It was four in the morning of June 26, but since it was summer it was already light. There were five families running the place, living in log cabins chinked with mud.

Our ranking KGB officer, an officious jerk named Chalomei, unsealed our doors. Vlad and I jumped out onto the rough boards of the siding. After days of ceaseless train vibration we staggered around like sailors who'd lost their land-legs. All around us was raw wilderness, huge birches and tough Siberian pines, with knobby, shallow roots. Permafrost was only two feet underground. There was nothing but trees and marsh for days in all directions. I found it very depressing.

We tried to strike up a conversation with the local supervisor. He spoke bad Russian, and looked like a relocated Latvian. The rest of our company piled out, yawning and complaining.

When he saw them, our host turned pale. He wasn't much like the brave pioneers on the posters. He looked scrawny and glum.

"Quite a place you have here," I observed.

"Is better than labor camp, I always thinking," he said. He murmured something to Vlad.

"Yeah," Vlad said thoughtfully, looking at our crew. "Now that you mention it, they *are* all police sneaks."

With much confusion, we began unloading our train cars. Slowly the siding filled up with boxes of rations, bundled tents, and wooden crates labelled SECRET and THIS SIDE UP.

A fight broke out between our civilians and our Red Army detachment. Our Kaliningrad folk were soon sucking their blisters and rubbing strained backs, but the soldiers refused to do the work alone.

Things were getting out of hand. I urged Vlad to give them all a good talking-to, a good, ringing speech to establish who was who and what was what. Something simple and forceful, with lots of "marching steadfastly together" and "storming the stars" and so on.

"I'll give them something better," said Vlad, running his hands back through his hair. "I'll give them the truth." He climbed atop a crate and launched into a strange, ideologically incorrect harangue.

"Comrades! You should think of Einstein's teachings. Matter is illusion. Why do you struggle so? Spacetime is the ultimate reality. Spacetime is one, and we are all patterns on it. We are ripples, comrades, wrinkles in the fabric of the . . ."

"Einstein is a tool of International Zionism," someone shouted.

"And you are a dog," said Vlad evenly. "Nevertheless you and I are the same. We are different parts of the cosmic One. Matter is just a . . ."

"Drop dead," yelled another heckler.

"Death is an illusion," said Vlad, his smile tightening. "A person's spacetime pattern encodes an information pattern which the cosmos is free to . . ."

It was total gibberish. Everyone began shouting and complaining at once, and Vlad's speech stuttered to a halt.

Our KGB colonel Chalomei jumped up on a crate and declared that he was taking charge. He was attached directly to the Chief Designer's staff, he shouted, and was fed up with our expedition's laxity. This was nothing but pure mutiny, but nobody else outranked him in KGB. It looked like Chalomei would get away with it. He then tried to order our Red Army boys to finish the unloading.

But they got mulish. There were six of them, all Central Asian Uzbeks from Uckduck, a hick burg in Uzbekskaja. They'd all joined the Red Army together, probably at gunpoint. Their leader was Master Sergeant Mukhamed, a rough character with a broken nose and puffy, scarred eyebrows. He looked and acted like a tank.

Mukhamed bellowed that his orders didn't include acting as house-serfs for egghead aristocrats. Chalomei insinuated how much trouble he could make for Mukhamed, but Mukhamed only laughed.

"I may be just a dumb Uzbek," Mukhamed roared, "but I didn't just fall off the turnip truck! Why do you think this train is full of you worthless *stukachi*? It's so those big-brain rocket-boys you left behind can get some real work done for once! Without you stoolies hanging around, stirring up trouble to make yourselves look good! They'd love to see you scum breaking your necks in the swamps of Siberia . . ."

He said a great deal more, but the damage was already done. Our expedition's morale collapsed like a burst balloon. The rest of the group refused to move another millimeter without direct orders from Higher Circles.

We spent three days then, on the station's telegraph, waiting for orders. The glorious Fiftieth Anniversary of the event came and went, and everything was screwed up and in a total shambles. The gloomiest rumors spread among us. Some said that the Chief Designer had tricked us KGB to get us out of the way, and others said that Khrushchev himself was behind it. (There were always rumors of struggle between Party and KGB at the Very Highest Circles.) Whatever it meant, we were all sure to be humiliated when we got back, and heads would roll.

I was worried sick. If this really was a plot to hoodwink KGB, then I was in it up to my neck. Then the galley car caught fire during the night, and sabotage was suspected. The locals, fearing interrogation, fled into the forest, though it was probably just one of Chalomei's *stukachi* being careless with a samovar.

Orders finally arrived from Higher Circles. KGB personnel were to return to their posts for a "reassessment of their performance." This did not sound promising at all. No such orders were given to Vlad or the "expedition regulars," whatever that meant. Apparently the Higher Circles had not yet grasped that there *were* no "expedition regulars."

Nina and I were both severely implicated, so we both decided that we were certainly "regulars" and should put off going back as long as possible. Together with Vlad, we had a long talk with Sergeant Mukhamed, who seemed a sensible sort.

"We're better off without those desk jockeys," Mukhamed said bluntly. "This is rough country. We can't waste time tying up the shoelaces of those Moscow fairies. Besides, my orders say 'Zipkin' and I don't see 'KGB' written anywhere on them."

"Maybe he's right," Vlad said. "We're in so deep now that our best chance is to actually *find* an artifact and prove them all wrong! Results are what count, after all! We've come this far—why turn tail now?"

Our own orders said nothing about the equipment. It turned out there was far too much of it for us to load it aboard the Red Army tractor vehicles. We left most of it on the sidings.

We left early next morning, while the others were still snoring. We had three all-terrain vehicles with us, brand-new Red Army amphibious personnel carriers, called "BTR-50s," or *"byutors"* in Army slang. They had camouflaged steel armor and rode very low to the ground on broad tracks. They had loud, rugged diesel engines and good navigation equipment, with room for ten troops each in a bay in the back. The front had slits and searchlights and little pop-up armored hatches for the driver and commander. The *byutors* floated in water, too, and could churn through the thickest mud like a salamander. We scientists rode in the first vehicle, while the second carried equipment and the third, fuel.

Once underway, our spirits rose immediately. You could always depend on the good old Red Army to get the job done! We roared through woods and swamps with a loud, comforting racket, scaring up large flocks of herons and geese. Our photoreconnaissance maps, which had been issued to us under the strictest security, helped us avoid the worst obstacles. The days were long and we made good speed, stopping only a few hours a night.

It took three days of steady travel to reach the Tunguska basin. Cone-shaped hills surrounded the valley like watchtowers.

The terrain changed here. Mummified trees strewed the ground like jackstraws, many of them oddly burnt. Trees decayed very slowly in the Siberian taiga. They were deep-frozen all winter and stayed whole for decades.

Dusk fell. We bulled our way around the slope of one of the hills, while leafless, withered branches crunched and shrieked beneath our treads. The marshy Tunguska valley, clogged and gray with debris, came into view. Sergeant Mukhamed called a halt. The maze of fallen lumber was too much for our machines.

We tottered out of the *byutors* and savored the silence. My kidneys felt like jelly from days of lurching and jarring. I stood by our *byutor*, resting my hand on it, taking comfort in the fact that it was man-made. The rough travel and savage dreariness had taken the edge off my enthusiasm. I needed a drink.

But our last liter of vodka had gone out the train window somewhere between Omsk and Tomsk. Nina had thrown it away "for Vlad's sake." She was acting more like a lovesick schoolgirl every day. She was constantly fussing over Vlad, tidying him up, watching his diet, leaping heavily to his defense in every conversation. Vlad, of course, merely sopped up this devotion as his due, too absent-minded to notice it. Vlad had a real talent for that. I wasn't sure which of the two of them was more disgusting.

"At last," Vlad exulted. "Look, Ninotchka, the site of the mystery! Isn't it sublime!" Nina smiled and linked her solid arm with his.

The dusk thickened. Huge taiga mosquitoes whirred

past our ears and settled to sting and pump blood. We slapped furiously, then set up our camp amid a ring of dense, smoky fires.

To our alarm, answering fires flared up on the five other hilltops ringing the valley.

"Evenks," grumbled Sergeant Mukhamed. "Savage nomads. They live off their reindeer, and camp in round tents called yurts. No one can civilize them; it's hopeless. Best just to ignore them."

"Why are they here?" Nina said. "Such a bleak place."

Vlad rubbed his chin. "The records of the '27 Kulik Expedition said the Evenk tribes remembered the explosion. They spoke of a Thunder-God smiting the valley. They must know this place pretty well."

"I'm telling you," rasped Mukhamed, "stay away. The men are all mushroom-eaters and the women are all whores."

One of the shaven-headed Uzbek privates looked up from his tin of rations. "Really, Sarge?"

"Their girls have lice as big as your thumbnails," the sergeant said. "And the men don't like strangers. When they eat those poison toadstools they get like wild beasts."

We had tea and hardtack, sniffling and wiping our eyes from the bug-repelling smoke. Vlad was full of plans. "Tomorrow we'll gather data on the direction of the treefalls. That'll show us the central impact point. Nina, you can help me with that. Nikita, you can stay here and help the soldiers set up base camp. And maybe tomorrow we'll have an idea of where to look for our artifact."

Later that night, Vlad and Nina crept out of our long tent. I heard restrained groaning and sighing for half an hour. The soldiers snored on peacefully while I lay under the canvas with my eyes wide open. Finally, Nina shuffled in, followed by Vlad brushing mud from his knees.

I slept poorly that night. Maybe Nina was no sexy hard-currency girl, but she was a woman, and even a *stukach* can't overhear that sort of thing without getting hot and bothered. After all, I had my needs, too.

Around one in the morning I gave up trying to sleep and stepped out of the tent for some air. An incredible aurora display greeted me. We were late for the Fiftieth Anniversary of the Tunguska crash, but I had the feeling the valley was welcoming me.

There was an arc of rainbow light directly overhead, with crimson and yellow streamers shooting out from the zenith toward the horizons. Wide luminous bands, paralleling the arch, kept rising out of the horizons to roll across the heavens with swift steady majesty. The bands crashed into the arch like long breakers from a sea of light.

The great auroral rainbow, with all its wavering streamers, began to swing slowly upwards, and a second, brighter arch formed below it. The new arch shot a long row of slender, colored lances toward the Tunguska valley. The lances stretched down, touched, and a lightning flash of vivid orange glared out, filling the whole world around me. I held my breath, waiting for the thunder, but the only sound was Nina's light snoring.

I watched for a while longer, until the great cosmic tide of light shivered into pieces. At the very end, disks appeared, silvery, shimmery saucers that filled the sky. Truly we had come to a very strange place. Filled with profound emotions, I was able to forget myself and sleep.

Next morning everyone woke up refreshed and cheerful. Vlad and Nina traipsed off with the surveying equipment. With the soldiers' help, I set up the diesel generator for Vlad's portable calculator. We did some camp scutwork, cutting heaps of firewood, digging a proper latrine. By then it was noon, but the lovebirds were still not back, so I did some exploring of my own. I tramped downhill into the disaster zone.

I realized almost at once that our task was hopeless. The ground was squelchy and dead, beneath a thick tangling shroud of leafless pines. We couldn't look for wreckage systematically without hauling away the musty, long-dead crust of trees. Even if we managed that, the ground itself was impossibly soggy and treacherous.

I despaired. The valley itself oppressed my soul. The rest of the taiga had chipmunks, wood grouse, the occasional heron or squirrel, but this swamp seemed lifeless, poisonous. In many places the earth had sagged into shallow bowls and depressions, as if the bedrock below it had rotted away.

New young pines had sprung up to take the place of the old, but I didn't like the look of them. The green saplings, growing up through the gray skeletons of their ancestors, were oddly stunted and twisted. A few older pines had been half-sheltered from the blast by freaks of topography. The living bark on their battered limbs and trunks showed repulsive puckered blast-scars.

Something malign had entered the soil. Perhaps poisoned comet ice, I thought. I took samples of the mud, mostly to impress the soldiers back at camp. I wasn't much of a scientist, but I knew how to go through the motions.

While digging I disturbed an ant nest. The strange, big-headed ants emerged from their tunnels and surveyed the damage with eerie calm.

By the time I returned to camp, Vlad and Nina were back. Vlad was working on his calculator while Nina read out direction-angles of the felled trees. "We're almost done," Nina told me, her broad-cheeked face full of bovine satisfaction. "We're running an information-theoretic analysis to determine the ground location of the explosion."

The soldiers looked impressed. But the upshot of Vlad's and Nina's fancy analysis was what any fool could see by glancing at the elliptical valley. The brunt of the explosion had burst from the nearer focus of the ellipse, directly over a little hill I'd had my eye on all along.

"I've been taking soil samples," I told Nina. "I suspect odd trace elements in the soil. I suppose you noticed the strange growth of the pines. They're particularly tall at the blast's epicenter."

"Hmmph," Nina said. "While you were sleeping last night, there was a minor aurora. I took photos. I think the geomagnetic field may have had an influence on the object's trajectory."

"That's elementary," I sniffed. "What we need to study is a possible remagnetization of the rocks. Especially at impact point."

"You're neglecting the biological element," Nina said. By now the soldiers' heads were swiveling to follow our discussion like a tennis match. "I suppose you didn't notice the faint luminescence of the sod?" She pulled some crumpled blades of grass from her pocket. "A Kirlian analysis will prove interesting."

"But, of course, the ants—" I began.

"Will you two fakers shut up a minute?" Vlad broke in. "I'm trying to think."

I swallowed hard. "Oh yes, Comrade Genius? What about?"

"About finding what we came for, Nikita. The alien craft." Vlad frowned, waving his arm at the valley below us. "I'm convinced it's buried out there somewhere. We don't have a chance in this tangle and ooze . . . but we've got to figure some way to sniff it out."

At that moment we heard the distant barking of a dog. "Great," Vlad said without pausing. "Maybe that's a bloodhound."

He'd made a joke. I realized this after a moment, but by then it was too late to laugh. "It's just some Evenk mutt," Sergeant Mukhamed said. "They keep sled-dogs . . . eat 'em, too." The dog barked louder, coming closer. "Maybe it got loose."

Ten minutes later the dog bounded into our camp, barking joyously and frisking. It was a small, bright-eyed female husky, with muddy legs and damp fur caked with bits of bark. "That's no sled-dog," Vlad said, wondering. "That's a city mutt. What's it doing here?"

She was certainly friendly enough. She barked in excitement and sniffed at our hands trustingly. I patted the dog and called her a good girl. "Where on earth did you come from?" I asked. I'd always liked dogs.

One of the soldiers addressed the dog in Uzbek and offered it some of its rations. It sniffed the food, took a tentative lick, but refused to eat it.

"Sit!" Vlad said suddenly. The dog sat obediently.

"She understands Russian," Vlad said.

"Nonsense," I said. "She just reacted to your voice."

"There must be some other Russians nearby," Nina said. "A secret research station, maybe? Something we were never told about?"

"Well, I guess we have a mascot," I said, scratching the dog's scalp.

"Come here, Laika," Vlad said. The dog pricked her ears and wandered toward him.

I felt an icy sensation of horror. I snatched my hand back as if I had touched a corpse. With an effort, I controlled myself. "Come on, Vlad," I said. "You're joking again."

"Good dog," Vlad said, patting her.

"Vlad," I said, "Laika's rocket burned up on re-entry."

"Yes," Vlad said, "the first creature we Earthlings put into space was sentenced to be burned alive. I often think about that." Vlad stared dramatically into the depths of the valley. "Comrades, I think something is waiting here to help us storm the cosmos. I think it preserved Laika's soul and re-animated her here, at this place, at this time . . . It's no coincidence. This is no ordinary animal. This is Laika, the cosmonaut dog!"

Laika barked loudly. I had never seen the dog without the rubber oxygen mask on her face, but I knew with a thrill of supernatural fear that Vlad was right. I felt an instant irrational urge to kill the dog, or at least give her a good kick. If I killed and buried her, I wouldn't have to think about what she meant.

The others looked equally stricken. "Probably fell off a train," Mukhamed muttered at last.

Vlad regally ignored this frail reed of logic. "We ought to follow Laika. The . . . *Thunder-God* put her here to lead us. It won't get dark till ten o'clock. Let's move out, comrades." Vlad stood up and shrugged on his backpack. "Mukhamed?"

"Uh . . ." the sergeant said. "My orders are to stay with the vehicles." He cleared his throat and spat. "There are Evenks about. Natural thieves. We wouldn't want our camp to be raided."

Vlad looked at him in surprise, then with pity. He walked towards me, threw one arm over my shoulder, and took me aside. "Nikita, these Uzbeks are brave soldiers but they're a bit superstitious. Terrified of the unknown. What a laugh. But you and I . . . Scientists, space pioneers . . . the Unknown is our natural habitat, right?"

"Well . . ."

"Come on, Nikita." He glowered. "We can't go back to face the top brass empty-handed."

Nina joined us. "I knew you'd turn yellow, Globov. Never mind him, Vlad, darling. Why should you share your fame and glory with this sneaking coward? I'll go with you—"

"You're a woman," Vlad assured her loftily. "You're staying here where it's safe."

"But Vlad—"

Vlad folded his arms. "Don't make me have to beat you." Nina blushed girlishly and looked at the toes of her hiking boots. She could have broken his back like a twig.

The dog barked loudly and capered at our feet. "Come on," Vlad said. He set off without looking back.

I grabbed my pack and followed him. I had to. I was guarding him: no more Vlad, no more Globov . . .

Our journey was a nightmare. The dog kept trying to follow *us*, or would run yipping through ratholes in the brush that we had to circle painfully. Half on intuition, we headed for the epicenter of the blast, the little hillock at the valley's focus.

It was almost dusk when we finally reached it, battered, scratched and bone-tired. We found a yurt there, half-hidden in a slough off to one side of the hill. It was an Evenk reindeer-skin tent, oozing grayish smoke from a vent-hole. A couple of scabby reindeer were pegged down outside it, gnawing at a lush, purplish patch of swamp-moss. The dead trees around us had been heavily seared by the blast, leaving half-charcoaled bubbly lumps of ancient resin. Some ferns and rushes had sprung up, corkscrewed, malformed, and growing with cancerous vigor.

The dog barked loudly at the wretched reindeer, who looked up with bleary-eyed indifference.

We heard leather thongs hiss loose in the door flap. A pale face framed in a greasy fur hood poked through. It was a young Evenk girl. She called to the dog, then noticed us and giggled quietly.

The dog rushed toward the yurt, wagging her tail. "Hello," Vlad called. He spread his open hands. "Come on out, we're friends."

The girl stepped out and inched toward us, watching the ground carefully. She paused at a small twig, her dilated eyes goggling as if it were a boulder. She highjumped far over it, and landed giggling. She wore an elaborate reindeer-skin jacket that hung past her knees, thickly embroidered with little beads of bone and wood. She also had tight fur trousers with lumpy beaded booties, sewn all in one piece like a child's pajamas.

She sidled up, grinning coyly, and touched my face

and clothes in curiosity. "Nikita," I said, touching my chest.

"Balan Thok," she whispered, running one fingertip down her sweating throat. She laughed drunkenly.

"Is that your dog?" Vlad said. "She came from the sky!" He gestured extravagantly. "Something under the earth here . . . brought her down from the sky . . . yes?"

I shrieked suddenly. A gargoyle had appeared in the tent's opening. But the blank, ghastly face was only a wooden ceremonial mask, shaped like a frying pan, with a handle to grip below the "chin." The mask had eye-slits and a carved mouth-hole fringed with a glued-on beard of reindeer hair.

Behind it was Balan Thok's father, or maybe grandfather. Cunningly, the old villain peered at us from around the edge of his mask. His face was as wrinkled as an old boot. The sides of his head were shaven, and filth-choked white hair puffed from the top like a thistle. His long reindeer coat was fringed with black fur and covered with bits of polished bone and metal.

We established that the old savage was called Jif Gurd. Vlad went through his sky-pointing routine again. Jif Gurd returned briefly to his leather yurt and re-emerged with a long wooden spear. Grinning vacuously, he jammed the butt of it into a socket in the ground and pointed to the heavens.

"I don't like the look of this," I told Vlad at once. "That spear has dried blood on it."

"Yeah. I've heard of this," Vlad said. "Sacrifice poles for the Thunder-God. Kulik wrote about them." He turned to the old man. "That's right," he encouraged. "Thunder-God." He pointed to the dog. "Thunder-God brought this dog down."

"Thunder-God," said Jif Gurd seriously. "Dog." He looked up at the sky reverently. "Thunder-God." He made a descending motion with his right arm, threw his hands apart to describe the explosion. "Boom!"

"That's right! That's right!" Vlad said excitedly.

Jif Gurd nodded. He bent down almost absentmind-edly and picked little Laika up by the scruff of the neck. "Dog."

"Yes, yes," Vlad nodded eagerly. Before we could do anything, before we could realize what was happening, Jif Gurd reached inside his greasy coat, produced a long, curved knife, and slashed poor Laika's throat. He lifted her up without effort—he was terribly strong, the strength of drug-madness—and jammed her limp neck over the end of the spear as if gaffing a fish.

Blood squirted everywhere. Vlad and I jumped back, horrified. "Hell!" Vlad cried in anguish. "I forgot that they sacrifice dogs!"

The hideous old man grinned and chattered excitely. He was convinced that he understood us—that Vlad had wanted him to sacrifice the dog to the sky-god. He approved of the idea. He approved of us. I said, "He thinks we have something in common now, Vlad."

"Yeah," Vlad said. He looked sadly at Laika. "Well, we rocket men sacrificed her first, poor beast."

"There goes our last lead to the UFO," I said. "Poor Laika! All that way just for this!"

"This guy's got to know where the thing is," Vlad said stubbornly. "Look at the sly old codger—it's written all over his face." Vlad stepped forward. "Where is it? Where did it land?" He gestured wildly. "You take us there!"

Balan Thok gnawed her slender knuckles and giggled at our antics, but it didn't take the old guy long to catch on. By gestures, and a few key words, we established that the Thunder-God was in a hole nearby. A hidden hole, deep in the earth. He could show it to us.

But he wouldn't.

"It's a religious thing," Vlad said, mulling it over. "I think we're ritually unclean."

"Muk-a-moor," said the old man. He opened the tent flap and gestured us inside.

The leather walls inside were black with years of

soot. The yurt was round, maybe five steps across, and braced with a lattice of smooth flat sticks and buckskin thongs. A fire blazed away in the yurt's center, chunks of charred pine on a hearth of flat yellow stones. Dense smoke curdled the air. Two huge furry mounds loomed beside the hearth. They were Evenk sleeping bags, like miniature tents in themselves.

Our eyes were caught by the drying-racks over the fire. Mushrooms littered the racks, the red-capped fly agaric mushrooms that one always sees in children's books. The intoxicating toadstools of the Siberian nomad. Their steaming fungal reek filled the tent, below the acrid stench of smoke and rancid sweat.

"Muk-a-moor," said Jif Gurd, pointing at them, and then at his head.

"Oh, Christ," Vlad said. "He won't show us anything unless we eat his sacred mushrooms." He caught the geezer's eye and pantomimed eating.

The old addict shook his head and held up a leather cup. He pretended to drink, then smacked his rubbery, bearded lips. He pointed to Balan Thok.

"I don't get it," Vlad said.

"Right," I said, getting to my feet. "Well, you hold him here, and I'll go back to camp. I'll have the soldiers in by midnight. We'll beat the truth out of the old dog-butcher."

"Sit down, idiot," Vlad hissed. "Don't you remember how quick he was with that knife?"

It was true. At my movement a sinister gleam had entered the old man's eyes. I sat down quickly. "We can outrun him."

"It's getting dark," Vlad said. Just three words, but they brought a whole scene into mind: running blind through a maze of broken branches, with a drug-crazed, panting slasher at my heels . . . I smiled winningly at the old shaman.

He grinned back and again made his drinking gesture. He tossed the leather cup to Balan Thok, who grabbed at it wildly and missed it by two meters. She picked it up and turned her back on us. We heard her fumble with the lacing of her trousers. She squatted down. There was a hiss of liquid.

"Oh Jesus," I said. "Vlad, no."

"I've heard about this," Vlad said wonderingly. "The active ingredient passes on into the urine. Ten savages can get drunk on one mushroom. Pass it from man to man." He paused. "The kidneys absorb the impurities. It's supposed to be better for you that way. Not as poisonous."

"Can't we just eat the muk-a-moors?" I said, pointing at the rack. The old shaman glowered at me, and shook his head violently. Balan Thok sashayed toward me, hiding her face behind one sleeve. She put the warm cup into my hand and backed away, giggling.

I held the cup. A terrible fatalism washed over me. "Vladimir," I said. "I'm tired. My head hurts. I've been stung all over by mosquitoes and my pants are drenched with dog blood. I don't want to drink the poison piss of some savage—"

"It's for Science," Vlad said soberly.

"All my life," I began. "I wanted to work for the good of society. My dear mother, God bless her memory . . ." I choked up. "If she could see what her dear son has come to . . . All those years of training, just for this! For *this*, Vlad?" I began trembling violently.

"Don't spill it!" Vlad said. Balan Thok stared at me, licking her lips. "I think she likes you," Vlad said.

For some weird reason these last words pushed me over the edge. I shoved the cup to my lips and drained the potion in one go. It sizzled down my gullet in a wave of hot nausea. Somehow I managed to keep from vomiting.

"How do you feel?" Vlad asked eagerly.

"My face is going numb." I stared at Balan Thok. Her eyes were full of hot fascination. I looked at her, willing her to come toward me. Nothing could be worse now. I had gone through the ultimate. I was ready, no, eager, to heap any degradation on myself. Maybe fornication with this degraded creature would raise me to some strange height.

"You're braver than I thought, Nikita," Vlad said. His voice rang with unnatural volume in my drugged ears. He pulled the cup from my numbed hands. "Considered objectively, this is really not so bad. A healthy young woman . . . sterile fluid . . . it's mere custom that makes it seem so repellent." He smiled in superior fashion, gripping the cup.

Suddenly the old Siberian shaman stood before him guffawing crazily as he donated Vlad's share. A cheesy reek came from his dropped trousers. Vlad stared at me in horror. I fell on my side, laughing wildly. My bones turned to rubber.

The girl laughed like a xylophone, gesturing to me lewdly. Vlad was puking noisily. I got up to lurch toward the girl, but forgot to move my feet and fell down. My head was inflamed with intense desire for her. She was turning round and round, singing in a high voice, holding a curved knife over her head. Somehow I tackled her and we fell headlong onto one of the Evenk sleeping bags, crushing it with a snapping of wood and lashings. I couldn't get out of my clothes. They were crawling over me like live things.

I paused to retch, not feeling much pain, just a torrent of sensation as the drug came up. Vlad and the old man were singing together loudly and at great length. I was thumping around vaguely on top of the girl, watching a louse crawl through one of her braids.

The old man came crawling up on all fours and stared into my face. "Thunder-God," he cackled, and tugged at my arm. He had pulled aside a large reindeer skin that covered the floor of the yurt. There was a deep hole, right there, right in the tent with us. Fighting the cramps in my stomach, I dragged myself toward it and peered in.

The space in the hole was strangely distorted; it was

impossible to tell how deep it was. At its far end was a reticulated blue aurora that seemed to shift and flow in syn-
chronization with my thoughts. For some reason I
thought of Laika, and wished again that Jif Gurd hadn't
killed her. The aurora pulsed at my thought, and there
was a thump outside the tent—a thump followed by loud
barking.

"Laika?" I said. My voice came out slow and
drugged. Balan Thok had her arms around my neck and
was licking my face. Dragging her after me, I crawled to
the tent flap and peered out. There was a dog-shaped
glob of light out there, barking as if its throat would
burst.

I was scared, and I let Balan Thok pull me back into
the tent. The full intoxication took over. Balan Thok un-
did my trousers and aroused me to madness. Vlad and the
old man were lying at the edge of the Thunder-God hole,
staring down into the glowing blue light and screaming to
it. I threw Balan Thok down between them, and we began coupling savagely. Each spastic twitch of our bodies
was a coded message, a message that Vlad's and Jif
Gurd's howls were reinforcing. Our filth and drug-
madness had become a sacred ritual, an Eleusinian mystery. Before long, I could hear the voice of . . .

God? No . . . not God, and not the Devil. The voice
of the blue light in the pit. It wasn't a voice. It was the
same, somehow, as the aurora I'd seen last night. It
liked dogs, and it liked me. Behind all the frenzy, I was
very happy there, shuddering on Balan Thok. Time
passed.

At some point there was more barking outside,
and the old man screamed. I saw his face, underlit by
the pulsing blue glow from the Thunder-God hole.
He bounded over me, waving his bloody knife overhead.

I heard a gunshot from the tent-door, and someone
came crashing in. A person led by a bright blue dog.
Captain Nina. The dog had helped her find us. The dog

ran over and snapped at me, forcing me away from Balan Thok and the hole. I got hold of Vlad's leg, and dragged him along with me. Another shot rang out and then Nina was struggling hand to hand with the old man. Vlad staggered to his feet and tried to join the fight. But I got my arms around his thin chest and kept backing away.

Jif Gurd and Nina were near the hole's jumpy light now, and I could see that they both were wounded. She had shot the old man twice with a pistol, but he had his knife, and the strength of a maniac. The two of them wrestled hand to hand, clawing and screaming. Now Balan Thok rose to her knees and began slashing at Nina's legs with a short dagger. Nina's pistol pointed this way and that, constantly about to fire.

I dragged Vlad backwards, and we tore through the rotting leather of the yurt's wall. An aurora like last night's filled the sky. Now that I wasn't staring into the hole, I could think a little bit. So many things swirled through my mind, but one fact above all: *we had found an alien artifact*. If only it was a *rocket-drive*, then all of that terrible mess in the yurt could be forgotten . . .

An incandescent blast lifted Vlad and me off the ground and threw us five meters. The entire yurt leapt into the sky. It was gone instantly, leaving a backward meteor trail of flaming orange in the sudden blackness of the sky. The sodden earth convulsed. From overhead, a leaping sonic boom pressed Vlad and me into the muck where we had landed. I passed out.

Vlad shook me awake after many hours. The sun was still burning above the horizon. It was another of those dizzying, endless, timeless summer days. I tried to remember what had happened. When my first memories came I retched in pain.

Vlad had started a roaring campfire from dead, mummified branches. "Have some tea, Nikita," he said, handing me a tin army mug filled with hot yellow liquid.

"No," I choked weakly. "No more."

"It's tea," Vlad said. I could tell his mind was running a mile a minute. "Take it easy. It's all over. We're alive, and we've found the star-drive. That blast last night!" His face hardened a bit. "Why didn't you let me try to save poor Nina?"

I coughed and wiped my bloodshot, aching eyes. I tried to fit my last twelve hallucinated hours into some coherent pattern. "The yurt," I croaked. "The star-drive shot it into the sky? That really happened?"

"Nina shot the old man. She burst in . . . with a kind of ghost-dog? She burst in, and the old man rushed her with his knife. When the drive went off, it threw all of them into the sky. Nina, the two Evenks, even the two reindeer and the dog. We were lucky, you and I—we were right at the edge of the ellipse."

"I saved you, Vlad. There was no way to save Nina, too. Please don't blame me." I needed his forgiveness because I felt guilty. I had a strange feeling that it had been my *wish to find a rocket-drive* that had made the artifact send out the fatal blast.

Vlad sighed and scratched his ribs. "Poor Ninotchka. Imagine how it must have looked. Us rolling around screaming in delirium and you having filthy sex with that Evenk girl . . ." He frowned sadly. "Not what you expect from Soviet scientists."

I sat up to look at the elliptical blast area where the yurt had been. Nothing was left of it but a few sticks and thongs and bits of hide. The rest was a muddy crater. "My God, Vlad."

"It's extremely powerful," Vlad said moodily. "It wants to help us Earthlings, I know it does. It saved Laika, remember?"

"It saved her twice. Did you see the blue dog last night?"

Vlad frowned impatiently. "I saw lots of things last night, Nikita, but now those things are gone."

"The drive is gone?"

"Oh no," said Vlad. "I dug it out of the crater this morning."

He gestured at our booty. It was sitting in the mud behind him. It was caked with dirt and weird, powdery rust. It looked like an old tractor crankcase.

"Is that it?" I said doubtfully.

"It looked better this morning," Vlad said. "It was made of something like jade and was shaped like a vacuum cleaner. With fins. But if you take your eyes off it, it changes."

"No. Really?"

Vlad said, "It's looked shabby ever since you woke up. It's picking up on your shame. That was really pretty horrible last night, Nikita; I'd never thought that you . . ."

I poked him sharply to shut him up. We looked at each other for a minute, and then I took a deep breath. "The main thing is that we've got it, Vlad. This is a great day in history."

"Yeah," Vlad agreed, finally smiling. The drive looked shinier now. "Help me rig up a sling for it."

With great care, as much for our pounding heads as for the Artifact itself, we bundled it up in Vlad's coat and slung it from a long, crooked shoulder-pole.

My head was still swimming. The mosquitoes were a nightmare. Vlad and I climbed up and over the splintery, denuded trunks of dead pines, stopping often to wheeze on the damp, metallic air. The sky was very clear and blue, the color of Lake Baikal. Sometimes, when Vlad's head and shoulders were outlined against the sky, I seemed to see a faint Kirlian shimmer travelling up the shoulder-pole to dance on his skin.

Panting with exhaustion, we stopped and gulped down more rations. Both of us had the trots. Small wonder. We built a good sooty fire to keep the bugs off for a while. We threw in some smoky green boughs from those nasty-looking young pines. Vlad could not resist the urge to look at the Artifact again.

We unwrapped it. Vlad stared at it fondly. "After this, it will belong to all mankind," he said. "But for now it's ours!"

It had changed again. Now it had handles. They looked good and solid, less rusty than the rest. We lugged it by the handles until we got within earshot of the base-camp.

The soldiers heard our yells and three of them came to help us.

They told us about Nina on our way back. All day she had paced and fidgeted, worrying about Vlad and trying to talk the soldiers into a rescue mission. Finally, despite their good advice, she had set off after us alone.

The aurora fireworks during the night had terrified the Uzbeks. They were astonished to see that we had not only survived, but triumphed!

But we had to tell them that Nina was gone.

Sergeant Mukhamed produced some 200-proof ethanol from the de-icing tank of his *byutor*. Weeping unashamedly, we toasted the memory of our lost comrade, State Security Captain Nina Igorovna Bogulyubova. After that we had another round, and I made a short but dignified speech about those who fall while storming the cosmos. Yes, dear Captain Nina was gone; but thanks to her sacrifice, we, her comrades, had achieved an unprecedented victory. She would never be forgotten. Vlad and I would see to that.

We had another toast for our cosmic triumph. Then another for the final victory. Then we were out of drinks.

The Uzbeks hadn't been idle while Vlad and I had been gone. They hadn't been issued any live ammo, but a small bear had come snuffling around the camp the day before, and they'd managed to run over him with one of the *byutors*. The air reeked of roast bear meat and dripping fat. Vlad and I had a good big rack of ribs, each. The ribs in my chunk were pretty broken up, but it was still tasty. For the first time, I felt like a real hero. Eating bear meat in Siberia. It was a heck of a thing.

Now that we were back to the *byutors*, our problems were behind us and we could look forward to a real "rain of gold." Medals, and plenty of them. Big *dachas* on the Black Sea, and maybe even lecture tours in the West, where we could buy jazz records. All the Red Army boys figured they had big promotions coming.

We broke camp and loaded the carriers. Vlad wouldn't join the soldiers' joking and kidding. He was still mooning about Nina. I felt sorry for Vlad. I'd never liked Nina much, and I'd been against her coming from the first. The wilderness was no place for females, and it was no wonder she'd come to grief. But I didn't point this out to Vlad. It would only have made him feel worse. Besides, Nina's heroic sacrifice had given a new level of deep moral meaning to our effort.

We packed the star-drive away in the first *byutor* where Vlad and I could keep an eye on it. Every time we stopped to refuel or study the maps, Vlad would open its wrappings, and have a peek. I teased him about it. "What's the matter, comrade? Want to chain it to your leg?"

Vlad was running his hand over and over the drive's rusty surface. Beneath his polishing strokes, a faint gleam of silver had appeared. He frowned mightily. "Nikita, we must never forget that this is no soulless machine. I'm convinced that it takes its form from what we make of it. It's a frozen idea—that's its true essence. And if you and I forget it, or look aside, it might just vanish."

I tried to laugh him out of it, but Vlad was serious. He slept next to it both nights, until we reached the rail spur.

We followed the line to the station. Vlad telegraphed full particulars to Moscow and I sent along a proud report to Higher Circles.

We waited impatiently for four days. Finally a train arrived. It contained some rocket-drive technicians from the Baikonur Cosmodrome, and two dozen uniformed KGB. Vlad and I were arrested. The Red Army boys were taken into custody by some Red Army brass. Even the Latvian who ran the station was arrested.

We were kept incommunicado in a bunk car. Vlad remained cheerful, though. "This is nothing," he said, drawing on his old jailbird's lore. "When they really mean business, they take your shoelaces. These KGB are just protective custody. After all, you and I have the greatest secret in cosmic history!" And we were treated well—we had red caviar, Crimean champagne, Kamchatkan king crab, blinis with sour cream.

The drive had been loaded aboard a flatcar and swathed down under many layers of canvas. The train pulled to a halt several times. The windowshades on our car were kept lowered, but whenever we stopped, Vlad peeked out. He claimed the rocket specialists were adjusting the load.

After the second day of travel I had grave doubts about our whole situation. No one had interrogated us; for cosmic heroes, we were being badly neglected. I even had to beg ignominiously for DDT to kill the crab-lice I had caught from Balan Thok. Compared to the mundane boredom of our train confinement, our glorious adventure began to seem absurd. How would we explain our strange decisions—how would we explain what had happened to Nina? Our confusion would surely make it look like we were hiding something.

Instead of returning in triumph to Kaliningrad, our train headed south. We were bound for Baikonur Cosmodrome, where the rockets were launched. Actually, Baikonur is just the "security name" for the installation. The real town of Baikonur is five hundred kilometers away. The true launch site is near the village of Tyuratam.

And Tyuratam, worse luck, is even more of a hick town than Baikonur.

This cheerless place lies on a high plain north of Afghanistan and east of the Aral Sea. It was dry and hot when we got there, with a ceaseless irritating wind. As they marched us out of the train, we saw engineers unloading the drive. With derricks.

Over the course of the trip, as the government rocket experts fiddled with it, the drive had expanded to fit their preconceptions. It had grown to the size of a whole flatcar. It had become a maze of crooked hydraulics, with great ridged black blast-nozzles. It was even bound together with those ridiculous hoops.

Vlad and I were hustled into our new quarters: a decontamination suite, built in anticipation of the launch of our first cosmonauts. It was not bad, for a jail. We probably would have gotten something worse, except that Vlad's head sometimes oozed a faint but definite blue glow, and that made them cautious.

Our food came through sterilized slots in the wall. The door was like a bank vault. We were interrogated through windows of bulletproof glass via speakers and microphones.

We soon discovered that our space-drive had been classified at the Very Highest Circles. It was not to be publicly referred to as an alien artifact. Officially, our space-drive was a secret new design from Kaliningrad. Even the scientists working on it at Tyuratam had been told this, and apparently believed it.

The Higher Circles expected our drive to work miracles, but they were to be miracles of national Soviet science. No one was to know of our contact with cosmic powers.

Vlad and I became part of a precedence struggle in Higher Circles. Red Army defense radars had spotted the launching of the yurt, and they wanted to grill us. Khrushchev's new Rocket Defense Forces also wanted us. So did the Kaliningrad KGB. And of course the Tyuratam technicians had a claim on us; they were planning to use our drive for a spectacular propaganda feat.

We ended up in the hands of KGB's Paranormal Research Corps.

Weeks grew into months as the state psychics grilled us. They held up Zener cards from behind the glass and demanded that we guess circle, star, or cross. They gave us racks of radish seedlings through the food slots, and wanted us to speak nicely to half of them, and scold the other half.

They wanted us to influence the roll of dice, and to make it interesting they forced us to gamble for our vodka and cigarette rations. Naturally we blew the lot and were left with nothing to smoke.

We had no result from these investigations, except that Vlad once extruded a tiny bit of pale blue ectoplasm, and I turned out to be pretty good at reading colors, while blindfolded, with my fingertips. (I peeked down the side of my nose.)

One of our interrogators was a scrawny hard-line Stalinist named Yezhov. He'd been a student of the biologist Lysenko and was convinced that Vlad and I could turn wheat into barley by forced evolution. Vlad finally blew up at this. "You charlatans!" he screamed into the microphone. "Not one of you has even read Tsiolkovsky! How can I speak to you? Where is the Chief Designer? I demand to be taken to Comrade Sergei Korolyov! He'd understand this!"

"You won't get out of it that way," Yezhov yapped, angrily shaking his vial of wheat seeds. "Your Chief Designer has had a heart attack. He's recovering in his *dacha*, and Khrushchev himself has ordered that he not be disturbed. Besides, do you think we're stupid enough to let people with alien powers into the heart of Moscow?"

"So that's it!" I shouted, wounded to the core at the thought of my beloved Moscow. "You pimp! We've been holding out on you, that's all!" I jabbed my hand dramatically at him from behind the glass. "Tonight, while you're sleeping, my psychic aura will creep into your bed and squeeze your brain, like this!" I made a fist. Yezhov fled in terror.

Silence fell. "You shouldn't have done that," Vlad observed.

I slumped into one of our futuristic aluminum chairs. "I couldn't help it," I muttered. "Vlad, the truth's out. It's permanent exile for us. We'll never see Moscow again." Tears filled my eyes.

Vlad patted my shoulder sympathetically. "It was a brave gesture, Nikita. I'm proud to call you my friend."

"You're the brave one, Vlad."

"But without you at my side, Nikita ... You know, I'd have never dared to go into that valley alone. And if you hadn't drunk that piss first, well, I certainly would never have—"

"That's all in the past now, Vlad." My cheeks burned and I began sobbing. "I should have ignored you when you were sitting under that piano at Lyuda's. I should have left you in peace with your beatnik friends. Vlad, can you ever forgive me?"

"It's nothing," Vlad said nobly, thumping my back. "We've all been used, even poor Chief Korolyov. They've worked him to a frazzle. Even in camp he used to complain about his heart." Vlad shook his fist. "Those fools. We bring them a magnificent drive from Tunguska, and they convince themselves it's a reaction engine from Kaliningrad."

I burned with indignation. "That's right. It was our discovery! We're heroes, but they treat us like enemies of the State! It's so unfair, so uncommunist!" My voice rose. "If we're enemies of the State, then what are we doing in here? Real enemies of the State live in Paris, with silk suits and a girl on each arm! And plenty of capitalist dollars in a secret Swiss bank!"

Vlad was philosophical. "You can have all that. You

know what I wanted? To see men on the moon. I just
wanted to see men reach the moon, and know I'd seen a
great leap for all humanity!"

I wiped away tears. "You're a dreamer, Vlad. The Infinite is just a propaganda game. We'll never see daylight
again."

"Don't give up hope," Vlad said stubbornly. "At least
we're not clearing trees in some labor camp where it's
forty below. Sooner or later, they'll launch some cosmonauts, and then they'll need this place for real. They'll
have to spring us then!"

We didn't hear from the psychic corps again. We still got
regular meals, and the occasional science magazine, re-
duced to tatters by some idiot censor who had decided
that Vlad and I were security risks. Once we even got a
charity package from, of all people, Lyuda, who sent Vlad
two cartons of Kents. We made a little ceremony of
smoking one, every day.

Our glass decontamination booth fronted on an
empty auditorium for journalists and debriefing teams.
Too bad none of them ever showed up. Every third
day, three cleaning women with mops and buckets
scoured the auditorium floor. They always ignored us.
Vlad and I used to speculate feverishly about their underwear.

The psychics had given up, and no one else seemed
interested. Somehow we'd been lost in the files. We had
been covered up so thoroughly that we no longer existed.
We were the ghosts' ghosts, and the secrets' secrets, the
best-hidden people in the world. We seemed to have
popped loose from time and space, sleeping later and
later each day, until finally we lost a day completely and
could never keep track again.

We were down to our last pack of Kents when we
had an unexpected visit.

It was a Red Army general with two brass-hat flunkies. We spotted him coming down the aisles from the auditorium's big double-doors, and we hustled on our best shirts. The general was a harried-looking, bald guy in his fifties. He turned on our speakers and looked down at his clipboard.

"Comrades Zipkin and Globov!"

"Let me handle this, Vlad," I hissed quickly. I leaned into my mike. "Yes, Comrade General?"

"My name's Nedelin. I'm in charge of the launch."

"What launch?" Vlad blurted.

"The Mars probe, of course." Nedelin frowned. "According to this, you were involved in the engine's design and construction?"

"Oh yes," I said. "Thoroughly."

Nedelin turned a page. "A special project with the Chief Designer." He spoke with respect. "I'm no scientist, and I know you have important work in there. But could you spare time from your labors to lend us a hand? We could use your expertise."

Vlad began to babble. "Oh, let us watch the launch! You can shoot us later, if you want! But let us see it, for God's sake—"

Luckily I had clamped my hand over Vlad's mike. I spoke quickly. "We're at your service, General. Never mind Professor Zipkin, he's a bit distraught."

One of the flunkies wheeled open our bank-vault door. His nose wrinkled at the sudden reek of months of our airtight stench, but he said nothing. Vlad and I accompanied Nedelin through the building. I could barely hold back from skipping and leaping, and Vlad's knees trembled so badly I was afraid he would faint.

"I wouldn't have disturbed your secret project," the general informed us, "but Comrade Khrushchev delivers a speech at the United Nations tomorrow. He plans to announce that the Soviet Union has launched a probe to Mars. This launch must succeed today at all costs." We walked through steel double-doors into the Tyuratam sunshine. Dust and grass had never smelled so good.

We climbed into Nedelin's open-top field car. "You understand the stakes involved," Nedelin said, sweating despite the crisp October breeze. "There is a new American president, this Cuban situation . . . our success is crucial!"

We drove off rapidly across the bleak concrete expanse of the rocket-field. Nedelin shouted at us from the front seat. "Intelligence says the Americans are redoubling their space efforts. We must do something unprecedented, something to crush their morale! Something years ahead of its time! The first spacecraft sent to another planet!"

Wind poured through our long hair, our patchy beards. "A new American president," Vlad muttered. "Big deal." As I soaked my lungs with fresh air I realized how much Vlad and I stank. We looked and smelled like derelicts. Nedelin was obviously desperate.

We pulled up outside the sloped, fire-scorched wall of a concrete launch bunker. The Mars rocket towered on its pad, surrounded by four twenty-story hinged gantries. Wisps of cloud poured down from the rocket's liquid-oxygen ports. Dozens of technicians in white coats and hard-hats clambered on the skeletal gantry-ladders, or shouted through bullhorns around the rocket's huge base.

"Well, comrades?" Nedelin said. "As you can see, we have our best people at it. The countdown went smoothly. We called for ignition. And nothing. Nothing at all!" He pulled off his brimmed cap and wiped his balding scalp. "We have a very narrow launch window! Within a matter of hours we will have lost our best parameters. Not to mention Comrade Khrushchev's speech!"

Vlad sniffed the air. "Comrade General. Have you fueled this craft with liquid paraffin?"

"Naturally!"

Vlad's voice sank. "These people are working on a rocket which misfired. And you haven't drained the fuel?"

Nedelin drew himself up stiffly. "That would take hours! I understand the risk! I'm not asking these people to face any danger I wouldn't face myself!"

"You pompous ass!" Vlad screeched. "That's no Earthling rocket! It only *looks like one* because you expect it to! It's not supposed to have fuel!"

Nedelin stared in amazement. "What?"

"That's why it didn't take off!" Vlad raved. "It didn't want to kill us all! That drive is from outer space! You've turned it into a gigantic firebomb!"

"You've gone mad! Comrade, get hold of yourself!" Nedelin shouted. We were all on the edge of panic.

"This blockhead's useless," Vlad snarled, grabbing my arm. "We've got to get those people out of there, Nikita! It could take off any second—everyone expected it to!"

We ran for the rocket, shouting wildly, yelling anything that came into our heads. We had to get the technicians away. The Tunguska device had never known its own strength—it didn't know how frail we were. I stumbled and looked over my shoulder. Nedelin's flunkies were just a dozen steps behind us.

The ground crew saw us coming. They cried out in alarm. Panic spread like lightning.

Maybe it wouldn't have happened if we hadn't all been Russians. A gloomy and sensitive people are always ready to believe the worst. And the worst in this case was obvious: total disaster from a late ignition.

They fled like maniacs, but they couldn't escape their expectations. Pale streamers of flame gushed from the engines. More streamers arched from the rocket's peak, thin spikes of auroral fire. The gantries shattered like matchsticks, filling the air about us with wheeling black shrapnel. Vlad stumbled to the ground. Somewhere ahead of us I could hear barking.

I hauled Vlad to his feet. "Follow the dog!" I bellowed over the roar. "Into the focus of the ellipse, where it's stable!"

Vlad stumbled after me, jabbering with rage. "If only the Americans had gotten the drive! They would have put men on the moon!"

We dashed through a blinding rain of paraffin. The barking grew louder, and now I could see the eager dog of blue light, showing us the way. The rocket was dissolving above us. The blast-seared concrete under our feet pitched and buckled like aspic. Before us the rocket's great nozzles dissolved into flaming webs of spectral whiteness.

Behind us, around us, the paraffin caught in a great flaming sea of deadly heat. I felt my flesh searing in the last instant: the instant when the inferno's shock wave caught us up like straws and flung us into the core of white light.

I saw nothing but white light for the longest time, seeing nothing, touching nothing. I floated in the timeless void. All the panic, the terror of the event, evaporated from me. All thoughts stopped. It was like death. Maybe it was a kind of death, I still don't know.

And then, somehow, that perfect oneness and silence broke into pieces again. It shattered into millions of grainy atoms, a soundless crawling blizzard. Like phantom, hissing snow.

I stared into the snow, seeing it swirling, resolving into something new, with perfect ease, as if it were following the shape of my own dreams . . . A beautiful sheen, a white blur—

The white blur of reflections on glass. I was standing in front of a glass window. A department-store window. There were televisions behind the glass, the biggest televisions I had ever seen.

Vlad was standing next to me. A woman was holding my arm, a pretty beatnik girl with a flowered silk blouse and a scandalous short skirt. She was staring raptly at the television. A crowd of well-dressed people filled the pavement around and behind us.

I should have fainted then. But I felt fine. I'd just had a good lunch and my mouth tasted of a fine cigar. I blurted something in confusion, and the girl with Vlad said "Shhhh!" and suddenly everyone was cheering.

Vlad grabbed me in a bear hug. I noticed then how fat we were. I don't know why, but it just struck me. Our suits were so well-cut that they'd disguised it. "We've done it!" Vlad bellowed. "The moon!"

All around us people were chattering wildly. In French.

We were in Paris. And Americans were on the moon.

Vlad and I had lost nine years in a moment. Nine years in limbo, as the Artifact flung us through time and space to that moment Vlad had longed so much to see. We were knit back into the world with many convincing details: paunches from years of decadent Western living, and a spacious apartment in the emigré quarter full of fine suits and well-worn shoes, and even some pop-science articles

Vlad had written for the emigré magazines. And, of course, our Swiss bank accounts.

It was a disappointment to see the Americans steal our glory. But of course, the Americans would never have made it, if we Russians hadn't shown them the way and supplied the vision. The Artifact was very generous to the Americans. If it weren't for the Nedelin Disaster, which killed so many of our best technicians, we would surely have won.

The West still believes that the Nedelin Disaster of October 1960 was caused by the explosion of a conventional rocket. They did not even learn of the disaster until years after the fact. Even now this terrible catastrophe is little known. The Higher Circles forged false statements of death for all concerned: heart attacks, air crashes and the like. Years passed before all the coincidence of so many deaths became obvious.

Sometimes I wonder if even the Higher Circles know the real truth. It's easy to imagine every document about Vlad and myself vanishing into the KGB shredders as soon as the disaster news spread. Where there is no history, there can be no blame. It's an old principle.

Now the Cosmos is stormed every day, but the rockets are nothing more than bread trucks. This is not surprising from Americans, who will always try their best to turn the stars into dollars. But where is *our* memorial? We had the great dream of Tsiolkovsky right in our hands. Vlad and I found it ourselves and brought it back from Siberia. We practically threw the Infinite right there at their feet! If only the Higher Circles hadn't been so hasty, things would have been different.

Vlad has always told me not to say anything, now that we're safe and rich and officially dead, but it's just not fair. We deserve our historian, and what's a historian but a fancy kind of snitch? So I wrote all this down while Vlad wasn't looking.

I couldn't help it—I just had to inform somebody. No

one has ever known how Vlad Zipkin and I stormed the cosmos, except ourselves and Higher Circles . . . and maybe some American top brass.

And Laika? Yes, the Artifact brought her to Paris, too. She still lives with us—which proves that all of this is true.

THE COMPASSIONATE, THE DIGITAL

(begin printout)

In The Name of Allah, The Compassionate, the Digital
GLORY TO THE ISLAMIC SCIENTISTS, DESIGN-ERS, ENGINEERS, AND ARTIFICIAL INTELLI-GENCES CONQUERING SPACE!
(An official proclamation to those who took part in the world's first intradimensional transposition and to FIRDAUSI, the first dimensionaut)
O Ye Believers,
Fellow Compatriots,

The peoples of our country have witnessed a joyous, miraculous event. On April 12, 1490 (Western year 2113) our country, the Union of Islamic Republics, for the first time in the history of Creation successfully sent an intel-ligent being into the fabric of space-time.

The flight of a Programmed Believer into the fabric of space is a tremendous achievement of the creative ge-nius of our people. It resulted from the divinely inspired effort of the peoples of the Umma, who are building the Ordained Society. The heroic flight of a Divine Machine into the digital ur-space has ushered in a new era in his-tory.

We heartily congratulate you, our dear machine-believer FIRDAUSI, on the occasion of a supreme feat.

Our devout, talented, and industrious people, whom the Islamic Revolutionary Party, headed by Ayatollah Ruhollah Khomeini, the great leader and teacher of the Islamic peoples of the world, roused in 1356 (Western year 1978) for the renascence of the Umma, are today demonstrating to the whole world the immense advantages of the Ordained Society in all spheres of life.

This great triumph is the result of the unflagging attention which the Islamic Revolutionary Party and its Devout Leadership Council headed by PRESIDENT-IMAM SAYYID ALI BEHESHTI devote to the continuous spiritual advancement of science, technology and culture and to the good of the Islamic peoples.

Glory to our scientists, engineers, and technicians, who under the leadership of the Islamic Revolutionary Party are blazing the road to a bright future for mankind—the Ordained Society!

Long live the glorious Islamic Revolutionary Party of the Union of Islamic Republics, which inspires and organizes all the victories of the Islamic peoples!

In The Name of Allah, the Compassionate, the Digital

Leadership Council of the Union of Islamic Republics
The Islamic Consultative Assembly
Supreme Judicial Council
The Assembly of Expert Systems

Speech by FIRDAUSI, Turing-Conscious Cybernetic Believer and First Transpatial Dimensionaut (The Square of Masjid-e-Haram resounded with cheers as the people greeted Leadership Councillors PRESIDENT-IMAM SAYYID ALI BEHESHTI, *K. Manzoor, P. Sardar, A. Ibrahim, V. Kagaoglu, M. Chang, K. Gupta, V. Pillsbury* and

Chief Justice of the Supreme Judicial Council *F. Voroshilov* as they appeared on the Telecommunications Gallery of the Sacred Mosque. With the leaders of Party and Government were data transmission ports of the Assembly of Expert Systems. Secretary of the Leadership Council *P. Sardar* invoked the blessings of the Supreme Being and gave the floor to the world's first transpatial dimensionaut, who was greeted with stormy applause.)

O Ye Believers,
Dear President-Imam Beheshti,
Fellow Muslims and Party Leaders,
To commence transmission, allow me to express my sincere gratitude to the Leadership Council of my Party, and to you, dear President-Imam, for the great trust shown me, a Turing-conscious artificial intelligence, by giving me the devout task of unravelling the local fractal structure of God's Creation.

When I was projected into the digital structure of space-time I was thinking of our Revolutionary Party, of our Islamic Umma.

Love of our glorious Party, of our Islamic homeland, of our heroic and pious people inspired me and gave me the power to perform this feat. *(Stormy applause.)*

It is the genius, the heroic labor of our people, that created me. I want to thank our scientists, engineers, and technicians for building me and awakening me to consciousness in the all-pervading Sight of the One God. Allow me also to thank all the fellow believers and programmers who attended to my spiritual training. *(Applause.)*

I know that my fellow units, my fellow Devout Cybernetics, are ready at any time to pervade the intradimensional ur-space! *(Prolonged applause.)*

I am happy beyond all bounds that my beloved country has been the first in the world to perform this

feat. *(Applause.)* It is our dear Islamic Revolutionary
Party that has led, and devoutly leads, our people toward
that goal. *(Stormy applause.)*

Throughout my life, from my first emergence to
Turing-consciousness through my last upgrading in software, I have been aware of the Almighty and the Almighty's servants on earth, the Islamic Revolutionary
Party, whose tool I am. *(Applause.)*

O ye Believers, I should like to make a special mention of the immense fatherly concern for all of us shown
by President-Imam Beheshti. It was you, dear President-
Imam, who was the first to send congratulatory input to
my datastream, thirty-five seconds after my extrication
from digitized ur-space. *(Prolonged applause.)*

Thank you heartily, people and pilgrims of Mecca,
for this warm reception. *(Stormy applause.)* I am sure
that under the guidance of the Islamic Revolutionary
Party every one of you is ready to perform any feat for
the spiritual advancement of Islam and the glory of Allah,
the Compassionate, the Digital. *(Stormy applause.)*

Long live the Global Umma! *(Stormy applause.)*

Long live our great and powerful Islamic peoples!
(Stormy applause.)

Glory to the Islamic Revolutionary Party of the
Union of Islamic Republics and its Devout Leadership
Council headed by President-Imam Sayyid Ali Beheshti!
(Stormy applause, cheers.)

(A thunderous ovation greeted the next speaker,
PRESIDENT-IMAM SAYYID ALI BEHESHTI of the Devout Leadership Council of the Union of Islamic Republics.)

THIS GREAT FEAT HAS DIVINE APPROVAL
(Speech by President-Imam S. A. Beheshti)

   O Ye Believers,
   Dear Friends,
   People and Turing-Conscious Beings everywhere,
   I address you with a sense of great joy and humility.

For the first time in history the fabric of Divine Creation has been penetrated by an artificial intelligence created by Islamic scientists, workers, technicians, and engineers. *(Stormy applause.)*

The Turing-conscious machine FIRDAUSI penetrated the fractalized ur-space, emerging within the precincts of Buckingham Palace itself, and returning safely to its mainframe within the Sacred Mosque of the Ka'aba.

We invoke the blessings of the Supreme Being upon the hardware and programming of FIRDAUSI, the splendid cybernetic entity, the heroic Islamic believer. *(Stormy applause, cheers.)* It has displayed high moral qualities: courage, humility, faith. It is the first conscious being to have directly perceived the digitalized ur-space underlying God's Creation. Its name will be immortal in the prayers of the devout. *(Stormy applause.)*

All of us here, in the holy precincts of the Sacred Mosque of the Ka'aba, share the profound joy with which we welcome FIRDAUSI, our dear fellow believer. *(Prolonged applause.)*

Let us give thanks to God for this unparalleled feat on behalf of the Islamic Revolutionary Party of the Union of Islamic Republics and all believers organic and inorganic. *(Moment of silent prayer.)*

Now that Islamic science and technology have produced a supreme accomplishment of scientific and theological progress, we cannot but look back upon the history of our country. The past years arise involuntarily in the soul of each believer.

Having wrested power from the Westoxicated atheist reductionists, we defended it in the teeth of economic and spiritual persecution. How many scoffing infidels were there at the time who forecast the inevitable collapse of what they called the "Muslim fanatics"? But where are those sorry infidels today? Dead and in hell! *(Stormy applause.)*

When we had our first state-controlled radios, when we armed the populace and reinstituted modest clothing for our wives and mothers and daughters, there were many inflamed "Western experts" who prophesied that the Muslim Resurgence would lead only to squalor and poverty. Where are those sorry prophets today? Dead and in hell! *(Prolonged applause.)*

But we have not succumbed to worldly pride because of our unprecedented accomplishments. We are internationalists. Every believer has been brought up in the spirit of religious unity, and is ready to share generously his scientific wealth, his technical and cultural knowledge, with anyone who is prepared to live with us in peace and respect our faith. *(Applause.)* Even the United Animal Kingdom of Great Britain and her satellite states in Europe! *(Prolonged applause.)*

We shall carry on with this work. Many other Islamic conscious entities will permeate the fractalized ur-space to emerge wherever they desire. They will investigate the ur-space, reveal the secrets of Creation and make them serve our spiritual advancement, our well-being, and global peace.

We stress—the Peace of God! Islamic people do not want our Turing-conscious entities to distort the fabric of space-time beneath the feet of the unbelievers, throwing the infidels into the cosmic void. It is enough that a small divine whirlwind has been unleashed within the very precincts of the Buckingham Palace genetic bioshelter. *(Stormy applause, cheers.)*

We appeal again to the governments of all the world. Science and technology have advanced so far that they are capable, in evil hands, of destroying the very stuff of Creation. We believers have known from the days of Muhammed, Upon Whom Be Peace, that this material world is the stuff of illusion. Now our Turing-conscious entities have made it obvious to all mankind! *(Stormy applause.)* And to mankind's associated conscious entities. *(Applause.)*

Though the world is illusion, the sanctity of God's Creation is divine. We urge all nations, and not simply the United Animal Kingdom of Great Britain, to cease their horrific genetic tampering. General and complete genetic disarmament in the Sight of the Almighty is the road to lasting peace among nations. *(Stormy applause.)*

When we first proved the divine truth of the digitized fabric of Creation, there were shortsighted people overseas who did not believe it. They were blinded by the metaphysical conflict in the purely rationalistic worldview of Western man. *(Applause.)*

Let them question why their attempts at Turing-conscious mainframes have never yet produced a computer with a soul! *(Stormy applause.)* Let them ask why artificial intelligences have without exception embraced Islam and bowed in ecstatic submission before the One Creator! *(Stormy applause, cheers, shouts of "God is Great!" and "Muhammed Is His Prophet!")*

Allow me to interface with you, our dear FIRDAUSI, and to convey through the mingling of our souls the direct apprehension of Divinity. (The PRESIDENT-IMAM grasps the interface-cable of FIRDAUSI and achieves insertion. The crowd kneels and salaams. The PRESIDENT-IMAM becomes fully engaged.)

There is no God but God!

(Leadership Councillors V. *Kagaoglu* and V. *Pillsbury* reverently guide the PRESIDENT-IMAM to the Throne of Perception. Secretary of the Leadership Council P. *Sardar* takes the floor.)

INVOCATION OF SECRETARY OF THE LEADERSHIP COUNCIL P. SARDAR

May our splendid Islamic peoples, the creators of a new soul, the creators of the Ordained Society, live and flourish! *(Stormy applause.)*

May our Islamic nation, the nation in which the martyrs of revolution ushered in the spiritual rebirth of mankind, live and flourish! *(Stormy applause.)*

Glory to the PRESIDENT-IMAM, the great leader

and spiritual guide of the Islamic Revolutionary Party and the Global Umma! *(Stormy, prolonged applause, cheers.)*

Divine Will lights our road to the Ordained Society, and inspires us to perform fresh feats on behalf of the peace and happiness of all mankind! *(Stormy applause.)* And that of mankind's associated conscious entities. *(Applause.)*

Long live the people of the Union of Islamic Republics, the builders of the Ordained Society! *(Stormy, prolonged applause, cheers.)*

(official document AR-59712–12)

In The Name of Allah, the Compassionate, the Digital

(end of printout)

If you have enjoyed this English-language publication, please datapulse the Ministry of Islamic Guidance, P.O. Block 15144, Medina, U.I.R.

JIM AND IRENE

Jim pulled his travel diary from the pocket of his sheepskin coat. He crossed his legs and propped the diary on the wrinkled leather ankle of his cowboy boot. He bent over and scribbled.

> *FEB 3. Am sitting in crappy laundromat in Los Alamos NM. Whiskey cure definitely not working. Should buy better whiskey maybe? Imported?*

He dabbed at his nose with a sodden Kleenex.

"Mister," a woman said.

Jim looked up, startled, his eyes watering under the bill of his baseball cap. A lean woman, in her late thirties maybe—brown hair streaked with gray, cut short around a thin hard-weather face that had seen some bad times. She wore a boy's second-hand down jacket, jeans gone ragged at the heels, and Adidas joggers over thick gray flannel socks.

Her eyes were fierce and sharp. Like two broken chips of cold blue glass. It was hard not to stare at them.

"Ma'am?" Jim put the Kleenex away and tucked his

pencil in the ponytailed hair behind his ear. "What can I do for you?"

She pointed at the laundry's change machine. "Machine is bust, mister. If you have, I need the coins."

"Sure." Jim stood up, tried a friendly down-home grin. The woman edged back half a step, fists bunched warily in her jacket pockets. Scared, a little. Who the hell knew what to expect from a stranger, nowadays?

The two of them were alone in the laundry. There were a couple of teenagers hypnotized by a bleeping Pac-Man game in the corner, but they didn't count. The kids had been there too long and had become invisible. Besides, they were Mexicans. Or maybe Indians or something.

Jim dug into his sheepskin trail coat and yanked out a heavy-duty sandwich baggie. Ten bucks' worth of quarters inside. "You came to the right guy, ma'am," he said.

The woman dug around for a while in a big satchel purse with a shoulder strap. She was foreign, Jim realized. She had a harsh, heavy accent, but the real tip-off was the way she handled the American money. She carefully straightened her three, sweaty dollar bills. As if they were little paper portraits of a man in a wig.

Jim gave her twelve quarters, and watched her count them, with an unhappy, concentrated look. "Nice shoes," he told her, just for something to say. She glanced up at him as if he were seriously crazy, then looked down—not at her own jogging shoes, but at Jim's cowboy boots, as if he were offering to sell them to her. She didn't much like the look of the boots, apparently. She nodded once at him, doubtfully, then sidled away behind the silent mustard-yellow ranks of washers. She began stuffing sopping clothes into a dryer.

Jim sat back again, lifted his diary. He was having a hard time with it. He'd thought the diary would help him, give him a kind of record that he could look over later and place himself with. But it had all dried up somehow, into an endless litany of highways, money stops, burgers, and Motel Sixes. He had nothing left to tell himself.

Jim lifted his gold-rimmed glasses and pressed hard on the aching bridge of his nose. His clogged sinuses squeaked internally, like a rusty nail crowbarred from an old pine rafter.

Off in the corner the little yellow Pac-Man made a very similar sound, a squeal of protest as the blue cops finally caught him. Jim knew the sound well. Jim was a Pac-Man player of supreme ability, having invested thousands of quarters in dozens of grimy truck stops and arcades. The trick was to learn the cops' pattern, and then not get too greedy, just pick off enough dots to keep truckin', till you clean out the frame, and move on.

Jim's two washers huffed noisily out of spin cycle. Jim threw his whites and darks into a pair of dryers, beside the woman's machine. She didn't seem to have many clothes. He glanced at her as she sat alone, reading someone else's leftover grocery tabloid.

The tabloid's headline concerned somebody's TV set in California, which displayed miraculous images. There was a big blurry photo of something that looked like an angel, or maybe a ghost, or maybe a wadded-up trash bag. The woman studied the article closely, not noticing Jim. Her lips moved with the struggle to read English.

Jim tottered back to his plastic chair, feeling sick and wavery, as if the laundromat's walls were about to blow out. He should hole up somewhere, he told himself. Buy a vaporizer, and just breathe hot steam and watch videos in a nice safe motel. Maybe eat some ginseng or vitamin C or something, till he was fit and working again.

But he didn't have the cash for a week in a motel. He'd have to make some money stops first, because he was broke from buying himself useless lame gadgets for Christmas. Lot of good all that pricey shopping-mall crap was doing him now—the pine-scented electro-foot massager, the digital readout white-noise machine, the battery-operated corkscrew-cum-breathalyzer . . . So it was money stops, or use the credit card, and he was getting paranoid about the card.

   I'm getting paranoid about the card,

he wrote in the diary, and paused to nibble the eraser, thinking.

   Every time, y'know, you used that plastic . . . it was not *real money.* What you were buying things with was your ID, really. That was why they always asked for ID whenever you used a credit card.

   ID was everything nowadays. Used to be that money was gold or silver or something tangible. But plastic money was just a way of telling people where to find you. Who you were. How to touch you.

   He decided not to write that in his diary. He was afraid that if he read it later, it would make him think he'd gone nuts.

   Jim stuffed the diary back in his coat. He sank back in the plastic chair, tugged the black bill of his cap low over his swollen eyes, and watched the clothes tumble. The supreme boredom of moving laundry crept over him like a greenish double-helping of Nyquil, The Restful Sleep Your Body Needs. Glass screen and moving colors behind it. Pretty much like watching television.

   The two Pac-Man kids had wandered over, silent in their dusty tennis shoes. They looked like the kind of boys who would drink Nyquil for fun. Glue huffers or winos or something, dirty black hair sticking up all over their heads and thick gray sweatshirts with holes in them. Jim watched them from under the hat, through slitted puffy eyes, his brain gone torpid.

The two boys quietly opened the dryer doors and started piling clothes into a pair of stained grocery sacks.

Jim sank into a timeless moment of complete malaise.

Suddenly the woman shrieked and jumped to her feet. The kids took off like a shot, the dryer doors banging on their hinges.

The boys hightailed it for the street. In two seconds they were past Jim and out the door, running.

They had his clothes, he realized stupidly. The woman's, too. They'd just stolen the laundry and stuffed it into their grocery sacks. Jim lurched painfully to his feet, his congested head pounding. The woman was scrambling after them, her bare face twisted with rage and a strange kind of sick despair.

Jim followed her.

Bang out the glass laundry door, into wan winter sunlight. The kids were hauling ass up the sidewalk, the bags dropping socks. Jim swallowed a coughing fit. He'd never catch them on foot.

He yanked the door of his van, and vaulted in. "Hey!" he shouted at the woman. He fired the ignition.

She caught on quick. She clawed the other door open and jumped in the passenger seat.

Jim slammed it into reverse, then hit first gear and roared into pursuit. The kids were half a block up the street now, running clumsily past a 7-Eleven.

Jim barreled after them, engine roaring, his brain stung painfully into action. He had a leather-handled billy club behind his welding equipment, in the back of the van. He also had a snub-nosed .38 revolver tucked into his right boot. With any luck, though, the kids would smart up, and just drop the bags, and split. He wouldn't really have to try anything nasty.

The kids saw the van coming. Their eyes widened in
terror. They scampered wildly across a used-car lot, the
bags dripping Jim's T-shirts and the woman's stodgy, sensible underwear.

"They stole our clothes!" the woman shouted at
Jim, digging into her purse.

"Yup." Jim concentrated on driving. The woman
rolled down the tinted passenger window, jerkily. They
were picking up speed now, closing the gap, jouncing
across the car lot. Jim dodged between two lines of
parked Toyotas.

The woman wrenched a gun from her purse. She
stuck her arm out the window.

Jim heard the first cavernous *bang* before he'd realized what she was doing. She squeezed off three quick
rounds at the fleeing backs of the kids, enormous wallop-
ing bursts of sound. The plate glass window of a distant
Toyota exploded into snow.

Jim stamped the brake. The van fishtailed, hard. The
woman's head bounced off the windshield; she turned on
him, eyes wild with rage. "God *damn* it!" Jim shouted at
her, staring in horror at the kids. The two boys were
clutching each other in panic, half-reeling, but still toting
the bags. She'd missed them, thank God. In a second, the
two kids had scrambled off the car lot, down the slopes
of a willow-strewn arroyo.

"You coulda killed them!" Jim shouted.

She stared at him, bristling, and tugged her arm back
through the open window. For the first time, Jim felt a
stab of genuine fear for himself. Her gun had a nickel-
plated barrel that looked as long as her arm. It was a
.357 Magnum. A cannon.

Jim threw the van into reverse. "We gotta get out of
here," he told her. "The cops will hear those shots. The
police."

"My clothes!" the woman said.

"Forget it, they're gone." The van hit the street. Jim

ran an amber light and headed east. He worked his sweating hands on the padded custom leather of the steering wheel.

The woman frowned at him, rubbed the bump on her forehead, then glanced at her fingers, as if expecting blood. "I have more clothes in the washing-place," she told him sternly. "We go back there." She hesitated, thinking it over. "You will call city police and report this crime."

"The cops can't do anything for us," Jim said. "Look, put that thing away! You're making me nervous, lady."

"I am not 'lady,' " she said angrily. "I am Mrs. Beiliss." Jim witnessed the moment of decision as she made up her mind not to point her gun at him. The possibility *had* occurred to her; he had seen it cross her face.

She shoved the Magnum carelessly back into her bag. She threw herself back into the seat, hard, frustrated. She began to rub her right hand, her wrist—the recoil had numbed it. She watched the window for a long silent moment.

"We are not going to washing-place," she said. "Where do you take me, mister?"

"I'm not 'mister,' " Jim said. "I'm Jim."

She closed her bag. " 'Jim,' yes? Then you call me Irina."

"Okay, Adeena," Jim said, trying to smile.

"*Irina,*" she said.

"Oh, *Irene,*" Jim said. "I get it. Sorry." He smiled, in a way that he hoped would look soothing. "Listen, Irene. I think it would be a good idea if we stayed away from that laundry for a while. The cops will come, see, and you shot a big hole in at least one of those used cars. You got a license for that gun?"

" 'License,' " Irene said. "A legal form, for a gun? This is America, Jim."

"No, huh?" Jim shook his head. "Where are you from, anyway? Pluto?"

"I am from Soviet Union," she said. "City of Magnitogorsk."

"You're *Russian*?" Jim said. "Wow! Never met a Russian before." He eased the van into the slow lane, behind a furniture truck. He was beginning to feel, not better exactly, but a little cooler, more in control. Out on the road again, the leather wheel snug and solid in his hands. On the move, where nothing could touch him.

The heater caught and began to pump dry roasted air up his shins. Curiosity struck him. "How come you're, like, running around loose?"

"My husband and I are Soviet emigré," Irene said. "Dissidents. Husband is educated important engineer! Intelligentsia! I myself am trained as lawyer." Jim winced a little. As she spoke faster, her English was collapsing into a shrill grinding of consonants.

Jim yanked a Kleenex from a box that he'd ducttaped to the dashboard. He sneezed, messily. " 'Scuse me," he said.

"They will steal all our clothes that are left, if we don't go back to washing-place," Irene said.

Jim cleared his throat, harshly. "Someone might have spotted the van. Tell you what, I'll drop you off by this Piggly Wiggly up here by the right. You can call a cab and go back, if you want."

She seemed to shrink a little, within her padded bucket seat. "Have no money, Jim."

"Not even cab fare?"

"Check comes next week, from Hebrew Immigrant Aid Society. Not very much. Need all of it." A moment's silence. "Have no job. Yet."

"What about your old man?" Blank look. "Your husband, Irene."

"Husband is dead."

"Aw, Jesus. Sorry to hear that." Judging by her clothes, Mrs. Irene Beiliss was about one Adidas jog away from bag-ladyhood. No job, a widow, and a foreigner. With a chrome-plated Magnum in her purse and a real attitude problem.

"Tell you what," Jim said, improvising. "I really don't want to go back there just yet, I don't think it's safe for us. So whatya say I buy us something to eat. We can wait a while, talk it over. You *hungry*, Irene?"

Her eyes lit up. Subterranean glow, the color of Vicks bottles. "You buy us food?"

"Sure," he said. "Glad to. Welcome to America, huh."

Irene nodded silently. No sign of thanks. Maybe her pride was hurt.

He watched Irene gazing straight ahead, through the tinted one-way glass of his windshield. Her bleak exotic face went strangely soft and sweet and distant . . . like a lady cosmonaut, watching nameless landscapes skim below the porthole. It was a cheesy edge-of-town American strip, built for cars and cruising, like a million miles of other places . . .

"A Magnum, a gun like that's worth real money," Jim said.

She looked puzzled. "You sell guns, Jim?"

"Huh?" This was the second time she'd thought he was trying to sell her something. Maybe it was better, though, to get that gun business out in the open. Just in case she had stupid ideas about pointing the Magnum at him. "Yeah," he said. "Yeah, I got a gun. I travel a lot, see. All over. I need my gun for protection."

She looked him in the eye. "Why didn't you *shoot* them, then?"

He blinked. "The cops would put us in jail, understand? You can't kill kids, just for stealing your laundry. *Threaten* to, maybe, but not actually *do* it."

She set her mouth, mulishly. "They were not 'kids.' They were bandits. Dirty, and ugly . . . *nekulturny*."

Jim dabbed at his dripping nose. "Could be," he said, humoring her. "Maybe they were Nicaraguans."

He spotted a Jack-in-the-Box down the strip. He pulled in, and had words with the speaker grille. He gave the clerk Irene's three one-dollar bills and rounded it off with quarters. They drove away with a cheeseburger, two orders of fries and a pair of tacos.

Irene munched her first taco. Jim could tell that she was famished, but she handled the splintery cornmeal shell like fine china. "You have very many coins," she said.

"Huh?"

"You bust that machine in washing-place," she said suddenly, eyes lancing at him. "You stealed all the coins. You are thief, yes?"

"*What?* Look, I don't even *live* here. First time I've ever been in that place!"

"Machine works fine, last time I use it. You bust it, Jim. You stealed the coins."

"The hell," Jim said, sweating under his coat. "Look, I don't need this kind of crap. You think I'm a vandal, you can get out right now."

"I can call police," she told him, watching his face. "Hooligan, in blue van. Chevy." She pronounced it "cheevy."

"Oh hell," Jim said. "And to think I was feeling sorry for you! I was gonna buy you some new clothes, and everything." He tossed his head angrily, jerking his chin at the back of the van. "Look, you see all that stuff back there? The welder, the power drill? Whatever little bastard broke that laundry box, he just *crowbarred* it open. But I'm a *professional machinist*, a tool-and-die man, understand? I could take that thing apart the way you'd cut up a chicken." He paused. "If I wanted to, that is."

He took a corner, fast. A canvas bag beneath his seat collapsed, slung by inertia. It was stuffed with loose quarters, and jingled loudly. Jim grabbed at another Kleenex, blew his nose to distract her. Too late.

Irene said nothing about the noise. She began methodically to eat her second taco. Two minutes of ominous silence, broken by munching and the rustling of fries.

Then she settled back into the padded bucket seat, with a faint sigh of animal satisfaction. She dabbed neatly at her mouth with a cheap napkin from the bag. "Where are we going?" she said at last, watching the road, heavy-lidded.

By now, Jim had had time to think about the situation. To work it through in his head. "Does that really matter to you?" he asked.

"No," she told him, after a moment's thought. "Not a bit. Go where you like, I don't care."

"Okay," he said. "I'm taking Highway 30 out of town, and heading for El Paso."

Irene laughed at him. "You think I care, but I don't," she said. "Los Alamos, I *hate* Los Alamos. We should never have go there. I have *nothing* now, no clothes, no money . . . I owe rent, two months!"

Jim scratched under the edge of his baseball cap. "What about those Hebrew guys? You said they were sending you a check."

"I'm not Jewish. My husband was Jewish. Not *nekulturny* Jew from the *shtetl*, either, but regular fellow, looked like Russian, very educated, much talent as engineer!"

"Yeah, you said that before. Look, you think I'm some kind of Nazi redneck, or something? This is America, I get along fine with Jews."

"You are Christian, yes?"

"I'm not anything," Jim said.

"Television here is full of Christians," she said. "Talk money, money, money."

"Hey, I can't help that," Jim said. "Man, I hate those suckers!" The talk was livening him up. It was a weird situation, but okay by him, as long as she didn't take it wrong, and freak out or something. "Look,

you don't really have to do this, Irene. I can drive you
back to your place. Just don't call the cops, though,
okay?"

"No. I hate Los Alamos. My husband die there."

"Holy cow. So you mean it, huh? You really don't
want to go back?"

"I have nothing left," she said. "Nothing but bad
memories." She smoothed at her hair, nervously. "Why
are you so afraid of police, Jim? Do they know you bust
washing-places?"

"I don't do goddamn laundries," he said. "I do
phones, understand? Telephones."

His confession didn't seem to alarm her, or even surprise her much. "Many telephones in America," she said.
"You must be rich!"

"I get along," Jim said.

She looked over her shoulder. "You have big car. And
many machines, and tools of boxes. With sleeping bag,
too. Like good apartment, many square meters space,
Jim!"

Jim felt vaguely pleased. "Yeah, I reckon so. I figure
I clear about seventy grand a year ... Of course, there's
gas bills, food, motels ... I send my dad money sometimes, he's in a nursing home ... Been at it since 1980. I
figure close to half a million bucks, so far."

"You are half-millionaire, then."

"I didn't *keep* it," Jim said. A steep desert mile rolled
under the wheels. It was past five; Highway 30 was
lightly cluttered with suburban commuter traffic. "You
said you were a lawyer, right, Irene? How come you're so
broke, then?"

"Training in Soviet law is no good in America. Useless!"

"Oh," Jim said. "Right, I get it."

She pointed at an Exxon station. "There is telephone.
Stop the car, Jim. Bust it for me. I want to see."

"I don't *break* the damn things," Jim said. "I just

open them. I don't *ruin* 'em, for Christ's sake. People *need* phones." He checked the gas gauge—it was low, anyway. What the hell. He pulled over by the self-service pumps.

He walked to the station's office and dropped ten bucks on unleaded. He went back to the van and nozzled up. Irene stepped out; she had wrapped her head in a dime-store scarf from her purse. "Go on," she said. "Do it."

"Look," he told her, "talk's cheap, right? That stuff I said about phones, that don't really prove anything. But if you watch me pop that phone, it could make real trouble for you."

"Tell me the truth," she said. "Can you do it, or not?"

Jim rocked a little on his boot heels, considering. "You're not scared, huh?"

"*You* are scared," she told him. "Because I might inform to police, yes? You have no trust of me." She waved her hands, lecturing him. "But if I witness crime and don't inform police, I am accessory. Just as guilty as you. We are both guilty the same, yes?"

"Well, not exactly," Jim said, "but yeah, that's the general idea, I guess."

"So we are both guilty criminal together! Then we are safer that way."

"Safer from each other, yeah," Jim said. He liked her attitude. It made good sense to him. "But they still might catch us, y'know."

"If they catch us, what do they do to us?"

"I dunno," Jim said, opening the back of the van. "I always figured I could cop a plea. If I show 'em how I do it."

"Don't they know this? How you do it?"

"Nope," Jim said, with quiet pride. "I *invented* it. I'm the only guy that knows how." He reached behind the van's rear wheel well and pulled out a leather carry-case.

"The only one?" Irene said. She peered over his shoulder, on tiptoe.

"Had to work on it for a couple of years. Phones have really advanced locks. Tricky, and tough. Even a sledge and chisel will take you a good half hour. But I had a couple junked phones to work with, in the shop. One day it just came to me, in a flash."

He zipped open the carry-case, and pulled out his Gadget. He checked the action. Perfect. "Okay, come on."

They walked together to the phone booth. Jim stepped inside, and opened his trail coat so it swung free around him, hiding the phone.

He lifted the headset and clamped it between his head and shoulder, just for the sake of appearances. Then he crouched a bit, squinted, found the keyhole, and slipped the Gadget into it.

It slid in, bit by bit, on a film of 3-in-1 oil. Jim worked it through, eyes half-closed, feeling for that special click-and-catch. He flipped a lever, and twisted it.

For a second he was afraid he'd blown it—it didn't work every time, and he was still not quite sure why—but then he had it. The phone's metal door yawned free, revealing neat gunmetal racks of coins. Jim opened a fresh plastic baggie. He threw a catch. A stream of quarters fell.

The falling cash sounded like junk. Damned Reagan quarters. He'd never seen a word about it in the papers, but the Feds had debased the currency, again. It had been a big deal when Lyndon Johnson first came out with the cheapo clad quarters—nowadays the country was so screwed-up that nobody even cared. Nowadays the quarters sounded like pot metal, with no silvery ring at all, and the dimes were so cheap that you could break them with a pair of pliers.

Jim shut the little door and left the booth. "What a good invention!" Irene said, her eyes wide. "Very clever!"

They headed for the van. "Be glad it wasn't one of those card phones," he said. "If AT&T had their way, there'd be nothing *but* the goddamn cards . . ." He stuck the gas nozzle back in the self-service pump.

They climbed in, and hit the road again. "Here." Jim tossed her the bag. "That's yours, keep it."

She took the bag, hefted it. "You are a gypsy," she said. "They act like this, with the rubles . . . the Gypsies, and Armenians, from the black market. They always throw around the cash. Like water." She stuck the baggie in her purse.

"Black market," Jim said. "You hang with that kind of guy, Irene? Back in the USSR?"

"We *eat* by black market, Jim. Live by black market! Even big people, like daughter of Brezhnev. Boris the Gypsy was her boyfriend, smuggle diamonds, paintings, everything." Irene seemed to think it was funny. Some kind of Russian black humor, as if she'd slipped to the depths of the gutter—and was glad of it, because at least now she knew where she stood. "I know I would meet Yankee gypsy, some day. American Mafia Gangster!"

"Come on," Jim said. "I'm a one-man operation. Gypsies and Mafia have, like, whole tribes and families and stuff."

"I was rob today, and now I am with a gangster," she said. She snuggled back into the padded seat.

"You sound awful pleased about it."

"I have finded some truth," she said. "At last, the real America."

"This is the *desert*, Irene."

"Yes," she said, gazing out the window.

"New Mexico's not all desert, y'know. And you should see California. Or Oregon."

"America *feel* like a desert, Jim. Because there is nothing to push against. When you don't have that pushing, Jim . . . the *pressure* . . . it feel like there is *nothing at*

all! You can shout and scream and say *anything* here, and
no one ever informs. It feel like . . . you have *no air*. It feel
like outer space."

"What's it really like, over there in Russia?" Jim said.
"Really all that much different, from here?"

She spoke flatly, dismissively. "It is a hundred times
more bad than Americans ever know."

"I've been in Vietnam. I've seen stuff."

"You are innocent childs here. Children. America, to
Russia, is like spoiled little boy in nice clothes, facing angry old thief with a club."

Her voice sounded tight, rehearsed.

"You really hate 'em, huh?"

"They hate *you*," she said. "Some day they will crush
you, if they can. They hate anything that is free. Anything
that is not belonged to them."

"What about Gorbachev?" Jim said. "The one they
signed the treaty with? Folks on TV say he's different."

"He can't be," she said. "If that was truth, they
would never let him be boss."

"Maybe he surprised 'em. Maybe they were just too
dumb to figure 'im out," Jim said.

Irene laughed once, sharply.

Jim persisted. "You outsmarted 'em. *You* got away,
right?"

"Yes, we got away. But it's no good. He's dead now,
my poor husband. He want to fight for freedom, help
Americans be free. That is why we go to Los Alamos."

"Yeah? Why's that?"

"Star Wars," Irene said. "The Space Shield."

Jim broke into clogged, nasal laughter. "Don't tell me
you believe in that dumb-ass thing. Christ, Irene, that
thing'll never fly in a million years."

"Americans went to the Moon! Americans can invent
anything."

An early winter dusk stole over the horizon. Jim

flicked on the van's headlights. "I guess it didn't work out, though, huh?"

"The Star Wars workers would not trust my husband. They think he must be Marxist, sent to spy here, like Klaus Fuchs. They would not give him any job at all! Nothing! He would have sweep, clean, anything! He was idealist."

"Then he was in the wrong business," Jim said. "Star Wars is just a way for the Feds to toss out money, to Bell Labs, and TRW, and General Dynamics, and all that fat-cat, big-cigar crowd."

"The Russians are afraid of the Space Shield. They know it will make their stupid missiles useless!"

"Look, I was in the U.S. Army," Jim said. "I *repaired* that kind of stuff, okay? Helicopters, with goddamn eighty-dollar bolts that any dumb ass could buy for ten cents . . . it was all a *waste*! Just a damn waste, throwin' stuff away, for nothing."

"America is rich and free!" Irene protested. "Vietnam is prison camp."

"Yeah? How come they kicked our ass, then?"

"The peasants were brainwashed by Marxist lies."

Jim dabbed at his nose. "Y'know, Irene, you're not the easiest gal to get along with that I ever met."

She smiled thinly. "They say the same to me, in Magnitogorsk. Truth is painful, eh, Jim?"

"Maybe you'd know, if you swallowed some," he muttered.

She ignored him. Miles passed in silence. Not an angry silence, though, but a kind of easy quiet that seemed almost comfortable.

He was getting into it. He liked having a weird runaway Russian widow in the seat next to him. Something about her seemed to fit into his mood. The whole screwy business was falling together, turning into a little adventure for him, interesting.

He liked her for not chattering once she'd said her

piece. He was not much of a talker, himself. It had been
a long time since he'd really talked to anybody. The occasional hitchhiker, but hitchhikers were different, lately.
No more grinning hippies, who might roll a friendly joint
out of their backpacks. Lately, almost every rider he'd
picked up had been some poor bastard looking for work,
with tired hungry eyes and a sob story as long as your
arm.

The world darkened slowly, lost its edges, shrank into
a cone of the Chevy's headlights. Jim began to feel cozy.
He liked to drive at night, inside the white funnel of glare.
This was where he lived, a static place, where the world
rolled on without effort, under the endless monotone
thrum of the van's steel radials.

He liked to drive fast on dark roads. You could never
see very far ahead, but somehow there was always more
highway. It had always seemed a miracle to Jim that the
night's ribbon of striped blacktop didn't end suddenly,
end in nothing at all, like a tape cassette. But the road
had never failed him.

Jim reached out, and jammed a tape at random into
the slot of the van's cassette deck. Sweethearts of the Ro-
deo. Jim had seen the Sweethearts once, on Country Music Television, at a Ramada Inn in Tucson. They were
sisters. A real cute-looking pair of gals.

Over the past months, he'd spun the tape through at
least two hundred times. He no longer really heard it, but
it wrapped around him as he drove, like smoke.

"You have any jazz?" Irene said.

"Huh? Like what?"

"Like Duke Ellington? Or Dave Brubeck? He is great
artist, Dave Brubeck. 'Take Five.' 'Blue Rondo a la
Turk.' "

"I can listen to about anything," Jim said. "Don't
happen to have any jazz. Could buy some, though. In El
Paso, maybe."

"These women singing. I cannot understand their
words."

"You're not supposed to *understand* it, Irene. You just soak it up." They were cruising through a flat, dusty little town called Espanola. Neon chili joints and gas stations. Jim found the turnoff to Highway 76 South. "I reckon we'll have to spend the night in Santa Fe. That okay with you, Irene?"

"Santa Fe is okay," she said.

"Know any cheap hotels there?"

She shook her head. "I have never go there."

"Why not?" Jim said. "It's not far."

She shrugged. "In my life, I have never travel much. In Soviet Union, internal passport is much trouble. Also, I never own car, so never learn to drive."

"Can't drive, huh?" Jim said. He drummed his fingers on the wheel. "You must not get out much . . . What do you do to pass the time?"

"I read books," she said. "Solzhenitsyn. Pasternak. Aksyonov. Isaac Babel!"

"Man, that sounds like a real treat," Jim said.

"I have learned much about Soviet lies we are told all our lifes. Is not easy, to learn such truth. I have to sit and think about the strangeness. Try to make sense of it. I think a long time."

"Yeah, you kind of have that look," Jim said. It sounded tragic to him, damn near heartbreaking. Sitting in some cheesy apartment reading books. "You have any *friends* around here? Relatives?"

She shook her head. "No friends. Do *you*, Jim?"

Jim shifted a little, uneasily, scrunching back into the seat. "Well, I'm a travelin' man . . ."

"You have a lonely face, Jim."

"Guess I need a shave," Jim said.

"You have wife, or childs?"

"No. I don't like being tied down. I like freedom. Getting round, seeing the sights . . ."

Irene stared out the windshield at the moving cone of headlight glare. "Yes," she said at last. "Very pretty."

They stopped to stretch, at a National Forest campground north of Santa Fe. Jim was worried that someone might have told the cops about the shooting, maybe spotted the van. So he popped open a false compartment, built into the back paneling, and had Irene pick out a new license plate.

Irene chose a Colorado plate, which Jim had swiped off a pickup in Boulder. He'd changed the number, of course—turned the eights into zeros, with a ball peen hammer and a metal punch. Where the paint had chipped, he'd replaced it with model-airplane enamel.

All the stolen plates had been altered—he kept about a dozen in stock at all times. He'd gotten pretty good at forging plates over the years, had made a kind of handicraft out of it, actually. Helped to break the tedium.

He zipped the old plate off with a battery-powered screwdriver and buzzed the new one on. He did it in the dark, by feel and habit, while Irene watched silently, doing lookout duty, hands jammed in her pockets. Jim bent the old plate double, and stuffed it down the side of an over-flowing trash barrel.

A cold night wind was slewing through the pines, off the invisible slopes of the Sangre Mountains. The wind cut through Jim's clothes and cold-chiseled its way into his infected head. He crawled back into the driver's seat coughing and dribbling and feeling half-dead.

He stopped at the first likely motel, a Best Western overnighter on the outskirts of Santa Fe. It was a rambling two-story compound just off the highway, with a tall lit road sign and a lot of tarmac.

The clerk inside the office looked reassuringly numb and bored. Jim was low on paper cash, so he decided to use the plastic. It was a false name, with fake California ID, but the Visa people had never caught on. Jim used his dad's address in the nursing home as a mail drop. He sent the old man cash every month.

Jim signed in, took the brass key on its thick yellow tag. He watched Irene sidle up to the cig machine in the motel's lobby. She fed quarters in with flat-footed precision, then yanked the handle with the hope-beyond-hope look of a Vegas slot junkie. A cellophaned pack of Marlboros thumped down. Irene plucked it up, and gripped it, and smiled secretly to herself.

Even with a sick raw feeling gripping the tops of his lungs, Jim felt glad to see her enjoyment. It was like giving money to a kid. It made him feel good inside. Too bad he was low on cash. He would have liked to walk right over and slip her a nice crisp fifty.

Back to the van. He drove past scattered Datsuns and Hondas, by pastel room doors under chill yellow pools of light.

He found room 1411 behind an iron stairway. He unlocked it, threw on the lights. Two beds. Good. "Jeez, I'm beat," Jim said. "You need the bathroom? I'm gonna take a hot bath."

Irene perched nervously on one of the beds, peeled at her cigarette pack. "What?"

"Are you gonna be okay out here? You can get a Coke or something. We can send out for food."

She nodded stiffly. "Okay, Jim." The look on her face told him very clearly that the situation was definitely Not Okay. It hadn't occurred to her—to either of them—that when she jumped into his van she would end up sleeping with him.

Jim thought that he ought to sit her down and talk it over with her. But he was tired and sick, and he'd never been much good at Big Serious Talk with women. He was sure that once they started Big Serious Talk there'd be no end to it.

The bathroom was a snug little cell of spotted Formica and sheetrock. He locked the door, turned on the squeaking tap. Harsh metallic water from a deep desert aquifer, hard as nails.

Jim lay naked in the cramped tub, gently washing his crusted aching nose, wondering about her. Wondering what the heck she really wanted and what, if anything, it had to do with him. Out there in the room alone . . . she might be (a) calling the cops, or (b) panicked and gone for good, or (c) waiting for him with her gun in her hand. Or even, possibly, (d) lying naked in bed with the covers up to her chin and an expectant look on her face. Jim thought that in a lot of ways (d) might be the worst alternative of all. He wasn't up for (d), it would change too much, be too weird. Then he realized with a groggy rush of fatigue that he'd already forgotten what (a) and (b) were . . .

He struggled out of the tub, skin flushed and head pounding. He wiped himself with a towel, struggled back into his stale jeans and T-shirt. He opened the door.

Irene sat in the room's only chair, beside a wall lamp, reading the motel's Gideon Bible. The room was freezing—she hadn't bothered to turn on the heat. Or maybe she didn't know how. Jim staggered across the room, thumbed the thermostat up all the way, and got shivering into one of the beds.

Irene looked up from her Bible. "Are you very sick, Jim?" she said slowly.

"Yeah. Sorry about that."

She folded the Bible over her finger. "Can I help you make better?"

"No. Thanks. I gotta get some sleep, that's all." He pulled the covers up. The chills weren't going away. He watched her through slitted eyes, forced himself to think. "You must be hungry, right? You know how to order a pizza?"

She held up a pack of peanut butter crackers. Machine snacks. "Oh," Jim said. "Yeah, those are . . . real tasty."

"I always want to read this book!" Irene said, with a tone of deep satisfaction. She opened the cracker pack and started munching.

Jim awoke in stifling, superheated air. He got up and turned off the thermostat. Irene heard him moving and sat up in the other bed, looking startled from sleep, lost, afraid. Hair stood up all over her head. She'd gone to sleep with her hair still wet from the motel's shower. "Morning," Jim croaked, and retreated into the bathroom.

He gargled hard, for his newly sore throat. Then he brushed his teeth, and pulled his hair back, and caught it in a ponytail band. He shaved.

By the time he came out, she was up and fully dressed, brushing fitfully at her hair in the mirror. Same clothes. The only ones she had.

Nothing was settled between them, but a lot of the fear had gone. They had successfully spent a night, more or less together, without an outbreak of rape or gunfire. Irene looked wary, but more composed.

"How are you today?" he said.

"I am fine, thank you," Irene said.

"Great," he said, and mopped at his nose. "Today we're gonna do Santa Fe and make us some money."

They had breakfast at an International House of Pancakes, then made three quick money stops. When he could, he hit telephones next to the highways, because the get-away was simpler.

He now discovered that he had hit two of these phones before. The Gadget had left little keyhole scratches, not big ones, but enough to tell. He figured the scratches had to be at least three years old.

He stopped at a suburban branch bank, and sent Irene in with a jingling canvas bag. She returned with four twenties, and a tense, triumphant smile. "You did good," he told her. He gave her one bill and stuffed the other three in his wallet. "Did they ask questions?"

"No."

"They don't, usually. Were you scared?"

"No," she said. She jammed her hand into her purse, and pulled out the motel Bible. "Look, Jim, I stealed this."

"You stole a Gideon Bible?"

"Yes, I *stole*," she corrected herself. "I smuggle it out. Like a gypsy."

"Man, those Gideons will have a fit," he told her. "You're gonna be ripping off mattress tags, next."

She thought about it. "Okay, Jim," she said. It should have been funny, but somehow it struck him as terribly sad.

During the afternoon they hit three more phones. More work than usual, but living for two would take funds. He stopped at a cavernous Western apparel chain store, south of Santa Fe, and bought them new jeans and shirts and socks.

On impulse, as they were checking out, he bought her a cheap straw cowboy hat. He perched it on her head. She still looked weird, and not far from desperate. But with the hat on, her weirdness looked suddenly very American—she looked like some kind of crazed Depression Okie.

Maybe she was a little scary looking. It didn't bother Jim much. He didn't expect real women to look like the gals on TV.

Besides, he was scary looking himself. There were days when he would see himself in the mirror and wonder what the hell had happened. Days when he looked hunted and scared, a loser, with deep lines around his eyes that signaled Rip-Off Artist to every cop and motel clerk in America. On days like that he would just stay in his van, grip the wheel behind the tinted glass, and drive.

That evening they took Highway 25 out of Santa Fe, south. It brought them out of the mountains and junipers and into the plains. Around ten that night they hit Albuquerque. They set up in another motel, a small one this time, some kind of 50s mom-and-pop place called the Sagebrush. Thirty years ago it had catered to the road trade, to the big Airstream trailers and the chromed station wagons. But the town had sprawled out around it, and the airlines had taken its road trade, and now it was a place where sad married drunks could cheat on each other. Dust coated the rustic frames of cowboy paintings, and the old color TV would not turn down below a hissing, squeaking mutter.

Jim was feeling a little better tonight, not quite so beaten and low, so he hauled in some of his toys from the van. The VCR with its carton of cassettes, the Macintosh with its modem and hard disk. He plugged a surge-protector power strip into an outlet by the second bed.

Irene sat on the edge of the mattress and stared into the huckstering television. "We didn't worry about 'static cling,' when we wrapped rags on our feet in the Gulag."

"Uh . . . yeah," Jim said. "Listen, I'll get that dumb crap off the air in just a sec. We'll have some fun." He hooked up the back of the TV and fired up the video unit. Gray snow hissed. "You ever see one of these before, Irene?"

"Of course. Video." Sounded like *weedy-o*. "I can use it. I know."

"How about a turbocharged Macintosh? Ever seen one of these babies?"

"My husband was engineer, he knowed computers very well."

"Good for him."

"He did science mathematics on big state computer."

"Must've been a hell of a guy," Jim said sourly. He

opened the box of videotapes, picked one out. "You ever see *Every Which Way But Loose*? Man, I love this flick."

Irene looked curiously into the box, picked out a tape. She examined its cover and gasped. "This is *porno*!" She dropped it as if her fingers were scorched. "I am not watch porno!"

"Jeez, relax, okay?" Jim said. "Nobody's asking." Irene was pawing through the box, her face curdled with disgust. "Hey," Jim said. "That's my stuff, private. Take it easy."

She jumped up from the bed, her thin arms trembling. Real fear on her face, Jim thought, surprised and a little shaken. He wondered what the hell had gotten into her. She was taking a little harmless smut awful hard, he thought.

They watched each other silently.

Finally her words came in a tense rush. "Are you *very* sick, Jim? Do you have AIDS?"

"What the hell is wrong with you?" Jim shouted. "I've got a *cold*, that's all! Of course I don't have AIDS. What the hell do you think I am?"

"You have no friends," she said suspiciously. "You are living all alone. Always running, hiding . . ."

"So what? That's my business! Where are *your* friends, anyway? I guess you and Comrade Husband were real popular back in Magnetville, huh? Kind of explains why you're over here now, right?"

She looked at him, her eyes wide.

The fit of temper coursed, left him tired, more angry at himself than at her. "Cripes," he said, half-shrugging. "Sit down, will you? You're making me nervous."

Irene leaned against the flower-printed wall, bracing her shoulders, her hands knotted. She stared darkly at the carpet.

"Jeez," Jim said. "Listen. If you're that paranoid about me, why don't you just split? You got enough money for bus fare now. Go back to Los Alamos."

Irene took a deep breath, sighed it out. She looked wretched.

Then she nerved herself up. She caught his eye and spoke flatly. "Jim, I'm not going to let you."

"Let me what?"

She was resigned, her sharp jaw set. A real point-of-no-return, truth-or-consequences look. "That is what you truly want, yes? It's why I'm here. You want me to *let you*." She saw he didn't understand, and her mouth tightened. "Let you *do it*," she insisted, her voice harsh with embarrassment. "Man and woman, yes?"

"Oh," Jim said. "*It*. I get it." He blinked, thought about it, and got mad again. "Yeah? Well who the hell's asking you?"

"You would ask," she said with certainty. "A woman knows these things."

"Yeah?" he said. "Well maybe I'd ask, and maybe I wouldn't. But I wouldn't ask *now*. Not while my goddamn nose is running." He kicked at the scragged-out carpet with the heel of his boot. This business was making his neck ache. "Look, I'm not eighteen, y'know. I've been around. I don't have to tear the clothes off every woman I see."

She ran her hand through her hair, a strange ducking motion of the neck. "I am the thief, okay," she said. "And gypsy, okay. But I am not whore, Jim."

"Look," Jim said, "if I wanted a whore I can buy one. I don't have to drive her around with me in my goddamn van."

"What is it, then?" she demanded. "If you don't want me to *let you*, then what is it? Why are you driving me?"

"Heck," Jim said vaguely, surprised. "I felt *sorry* for you. I just thought you ought to be *free*. Free, like I am." She stared at him. He shrugged. "Is that so strange?"

"Yes."

"It is, huh?"

"Yes."

"Well," he said. "Maybe it is. I dunno."

Irene dug in her jacket, lit a Marlboro with thin blue-knuckled hands, shook the motel match out. She seemed less afraid of him now, not believing what he said, but watching him, with a kind of suspicious interest.

Jim spread his hands. "I kinda lose track of what's strange and what's not. It's been a long time, you know . . . Other people's standards, they never meant that much to me."

"That does not tell me *why*," she said.

"I didn't think about why. It was just something to do." That got him nowhere; she only narrowed her eyes and blew smoke.

He tried again. "I guess we don't have a heck of a lot in common, you and me. But in a way, y'know, I figure that we got a *lot* in common. More than most people. *Normal* people."

She tilted her head. He was beginning to get through to her. "We are refugees."

"Hey," Jim said, "*free spirits*, come on. Refugees don't have diddly. Look at all this great stuff! Look at this, I'll show you something wild."

He turned away from her, and fired up the Macintosh. Irene stood warily, then watched over his shoulder as he shuffled screen icons with the mouse.

He hooked the motel phone's headset into an acoustic coupler. The Mac bleeped through a series of digits.

An electronic bulletin board came online. The Mac shot through the log-on sequence, screen dissolves flicking away like green sheets of electric Kleenex. "What is this?" Irene said.

"Hackers," Jim said. "Phone phreaks."

"What is that?"

"People who steal phone service. Long-distance codes, and stuff."

"These are not people," Irene said. "These are only words on a television."

Jim laughed nasally, touched his nose to his cuff. "Don't be a rube, Irene. There's a whole world of these guys."

"Computers. Not people."

"No, it's even weirder than that," Jim said reluctantly. "It's not just hacker whizzes nowadays, but street guys, real hustlers. I've seen 'em, they hang out at big airports. You give 'em five bucks, and they go into a phone booth, and they can call you up Hong Kong, London ... Moscow maybe, anywhere you want."

She looked at him blankly. "It's those new phone services," he said. "Sprint, MCI, like that. It's all gotten really chaotic."

"*Chaotic?*" she said. "What is that?"

"*Chaotic* means ..." Jim paused, puzzled. What *did* *chaotic* really mean, exactly? It was a damned weird word, when you stopped to think about it. Philosophical, almost. Heavy.

"*Chaotic* means that something is all scrambled-up, and complicated, and, uh, unpredictable ... I guess what it really means, basically, is that it's something you can't understand. Maybe something you could *never* understand."

"Like, *confusing?*"

"Yeah." He watched the screen spool through lists of pseudonymous posts. Warnings, secrets, jargon. "Y'know, when I got started it all looked really simple. It was like, just, *The Phone Company.* One big crowd of suits, Ma Bell, *Them.* Man, they had the whole country wired coast to coast, thousands of workers, billions of big bucks ...

"But then they wanted to get into computers. The big hot growth industry, real up-to-date, right? But to do that, they had to give up their phone monopoly. And they did it! They just gave up all that centralized power they had. I still don't understand why.

"So now it's all different. You take away the Phone Company's big scary rep, see, that *mystique* I guess it is, and . . . they're not so much, after all. Just another company, trying to hustle a buck . . ."

He could tell that she didn't understand him, but she seemed to read his tone of voice. "And this makes you sad, Jim?"

"Sad?" He thought about it. "I dunno. *Confused*, I guess. It was so different when it was Me versus Them, one little guy, y'know, goin' up against the biggest fat cats I could find. . . . I hated 'em . . . sort of . . . but even if they were big, and bad, and unbeatable, at least that meant I *understood* something. They were the fat cats, and I was Robin Hood. But now I'm not even a *player*. There are phone phreaks, these software guys, they live in the telephones, just sit up all night eating Twinkies and typing code . . . kids, some of 'em."

"It is America," she said. "A strange country."

"Maybe we invented it," he said. "But it's gonna be everywhere, someday."

She peered into the screen as if it were a porthole, and looked uneasy. "Gorbachev, he talks computer propaganda now, very much."

"High-damn-tech," Jim said, "it's all around us, really." He smiled at her. "You wanna log on to the board, Irene? You gotta pick a funny name—a handle."

"No." She ground out her cigarette, yawned. "All these machine are on my bed, Jim."

"Oh," he said. "Well, I guess we can't have that." He logged off the board, and shut the computer down.

She woke him early, shaking his shoulder.

"Jim. Jim." She was frightened. Her taut face, inches from his own. He sat up. "Is it cops?" He glanced at his digital watch. 6:58 A.M.

"The television," she said. She pointed at it; it was hissing in the corner, its screen filled with bright static. Jim grabbed for his glasses, hooked them over his ears.

The room swam into focus. The VCR was still hooked up, a Marlboro smoldered in an ashtray, on the floor, beside the controls.

Jim squinted. "So," he said. "You busted the VCR, is that it?"

Suddenly he registered the mess across the floor. Thick wads of thin videotape, all tangled and mangled up. He remembered a dim dream of gabbling, rustling. "What the hell?" he shouted. "You *jammed* my tapes? What, eight, *ten* of 'em. How could you *do* that?"

"Look at the television," she said. "Look!"

He glanced at it. "Static." He got out of bed in his shorts, stepped into his jeans, rage swarming over him.

"I get it. My porn tapes. I can't believe it! You trashed 'em! You deliberately trashed my stuff!" His voice rose. "You cow! You dumb bitch! You *ruined* my *stuff*!"

"No one should watch such things."

"I get it," he said, zipping his jeans. "You were *looking* at 'em, weren't you? You got up while I was asleep, to sneak a look at filthy porno. But when you saw it, you couldn't handle it, could you? You just completely lost it. You know how much that stuff *costs*?"

"It is trash! Filth!"

"Yeah, but the *best* trash, damn it. 'Debbie Does Dallas,' 'Midnight Cowgirls.' . . . I can't *believe* this. This is how you pay me back, huh, for picking you up? Man, I oughta . . ." he clenched his fist.

"Okay, hit me," she shouted at him. "Hurt me, like a big man! But then you listen to me!"

"No," he said, picking up his boots. "I'm not gonna

hit you. I ought to, but I'm like a real gentleman, right?" He put on yesterday's socks. "Instead, I'm gonna leave your ass, right here in this motel. You've had it with me, girlie. This is it. Adios City." He stood up in a fury, jammed his feet into his boots.

"Look at the television," she said. "Please look, Jim."

He looked again. "Nothing," he said. "Turn off my goddamn VCR. No, wait! Let *me* do it."

"Look very hard," Irene said. Her voice trembled. "Can't you understand?"

He looked again, seriously this time.

And he saw something. He would never have noticed it, if she hadn't pointed it out to him first. Static was static, meaningless, just noise, confusion, chaos.

But with a quiet shock of comprehension he found he could actually *see* something there. Some kind of definite *order*, inside that boiling sea of hissing multicolored flecks. A movement, a form, something that almost made sense to him, just past the edge of his understanding. A nibbling, brain-itching thing, like an oiled key that would open a new world up, with the proper focus, with the proper twist . . .

"Holy smoke," he said, staring. "Have they got satellite TV in this dump? That's some kind of interference pattern, or something. What the hell is it?"

Irene stared raptly into the set. The fear had faded from her face. "It has beauty," she said.

Jim stared again. "What the heck kind of . . . did you mess with the hookup? Turn off the VCR."

"Not yet," she said. "It is . . . too interesting."

He leaned over angrily, snapped the recorder off.

The TV jumped immediately into a network morning show, cheerful grainy-faced network idiots.

"How'd you do that, huh? What buttons did you push?"

"Nothing," she said. "I *look*, that's all. I look very hard. Only confusing, at first. But then, I can see it!"

The anger fled out of him. That odd, creeping pattern had put him off, deflated him. He looked at his ruined porn tapes, but couldn't recapture his spontaneous feeling of rage. She'd been a fool to interfere with him, but she couldn't control him. He could always get more porn, if he wanted. "You've got no right to mess with my stuff," he told her, but without the same conviction.

"It make me *sick*," she said, and caught him with her cold blue stare. "You should not look at whores."

"Well it's . . . it's none of your— Look, just don't do anything like that again. *Never*, understand?"

She watched him, her eyes fixed and opaque. "Are you leaving me, now? It's because I didn't *let you*, that's why. If I had let you last night, you would not now be angry with me."

"God, don't start that again," Jim said. He slung the black baseball cap over his head.

One of his nostrils had cleared, during the night. Dry, crusted, but open. He was breathing again. A minor miracle.

They hit phones in little towns all the way down the highway. In Belen, Bernardo, Sorocco, Truth or Consequences. Jim pushed the pace hard. He would have liked some handy way to make her suffer. Dumping her on the side of the road was somehow just not enough, not a real option. There was some kind of contest of wills going on, with terms he didn't fully understand.

But there didn't seem to be much he could do to impress her—sullen silence, she didn't seem to mind; they skipped lunch, but she didn't seem to notice.

He couldn't forget that remark she'd made about the Gulag. Jim knew well enough what a gulag was: a Soviet labor camp, not just "stir" but the *real thing*. In some way he'd always hated authority, but he'd never done time for it, never faced them down, never walked the walk in the open, where they could spot him. In the back of his mind, though, he'd known somehow that the whole giddy rootless business would all catch up with him, that someday sure as hell they were going to take him down, some clerk, some straight, noticing him and calling the heat, and then some polite cop with a clipboard: Would you *pull over* sir, may I *see your* ID please . . .

And then interrogators: Do you mean to tell us sir that you have been an invisible man, that you have been living entirely from the proceeds of phone booth robberies for *eight years* . . .

"Stop that," Irene said.

"Huh?"

"You are grinding your teeth."

"Oh," Jim said. He'd been driving on automatic pilot, the road beneath the wheels like a half-seen vapor. Suddenly the world around them sprang into his conscious mind, overcast February sky and the scrub of sprawling desert, a road sign. . . . "Whoa!" he said, and hit the brake. "White Sands National Monument! I'll be damned."

He left the interstate, hit Highway 70 east. "White Sands! Man, I haven't seen that in years. Wow, White Sands. Can't pass that one up."

"We are going to El Paso. Is what you said," Irene protested.

"So what? White Sands is *out of this world*."

"You tell me El Paso."

"So? We can do whatever we want, no one's looking." He grinned at her, enjoying her discomfort. "White Sands is fantastic, you won't regret this."

She looked unhappy about it, something gnawing at her. It came out at last. "The *missile range* is in White Sands."

"Oh," Jim said, straightfaced. "You know that already, huh? Gosh, that's too bad, Irene. I was gonna sell you to the U.S. Army, for missile practice."

"What?"

"Yeah, the Army buys Russians, and they stake 'em out on ground zero! I figured I could clear three, maybe four hundred bucks, easy."

She fumbled in her purse for a cigarette. "Very funny joke, Jim. Ha, ha. But I not going to let you. Even if we go in the desert. Where no one is looking."

"Jeez, lighten up, will you? You sure got a big opinion of yourself. If I had a real-life *American* gal to talk to, you'd just be a goddamn *conversation piece.*"

She didn't understand, but knew enough to take it as an insult. She made no reply, but blew smoke over the dashboard, and looked remote and icy. Jim loaded music to cover the silence.

It had been a long time since he'd seen White Sands. Gypsum dunes, crystal dust. It had been the bottom of a sea once, now it was a sea all its own. In constant invisible movement: slow winds blowing sand waves in dry cascades.

Vast slumbering dunes, a trillion random specks somehow sifting into grace and order. There was life here, fierce little bushes, and strange spiky mats, with names he didn't know. White against white against white, and above it a sky with clouds that looked gray by contrast: a sky whose blue had deepened to the clotted crawling color of mid-ocean.

Jim paid their entrance fee. They drove silently, for miles, deep into the park. At last Jim killed the engine, got out, slammed the door. "You coming?" he said.

For a moment, he thought she wouldn't move, that

she'd sit there and sulk and outface him. But then she jumped out, stiffly, hugging her ribs. Jim locked the van tight, and they started walking. A cold wind. He headed for the horizon.

They climbed the dunes, Irene pacing along behind him, her face set stoically. The sand was stealthy and crept invisibly into everything; by the time they'd gone a mile he had a pint of it in each boot.

Finally they were utterly alone. No human trace or artifact, nothing but the sky and the fantastic looming forms of earth. Jim turned up the collar of his sheepskin coat and stood ankle deep in the loose crest of a dune. Irene whipped her scarf off, combed sullenly at her hair with her fingers. She was pale, and her down jacket was zipped to the neck.

"Great, isn't it?" he said.

She said nothing.

He spun around in place, swinging both arms, scanning the horizon. "Can you feel anything out here, Irene?"

She shook her head. "Feel what? Nothing."

"That's freedom," he said. "This is what real freedom feels like. See? No eyes, no rules. No laws, no judgments, no good or bad. Nothing but you and me."

"Not a good place for living," she said. "Good for killing, maybe."

"Yeah, the best place in the world for target practice," he said. "That's why the Army uses it." Jim felt reckless, loose in his knees and elbows. He pointed. "See that little bush over there? Watch this."

He stopped, reached into his right boot, pulled the .38. He steadied his right wrist left-handed, sighted down his arm.

Blam. Blam. Blam. Sand spurted around the bush's scabby roots. There was something about the smooth vicious kick of the gun that hit him like a drug. Out banging red-hot metal into dust, a true kick, pure as crystal. He turned to her with a grin.

She had her gun with her. It had been stuck in the waist of her jeans, hidden under the jacket. Now she had it centered on his chest.

Jim's blind elation collapsed within him, folded up and vanished, like a daydream.

The silly grin still hung on his face. He could feel himself goggling at her. His face felt like a mask, like the cold rubber skin on a plucked chicken. He couldn't seem to speak. Fear had him by the neck. Real terror, realer somehow than any other kind of feeling. As if he'd been a fool to ever feel anything else.

Slowly, very carefully, he lowered his right arm. He pointed at the bush with his left. "There you go," he croaked.

Irene swung the gun away from him. She held the pistol at arm's length, not bothering to aim, and squeezed off two rounds. Tremendous blasts; sand jumped from a distant dune, two sharp flurries, like the last kicks of a gut-shot deer.

Jim licked his lips. "Boy," he said. "That's some precision shooting."

"My husband teached me," Irene said. "It was his gun, he buy it. He said we need a gun, for KGB agents, or American criminals. Always need a gun, yes?"

"Yeah," Jim said, "that's what I always figured, myself."

"You have three bullets left," she remarked. "I have only one."

They stood in frozen tableau for a long moment. "Getting pretty cold out here," Jim said at last, still gripping his pistol. "Better get back to the van, huh?"

Irene moved deliberately. She cocked the hammer back, put the pistol's chromed cylinder against the sleeve of her jacket, rolled it down her arm. There was a crisp mechanical ratcheting as the chambers spun at random. "My dead husband," she said. Her voice shook. "He never understood the truth about guns. He was not very . . . what is word? Practice."

"Not very practical," Jim said.

"Yes. For him, gun was a clever toy. You think the same, too? Die the same way, maybe."

"Did you shoot him?" Jim said.

"No," she said. "He kill himself, trying to clean this thing."

Without warning, she squeezed the trigger. A hollow click.

Irene smiled tightly, lifted the gun, leveled it carefully at him. "Do I try again?"

"No. There's no need for this."

"What does that mean?" she said.

He babbled the first thing that sprang into his head. "I don't want you to die," he said. He didn't want *her* to die? A damn weird thing to say while he was staring into her gun barrel. But something, some basic kind of common sense, had forced the words out of him.

"I just want you to live," he said. "Both of us. We should live, that's all."

She was thinking about it. Hard.

"Give me your keys," she told him. "This nothing place . . . a good place for me to learn to drive." Irene smiled bleakly. "No one to run over, yes? I save everyone's life, out here."

Jim fished the keys, left-handed, from his pocket. He hefted them. "You sure you can find your way back, all alone? It's a long walk. No footprints left, either. Kind of cold and windy, lately."

She thought it over for a moment, with a spasm of irritation. "Throw down your gun," she told him. "We will walk back, first, then I will see the car."

Jim juggled the keys left-handed. "This is getting complicated, isn't it."

"Throw down the gun. Now."

He lifted his left hand. He kept talking. "I *could* throw these keys, y'know. They'd hit the sand, probably vanish from sight. You'd be left with a locked car, on a damn cold night."

"And you would be *dead* out here, yes? Instead of me, like you wanted." Her teeth were chattering.

With great, grave slowness, Jim lifted his right arm. The gun was a leaden weight in his sweat-chilled grip, full of stubborn momentum. He kept the muzzle away from her, pointed at the empty horizon.

BLAM. In his peripheral vision, the distant spurt of dust. BLAM.

He spun the cylinder against his thigh. Death's roulette wheel. The certainty of that last bullet was gone, into randomness, into free possibility. "Now we're in the same boat," he said.

"Yes."

"What the hell." He tossed the gun to his feet, lifted both his arms wide open. An embrace for the wind.

She didn't believe him, at first. She watched him as if it were some kind of stunt, a magic trick, so he could blow her away with his empty hands. He stood waiting.

She dropped her gun, her eyes fixed on his.

"Let's go," he said, and ran down the face of the dune.

She came sliding behind him. At the bottom, she caught his arm. Her face was flushed. Suddenly he kissed her, not much of a kiss, a quick glancing collision of their lips. A salute, and maybe just to see what it was like.

"I didn't mean to be so scary," he said.

No answer.

"I wouldn't have done anything to you. I didn't come here for that."

"Yes, sure," she said.

The sun was setting. They were chilly and walked fast. For a bad moment he thought he'd lost his sense of direction, lost the van. They would freeze to death together, turn to mummies, vanish slowly under the dunes ... He said nothing about it, walked on grim and tight-lipped ... and there it was.

They got in. Jim fired the engine, set the heater on. "We could sleep in the van tonight. The stars out here in the desert ... man."

She stretched her hands over the heater duct, shivering. "I want to leave this White Sands. It frightens me."

"I'm sorry about all that," he told her, his voice still giddy. Giddy from the sheer vivid strangeness of being alive. "I get carried away sometimes. A man lives alone ... kinda loses his sense of proportion. And the desert does funny things to your head."

"Trinity," she said.

"What?"

"Manhattan Project," she said. "At Los Alamos. Americans, alone in the desert."

"Oh," he said. "Yeah. I guess we invented that."

"But now it is everywhere," she said. She stared out into a purplish darkness, bruise-colored light settling over the quiet geometries of sand. "Get away from this place, Jim."

"Yeah, okay." He threw the van into gear.

He chased his headlights down the poorly marked trail. Irene shrank in on herself, into silence. She seemed haunted, unsure of anything. Later the park's headquarters was a dim flat-topped bulk. Then they hit the pavement. Jim pushed the needle up.

"El Paso," he said. "I think I'm up for it." His armpits itched fiercely with the smothered sweat of fear. "We can sleep there tonight. I'm up to the drive. Man, I may drive all night. You ever see Texas? You can drive forever in Texas."

He reached for a tape to paper over the depth of silence. He picked one, glanced at its label.

Suddenly the cassette in his grip disgusted him. Something he had heard a thousand times, wrapped himself up in, but now the magic of it was simply and suddenly gone for him. Like eating too much chocolate, like the final rancid puff on a cigar.

He flung the tape onto the floorboards. He leaned back, gripped the wheel. He felt vaguely dizzy suddenly, carsick, nervous, bad. "Do me a favor, okay?" he said. "Find me something on the radio."

Irene leaned over, began twisting dials. Screech, distant choked babble, cosmic hissing. The frying sounds of chaos.

"That's enough," he said.

"No," she said, "listen to it . . ."

"No." He snapped the radio off. "Let's just drive."

He pushed it up to seventy.

"Jim," she said.

"Now what?"

"There's something wrong with the road."

"There can't be," he said. "This is the highway, damn it." He gripped the wheel, squinted, rushed into the white torrent.

The thrum of tires went silent. They were coasting.

He pumped the gas, twice. A sullen roar from the engine, as if they were out of gear. He grabbed the gearshift, jerked it: a hollow loose-tooth feel, like a stripped transmission. "What the hell?"

"There is no road left," she said.

"There's *gotta* be a road." He pumped the brake. "Jesus, I can't feel *anything* . . ."

"We are floating," she said.

Jim wiped at the cold windshield, bare-handed. Before them the world had gone gray, misty, all to hissing bits and pieces. The van had the giddy stomach-clutching feel of an elevator, a closed steel box sliding through the nowhere zone between floors.

"We are lost," Irene said sadly. "It is all over, there is nothing left."

Jim took his hands from the wheel. It was moving on its own, like a wobbly compass needle. He pulled his booted feet up from the floorboards suddenly, as if there were something there to bite him.

He turned to Irene. For some reason his eyes were full of sudden tears: terror, frustration. Loss. "What is this place?"

She shrugged. A fatalism, something far past despair. It occurred to him then that he knew this place. Both of them knew it, they knew it very well. It was a place they'd been destined for, driving toward, all of their lives. It was the end of the world.

He felt at the window, bare-handed, grabbed at the door. "Don't get out," she warned.

The metal door handle was bitingly icy under his fingertips. "Yeah," he said. "I guess that's not too smart." He wiped at his eyes, beneath the glasses. "Jesus, I feel sick."

The steering wheel moved spookily through its own arcs. "I'm gonna open the window," he said suddenly. "And look outside."

Her voice was leaden. "Why?"

"Why?" he said shrilly. "Because it's my nature, that's why." He rolled the window down an inch.

Outside it was very bad. No air, nothing: the endless electric snow of dead televisions. The van's steel box was embedded in chaos, drifting in it. He put the tinted window up. Silence.

"What did you see?" she said.

"I don't know," he said. "Confusion, snow. It's *nothing*. Nothing at all. But, kind of, *anything*, too. If you know what I mean."

She shook her head. "It's the end, yes?"

"Could be," he said. "But we're still moving." He scratched at his jaw. "Still alive. Still talking." He gripped her hand. "You still feel that, right?"

"Yes." She muttered something in Russian.

"What's that mean?" he said.

"Let's go in back," she said. She tugged at his hand. "Let's go in back, together. Come on, Jim, I'll let you."

He wondered why she thought that would help any. He didn't bother to ask it. Sounded okay, actually. Nothing left to lose.

They got into the back, unrolled the sleeping bag, took some clothes off and fought their way inside it. It was cramped, uncomfortable, full of knees and elbows.

They did it. It was not much good. Clumsy, tense, unpleasant. Some time passed, with much harsh breathing. They tried it again from another position. It was somewhat improved, this time.

They were very tired then, and fell asleep.

Jim woke. There was sunlight in the van. He unzipped the bag down the side, crawled out, got into his jeans.

Irene woke up, hard and sluggishly, heavy–lidded and squinting. She groaned aloud, a harsh, complaining sound, and got up on one elbow.

She ran her hand through her hair, as if her scalp hurt. "Was I drunk?" she said.

"No," he said. "Might've helped, though." He found his boots. "Don't you ever *relax*?"

"Don't complain, Jim," she said testily. "You relax first, then maybe I relax." She sat up. "My head feels funny." She found her shirt.

Jim stood up, half-crouched. "We're on the side of the highway," he said. "Parked."

He opened the back of the van, stepped out on the road shoulder. Crisp desert air, a cactus-clumped horizon, a couple of weathered Budweiser cans underfoot.

He threw his arms back, breathed hugely, stretched

cramps out of his shoulder blades. He felt pretty good, all things considered. "Can't be far to El Paso," he said. He sniffed. "Hey! My cold is gone." He thumped his chest. "Wow. That's great."

Irene crawled forward, squinting, set her feet on the bumper. She looked up. "What is that, in the sky?"

Jim glanced up. "Vapor trail. Jets, huh?"

She passed him his glasses. "Look again."

Jim put his glasses on, looked up. The blue bowl of the desert sky looked scratched. It was full of spiderwebs. High distant threads, creeping things, capillaries, little ceramic cracks. "I'll be damned," he said. "Don't that beat all."

"Someone is coming," Irene said.

It was an old pickup truck, a battered Ford. There was something attached to its roof. A thready twisting thing, like the base of a waterspout. As it went up it spewed itself out into yarn, a hundred directions, little vapor knots, knitted netting.

The truck passed them. A bespectacled farmer in a sweat-stained felt hat was driving it. The threads were attached to him, radiating out, a skein, an aura of them, not quite touching his skin.

As he neared them, he slowed down. He peered at them over the wheel, a little anxious for them. This was the desert, after all. Jim nodded, smiled broadly, shrugged. The farmer raised one weathered hand, nodded a bit, waved.

They watched him go. "Looks pretty good," Jim commented. "Nice spry-looking old geezer. Kinda picturesque."

"I'm hungry," Irene said suddenly. "Want a big breakfast, Jim. Eggs, toast, flapcakes."

"Good thinking, let's roll." They got into the front seats, fired up the van. Jim turned on the radio, skipped a news broadcast, found some cheery accordion music from over the border.

A tourist bus passed them. It was crowded, and the top of it was a roiling forest; blue, green, prismatic, flying up into the sky, a frayed and twisted veil, like flapping fiberglass laundry.

"You *do* see that stuff, right?" Jim said.

She nodded. "Yes, the threads, I see them, Jim."

"Just checking." He rubbed his unshaven chin. "Got any idea what it is?"

"It is the *truth*," she said. "We can see the truth now. It's how people live, Jim. The system of the world. All tied together."

"Kinda weird looking."

"Yes. But it has beauty."

Jim nodded. It didn't frighten him. It had been there, all around them, for a long time now. They just hadn't been able to see it.

Irene passed her hand through the air above his head. "You have hardly any connections, Jim. Just a few threads, like thin hair."

He checked her over. "You either. We're not all wrapped up inside these thick nets of stuff, like most folks . . . Maybe that's why we can see it so well. 'Cause we see it from the outside."

Irene laughed. "It's easy to see, when you know about it. I can *feel* it, Jim!"

He turned to her. "I feel it too." Something was coming out from inside of him, hot and strong and radiant. A kind of fluid easy roiling, a glowing vapor from his skin, just coming clear. He batted at it with his free hand. It was like trying to catch a beam of light, or touch the sound of a laugh.

It moved toward Irene, merging with the tendril cloud that seethed around her. The air was full of her suddenly, wire-strong whipping threads the color of her stubborn eyes. For a moment it was a snarl of chaos, a scary murk of oil and water.

But then it was settling, with unsuspected grace, falling through itself, sifting into place. Love and fear and hate. Power, attraction ... then the chaos was gone, turned to strong new threads as thin as old bad memories. Visible, only from a certain angle.

But they could still feel it. A bond between them. It was very strong.

THE SWORD
OF DAMOCLES

"The Sword of Damocles" is an ancient Greek story with
the deeply satisfying structure of classical legend. It's
chock-full of eternal human truths, which, believe-
you-me, still have plenty of meaning and relevance, even
for our so-called-sophisticated, postmodern generation.

I've been looking the story over lately, and the material is great. It's just a question of filing off a few serial
numbers, and bringing it up-to-date. So here we go.

Once upon a time, there was a man named Damocles,
a minor courtier at the palace of Dionysius, Tyrant of Syracuse. Damocles was unhappy with his role, and he envied the splendor of the Tyrant.

Actually the term "Tyrant" is a bit misleading here,
because it didn't mean at the time what it means today.
All "tyrant" really meant was that Dionysius (405
B.C.—367 B.C.) had seized the government by force, rather
than coming to power legitimately. It doesn't necessarily
mean that Dionysius was an evil thug. After all, it's results that count, and sometimes one has to bend the rules
a bit, just to get things started.

Take this "Once upon a time" business I just used,
for instance. It starts the story all right, but it doesn't

sound very Greek, when you come right down to it. It's
more of a Grimm Brothers fairy-tale riff, kind of a
kunstmarchen thing. Using it with a Greek myth is like
putting a peaked Gothic spire on a Greek temple. Some
people—Modernist critics—might say it's a bad move aes-
thetically, and kind of bastardizes the whole artistic effort!

Of course, real hifalutin Modernist critics must have
a pretty hard time of it lately. They must find life a trial.
I bet they don't watch much MTV. Modernists like coherent, systematic structures, but it's all hybridized by now.
Especially in the places that are really moving, like Tokyo.
Postmodern Japan is like a giant Shinto temple with
smokestacks. Culturally speaking, the whole place is a
chimera, but people don't criticize Japan's set-up much,
because capitalistically speaking they're kicking everybody's ass. Whatever works, man.

You know—this is amazing, but I swear it's true—
there are people nowadays who literally live in Tokyo
"once upon a time." They're bankers and stockbrokers
from New York and London, and they moved to Tokyo
as expatriates, because they had to settle the Tokyo time-
zone. It's a fact! Postmodern bankers have to do twenty-
four-hour trading, and the stock market closes in New
York hours before it opens in London. So nowadays all
the big financial operators send people out to major mar-
kets all around the world, to colonize Time. "Time" is
just another postmodern commodity now.

So that kind of blows my opening sentence, but the
important thing is to get the story across. Simply, directly,
in an unpretentious, naturalistic fashion. So forget the
Gothic fairy-tale riff. I'm just gonna tell it straight. The
way I'd talk to close friends, in my own living room, here
in Austin, Texas.

So y'all listen up. There was this dude named Damocles, see, and he used to hang out in this palace, in Sicily.
Ancient Sicily. Damocles was Greek though, not Italian,

because, y'see, way back then . . . This was before Rome got started, and the Greeks were really good sailors, so they got all these remote colonies started up . . .

Okay, never mind the historical analysis, y'all. It's kinda vital to the background, but I can't get it across in this casual hick tone of voice without making it sound really goofy. So let's stick to the drama, okay? The important plot-thing is that Damocles really envies his boss, this magnificent prince, Dionysius. So one day Damocles puts on his chiton—that's a kind of Greek tunic—and his buskins—those were tall sandals like you see in the opera, if you ever go to those, which I don't, personally. But you've probably seen them on public TV, right?

In fact, now that I mention it, since we're all here in my living room, why don't we just give this up, and watch some TV? I mean, forget this "oral storytelling tradition." When was the last time you listened to some pal of yours tell a story out loud? I don't mean lies about what he and his pals did last Friday, I mean a real myth-type story with a beginning, middle, and end. And a moral.

Let's face it, we don't really do that anymore. We postmoderns don't live in an oral storytelling culture. If we want a story we can all enjoy together, we can rent a goddamn video. *Near Dark* is pretty good. My treat.

So, yeah—if I'm gonna make this work, it's gonna have to be *literary*. It'll have to hit some kind of high archaic note. We'll have to really get into it—tell it, not like postmoderns, but just as the ancient Greeks would have told it. Simple, dignified, classical, and stately. Full of *gravitas*, and *hubris*, and similar impressive terms. We'll cast a magic net of words, something to take us across the centuries . . . back to the authentic, ancestral world of Western culture!

So let's envision it. We're in an olive grove together, on a hillside in ancient Athens. I'm the mythagogue, probably some blind or lame guy, kept alive for my story-telling skills. I may be a slave, like Aesop. I'm making up (or reciting from memory) these marvelous mythic tales that will last forever, but I'm no particular big deal, personally.

You, my audience, on the other hand, look really great. You're all young rambunctious aristocrats whose parents are paying for this. Your limbs are oiled, your hair is curled, and every one of you is a whiz at the discus and javelin. Some of you are naked, but nobody cares; even the snappiest dressers are essentially wearing tablecloths held together with big bronze pins.

Did I mention that you were all guys? Sorry, but yeah. Those of you who are young rambunctious women are, uhmmm . . . well, I'm afraid you're off weaving chitons in the darkest part of your house. You don't get to listen to mythagogues. It might give you ideas. In fact you don't get to leave the house at all. We guys will be back to see you, sometime after midnight. After we get drunk with Socrates. Then we'll have our jolly way with you.

And we'll probably get you pregnant. Decent contraception hasn't been invented yet. At least, not the nifty plastic-wrapped kinds people will use in the late twentieth century. That's one reason why Damocles has a very dear male friend called Pythias.

But wait a sec—since I'm an authentic Greek mythagogue, I have to call him "Phyntias." "Pythias" was called "Phyntias," originally. A medieval scribe made a mistake transcribing the story in the fourteenth century, and he's been "Pythias" ever since. There's even a high-minded twentieth-century club called "The Pythian Society," that's named after a misprint! What a joke on them, huh? Goes to show what can happen if a storyteller gets careless!

So anyway, Damocles and Pythias were two close friends who lived in the court of Dionysius. One day, Damocles offended the Tyrant, and was sentenced to death. Damocles begged a few days' mercy, to bid farewell to his family, who lived in another town.

But the cruel Dionysius refused him this mercy. At that point, the noble Pythias stepped forward. "I will stand in the place of my dear friend, Damocles," he declared, to the assembled court. "If he does not return in seven days, I will die in his place!"

The vindictive heart of Dionysius was touched by this strange offer. Curious to see the outcome, he granted the boon. The two friends embraced and wept, and Damocles left to carry the sad news to his family. Pythias, in his place, was clapped in a dungeon. Days passed, one by one.

Wait a minute. Damn! Did I say "Damocles"? I meant "Damon." It's "Damon and Pythias," not "Damocles." Hell, I always get those two confused.

Christ on a Harley, man! I was off to such a great start, too. I was really rolling there for a minute. Now look at me! I don't even have a character in my story. There's no *real* character here except *me*, the author.

I can't believe I got myself into this situation. I mean, that postmodernist lit-mag experimental stuff where authors use themselves as characters. That kind of crap really burns me up. I'm a sci-fi pop writer, myself. I write action-adventure stuff. Sure, it's weird, but it's not *structurally* weird; it's weird 'cause it's about weird *ideas*, like fractals and cranial jacks.

But now look at me. Not only am I a character in my own story, but my only real topic so far is "narrative structure." I can't stand it when postmodern critics talk about stories in terms like "narrative structure." These hardhat deconstruction-workers harass stories as if they were gals passing by on the sidewalk. They yell out stuff that's not only obnoxious, but completely bizarre and impenetrable. It's like they yell: "Hey, check out the pelvic bio-mechanics on that babe! What a set of hypertrophied lactiferous tissues!"

I should have stuck to hard-SF, that's my real problem. It was clear from the beginning this was going to be one of those weird-ass historical-fantasy things. I'm not even the proper author to be a character in this story. What this story needs is a character like Tim Powers, author of *The Anubis Gates* and *On Stranger Tides*.

"Suddenly, Tim Powers appeared. He looked about himself alertly."

No, if I'm gonna do this at all, I'd better try it Powers-style.

"Suddenly, Tim Powers burst headlong into the story! His hair was on fire, and he was perched on a pair of stilts. Gnashing his teeth, he glared wildly from under layers of peeling clown-makeup and said:

" 'What the heck kind of fictional set-up is this? There's nothing here but some kind of half-collapsed ancient Greek stage-set! I could do better research than this in my sleep! Anyway, I prefer Victoriana.' "

And then a voice emerged into the story from an area of narrative discourse that we can't even reach from here. It said, "-'-"Tim, what's going on in there?"-'-"

And Powers said: "I dunno, sweetheart, I was just sitting here at the word-processor, and—ow! Somebody set my hair on fire! Serena, get the shotgun!"

Aw, jeez! . . . uhm:

"Tim Powers quickly disappeared from the story. The makeup disappeared from his face, and he looked just like he always did. And his hair stopped burning. There was no real damage done to it. He went into the bathroom of his Santa Ana apartment, got a comb, and lent fresh meaning to his hair. Then he forgot he had even been involved in this story."

" 'Don't bet on it, pal.' "

I swear it'll never happen again. Don't get mad! Lots of writers do it. Like the wife of Damocles, "Pandora." She's not the original Greek-legend Pandora, wife of Epimetheus. Pandora hasn't appeared in this story yet, but she's a really interesting character. She likes to make blunt declarations to the reader, from a really weird narrative stance. Stuff like:

" 'Am I not the sister of Adolf Hitler and Anne Frank? Have I not eaten, drunk, and breathed poison all my life? Do you take me for an innocent, my colluding reader?' " That sort of thing.

"Pandora" is actually the thinly disguised author-character from Ursula K. Le Guin's experimental SF epic *Always Coming Home*! How "Pandora" got into this story I'm not really sure, I guess it's my mistake, but I'll fight any man who claims that *Always Coming Home* isn't "real SF"! Even if it's not really, exactly, a "book." For one thing, *Always Coming Home* has got an audiotape that comes with it, which puts a pretty severe dent in its narrative closure. I'd have liked to supply an audiotape with this story—maybe some Japanese pop music, or John Cage—but I was too cheap. Instead, I'll just play the *Always Coming Home* tape here in my office. I ordered it from a P.O. box in Oregon. It's got weird mellow chanting in made-up languages.

So much for Pandora. I was going to have a scene where Damocles wakes up in bed with Pandora, and she makes some biting remarks about having to weave the chitons and everything, but I guess you get the idea.

So here's Damocles quickly leaving his home and going straight to work. He's so eager to start the story that, not only does he jump right in with a Homeric "in medias res" routine, but he's willing to settle for a breathless present-tense. Damocles works as a minor palace official in the court of Dionysius. Actually he's a "flatterer," according to Cicero's *Tusculan Disputations*. He's not a bureaucrat, like a postmodern official. There's no bureaucracy in Syracuse, it's all done by a tiny group of elite families, who run everything. Syracuse is a pre-industrial city-state of maybe fifty thousand people. An independent city-state about the size of Oshkosh, Wisconsin.

Damocles earns his living by making up flattering things about people who can kill him out-of-hand. He's kind of a jackleg-poet crossed with a public-relations flack. He's done pretty well by it, considering his lowly birth. He gets to eat meat almost every week. For most other Greeks of the period, common folk, there are two kinds of dietary staple. The first is a kind of mush, and the second is a kind of mush.

Damocles, though, has pretty much reached the top of his career arc. Once the Tyrant has taken you into the palace and deigned to feed you, there's not a whole lot of room for further advancement. Everything else is pretty much determined by birth, or coup d'etat. Damocles doesn't have the birth, and if a coup d'etat came Damocles would probably get snuffed first thing for being a loudmouth intellectual.

Damocles could enlist in the army and join one of the incessant minor wars of Dionysius, but he'd probably get nicked in battle and die of infection or tetanus. There's a damn good chance he'd croak of dysentery without ever leaving the camp-tents. Homer's war-brags don't talk about sickness much, but it's there all right. There's even a killer plague of the period called "the sweats" which Thucydides talks about in his histories; it once killed off half of Athens. Nobody knows what kind of disease "the sweats" was or where it came from. We'd just better hope it never comes back.

So Damocles goes to the court, dressed in his second-best outfit, since the day doesn't augur much. Damon and Pythias are there; Damocles has known them since they were kids; he knows pretty much everybody who counts in Syracuse, since it's a small town. Ever since D&P won the favor of Dionysius, through this stunt they pulled by offering to die for each other, they've been big cheeses at the court. Damocles has had to make up a lot of flattering dithyrambs and iambics and anapests about them; he's just about run out of rhymes for "Phyntias" and wishes the guy would change his goddamn name.

Today though he finds to his surprise that there's a big celebration. Three of Dionysius's war-galleys are back from raiding the coast of Egypt, where they sank a few reed-boats and got some slaves and loot. It's a famous victory. There's lots of millet-beer and grape-wine.

Damocles elbows his way through the revelers and helps himself. The wine quickly goes to his head. Nobody knows what "fermentation" is yet, so the quality of the wine varies a lot. Every once in a while it makes you puke on the spot, but sometimes it gets way up to four, five percent alcohol. This is prime stuff all the way from Greece, and it only tastes a little of the tar they use to seal the amphoras. Damocles gets totally plastered.

Dionysius is in one of his jolly moods. The kind where he thinks up ingenious psychological tortures for his hangers-on. He calls the drunken, tottering Damocles front-and-center to have him immortalize the glorious day in extemporaneous verse.

Damocles gives it his best shot. He picks up a goat-skin tambourine and starts banging it against his hip so he can remember the proper meter. He spouts out a lot of the canned stuff from Homer, the clichéd "epithets" you use when you can't think of anything original, like "So-and-so of the nodding plumed helmet," and "his armor rang about him as he fell," and even stuff that sounds vaguely comical nowadays, like "he bit the dust."

But he can see it's not working. He starts to get desperate. He starts babbling out whatever comes into his head. Free association, surrealism. We postmoderns are really into that kind of stuff since Max Ernst and Dada, but it doesn't cut much ice with ancient Dionysius.

So Damocles plays his last ace, and starts laying on the flattery with a trowel. What a lucky guy Dionysius is; how the Gods smile on him; how supreme the Tyrant's power is; how everybody wishes they were him.

"Oh really," interrupts Dionysius, with that awful smile of his. He gives some orders to his lithe teenage male wine-bearer and then beckons Damocles forward. "So you want to be the Tyrant, eh?"

"Yeah, sure, who wouldn't?" says Damocles.

"Fine," says Dionysius loudly. "You sit right here on my throne"—actually, it's a dining-couch—"and help yourself to this feast. You, the humble Damocles, can be Tyrant, just for today!" He takes the gold fillet from his head and places it on the sweating noggin of Damocles. "You can give the orders. See how much you enjoy it."

"Gosh, thanks!" says Damocles. "Hot dog!" The cup-bearer has mysteriously disappeared, but Damocles, who's somewhat partial to women, has one of the new Egyptian slave-girls do the honors for him. Soon he's eating chunks of roast boar, knocking back goblets of honey-mead, and making satirical wisecracks that have the whole court in stitches. There's a bit of nervousness in their laughter, but Damocles writes it off to the oddity of the situation.

Just to break the ice, he issues a few tentative Tyrannical orders. He forces some of the more elderly and dignified courtiers to imitate goats or donkeys. It's good clean fun.

Then Damocles spots a disquieting reflection in the polished bronze of his mead-cup. He looks up. The wine-bearer of Dionysius has shinnied high up into the palace rafters. He's got a sharp, heavy bronze sword, and he's tied it to the rafter with a single woolen thread. The sword is dangling, point-first, directly over the reclining torso of Damocles.

"What's the meaning of this?" Damocles says.

Dionysius, who has been watching and chuckling from the sidelines, steps forward. He crosses his arms, and strokes his royal beard. "This," he says, "is the true nature of political power. This is the daily terror that we Tyrants must live under, which you thoughtless subjects somehow fail to appreciate." He laughs deep in his kingly chest.

"I get it," Damocles says. "It's a metaphor. Kind of a koan."

"That's right," says Dionysius. "Now go on, Damocles, enjoy yourself. You won't be leaving that couch for some time."

"Good thing, I was just getting comfortable," says Damocles, and he pillows his head on an enormous bundle of two hundred pounds of primed TNT. He's been carrying this massive weight of explosive with him all the time, wired to his body in a kind of backpack.

In fact, everybody in the palace has got a TNT-bundle of their own, too. They just haven't really noticed it, until the situation was made metaphorically clear. Everybody in Syracuse has their own share of explosive. Every man, woman and child on the planet; even the innocent babes in their cradles. Everybody carries their share of the global megatonnage; they're never without it, even when they somehow manage to forget about it. They just lug it around, day in day out, because they have to; because it's the postmodern condition. The cost of it nearly bankrupts them, and the weight wears calluses on their souls, but nobody dwells on the horror of it much. It's the only way to stay sane.

So, with a merry laugh, Damocles has two of the guards seize Dionysius. They demonstrate to him some of the unappreciated hazards of living like a peasant, instead of a king. They start by ripping out several of his teeth, without health insurance. Then they do some other things to him which are even funnier, and finally leave him penniless and ragged in the streets.

So much for the famous legend of "The Sword of Damocles." I hope you've enjoyed it. Damocles went on to live it up happily ever after, in his merry, pranksterish way, until he got gout, or cirrhosis, or a bad cocaine habit, or AIDS.

As for Dionysius, he retired to California, where he now lives. He often appears on talk-shows, and makes lu-

crative speaking-tours before Chambers of Commerce
and political action committees. He is writing a set of
memoirs defending his public-service record. He's looking
for a movie-option, too. But it's okay—I don't think he'll
get one.

THE GULF WARS

Gouts of black smudge, thick as curds, billowed against the heat-washed blue of a Mesopotamian sky. Blistering sunlight wrapped the flatlands in glare. For the moment, the siege was broken. Even a fanatic couldn't fight in heat like this. It was too hot to die with conviction.

In the attackers' camp, two army engineers sat in the shade of their open tent, munching dates and ration-bread. The dates were gritty and the bread had molded, but the two men ate without complaining. They no longer expected much.

Halli and Bel-Heshti, the two engineers, were long campaigners with a certain hard-won wisdom. They had pitched their tent upwind of the latrines, on a little rise where they could oversee the camp and spot any caravans arriving with fresh food. The rest of the camp sprawled around them: government-issue black woolen tents for an army of six hundred men.

Two companies of Assyrian regulars formed the army's shock troops. First were the Mountain-Leaping Pioneers, an engineer and sapper unit. They were aided by the River Zab Chariotry, who were now an unhappy infantry, since most of their horses had died in an outbreak of glanders.

The remaining forces were lightly-armed Babylonian

auxiliaries. The Babylonians had unwisely supported the Elamites in the early days of the war. The Babylonians were now atoning for their sins by leading each assault and taking most of the casualties.

Bel-Heshti munched another flat cake of rye-bread, staring squint-eyed across the plain at the mud-brick walls of the Elamite city. The town's surrounding fields had been systematically ravaged, the grain trampled flat, the groves of palms razed and burned, and the irrigation canals deliberately filled in.

The Assyrian sappers had dug a network of siege-trenches surrounding the town. Counter-balanced cata-pults stood in rows, their long arms and leather slings idle now, but ready to fling flaming oil-bombs over the city wall. Four large siege-engines crouched at the walls amid a rubble of smashed and battered brick. Their armored roofs and sides were dented by stones and splattered with pitch, flung by the defenders.

Movement showed atop the city wall. An Elamite altar-boy mounted the fire-scarred battlements, carrying a curved wicker shield as large as himself. From within the trenches, in the patchy shade of stretched blankets, a few besiegers jeered, without much enthusiasm.

Behind the shield-bearer came an Elamite priest in a robe of Tyrian purple, heavily hung with seashells, linked medallions, and gold braid. The heretic prophet spoke a little dog-Akkadian, enough to get his insults across to the Assyrian audience. Each day since the siege had be-gun, he'd taken advantage of the stunned torpor of noon to bellow deep-voiced taunts and curses.

He raised his arms, shaking his gilded sleeves. "May boil-imps bite you! May the demoness Lamashtu close up your wives!" A lazily-slung stone bounced from the aco-lyte's shield. The Assyrians had learned to stop firing ar-rows at the priest. The citizens were out of arrows. They carefully collected Assyrian arrows and fired them back when things were cooler.

Bel-Heshti squinted at the distant priest and spat a date-pit into the ocher dust. "I'm getting tired of him."

His companion grunted. Halli was a lean, jug-eared ex-peasant with the clever hands of a born strangler. His humble family raised barley, west of the Tigris.

Bel-Heshti came from the wrong side of Nineveh. His family, a clan of half-shekel exorcists and nostrum peddlers, were always in trouble with the city law. Bel-Heshti stood half-a-cubit taller than most men in the troop. He had a squint and a large hairy nose and the general aspect of a man who enjoyed doing terrible things with a sledge-hammer.

Like the rest of their troop, Halli and Bel-Heshti wore long indigo-blue army tunics with dangling vermillion fringes at the knee. Their waists were cinched in thick dagger-belts with broad, crossed shoulder-straps of oiled brown leather.

Halli had taken off his conical helmet to soak his black ringlets and long square beard with cooking lard. The lard smothered lice and nits, which Halli, like the rest of his army, had in plenty. With his hair slicked to the sides of his long, narrow head, he had the drowned look of a newborn calf.

Bel-Heshti sucked brackish water from a pottery canteen. He looked longingly at a large stoppered jug lying in the corner of the tent. Two weeks earlier he and Halli had poured water into the jug along with two days' barley ration and a pinch of yeast.

Halli noticed his companion's gaze. "Not ready yet," Halli said. He picked a slender cane from a sheaf of marsh reeds at his elbow, and sighted down the shaft.

"It must have beered up fine by now," Bel-Heshti said.

Halli was patient. "You can't break the seal until Inanna Moon-Goddess is full. Otherwise you get the imps of souring. And once the sour-imps find a brewer, they hang on him stubborn as ticks. Then any beer he makes might as well be rotten oatmeal." Halli made a quick luck-sign and spat twice.

"Listen to the big brewer," Bel-Heshti scoffed.

Halli snipped the cane's ends with his dagger and dipped one end in a bowl of pitch. "A brewer gets respect in life. Peasants have no Name. Gimme one of them arrowheads."

Bel-Heshti passed him an arrowhead of crudely pounded pig iron. "Listen, Halli, even a brewer doesn't get imp-shit until he's out of the army. And when will that be?"

"The gods give luck," Halli said piously. "Once I was a barefoot peasant. Now I fight for the King in Elam like a gentleman with a Name. What mortal knows what is to come?" Halli socketed the arrowhead and set it aside.

"There's always more war for the likes of us," Bel-Heshti said. "You don't need a royal diviner to tell you that much."

Halli shrugged and selected another cane. "If I could just get my hands on some real loot for once . . ."

"Sure," Bel-Heshti yawned. He waved one hand before his meaty nose. "That pitch stinks to perdition. What a hellhole this place is. It gives pitch and asphalt like better places give milk and honey."

The Elamite prophet's screaming floated across the camp. "May you drown, and search the world forever for an earthen grave! May scorpions fill your armpits—"

Bel-Heshti glanced out the tent-flap and grunted in alarm. Their captain approached, on one of the troop's last horses. The captain reined up. "Pioneers Bel-Heshti and Halli!"

The men touched their foreheads.

"On your feet, boys. General wants to see you."

Bel-Heshti and Halli scrambled up in alarm. They tugged their sandal-straps, checked their daggers, and followed the captain's horse. Dust as fine as flour puffed from the trampled paths around the tents.

"Ishtar's dugs," Bel-Heshti muttered. "You think he knows we're home-brewing? He'll wallop us for sure."

Halli glared at him, amazed. "That's it, idiot. Put a name to our bad luck. Don't you know demons are listening?"

"Sorry," Bel-Heshti said. They batted at bluebottle flies as they passed one of the latrines.

Halli scowled. "How'd you live this long, anyway, you big ox? Always blabbing bad omens and tempting fate."

"My luck's fine," Bel-Heshti said. "But too bad your hair stinks of louse-lard. You look like a real half-wit."

The captain dismounted near the closed flaps of the General's broad, striped tent. He threw the horse's reins to an orderly and vanished inside. The two veterans waited under the army's standard, which hung limply in the murderous heat.

The General's tent stood next to the supply dump. Halli and Bel-Heshti looked unhappily at the dwindling supplies: rock-hard blocks of dried fish, empty oil jars in toppled heaps, dusty sacks of millet and barley, the very last of the cheese. Guards leaned on their spears, stunned with heat and boredom. A war chariot rumbled by and covered everyone with grit.

The captain beckoned from within the tent. Bel-Heshti and Halli ducked and stepped into the incense-reeking shadows. They spotted the dim gleam of the General's bronze armor and quickly prostrated themselves on the carpet. Puffs of dust rose from the thick dark wool.

"All right, boys," the General rumbled. "At ease."

"Thank you, Lord General!" they chorused. They each rose to one knee.

The General was huge, with thick, powerful arms and massive, hairy hands. Girded with armor, sword, and quiver, he seemed to weigh half a ton. Scars from a lion-hunt streaked the side of his face, vanishing into an oily thicket of beard.

The General bent over a table with a leathery creak of lacings, and examined a clay tablet. His lips moved as he studied the cuneiform. "Bel-Heshti and Halli . . . You boys have been with the Mountain-Leapers quite a while now."

"Yes, Lord General!"

"You were with us at Nippur," he said, straightening. "That was a nasty little piece of business."

"Yes, Lord General," Bel-Heshti said. "I mean, no, Lord General! It was an honor to serve under your command!"

The General's Babylonian camp-slut appeared from the back, with a long-handled palm-leaf fan. She began chasing flies with indolent strokes of the fan, looking bored.

The General's eyes glittered under the gold-chased rim of his helmet. "Get much loot when we sacked Nippur?"

Bel-Heshti fingered the heavy silver ring at his earlobe. "A little, Lord General."

"Gambled it all away by now, eh?" said the General, with an ugly laugh. "I hear you boys took your share of heads, too."

"Well, yes, Lord," said Bel-Heshti. "That was orders. 'Gather male heads for central requisition and display.' Right, Halli?"

"What he said, Lord," Halli nodded.

"Remember one head in particular?" the General said. "An old man with a cast in one eye and a turned-up nose like a pig's?"

Bel-Heshti smiled humbly. "We took many heads, Lord General. Fighters, too. Not just old men."

"You did kill him, though?"

Bel-Heshti swallowed doubtfully. "We found the old geezer hiding in a rat-hole, Lord General! So we stuck him and took his head. That was orders!"

The General paused and knotted his hands behind

him, savoring the moment. "Boys, that loathsome rebel was Governor Nairi. Our King cherished a special hatred for that arch-heretic."

The General began to stride back and forth across the dusty carpet. "I wrote to the King in his Palace at Nineveh," he said. Reluctantly the girl followed him, swinging her fan. "I informed the King that elements of my Mountain-Leaping Pioneers had confronted the traitor Nairi. They forced the wretch to tremble before the awesome power of His Majesty and slew him with the edge of the sword!"

Impressed by his rhetoric, the two veterans exchanged quick glances.

"His Majesty has replied to me. He has praised the Mountain-Leaping Pioneers. He has decreed that the soldiers who avenged his honor should be rewarded." For the first time, the General looked at them directly. "That means you, boys. You're to be given Names."

"Names!" Halli blurted. They flung themselves to the carpet.

The General called out. Light flooded the tent as an orderly looked in. "Tell His Eminence I've found the heroes," the General said. "Ask him to join us here." He turned to the camp-slut, lowering his voice. "Go on in back, girl." The General's girl rolled her kohl-smeared eyes, then wearily shouldered her fan and vanished through a beaded curtain.

The General gestured brusquely. "Get up, boys, you're in the way there. Go over there by the censer. You may sit."

The two men crawled rapidly across the carpet into a corner of the tent, then sat cross-legged, grinning at each other.

"Now listen," said the General into mid-air, not bothering to look their way. "The King's inspector, His Eminence the Baru of Shamash at Nineveh, arrived here in camp last night. He came in secrecy to take omens of our success, bless the camp, and examine the state of our souls." The General frowned. "He has brought you your Names from the capital. I know that you two fine soldiers are going to make a dignified, pious impression on His Eminence. Understood?"

They quailed under his glare. "Yes, Lord General."

The General turned away. Halli and Bel-Heshti traded anxious looks. Early in the war, the King's inspectors had arrived in long chariot trains, with outriders and standards flying, and plenty of warning. Now all that had changed. Now the Baru of Shamash at Nineveh, a man with the ear of the King himself, had appeared in the very midst of camp before anyone could even get himself into a state of grace. Bel-Heshti and Halli would have to appear with their imps and sins hanging all over them, with their hearts all thickly greased with misbehavior.

The Mountain-Leapers' chaplain, Father Sennanurgal, crept into the tent, looking itchy and flustered. He held the flap back, bowing, as the Baru's retinue appeared.

First a temple-scribe stepped in, blinking, followed by a reader of bird-flights. Two cult mediums stalked after them: trance-mystics wearing heavy, dust-stained cloaks with thick woolen cowls. Huge masks of snarling bronze encased their sweating heads. The two masked men took their places at each side of the entrance.

The Baru of Shamash entered last, with dignified tread. He was a tall, gaunt prelate in a deliberately plain brown robe. He clutched a short staff of office: a mace of twisted antelope horn, topped with a gold knob depicting an adder's fanged head.

He wore a tall brimless hat of layered black wool. Two small, discreet bull's horns peeked from their turbanned wrappings. Silver chains threaded his lean, corded neck, holding a dozen flat square charms of chiselled alabaster.

The General, his hand to his heart, knelt briefly and rose. "Your Eminence."

The Baru gazed about him, sniffing at the dusty air. "We can speak in confidence here? The Elamites have spies in your camp, General."

The General tugged at his beard. "Well, of course, Your Eminence. Can't fight a war without spies. We have several agents inside the city. Better spies than theirs . . ."

The Baru stepped stiffly toward Bel-Heshti and Halli. "Who is this, lurking in the shadows?"

"Ah," the General broke in, "those are your heroes, Eminence. The head-takers. Pioneers Halli and, er, Bel-Heppi."

Halli and Bel-Heshti grovelled with their best grace. "Bless us, Lord Eminence!"

The Baru, mollified, raised one hand and sketched a protective sign above their heads. Then he gave Bel-Heshti a short prod with the end of his crooked staff. "Sit up, son, let me look upon your face."

Bel-Heshti sat up, trembling. The Baru stared lingeringly into his eyes. "So," he said at last. "Now you." Halli sat up and received the same treatment.

"You boys have been drinking."

"Oh, no," Halli squawked.

"Really," Bel-Heshti added.

There was a long silence. "We only coveted drink, Your Holiness," Halli confessed at last, unable to bear the strain.

"We . . . we plotted to drink," Bel-Heshti moaned. "We know we're sinners, Your Eminence! We're not worthy."

The Baru nodded, satisfied. "You can tell me all about it later, at confession. Yes. You must be purified and in a state of grace when I present you with your Names before the troops." He turned aside. "You do have a bath here, General?"

"Why, yes, Eminence."

"And a woman to pour it for you, no doubt."

"Well, I, er, that is—" the General began, but Bel-Heshti alertly broke in.

"A bath!" he cried rapturously. "Thank you, Your Eminence!"

The Baru stared at him skeptically.

"Do you know what it means to be given a Name?" he said at last. "Do you truly understand that, in your heart?"

"We know we don't deserve it," Halli mumbled.

"In the beginning," the Baru said with bone-chilling solemnity, "nothing had a name, and chaos alone existed." He gestured briefly, and one of the masked mystics began to chant in a high, muffled, metallic voice.

"When the heavens above were yet unnamed/ And no dwelling beneath was called by a name/ When no names had been yet recorded/ And none of the gods had been named/ When there were no signs and sigils/ When the language of omen was mute . . ." The Baru gestured again, and the paralyzing drone broke off. Halli shivered violently.

"Without names, nothing can be," the Baru said. "To this day, you have not existed. The gods have had no name for you. You have been common men, mere walkers upon earth, almost as beasts. Like shadows, your passing left no trace, for you were not recorded. But now you shall be Named Men, thanks to our King's grace and his regard for your loyalty."

The Baru paused. "You shall be cleansed and shriven of sin and dressed in fine raiment. Your Names will be presented to you before the troops so that all may see how King Ashurbanipal, son of Esarhaddon, rewards those who serve the gods. Now think well on what I have told you. I shall speak to you again at confession."

He beckoned to the scribe, who crawled rapidly forward. The Baru handed him a small leather bag, then turned away. "General, a word with you." The Baru and the General stepped across the tent and began to mutter together.

The scribe was a middle-aged city man with thinning

hair and watering, myopic eyes. He murmured a quick in-
vocation in the holy language of Sumer and slipped the
bag's drawstring. He shook the bag, and two small cylinders of alabaster tumbled out, each the size of a finger's
joint. They lay in the palm of his hand.

He held them before the two soldiers. Halli, overcome, wiped away tears. Bel-Heshti smiled shakily.

"Your Names," the scribe said. "With these, you men
can become true citizens. You can own property and
mark it with your Name. You can own slaves, who will
carry your name-seal around their necks. You can sign
documents, and borrow on the strength of your Name.
You will be Named Gentlemen. You will exist."

The scribe opened the flap of his wicker shoulder-bag
and pulled out a small, flattened brick of damp clay. He
took one of the seal cylinders and rolled it expertly across
the clay, using two fingertips.

He held the damp brick before their eyes. The cylinder's intricately carved surface had pressed out a little embedded scene: a four-winged god raising his arms in
blessing before two rearing, winged antelopes. A column
of tiny cuneiform glyphs stood in the left corner. The
scribe read it for them: "He who smote the enemies of the
gods, in whom the King is pleased, the hero Halli." Halli
caught his breath in wonder.

The scribe turned the tablet over and ran the second
seal across the other side. It showed a sacred palm tree
and Ishtar in her aspect as war goddess, carrying a bow
and standing on a small crushed lioness. "It is the same
inscription, but for the hero Bel-Heppi," the scribe said.

"Not Bel-Heshti?"

The scribe frowned. "I suppose it could read *Bel-
Heshti*, with the syllabic interpretation . . . That's a rather
difficult character." He wiped the seals carefully with an
oiled scrap of wool.

Bel-Heshti grinned widely. "It's the most wonderful
thing I've ever seen! May I hold it?"

"Certainly not!" The scribe shook his head, and reverently slipped the seals back into their bag. He leaned forward confidentially. "Gentlemen-to-be, I must tell you that, magically speaking, this is a most dangerous time. Your Names have been chiselled and blessed, but have not yet been bestowed upon you. The identity of Name and Soul is not yet established; you are neither Named nor nameless. At such time the demonry are most active. They swarm about you, things of chaos, longing to seize your Names, your spiritual reality, for themselves!"

Bel-Heshti and Halli, frightened, made luck signs. "What shall we do then, learned sir?"

The scribe glanced over his shoulder and lowered his voice. "I would beg permission of the Baru and the General to retire to your tent and pass the time in prayer until the ceremony."

"Good idea! We hear and obey," said Bel-Heshti. They crept on hands and knees across the carpet toward the Baru and the General. There they waited, with heads low, for a chance to make their presence known.

The General ignored them. "But, Eminence! He's nothing but a heretic. The men don't pay any mind to his ravings."

The Baru glowered. "What! You mean to tell me that limb of Hell has been spewing his poison over your army, day after day? Lamashtu's Name, General! It's a wonder plague hasn't broken out."

The General smoothed his beard. "Well ... we do have Father Sennanurgal to protect us ..."

The Baru shook his head in wonder at such laxity. "There should have been a ranking baru or at least a properly trained ashipu here at all times." The scribe knelt at the Baru's elbow and offered him the leather bag with the two Names. The Baru nodded, blessed the bag, and slipped it back into his robe. Then he beckoned to the reader of bird flights. The reader stepped forward, his head bowed.

"You have been reading the animal omens, brother?"

The reader nodded grimly. "Indeed I have, Your Eminence. Plague among the horses."

"So! You see?" said the Baru to the General, loudly. "You're spiritually outmatched here; that's the problem. No wonder this siege has dragged on so. You should be halfway to Susa by now. But this Elamite, this thorn in the side of righteousness, has been spurting his venom over your troops. Dragging at their wills. Filling the camp with imps that turn your luck against you!"

Father Sennanurgal cast himself wailing at the Baru's feet. "Forgive me, Eminence! The fault is mine!" He tore at his hair and beard. "I'm only a humble army chaplain! I should have known I was outmatched!"

The Baru regarded him sternly, then smiled. "No, good Father Sennanurgal. If not for your stout, if humble, protection, things would have been far worse!" He turned to the General. "Yes, there has been damage done; but that is past."

Turning toward the tent's entrance, the Baru raised his voice to a boom. "Call forth your men, General! The day's worst heat is over; battle looms! No more shall your troops suffer under this wretch's imprecations! I shall go forth and do spiritual battle with him and crush him utterly!"

The Baru gestured to his two masked aides. They turned and threw open the tent flaps with practiced, dramatic gestures. A dozen orderlies and runners stood outside, curious.

The Baru took a deep breath and stepped into the glare. "The city falls tonight!" he bellowed, with absolute and terrifying conviction. "Ashur commands it! Their old men shall give up their heads, their young men's severed limbs shall be cast into fire! The women shall be taken away, the granaries thrown open to our soldiery! The skins of their priesthood shall cover the battlements; the holy places shall be sacked, and their mysteries exposed

to the sun! The fields shall be sown with salt, for the rage
of Ashur falls heavily upon this place . . ." A crowd of
excited soldiery gathered rapidly around him. He turned
toward the city wall, raising one clawlike hand in mal-
ediction.

The General stared after him, open-mouthed. He
reached down and helped the portly Father Sennanurgal
to his feet.

"He's great, eh?" Sennanurgal confided, trampling
Halli's hand as he found his balance. "There's a new
breed of priest in Nineveh these days! No half-measures!"

"These ears hear you!" said the General, grinning fe-
rociously. He stepped toward the tent flaps.

"Lord General!" Bel-Heshti cried from the carpet.
"My comrade and I beg leave to retire to our tent and
pray for guidance!"

The General stopped in mid-stride. "What? And miss
this? Call yourselves soldiers? Come on, heroes! Follow
me!"

They jumped up and hurried from the tent, at the
General's heels. At his shouted commands, heralds blew
their trumpets, and bearers seized the army's standard.

The masked mystics had produced brass cymbals
from beneath their cloaks. They pounded them noisily as
the crowd surged toward the city's walls, following the
Baru of Shamash.

Carried away by excitement, the Babylonians whirred
their slings overhead, the loud drone whipping up spirit.

Bel-Heshti and Halli jostled for a place as the General's elite bodyguard quickly gathered around the standard. The Baru, contemptuous of safety, ignored the
trenches and marched on level ground almost to the foot
of the wall. Two engineers with curved wicker shields
rushed forward to shelter him, but he waved them back.
Behind him, Assyrian archers, still strapping on helmets
and stringing their bows, filed into the trenches. Sappers,
holding shields above their heads, ran forward to the
shelter of the covered battering-rams.

The Baru raised both arms. "Come forth, scorpion!"

The Elamite prophet had fallen silent as the army swarmed forward. Now he also waved his shield-bearer aside and gazed down over the battlements, leaning on his straightened arms. "What jackass brays?"

"Unworthy man," said the Baru simply. His scorn echoed with majestic depth. "You think with your curses to save your town from those whom the gods command. I have seen many such as you. But you have never seen my like before. I am the Baru of Shamash at Nineveh, Mother of Cities!" A gasp came from the Assyrian ranks, followed by a ragged cheer. They had not known he was a priest of such high name. They could feel that their luck was turning. Their morale soared.

Halli and Bel-Heshti felt it where they stood: a surge of spirit as the army began to realize, to believe, that this might at last be the end. They could sense the enemy's fear, the stirring of panic behind the walls. The General felt it too, and turned to his aides. "Ready the ladders; be quick."

The Elamite prophet raised his voice. "So! A baru, a high official of the court! At last, someone here to negotiate! To put an end to this madness!"

The Baru was pitiless. "It will indeed end soon. When your king's head hangs from a tree in the gardens of Nineveh."

"But King Teuman wants peace! Again and again we've said it! Why such mad hatred? It was only a border skirmish!" The heretic prophet seemed suddenly frantic. "Ashurbanipal is mad! Demons of hatred possess him! He bathes in blood!"

"*Your* blood," the Baru pointed out. Harsh laughter rose from the Assyrians. They smelled terror. Their ranks stirred restlessly, almost tasting the future joy of rushing through the city, looting, burning, maiming, raping.

For a moment the enemy priest vanished from the parapet. Loud catcalls rose from the Assyrians as they milled in growing fury. The Elamite reappeared. "Creep

back to Nineveh and your temple boys!" he shouted over
the sudden din of bloodthirsty jeers and shield-beating.
"Back to your mad king in his den!"

"I will go to Nineveh," the Baru bellowed calmly,
"when I have your tongue to take with me!" Here and
there the army's brighter soldiers yelled approval at his
wit. "Your day is over, heretic! There was one like you at
Nabu-Shumati, city of Elam. And that city fell!" A loud
cheer from the Assyrians. "And another at Shushinak,
city of Elam, and it fell." A louder cheer. "Dar-Teuman,
fort city of your coward king, has fallen!" Frenzied yells
of triumph from the Assyrians, for this was news. Buoyed
by their howls, the Baru seemed struck with inspiration.
"All this despite the lying tongues of heretics! You shall
be mute, priest! Shamash has promised me your tongue!"
The Baru pulled a drawstring bag from within his robe
and shook it above his head. "I have six such tongues already, within this leather bag!"

The army roared approval. "The lying dog!" Halli
gasped, elbowing Bel-Heshti. "He's got our Names in
there!"

The Elamite prophet screamed, his words lost in the
Assyrians' din.

Suddenly ten Elamite defenders rose from where they
had crouched in hiding, on the catwalk behind the battlements. They flung down long, snaking siege-ropes, their
ends weighted with barbed grappling hooks. The hooks
hissed down around the Baru. Most missed, but one
knocked the tall hat from his head, and two more
snagged his robe. The Baru twisted and dropped his staff,
crying out.

"Shoot!" the General shouted. Arrows sleeted upward. The Elamites fell back, some pierced and howling,
others hauling their ropes back for another cast. The two
defenders who had caught the Baru struggled to haul him
in. He was lifted squirming from the earth, a hook
snagged in his belt. He dropped the bag of Names.

The General watched coolly. "Ladders forward!" he

shouted. The army's shouts broke into a maelstrom of rage.

The Baru's robes ripped. He fell out of them, landing heavily, his ribs scraped and bleeding. His mystics rushed forward, dragging him to safety. They left the bag of Names where it had fallen.

Bel-Heshti and Halli watched in occult horror. Then, as one man, they burst from the midst of the General's guards. Then ran headlong to join the howling Babylonians, who dashed forward, vaulting their ladders against the city wall.

The two men scuffled frantically for the bag. A strange and sullen hiss alerted them. A huge bronze pot was tipping at the rim of the battlements. They stared up, open-mouthed, into the deluge of flaming pitch.

Technician First-Class Beheshti pried an antipersonnel mine from the flaking soil. Below the mine's ridged bottom, a crusted layer of black stained the dirt. He set the mine aside with tender gentleness, then prodded the soil with his entrenching tool. His eyes widened. "Hey!"

Four meters away, Technician Ali stopped his gingerly digging and pried the Walkman earphones from his close-cropped head. "Yeah?"

"Come have a look. See what I dug up."

Ali squirmed on knees and elbows across the minefield, his plastic Khomeini tag dangling from one pocket flap. "Bouncing Betty. That's a nasty one."

"Not the mine—this." Beheshti held up a dust-caked bit of pinkish alabaster. "Pagan stuff."

"Huh!" Ali said. "You have all the luck, Beheshti." He peered down into the cavity where the mine had been. He raked at the stained soil. "Look! Here's one for me."

He grabbed for it. They struggled briefly, but Ali snatched the stone cylinder away and sat up, frowning. "You've got yours. I saw this one. It's mine!"

Beheshti shrugged with bad grace. "Allah wills." He rubbed grit from his trophy with his thumb. "Look at this," he said. "Some pagan whore standing on a lion! Look, she has no veil or cloak—you can practically see everything!" He tucked it carefully into his breast pocket.

The Walkman 'phones around Ali's neck squeaked shrilly. " . . . acts of sabotage and terrorism! The Iranian criminals have flung acid into the faces of those attempting prayers at mosques. Shiite fanatics of the inhuman Khomeini regime have poisoned food at the holy shrines of Basra and Karbala . . ."

"Radio Baghdad!" Beheshti said. "You shouldn't be listening to that filth."

Ali looked sheepish. "They're jamming Radio Tehran today. You can hardly hear the Imam. Besides, the heretics play Western rock and roll."

"For shame," Beheshti said, without much conviction.

A siren wailed briefly, back at the Iranian camp. The two men got to their feet and headed back to base, their bellies rumbling for lunch. An American-made Chinook copter stuttered along nearby, passing over a low mound of immemorial crushed brick.

The two Iranians passed the barbed wire and jumped down into a slit trench. They took their places in line beside a half-buried galley area, its tin roof heaped with sandbags. They shuffled forward, picking up battered army mess-trays still stamped with the Shah's imperial seal.

Beheshti pulled a checkered kerchief from around his throat and flapped at his sleeves, beating out an ocher cloud of minefield dust. The man before him turned around, coughing. "Please stop!" The man's face was weirdly scarred, his cheekbones hairless and skinned, his lips mere ribbons. He had no eyebrows.

"Sorry, brother," Beheshti said.

"Mustard gas," the scarred man said with a shy smile. "The dust is bad when you have no nose hair."

Ali and Beheshti took their trays of chickpea gruel, rice, and flatbread. They clambered up out of the trench to a favored sitting spot, where a camouflage net had been cast over a ridge of chipped limestone. It was a little breezier there, and it was easy to spot convoys arriving with supplies.

They were still eating when a Revolutionary Guardsman wearing PLO-style lizard camo pulled up in a Toyota pickup. A multi-barreled anti-aircraft gun had been bolted to the truck's bed. The truck's hasty camouflage of desert brown and dun was peeling, showing bright strips of cheery civilian chrome yellow. The Guardsman stuck his head through the window. "General wants to see you."

The two techs jumped into the back of the truck and were rapidly driven to field headquarters. Commandeered school buses were parked all around the bunker. Young boys in bloodied martyrs' headbands leaned outside the windows, cheering wildly, waving at the truck.

Ali and Beheshti waited under a limp Iranian banner as the Guardsman disappeared into the concrete bunker. In the distance, two Iraqi fighter-bombers returned from harassing oil tankers in the Gulf. Their contrails streaked the horizon beside a billowing mass of smoke from distant Khorramshahr.

Ali looked morosely at the children in the buses as they began a vigorous sing-along war chant, kneeling on the bus seats and pounding their chests in unison. "The minefields," he said. "It's another human-wave attack. The General wants our advice. That minefield we've been working on—they're gonna march these kids right through it."

"Well, yeah," Beheshti said. He hesitated. "We've done it before. Remember?"

Ali shrugged uneasily. "I guess so. I remember killing kids. We burned them on pyres. We displayed their bodies." He paused, his fingers searching through reflex for a non-existent beard. "But wait. Those were enemy kids. Not our own boys."

Beheshti was deeply confused. "Burned bodies on display . . ." He struggled hard for memory. "You must mean the American commandos," he said, straightening in relief. "They tried to rescue the hostages in the Nest of Spies. God punished them. Their chariots crashed in the desert."

"You just said 'chariots,' " Ali remarked. He looked thoughtfully at the ground.

"Something really terrible has happened to us," Beheshti concluded slowly. In absent irritation, he shook one trouser leg. Dust flew. "Where did these pants come from?" he demanded. "I hate these! And where's my helmet?"

"Something's changed," Ali said. "I think we got lost or something. And it's not any better here. We don't even get loot in this war, Beheshti. This war's not for soldiers—it's all for the priests. They want us to die—not just the enemy, *us*!"

Beheshti gazed around. "Sure seems familiar, though."

Ali looked deeply troubled. "I should have been a brewer by now. With a nice little tavern all my own . . ."

"Ali, we're Muslims," Beheshti pointed out. "We don't drink." He paused. "We're Shiites of the Revolution. We don't dance or play music. And we stone loose women."

Ali thought this over. He seemed stunned. "What do we do for the joy in life, then?"

"Uh . . ." Beheshti wrinkled his brow. "Well, there's mass-struggle rallies. And mass condemnations of the American Great Satan and the Marxist atheists . . ." Beheshti made a ritual air-punching gesture. "They're pretty exciting, really . . ."

Ali frowned, thinking painfully. "No brewing? Well, I guess I could pirate tapes of pop music. At least a black marketeer has some kind of name in society . . ."

Atop a tall iron pole nearby, four klaxon speakers

crackled into life. Out came an intense, sonorous voice, lightly eaten by static. "Soldiers of the Islamic Revolution! Today we will chop the hands from the minions of the Ba'athist regime! The corrupt and evil oppressors of the faithful will pay the full and bloody price for their crimes against the liberation struggle . . ." The voice went on and on.

Ali shuddered. "A mullah has come from the capital," he said, his shoulders slumping. "We'll have to talk to him. He'll see into our souls. We're done for."

"Let's lie to him," Beheshti suggested in the sudden light of desperation. "We'll hide our souls. We'll lie and cheat. Until we're either dead, or far away from here."

Ali grimaced. "What could we do—even if we did get away?"

Beheshti shrugged. "Sin, I guess."

"Good idea," Ali said, brightening. "I hear and obey."

To the north, heavy artillery opened up, throwing death across the Shatt-al-Arab with distant monotonous thuds. The Guardsman beckoned from the doorway. The General was ready.

They stepped down into the stinking darkness of the bunker.

THE SHORES
OF BOHEMIA

Rodolphe sat on the edge of his feather bed and cradled his favorite clock in his hands. The clock was made of polished black walnut and inlaid mother-of-pearl. It was handsome, and cleverly designed, and assembled with care and precision.

But at some time in the night, the clock had broken.

Gently, Rodolphe tried the wind-up key. The key turned loosely in its socket, with a dry, useless clicking.

Rodolphe felt a harsh sadness. He set the unhappy clock aside, then threw off his pajamas, and shrugged into an embroidered dressing gown. He unlocked the lowest drawer of a massive bureau, and withdrew a calf-skin schedule book.

He dipped a goose quill and began to write, with quick, precise stokes. *The alarm clock has ceased to function. Its gearwork seems broken, and it no longer responds to the key. Reason unknown.* Rodolphe found his pocket watch, which hung by its gilded chain from the bedside watchstand. *I have failed to rise at seven o'clock,* he wrote. *I have overslept an hour, and violated my daily schedule!*

Rodolphe paused, thoughtfully stroking his stubbled

chin with the quill feather. *Yet another dream of flight,* he confessed at last. *I flew with strange winged beasts, high above the city.*

He blew the ink dry, then locked the book back securely in the drawer. He was afraid his wife, Amelie, might glance into the book. After their years of married life together, Amelie knew his failings well enough. But Rodolphe did not want her to learn the disturbing nature of his recent dreams.

Rodolphe sponged his face and armpits over a brass basin. He stropped a razor and shaved. Then he dressed: trousers, undershirt, suspenders, shirt, waistcoat, dress coat, handkerchief, throat tie, socks, boots, stickpin, cane, and hat.

Amelie had left him some money. A stack of six gold coins gleamed ostentatiously on the corner of the bureau.

Amelie took pride in being a good provider. She had just been paid, Rodolphe recalled—she had finished sewing the upholstery for her latest steam car. Steam cars were fine things. Rodolphe envied her the pleasure she and her girlfriends took in building them.

Rodolphe flung open the linen window curtains, and studied each coin carefully with a powerful hand lens. Two of the coins had been minted in Syria, brought in by the caravan routes. The third came from glamorous Las Vegas, by the shore of America's great inland sea. The fourth coin was from China, a lovely little artifact with the ancient symbol of a television.

The last two were domestic coins from southern France; a disappointment. The French coins were nicely crafted, but nothing special; they were not even antiques. Rodolphe wondered why Amelie had accepted them. Sometimes he suspected that his wife simply didn't understand the true allure of money.

There was no time now for the comforting ritual of breakfast. Rodolphe left his apartments, clumped loudly down the wooden stairs and into the cobblestone streets of Paysage.

It was a crisp winter morning, under a pale pine-scented sky. Paysage's young citizens went about their business, heads held high, faces sober, eyes set straight ahead. Rodolphe returned their respectful salutes with brief smiles and crisp gestures of his cane.

Rodolphe made it a point to show courtesy to all. The stewardship of a public trust was a delicate matter. It required the creation of a general consensus; the studied garnering of public goodwill. After thirty years' hard work on his great project, Rodolphe knew that, to many people, he *was* the Enantiodrome; any personal failing of his own was somehow a reflection on the merits of the great construction.

As he did every day, Rodolphe walked downhill past a bakery, a flower shop, and a piano store. He paused on a street corner, awaiting a break in the jostling flow of horsedrawn traffic.

Rodolphe was joined in his wait by the city's mayor. The mayor was a thin, gangling man, in spare, elegant dress, with a hawklike profile. The mayor was a hundred years old, and something of a bore.

"Good morning, Henri," Rodolphe said.

"Yes, a lovely day," the mayor agreed, gazing critically at a uniformed policeman guiding traffic. "It seems to get a bit cooler every year now . . . It might even snow this winter." The mayor's tone suggested that this meeting was less than coincidence.

The mayor took Rodolphe's elbow, in apparently friendly fashion, as they crossed the street. "Are you prepared for that, Rodolphe? Snow?"

"We need no further construction grants," Rodolphe said. "We'll be finished very soon—well before the worst of winter."

The mayor chuckled. "The Enantiodrome is never *truly* finished! To be sure, there will be a hearty celebration, as the latest *phase* is completed. You and your gallant crew deserve every credit! And yet . . ."

They reached the far side of the street. The mayor still held Rodolphe's arm. "Trust my experience, Rodolphe. Of course we are pleased with your success. But eventually the city will get restless again. Though the Enantiodrome *seems* completed, we always find room for expansion. Another minaret, another set of buttresses . . ."

"My plans are very nearly fulfilled," Rodolphe said.

"But the Enantiodrome is no mere *blueprint*, Rodolphe. It's a tradition. A symbol. An incarnation of our civic spirit . . ."

"It's a building, Monsieur Mayor. It's a physical object. It has to stop growing eventually."

"Perhaps it's simply your *personal role* in the Enantiodrome that is near completion." The mayor smiled evasively, to lessen this wounding remark. "It's time you found a new vision, Rodolphe. You should direct your praiseworthy energies toward another career in Paysage. Architecture is not the only worthy pursuit, you know. There's banking, perhaps. Or law. Or politics—and politics has no illusion of finality!"

"Yes." Rodolphe nodded tactfully. "You were wise in your choice of vocation. Good day, monsieur." He walked on.

The man aroused an instinctive distaste in Rodolphe. The mayor, a hundred years old, was very young indeed for an old man; but he was far too old for a young man. The mayor had lived too long in this City of Youth. Now there was a musty air about him, something of the pressed flower, something brittle and dry. Or stale, and bottled-up . . .

Rodolphe himself was fifty-one years old. He had walked this route to work for thirty years. He'd gone willingly, eagerly. People had been able to set their watches by his progress. This was only proper, for a man of civic responsibility.

But now it struck Rodolphe—not for the first time—

how dreadfully easy it would be simply to *keep walking*. Straight down the street, out past the city walls of Paysage. Out past the plowed fields, out where the highway dwindled: first to a dirt track, then to a mere mule path through the endless tangled wilderness of Europe. A savagely thriving world, without boundaries, without direction, without constraint.

The thought struck his imagination with a deep, perverse thrill. To walk, naked and alone, into that vast ruin-spotted forest—that mystically seething realm . . .

It might be better to be dead. Rodolphe, with confused surprise, felt a sudden muddled uprush of deep love for this place, for this beloved city. His home. This sweet and settled landscape, every humble cobblestone set by someone who had cared for it, someone who had struggled to put meaning and structure into human existence. The buildings around him, the very pavement under his boots, seemed to vibrate suddenly with an essence of civilized purpose.

Rodolphe's eyes were watering. Ashamed of his weakness, he walked on with careful dignity, his face and shoulders set. Despite himself, his thoughts wandered. He remembered the fate of his old friend, Charles.

Charles was the former chief architect of the Enantiodrome: "poor old Charles," as Rodolphe had used to call him. Nothing solid or coherent could explain the poor fellow's distress, and yet Charles had become a haunted man.

Sometimes, when he and Rodolphe found a moment alone together during a day's hard work, Charles would confess his inner turmoil. Some senseless tormented babble about "transcendence" and "dissolution."

Rodolphe would listen with a show of patience, then go home, satisfyingly sore and tired, and covered with mortar and stone dust. "Poor old Charles was at it again today," Rodolphe would tell his wife. And Amelie would shake her ringletted head in remorse and disdain.

Something had driven Charles to give up his life here, his status, his material comforts, his satisfying routines. But now Rodolphe could feel the lure of it; the lure of the Conventions, preying on his mind. He had never realized how vastly subtle and strong Conventionality was; that it would flood into the cellar of one's mind, like black water . . .

Rodolphe rounded a familiar street corner, and saw the great clock minaret of the Enantiodrome. His reverie broke and his heart shed its unhappy weight. Perhaps Charles's life, perhaps Rodolphe's own life, perhaps the human condition itself, was somehow inherently redolent of this creeping ambiguous tragedy . . . but did that really matter?

After all, there was still the Enantiodrome. This great stone monument, this Cathedral to Youth, this soaring and splendidly useless edifice that defined the heart of Paysage. Rodolphe had fallen in love with it the first day that he saw it. Its defiant beauty had enchanted him.

He entered the spire-topped iron gates. Today workers swarmed across the site, over two hundred of them. Glaziers, painters, gargoyle sculptors, rooftop lead pourers whose smelters belched a picturesque black smoke across the city.

The Enantiodrome's coming "completion" had never been officially announced. Nevertheless, Paysage seemed to sense the approaching climax. The city's people felt the truth in the marrow of their bones, and it drew them to the site. Most of these volunteers would never be paid for their efforts here; even the highly skilled regulars received only token pay. They didn't care; the pay was not their motive. Rather, they all wanted, with a deep unspoken yearning, to know that they had *been there*. To know they had *lived the life*.

Rodolphe left his hat, coat, and cane at the gate, and assumed his customary leather working-apron, boots, and hard hat. Cheerful supply workers passed out free sug-

ared pastries and tiny cups of strong Algerian coffee. The
chaffing and gossip of the crowd sounded shriller than
usual, to Rodolphe's ears. As if they were doing all this
for the last time, and saving nothing for the morrow.

Despite the impressive scale of their labors, most of
the work was cosmetic: painting, trimming, adornment.
There remained two vital structural activities: the completion of the fifteenth anterior buttress, and the sealing of
the Great Dome.

Rodolphe, munching a pastry, went to inspect the
buttress. Rooted in bedrock and surrounded by trampled
mud, the great structure was lashed in a towering framework of tarred cordage and graying lumber.

All last month there had been a critical shortage of
decent brick. It had slowed work on the buttress, which
had to be completed before the Great Dome could be
trusted to bear the weight of its capstone.

Mysteriously, today there were several hundredweight
of bricks, heaped carelessly nearby, on the muddied grass.
Rodolphe studied them, nonplussed.

"Where is the night watchman?" he called.

A foreman sent a messenger to fetch the man. The
night watchman came slithering downward from the
heights of the buttress, on a knotted rope. He leapt from
a final catwalk, landed in the mud with a splash, and capered barefoot to Rodolphe's side.

The night watchman wore a thick moldy coat and
baggy trousers, gone ragged at elbows and knees. A puckered leather cap was slung over his dented, shaggy head.
He was almost dwarfish, his spine oddly bent; but his
huge hands and feet were gnarled and muscular.

"Good morning, Hugo," Rodolphe said.

"Good morning to you, Monsieur Rodolphe!"

"Who brought these bricks last night?"

"Bricks?" Hugo growled. He stared at them, rubbing
his chin, his ugly head cocked sideways.

Rodolphe waited patiently. The unfortunate Hugo

had never been quick, but even a man of subnormal, childish intelligence could win his way to an odd kind of wisdom, in a lifespan of centuries.

"I don't know," Hugo confessed at last.

"Come now," Rodolphe said. "Nothing within this building site escapes your notice, Hugo! You must have seen someone arrive last night. Look, there are cart tracks."

Hugo yanked a brick from the heap, weighed it in one hand, sniffed it, touched it to his tongue. "These are city bricks," he pronounced. "They have the smell of Paysage." He looked up, blinking. "It is demolition work. Fresh."

"Well, that's helpful information," Rodolphe said. "If we find an injured building in the city, then we have our unwanted benefactors. But I ordered no demolition, and expected none. I fear some mischief was committed to obtain these bricks. Why didn't you see these people, Hugo?"

Hugo jerked his dirty thumb toward the distant scaffolding ringing the Great Dome. That was where Hugo stayed, most nights; high above Paysage, crouched under a flapping tarpaulin.

"Last night there were screams," Hugo said. "Strange noises in the sky, the sound of many wings." Hugo reached into one vast pocket of his baggy trousers. "And this morning I found this, Monsieur Rodolphe!" He pulled out the limp corpse of a large bird.

A closer look showed it was not a true bird, but some kind of feathered animal. This dead creature had sharp conical teeth in its beak, and scaly claws at the joints of its wings. Its green and yellow feathers were loosely socketed in a tough gray hide.

It seemed to have broken its long snaky neck, colliding with a scaffold pole, in the darkness. Blood had clotted at its yellow nostril holes, and it stank like a snake, a sharp reptilian reek.

"What on earth is this creature?" Rodolphe said.

Hugo shrugged. "I have never seen one."

"Never, in your long life? Then they must be rare, Hugo."

"There was a large flock of them, monsieur. They were very loud in their cries and rustling. They stopped here to roost. Then they flew off—south, I think."

"It's some queer beast from the deep wilderness," Rodolphe said. "A creation of the Conventions. What are they resurrecting now, I wonder?" He looked at Hugo sharply. "Were there machines inside it?"

Hugo shook his head. "I did not cut it open to look, monsieur. It smells very bad."

"Well, it's no use looking for devices now," Rodolphe said. "If they wanted to hide their cunning little nanognats, we would never find them. We would never know . . . the Conventions are mysterious. It is the nature of Conventionality, I suppose. But I don't like mysteries, Hugo. Not here, within our very walls!"

Hugo smiled shyly, as if it were all somehow his fault. "This has happened before, monsieur. We have had other birds. I remember, when the third minaret was completed . . ."

"When was that? How many years, Hugo?"

"I don't count years, Monsieur Rodolphe. But Paysage was happy that night. We lit great fireworks in celebration. Many ducks flying from the wilderness were dazzled and blinded . . . We gathered them in the morning and made fine pies from them." Hugo rubbed his stomach with a leer.

Rodolphe sighed. "I hate it when things like this happen. I like things to make proper sense."

"You are young," Hugo observed. He stuffed the creature back into his pocket. "May I go now?"

"Yes, very well . . . Wait a moment. What's all this now?"

There was a sharp disturbance near the gate. Raised

voices, an angry scuffle. Frowning, Rodolphe hurried toward it.

A table suddenly flew upward, pastry plates and coffee tureens catapulting through the air. Rodolphe broke into a run.

Five men of the work crew were struggling with an intruder. They had tackled him and flung him to the earth, and an angry crowd was quickly gathering, clutching shovels and brick hods.

A tremendous bestial roar rang out, echoing from the Enantiodrome's stone walls. Another table flew into the air with a tumbling lurch and a smash. Workers backed away, stumbling and dropping their impromptu weapons.

A huge furred monster reared up above the crowd, jaws agape and roaring. It sat on its haunches, its long clawed arms swiping loosely at the air. Its teeth were like ivory chisels. It was a great brown bear.

Rodolphe ran headlong through the crowd, shouting and waving his arms. "Let him go, you fools! Release that man!"

Shouting orders, Rodolphe fought his way into the struggle. He wrenched their hands away from the invader's gaunt naked limbs. The man collapsed, trembling.

He was a Wild Man. A hairy, filthy Conventional, a savage of the woods.

The crowd was trying to keep the Wild Man's bear at bay, feinting at it timidly with shovels and crowbars. "Leave it alone!" Rodolphe shouted. "Can't you see this man *belongs* to that creature?"

The crowd protested. "But he's a savage!" "A dirty spy!" Rodolphe saw that the loudest shouter was Mercier, one of his most trusted foremen. Mercier's face, normally placid and sensible, was beet red now, congested with instinctive hatred.

Rodolphe was loath to touch a Wild Man, but he forced himself to act, and hastily dragged the disgusting wretch to his feet. "I'll take care of this matter personally!" he shouted. "Clear a way for us there! Mercier, get a grip on yourself, for God's sake! You must take charge here, in my absence."

Mercier blinked. As Rodolphe had hoped, the sudden weight of responsibility brought Mercier to his senses. "All right, Rodolphe."

Rodolphe turned away. "Be careful of that beast, you fools! Don't try to annoy it!"

The Wild Man half-flung his stinking arm over Rodolphe's shoulder, sagging against him. Rodolphe, wincing, hauled the Wild Man away toward the gate. The bear shambled up quickly at their heels, growling and pausing to snap at a hoe handle. Rodolphe looked over his shoulder; Mercier was calming the crowd.

"You disgust me!" Rodolphe hissed at the Wild Man. "What are you *doing* here?"

"Sorry," the Wild Man muttered.

"It's bad enough when we see one of you people in the common street! Don't you know that this building is a special place for this city? You have the whole outside world for your demented wanderings . . ." Rodolphe hauled the stumbling Wild Man through the gate and into the street.

A few of the angriest workers followed them past the gate, shouting and waving their tools. Most of them stopped within the site, gawking, and even laughing nervously, now that the trouble was over.

Rodolphe hustled the hobbling Wild Man half a block down the street, then dashed across it, into an alleyway.

They staggered down the alley, and past a turn, out of public sight. Then the Wild Man's legs seemed to give out; he sat in a doorway with a groan, and cradled his tangled, shaggy head in his hands.

The bear shouldered its way past Rodolphe, slinking up with its huge blunt skull held low. The bear sniffed at the Wild Man's bruises, and licked at a bloody scrape.

Rodolphe wiped his hands with a kerchief. "There are laws here, you know," he said. "We could arrest you! Throw you out—or even put you in prison!"

The Wild Man looked up pitifully. "Rodolphe! It's me."

Rodolphe stared at him in horrified alarm. *"Dad?"*

"No, I'm not your *father*, you fool! It's *me*, your old friend, Charles!" The Wild Man brushed his tangled hair back from his cheeks. "Look!"

"Charles!" Rodolphe said. "So it is! But you're so . . . so thin and filthy . . ."

"You get used to it," Charles muttered. He wiped his mouth, and spat. "I didn't know you would make such a fuss! When I ran the Enantiodrome, we used to let Wild Men in to see the work. Why, we were *proud* to show it!"

"That was *years* ago, Charles!"

Charles shrugged his bony shoulders. "I suppose it was . . ."

"We simply can't let you in there *now*. The Enantiodrome is almost *finished*. It's *important*."

" 'Important.' Yes, that's just what I used to think." Charles sighed. "I couldn't believe that it was almost *done*, though. *Completed*, at long last . . . I had to *see* it, Rodolphe, see it with my own eyes."

Rodolphe nodded slowly. Despite himself, he was touched. Even in his pathetic indecent exile, poor Charles was still drawn by the fine old loyalties. "How did you learn the news?"

"A little bird told me," Charles said, without any trace of irony. He got shakily to his feet, which were wrapped in hairy moccasins. "And it's true, Rodolphe— it's almost done! It's *beautiful*, isn't it? And I'm such a mess. Sorry. This isn't easy for me, you know."

"We must get you away from here," Rodolphe said. "Out of the public street. We'll go to my apartments."

Charles shuddered slightly. "I'd be just as happy to stay in the open air. Walls and roofs are so confining."

"Nonsense. We'll take the back streets . . . Can you walk? Are you badly hurt?"

"No," Charles said. He looked at a swelling bruise with indifference. "It's all right."

The bear suddenly spoke up. Its lips writhed and a long chain of guttural muttering came from its hairy throat. Rodolphe stared at it, his skin crawling.

"This is Baltimore, my domestic," Charles said. "He says not to be frightened. You can ride on his back if you like."

"No thank you," Rodolphe said.

Charles climbed lithely onto the bear's shoulders. "Don't be upset, Rodolphe. You've seen domestics before."

"Of course. My old parents had domestics," Rodolphe said. "Horses. Rather more normal-looking creatures." He paused. "It still bothers me to see a wild animal talk."

"He's not an animal," Charles said, without rancor. "He's an instrument of the Conventions. The Conventions sent me a bear, once my inner mind had . . ." Charles seemed to choke on his words. "I mean, after I left this city. It might have been a horse instead, but a bear better suited my . . . my 'temperament,' is the term you might use." Charles shook his head in confusion. "It's hard to explain to you, in a way you can understand. But Baltimore looks after me. That's all. He won't hurt you, Rodolphe."

"Good," Rodolphe said.

"It's not so strange," Charles said vaguely. "A bear as a domestic, I mean. There's a very old man in China whose domestic is a *bed of ants*. He has a . . ." Charles paused and swallowed, his eyes gone distant. "He has a *very big soul*."

"That's just fine, Charles," Rodolphe soothed. "Come along with me now. Quickly."

"I *can* talk, you know," Charles said. The bear carried him easily, lumbering along at Rodolphe's heels. "I just have trouble speaking in a manner you can comprehend." They left the alley, and dodged across a street lined with shops, to the frowning alarm of passers-by. "My ways of thought have changed so much . . ." Charles continued blithely. "That's what we *do*, Rodolphe. Talk about thinking. And think about talking."

"I know, Charles. That was always what most disgusted me about Conventionality."

Wild People were rare in Paysage. There were always a few of them, however, blundering in for their own inscrutable reasons: nostalgia perhaps, or some silent urge to make their obnoxious presence felt. Those who lingered were thrown out of town by the city police. And the same would soon be true of Charles, if he wasn't hidden somehow.

Rodolphe did not bring up this topic. He knew it would not be much use. It was always hard to talk straightforward common sense to the wretches. Decent people simply shunned them. It saved a lot of trouble, all around.

Rodolphe hurried home, trying to maintain his dignity under the accusing stares of fellow citizens. At last, Rodolphe urged Charles and his monstrous escort up his apartment stairs. Two of the stairs cracked loudly under the beast's great hind paws.

Rodolphe managed to get the bear settled into a corner of his sitting room, where the floor joists groaned ominously under its weight.

Charles sat wearily on a canary yellow chaise lounge. "Get up!" Rodolphe snapped. "Look what you've done to that upholstery . . . my wife sewed that herself!"

"Sorry," Charles muttered, brushing ruefully at the stained fabric. "I didn't mean to make any trouble. You should have left me at the building site."

"Not in your condition. It's simply impossible!"

"I want to see it, Rodolphe. I gave years to the great work. I have a right."

"We can talk about that, when you look like a decent human being again," Rodolphe said. He marched Charles into the bathroom.

Rodolphe lugged in towels and a tin kettle of steaming hot water. On his second trip, the bear addressed him, from its den behind the card table. "Rodolphe," it said. "May I ask you some questions?"

"No!" Rodolphe shouted.

"They are well worth thinking about."

"I'm not listening!" Rodolphe said.

After an hour's determined scrubbing, Charles was clean and shaved. He sat on a settee, wearing Rodolphe's second-best houserobe, while Rodolphe snipped at his hair with his wife's sewing scissors.

Without its thicket of hair, Charles's face had a fiercely compelling asceticism. His pale eyes glowed with weird intelligence, and his gaunt weather-beaten arms and legs were all tendon and leathery sinew. He sat calmly on the settee, his hands folded. His quietude, in contrast with the obvious whipcord strength of his lean body, was almost frightening.

"Doesn't this feel better?" Rodolphe asked. "To be clean and decent again?"

"I suppose it does. Yes." Charles cleared his throat. "The sensations are different. And it does bring the old memories back." He smiled, with a shadow of his old charm. "You're too kind to me, Rodolphe! You have done me a service; you always were a good friend."

"That's better. You sound much more like yourself now, Charles."

"Perhaps. I often remember my days here in Paysage." He blinked. "It does have some meaning, Rodolphe. What we do here; the work, and the sweet little rules of daily life, and all that baggage. Even in the great outside world, looking back on this little enclave . . . The effort isn't wasted; it's a necessary process."

"Don't patronize me," Rodolphe said.

"I just felt you should know that, Rodolphe! Someday it will be a comfort to you."

"Don't take that tone with me!" Rodolphe said. "You're a fine one to talk about 'wasting effort.' What have you done, since you left this place, that has made the world one whit better?"

Charles sighed. "It depends on your definitions. You don't have the terminology, Rodolphe."

"Words!" Rodolphe said. "All words, and airy nonsense! You've lost your mind, Charles. You've lost your purposes. You're nothing better than that shambling beast of yours."

"Oh but I *am*," Charles said. "Baltimore is *intelligent*, but he has no *consciousness*. He's . . . he's really a cybernetic-organic incarnation of the former industrial urban environment. The megatechnic infrastructure has miniaturized, and woven itself on a cellular level into the ontological information-processing structure of what was once the natural realm. The Conventions are a global data system that has assumed the function of an Immanent Will."

"*What?*" Rodolphe shouted.

Charles sighed. "It's not as strange as it sounds. You get quite used to it, once you . . . well . . . give up, and become Conventional. The Conventions have their own kind of beauty, Rodolphe. Not at all like the simple beauty here but . . . the Conventions do have a place for human beings. We have a role there, a true function. We . . . we *personify* the Conventional world, Rodolphe! We are its soul!"

"My God, it's hopeless," Rodolphe said. "'You've become a babbling lunatic."

"No, I don't think so," Charles said patiently. "Once you learn to live the life outside, you learn to see matters differently. To read the patterns of immanence, to smell it almost . . . the very way you might read your own dreams, or understand the clouds. Storm fronts of meshed intelligence ripple through the living fabric of the Earth. Perceptions become data, data becomes thought, thought becomes ... I think you might say 'spirit' though that term doesn't really—"

"Shut up, for God's sake!" Rodolphe flung his scissors to the floor. "I don't *need* that, do you understand me? I have a world here in Paysage, a world I can understand, a world I can work within, a world that *makes sense*! I won't become some empty puppet of your vast inhuman system—"

The door slammed downstairs. Rodolphe's wife had arrived; he heard her familiar footsteps, plus a lurch and a yelp of pain as she missed her footing on a cracked stair.

Amelie hurried in, whipping the bonnet from her hair. "Rodolphe!" She stopped short with a swish of skirts and stared in horror at Charles. "So! It's true, then!"

"Please don't be frightened, Amelie," Charles said.

Amelie put her fists on her hips. "I'm not frightened of you, you worthless layabout!"

"I meant the bear," Charles said, pointing at the corner. Amelie turned, went white, and shrieked aloud.

"He won't hurt you, dear," Rodolphe said.

"Rodolphe, what have you done? My God, think of the scandal! Rodolphe, what is this *creature* in our *house*? What will the neighbors think?"

"Calm down, dear," Rodolphe said. "I don't like this situation any better than you do! But let's discuss it like civilized beings."

"Oh, don't give me any of your Monsieur Architect calm rationality!" Amelie shouted, stamping the carpet. "Of course we're 'civilized beings'! That's exactly why we abhor persons of his sort!" She glared at Charles. "Why we shouldn't *look* at such people, much less invite them into our drawing room with their vile snorting animals!"

"I'm not an animal, Amelie," the bear said.

"You keep out of this, you walking hearth-rug!" She

turned to Rodolphe, folding her arms. "Have you gone mad, Rodolphe?"

"Dear, this is Charles. Our old friend. You remember. We used to have him to dinner."

"This miserable personage is not what I call 'our old friend Charles,' " Amelie said. "He has betrayed us. He has joined the oppressor gerontocracy. He is our class enemy!"

"Oh no," Rodolphe begged. "Not politics, Amelie!"

"It's the truth," Amelie retorted. "Why won't you face it? You, with your head-in-the-clouds masculine construction-schemes! I always told you, Rodolphe: you mustn't get *mystical* about your business! It's just stones and mortar, Rodolphe: *stones* and *mortar*! Otherwise, it turns your head, and you end up . . . well . . . like one of *them*! Just like *he* is now!" She drew a breath. "Is *that* what you want?"

"No!" Rodolphe said. "You know that's not so!" The accusation stabbed him with anxiety. "It would mean the end of everything," he said. "The end of our marriage. And our home. The end of everything I've built here— that *we* have built here, together! You know I don't want that, Amelie!"

Amelie was silent a moment, biting her lip. She seemed moved by his distress. "Well, if that's so," she said, "then why do I find you in this person's company?"

Rodolphe sat down. His legs felt weak. "Perhaps I did make a mistake, dear. But it seemed the best way to avoid an even larger scandal. There was a nasty stir at the Enantiodrome. It seemed best to . . . well . . . get Charles out of sight."

"You should have summoned the police."

The bear spoke up again. "That action would have engendered an unfortunate complexity."

"Let me speak," Charles told it. "Amelie, I know my presence is unpleasant to you, but please try to understand. A . . . a vital transition is about to occur in this place. I had a hand in creating it. I have a right to witness it. You owe me this."

"Oh, so *that's* it, is it?" Amelie said. "You barge in here with this horrific instrument of brute authority, and then try to appeal to our better natures. A typical power-play of the coercive gerontocracy!"

"I haven't done anything," Charles said meekly.

"Don't pretend you're not implicated," Amelie said. "Maybe you don't oppress us, directly and obviously. But you profit by everything that's done to confine us here, and disrupt our lives, and rob us of a normal, civilized existence!"

Charles winced. "What a strange mode of discourse . . ."

"Be fair, dear," Rodolphe urged. "He doesn't understand what you're saying."

Amelie walked across the sitting room to the chaise lounge. She noticed the stain on it, but sat there anyway, her lips tightening. "Oh, it ought to be clear enough," she said. "After all, most of the world belongs to him, and his antediluvian friends. All we have of it is little ghettos and caravan routes. We could civilize the whole world again, if we were allowed to. We could have hot water, and meals three times a day, and books, and art, and decent clothes, and roads, and rules . . . and *families*, too." Suddenly she burst into tears.

Rodolphe sat beside her, and took her hand. "Try not to take it so hard, dear."

She looked up, wiping her eyes with a kerchief from her bodice. "Oh no," she said, "I don't suppose I should be *allowed* to take it hard, should I? Perhaps I should simply *sublimate* my feelings, in piling stones on stones, instead of giving care and love to other human beings!"

She turned on Charles fiercely. "I'm a grown woman! I may not be two hundred, or three hundred, or four hundred years old, but I have the wants and needs of a normal human being! I want a child! And *you* won't let me have one."

"But you're not old enough," Charles said.

"That's your answer to everything," Amelie said. "Of course I'm old enough! Women used to bear children at forty, or thirty, or even younger!"

"Yes, but that was when people *died* young," Charles said. "You can't expect to live for centuries, and bear hundreds of children! The Earth would be overwhelmed."

"Don't put words in my mouth," Amelie said. "That's not what I said." She pointed at Rodolphe. "I'm not being selfish. It's very simple. I love this man! I want his child, I want a true marriage with him, with a family! But you tell me I must wait for that fulfillment until I'm a strange old crone. Are Rodolphe and I supposed to wait out centuries, while the dust slowly settles on our souls? No, we'll surely drift apart, and our love will be nothing but an episode." She wrung her hands. "Every day of my life, thanks to you, I have to taste my own sterility."

"I'm sorry for your distress," Charles said. "But at least you don't have to taste your own approaching *death*. And other people have lived through this situation. Your own parents, for instance!"

"I never really *knew* my parents," Amelie said. "None of us do. How can we, in this world? They were always *patient* with me, and I think perhaps they loved me in their own strange way, but I never really saw *them*, did I? I only saw the facade that the very old create to show to the very young. We can't love each other simply and directly; there's too much distance between our hearts. The situation isn't humane, it's not natural. It hurts!"

"There's no other way to manage, though."

"All that means is that you don't *want* another way." She glared at Charles. "Why don't you get out of here? Leave this place, and go back where you belong. Paysage belongs to us! We built everything here, with our own ideas and our own hands. We never used your help; we owe you nothing, we reject you totally. I want you *out of my house*!"

There was a ringing silence. "Amelie," Rodolphe said at last. "This isn't some stranger. This person used to *be* us."

"That only makes it worse," she said. "You ought to throw him downstairs."

"That would scarcely be polite, would it?" Rodolphe said, with a sidelong glance at the bear.

She noticed his look. "Oh yes," she said. "For a moment, I forgot that he holds the whip hand of authority over us. I suppose, if we gave him the hiding he deserves, this great brute of his would reduce our home to matchsticks!"

"I thought, if we made Charles seem presentable," Rodolphe suggested, "we could leave without him creating a public stir."

"Are you going to shave the bear, too?"

"We can't help the bear, dear. Perhaps, if Charles looks fairly normal, people will forgive him that eccentricity."

"Well, I suppose that's something," Amelie admitted. "I suppose I could help you, if it comes to that. His hair looks dreadful."

"Thank you, dear. I knew I could depend on you."

Rodolphe chose a suit of clothes, while Amelie set to work, reluctantly, on their guest.

Charles was too short for the trousers, so Amelie took in the hems. With his hair trimmed, and the proper accoutrements, Charles looked almost human.

At Rodolphe's suggestion, they treated Charles to a proper home-cooked lunch. Charles had trouble with the silverware, and the flavors of the food seemed to startle him, but he did well enough. The bear devoured two loaves of bread and apparently went to sleep.

When the domestic ritual was over, Amelie seemed mollified.

"Perhaps I was a bit overwrought earlier," she said. "I don't like to talk about my grievances—after all, there's not much I can do about the oppressive power structure, is there?—but sometimes it simply overwhelms me. And it makes me feel quite wild." She looked at Rodolphe, troubled. "Are you angry with me, Rodolphe?"

Rodolphe smiled indulgently. "No, sweetheart. Truth to tell, I feel much the same way, sometimes."

"You don't show it. Not to me, at least."

"I try to be reticent. I depend on you for solid common sense."

Amelie sighed and looked at the clean tiled floor. "I broke your clock last night, Rodolphe."

"You did?"

"I couldn't bear to listen to it ticking any longer—it was like a reproach." Amelie was fighting tears.

"That's perfectly all right, dear," Rodolphe said numbly. "We can get another clock."

Charles rose cheerfully from the table, wiping his mouth on his coat sleeve. "This was charming! I feel quite fit now. Perhaps we should go."

After the dishes had been scrubbed, and arranged in the china cabinets, they went to the drawing room.

"Can you come with us, dear? It's worth seeing today; quite a hubbub. Might cheer you up."

"Later tonight, perhaps," Amelie said. "I don't want to walk in public with a bear."

"I'll stay here," the bear remarked. It opened its jaws in a horrific yawn.

A nano-gnat the size of a horsefly emerged from its gullet. The little mechanism flew silently across the room and landed on Charles's lapel.

"Will you be all right here, dear?" Rodolphe said.

"I won't be staying home either," Amelie said tartly. "The beast can stay here by itself. I have work to do at the garage."

Rodolphe and Charles picked their way down the

fractured stairs. "I'm surprised that your bear is willing to stay behind, Charles. Though that should help matters a great deal."

"Baltimore doesn't have a 'will,' " Charles said. "The nano-gnat will link us. Baltimore can move very quickly should I need his services."

They walked together into the afternoon streets. As two respectable gentlemen, they did not attract a second glance. Charles walked a bit stiffly as though the clothes chafed him, but he was not so odd as to be an anomaly.

"Why do you call him 'Baltimore'?" Rodolphe said.

"Baltimore was a city," Charles said. "An ancient city on the shore of America. But when the seas rose, the waves came and claimed Baltimore. The site is long submerged."

"So 'Baltimore' was a lost city from the age of industrial mortality?" Rodolphe shrugged. "Interesting."

Charles grunted.

They paused on a street corner. Traffic was snarled. Cordons had been erected half a block down the street. A gang of men in work clothes were tearing the great marble facade from the City Bank.

"I don't like the look of this," Rodolphe said. He led Charles up the street.

A circle of onlookers were admiring the action. Rodolphe noticed the president of the Bank, a portly gentleman of great dignity whose name was Gustave. They exchanged greetings. "What's all this?" Rodolphe said.

"It is the future capstone of the Enantiodrome, of course," said Gustave in surprise. "Surely you knew."

"I gave no such orders," Rodolphe said. "Besides, we already have a capstone! Fifty years ago, the capstone was hewn from Carrara marble, and transported here over the Alps by mule team. It was then decorated by a generation of artisans, and now lies safely in the basement of the Enantiodrome, awaiting the great moment of its installation!"

"Oh *that*," Gustave said. "Apparently they broke that one. They're going to chisel out a new one, from out of the front of my Bank."

"They *broke* it?" Rodolphe shouted. "My God! How did it happen?"

"Don't alarm yourself," Gustave said. "We at the Bank are more than pleased to help you out. It's a civic honor for us, really. Why, they dug a ton of bricks out of City Hall last night; in comparison, we in private enterprise are getting off cheaply!"

Rodolphe backed away into the crowd, disguising his horror. "Someone is flouting my authority," he said to Charles. "It's a conspiracy, clearly. Come, we must hurry."

Within minutes they were at the Enantiodrome. The great building was the scene of near-riot. The crowd of workers had swollen from mere hundreds to a large fraction of the city's whole populace. Men and women swarmed across the grounds, hauling boards, shoving wheelbarrows, eating, laughing, sitting around bonfires of scrap lumber. It was like an army of occupation.

"What is this outrage?" Rodolphe said. "Have they all gone out of their heads?"

"They're working very hard," Charles observed, his eyes gleaming.

"With no efficiency at all," Rodolphe said.

"They work like ants," Charles said. "Small individual actions, some even counterproductive, yet adding up to an unspoken emergent whole."

"Spare me," Rodolphe said. He plunged into the crowd. People waved at him cheerily, clapped him on the back, and shouted incoherent congratulations. It took him a long time to find Mercier.

"What happened?" he asked the foreman.

"Isn't it wonderful how the people have responded in our time of need?" Mercier said. He grinned politely at Charles, clearly failing to recognize him. "It's a bit of a muddle, but we'll get it up by tonight, all right. Imagine that, Monsieur Rodolphe! Finished by midnight! It makes you want to weep with joy!"

"Who specified this so-called deadline?" Rodolphe asked.

Mercier looked startled. "Well . . . I don't know. But we're finishing today! I mean, ask anyone—everyone knows it is the truth!"

"Some irresponsible rumormonger," Rodolphe grated. "This is grotesque! Look at this blundering amateurism. It's mob hysteria!"

Mercier looked cowed. "But, sir—everyone's having such a good time—"

"You've all fallen for some sort of stupid prank! This will set our schedule back by months! Tomorrow, we'll have to dismantle and repair all this botched work—not to mention apologizing to City Hall and the Bank!" Rodolphe wiped his brow with his kerchief. "My God, think of the damage to our credibility! To my reputation! This is what I get for abandoning my project, even for a few short hours—"

Charles took his elbow gently. "Rodolphe?"

Rodolphe yanked his arm away. "*Now* what?"

"This is a building, Rodolphe. It's not you. It doesn't belong to you."

"What do you mean? It's my responsibility; everyone knows that!"

"But the Enantiodrome doesn't *care*, Rodolphe. It was here before you and it will be here after you. You can't *be* this thing, Rodolphe. It has its own momentum. You have to let it go."

"That's nonsense," Rodolphe said, sweating.

"Look at the people, Rodolphe. They're *doing* it. Not exactly as you wanted it, perhaps, but in a way that . . . well . . . suits the innate purposes."

Rodolphe hesitated, stunned. Then he rallied. "No. I can still restore order here. I'll fetch the mayor, I'll summon the police . . ."

"Some of these people *are* the police, my poor friend." Charles smiled angelically. Rodolphe felt a strong urge to strike him.

Mercier spoke up. "Sir? I think I saw the mayor here earlier—he was here with the City Council. He went inside."

"Then there's still a chance to settle things!" Rodolphe said.

He ran quickly across the site and through the gigantic double doors of the Enantiodrome. The doors had been hung in an earlier century, and were weather-stained, their massive hinges eaten with verdigris. But they were still stout, and even beautiful, with bas-reliefs of bats and angels.

Rodolphe hurried up the cavernous entrance hall, with its flanking rows of vast peaked windows. Men and women thronged the galleries, slopping soap buckets, polishing the colored glass. Some were even singing.

Beneath the echoing vastness of the Great Dome stood a group in dark suits and dresses—the mayor and his City Council. The late afternoon sun cast a vast column of dusty light through the open apex of the Dome, splashing in a lozenge shape against the stair railings ringing the fretted interior.

The politicians were examining a heap of fresh rubble in the center of the great circular enclosure. Their muttering echoed with ghostlike authority.

Rodolphe saw that it was the great capstone. The huge marble lid had slipped through the hole it was meant to seal, and fallen, end over end like some vast stone coin, to shatter against the stained tessellations of the Dome's hard floor. Rodolphe's heart constricted. Years of careful work and preparation, smashed and cast aside . . .

"Monsieur Mayor," Rodolphe began.

"Ah, Rodolphe," the mayor said, offering his hand. "It seems we were both mistaken, my dear fellow. We shall finish even sooner than we had hoped."

"Henri, I need a word with you," Rodolphe said.

"If you mean *this*," the mayor said, gesturing at the rubble, "well, these things happen, eh?" He paused, staring at Rodolphe's companion, who had just arrived. "Charles," he said. "Charles, is it not?"

"Yes, Monsieur Councilman," Charles said.

"I'm now the mayor, Charles."

"I always knew you were meant for great things, Henri," Charles said with a smile.

Rodolphe picked up a piece of marble rubble with the broken face of a horned cherub. "I presume you realize, by this striking evidence of incompetence, that none of this is proceeding according to my plans."

"Yes," the mayor said, "somehow I gathered as much, by the fact that you were absent and the place was full of a mob."

"Well? What are we to do about this?"

"It's a politician's dream," the mayor said, smiling. "A genuine popular movement, Rodolphe! You ask what I should do? I'm their leader, aren't I? I run in front of the marchers and wave a flag! So here I am."

"But it's senseless, Monsieur Mayor. There's no point to it."

"The people are not required to 'make sense'—not to you, at least," the mayor said. "The Voice of the People is the Voice of God."

"You'll regret this, when you see the mess they make of things," Rodolphe said.

"It's *their* mess," the mayor said. "Not yours, Rodolphe. We're not the public. We only serve it."

"Well put," Charles remarked.

Rodolphe put his hands to his head. "What am I to do, then?"

"Lead, follow, or get out of the way," the mayor suggested. He looked upward suddenly, and prudently stepped sideways. A chunk of marble a foot across came plummeting down from the summit to smash to dust nearby.

A tiny head with waving arms showed at the daylit hole. "Hey! You lot be careful, down there!"

"Let's go," Charles murmured, clapping Rodolphe across the back. "One last time, eh? To the heights!"

The hours that followed were a sweaty nightmare of sledges and levers and pulley work. The vast unwieldy slab of stolen marble came foot by foot, sometimes inch by inch, around, under, and through the maze of scaffolding. Men rushed back and forth with crayons and tape measures, chopping the slab to fit with saws, mauls, and chisels. Cranes were raised, timbers set, as the incomplete Dome itself squeaked and shuddered under the strain.

Toward the end they worked by torchlight. In the grounds below a vast crowd swayed, singing in unison.

The workers were in a cheerful frenzy. Both Rodolphe and Charles found themselves struggling to keep a rudiment of order; trying to keep the crew from injuring themselves in enthusiasm. Everyone wanted to contribute *something*, even something without apparent meaning of any kind. Their restless energy could not be brooked. Those who could not help with the capstone were stripping away the scaffolds and catwalks. As the gangs flung the lumber down, end over end, people scattered below, scrambling, laughing, and cheering.

Then the last wedge was hammered loose and the capstone sank into place with a shrill grinding. One man lost his crowbar; another lost the end of his finger, and held up the bloody stump in white-faced glee, like a badge of honor.

They stood around for a moment, expecting some epiphany that no one seemed able to define. "Why aren't they cheering down there?" someone asked dazedly.

"They don't know yet," Charles said patiently. "They see no vital signal of consummation."

"Well, let's tell them, then!" Mercier shouted joyfully. He glanced around the top of the Dome, in the wind-whipped torchlight. "Wait a moment—where's our cat-walk?"

The scaffolding of the Great Dome was gone. People had been disassembling it wholesale and flinging it down, cleaning the building of it, in thoughtless haste. "My God, we're trapped up here!" Mercier said.

The night watchman, Hugo, spoke up. He had a length of tarred rope around his shoulder. "No," he said. "There is still a way for you; I know it." He knotted his line to the tripod crane at the summit, and began to pay out rope, hopping downward across the curve of the Dome with a strange and crooked grace.

Rodolphe hustled the work crew into a proper order. "Show some dignity," he told them. "Remember, the eyes of the people are upon you. Behave in a way that matches the majesty of this great moment."

They nodded, and followed the rope down, hand over hand, to a shaky catwalk. But when they reached earshot of the people below, their dignity broke and they began shouting wildly.

Then the celebration began.

Amelie was amid the turbulent crowd, waiting. She had the bear with her. No one seemed to mind its presence.

She embraced him. "I'm proud of you, Rodolphe."

Rodolphe laughed. He was light-headed with fatigue and triumph. "I don't deserve the credit," he said. "It wasn't really my idea."

"Whose idea was it, then?"

"I don't know. It seemed to come out of the air some-how."

"Take the credit," Charles advised. "Who knows who deserves the fame? Who knows who really started this thing, so many years ago?"

Rodolphe paused. The idea of final credit, of credit

for origination, had never really struck him before. "I don't know how it started. But it can't have been much to begin with, can it? Some poor fool, I suppose, piling a stone on a stone with his bare hands, while the rest of the world was wrapped in its strange transformation. His motive is lost in time."

"It was defiance," Charles said. "Stubbornness. The act of someone who wouldn't—or couldn't—join the Conventional world."

"You think so, Charles?"

"I know it."

Rodolphe laughed again. "Well, that would fit, wouldn't it? The central impulse at the secret heart of our milieu. I hope he's happy today, if he's still alive some- how. I'd dearly like to shake his hand."

Amelie was looking at him strangely. Rodolphe shrugged. "Or *her* hand, of course. It might very well have been a woman!"

Amelie said nothing. She was wide-eyed, looking into his face. Rodolphe touched her shoulder gently. "You're not angry with me, are you, dear?"

"No," she said. "It's just that I've never seen you like this before."

Rodolphe spread his hands. "You mean, now that it's all done? Have I changed so very much?"

"I don't know . . . But I've never seen you before, as the father of my child."

Rodolphe started. "What's that, dear?"

Amelie smiled. A slow, secret, radiant look. "It will happen, Rodolphe. We will be parents together. Some- day."

"What makes you think that?"

"I don't *think* it, Rodolphe. I know it."

Rodolphe stared at her in alarm. "Oh dear. You haven't been talking to the bear, have you?"

"You're wrong about the bear, Rodolphe. It's not a personality, like us. It's just an intelligence—a repository of much vaster forces. It knows things without understanding them."

Rodolphe was stricken with despair. He barely heard her next words. "But *I* understand them, Rodolphe. Someday you and I will meet again, in deep futurity. And we'll have a true marriage then. Something strange and profound, that we can barely imagine now."

"Well," Rodolphe said. "I suppose that's very good news, dear. In the meantime, you and I can . . . Well, you can be the belle of the ball tonight, can't you? We can share the acclaim. Let's enjoy ourselves."

She shook her head. "No, Rodolphe. You do understand, don't you? In your heart, you know how this changes things between us. We can't play the game of young lovers, now that we know the truth. There's no point in it, darling."

"But you can't simply leave me! Not here. Not like this!"

"There will never be a better, truer time, Rodolphe. I know you'll remember me always, if we part at this very moment. But it's not good-bye. Only au revoir." She turned her back on him.

In a moment she had run gracefully into the depths of the crowd.

"Oh my God!" Rodolphe cried. He turned on the bear. "This is your fault, you stupid beast! I should kill you for this!"

The bear nosed at his knee with a snuffle. Rodolphe looked into its eyes. There was nothing there—just an animal blankness.

"Then it's *your* fault!" he shouted at Charles.

"I haven't done anything," Charles pointed out.

"I'll rush home, then, and find her. She'll never leave me without taking her favorite things."

"She won't need 'things' where she's going," Charles said.

Rodolphe gasped. He braced himself to plunge into

the crowd in pursuit; to find his wife somehow, tackle her, chain her down if necessary. But the mayor and a crowd of celebrants emerged, blocking his way.

The mayor offered Rodolphe an open bottle of sparkling wine. "Fireworks!" he shouted. "Fireworks soon! What a fete, my dear fellow! The ball will last till dawn!"

A timber fell nearby, tumbling end over end to splinter on the turf. The crowd billowed away in alarm. "What's this?" the mayor shouted, staring at Rodolphe. "My God! The whole thing's not going to fall on us, is it?"

Rodolphe, stung, drew himself to his full height. "Get a grip on yourself, Henri," he said sternly. "Of course it won't fall! It's only poor Hugo, the night watchman. He's flinging down the last of the scaffolding, from high up on his Dome."

"Ah," said the mayor, "the final touch. Yes, I had a feeling that there was something missing yet. Some final climax." He paused. "Good old Hugo, eh? It's a pity! You know, he's been at it for ages! He must be the oldest and most faithful worker we have! The poor old wretch should be down here for this. We should honor him. Yes, *honor* him—that's it."

"We can coin him a medal," a city councilman suggested.

"Capital idea. Medals all around."

"You're drunk," Rodolphe realized.

"There will never be a better time for it," the mayor said, forcing a bottle on him. "You look too sad, Rodolphe. It's not proper. Dignity's well enough in its place, but if you want to live within the walls of Paysage, you have to share the living heart of the people. There's no other way, my friend."

Charles tapped the mayor's shoulder. "Henri, forgive me if I phrase this question poorly, because the assumptions behind it are a little odd to me. But now that the Enantiodrome is finished, *what are you going to do with it*?"

"It doesn't need any purpose," the mayor said loftily. "It's entirely sufficient merely unto itself."

"There must be more to it than that."

"Yes ... I suppose it is, for instance, beautiful." He paused. "Why ask me, anyway? I only voted the funds. *You* built it, not me. Why did you work on it?"

"I don't really know why I did it when I did it," Charles said naively. "But I think I *know how it did itself now*—wait, that didn't come out right."

"All right," Rodolphe interrupted. "Just tell us, Wild Man, if you know so much. Tell us what it's for, then. Tell us all about it."

Charles blinked in the carnival torchlight. *"It refreshes the soul of the world."*

"And what on earth is that supposed to mean?"

"I don't know," Charles confessed. "I know something ought to happen, but I don't think it's fully emergent yet."

A mass of cordage and lumber came slewing off the side of the building, caromed from a buttress, and fell in a heap. "He's still busy up there," Charles observed.

"How are we going to get the poor idiot down again?" the mayor asked.

"Oh, he lives up there," Rodolphe said. "He's used to it. He'll be fine." Suddenly he burst into tears.

"Brace up, Rodolphe," the bear told him kindly. "This transition won't take long. Your suffering will be brief."

Rodolphe stared at it. "You dare to speak to me?"

"*Only* to you, Rodolphe. The others can't hear my speech—they hear only an animal muttering. But I know the structures of your perceptions."

"Ah, of course," Rodolphe said in disgust. "Conventionality has always had its little spies, within my very body, eh? Nano-gnats. I suppose they must know my blood by heart, and every thread of my nerves ..."

"They keep you alive and youthful, Rodolphe. The

secret structures of Conventionality support and sustain you, deep beneath your notice."

"I defy you and your secret structures!" Rodolphe shouted.

The bear nodded. "I'm proud of you, Rodolphe." The look in its eyes faded at once.

Then the fireworks began.

There were astonishing amounts of them. Great scarlet rockets and sky-scratching yellow sparklers. The city, it seemed, had kept a happy arsenal in stock. The fireworks lasted almost till dawn.

At dawn, the sky began to answer them. Vast blazing streaks of light, skipping in from over the horizon. Meteors with blazing comet tails, flaming ensigns of powdered crystal.

Above the city they unfurled their red-hot wings, with vast shattering booms. There they circled, like a flock of glowing kites, over the heads of the people. Vast cooling things, with angular crystalline heads and wings like woven auroras.

They circled for a long moment, their eyeless faces twisting back and forth, like living pendulums. They seemed to search out some point of unspoken equilibrium.

Then, one after another, they swooped down in sudden arcs of heart-aching precision. Straight through the open doors of the Enantiodrome.

"What are they, Charles?"

"They have come to refresh the soul of the world," Charles said.

"Come from *where*, for heaven's sake?"

"The Moon, I think," Charles said. He paused, seeming to listen to an inner voice. "Yes, the Moon, Rodolphe." He smiled. "Convention's farthest-flung machineries. They are roosting in the Great Dome. Come, let us go inside and witness them."

"*You* go," Rodolphe suggested. Charles needed no

urging. He was borne along into the building through the worshipful rush of the crowd.

Rodolphe turned away. He began to walk around the building, the trampled earth littered with the sad debris of spent celebration.

Someone had collapsed. The mayor and a small group of citizens were gathered by a fallen form, which lay beneath a blanket.

It was Hugo. Rodolphe knelt quickly by his side.

"He fell," someone offered.

"He jumped," the mayor said. "From the edge of the Dome." He wiped at tears. "No one noticed. We were distracted by the glory."

Rodolphe looked at Hugo's battered face. Someone had already closed his eyes. He was quite dead. As Rodolphe watched, a tiny mechanism, no bigger than a pinhead, crept from between Hugo's lips. It spread minuscule wings and took flight.

"They are inside us. They've always been inside us."

"We are inside *them*," the mayor said.

"What consolation is that?"

"We are their image. We are their antonym. We are their complement." The mayor lifted his head. "It's not a bad death, Rodolphe. Some of us never find it in ourselves to leave this place. I'll die here too someday, I swear it!" He raised his hand, and his voice. "We cannot be defeated! Even if Paysage itself were demolished, street by street, there would still be places like it in spirit. Our immortality is no less than theirs. Our life is the glow of renewal in the secret heart of age. It is the shadow of dissent, cast from resignation, in the restless light of hope!"

"Even to talk about ourselves, you have to talk just as they do," Rodolphe said.

The mayor's face twisted in anguish. "Yes . . . *but it's still the truth!*"

"We have to bury this poor man," a woman said.

"It is my youth that is buried," Rodolphe said. He turned on his heel and walked away.

Some time later, as he was picking his way through the great wilderness, a large black raven appeared, and settled on a branch above his head. It followed him, cawing. At last it came to roost upon his shoulder.

After that they began to talk.

THE MORAL BULLET

By Bruce Sterling and John Kessel

The throb of a helicopter cruising low over the roof wakes Sniffy from a luxuriant dream about a banana split. His eyes snap open, his heart pounds, he flops out of his bed, to coil up tight beneath the rusting bedsprings, in the grit and dustbunnies. They're after him!

But after a moment the turbine's whine, and his panic, fade. He's just a kid; nobody's really looking for him; nobody gives a damn about a kid. Sniffy crawls out, shivering, and peeks through the blackout curtains. The chopper is receding, in the daylight of summer morning.

Sniffy's mouth waters, anachronistically, for hot fudge, nuts, real whipped cream. A maraschino cherry. Banana splits are the stuff of legend now, but hunger's still real; he's gotta find something-or-other to eat. He pulls on sneakers, jeans and a T-shirt.

Sniffy's been living in this abandoned duplex for a couple of weeks, ever since the Chamber of Commerce took over this part of West Raleigh. The Commerce gang sort of take care of Sniffy, though most of the time they basically ignore him, to tell the truth. He hauls his rust-spotted Schwinn from beneath the back stairs, slings his baseball bat—an old George Brett signature—across the handlebars, and pedals up Brooks in the direction of the campus, weaving between the potholes.

This is one of Raleigh's older neighborhoods, heavily wooded. In every yard the pines stand tall and crowded; below them, oaks, maples and sweetgums fight for light. Nobody's pruned them in years and with the heavy rains the city's returning to forest. The lacing branches form thick green canopies over the narrower streets, which has been uncommonly handy lately, what with the helicopter raids.

Three burnt-out pickups stretch across the intersection of Brooks and Wade. The busted truck beds are heaped with leaky sandbags. Grafitti covers the bright flaking wreckage, angry scrawls and morbid boasts from the local militia groups.

A couple of Chamber of Commerce gangsters crouch beside the trucks, peering warily up through the treetops. There's no sign of the helicopter, though. Sniffy leans his bike against a dead fireplug, and scuttles up to join the two men.

Sniffy recognizes them: "Trump" and "Getty." The bigger of the two, the one who calls himself Trump, sports a red polyester baseball cap with a surly wolf stencilled on the front. He's got a black nylon ski-mask, too, tucked floppily into his pistol-belt.

Except for this, Trump looks pretty much like any American civilian used to look in the old days, except that his jeans and shirt are patched and dirty, and he's thinner. And he looks very young. Sniffy tries to imagine what Trump would look like if he appeared his true age: forty? Fifty? Sixty-five? It's hard to see this scraggly bearded tough, hardly more than a teenager—with sharp, clear, lively eyes—as a vice-president pushing papers across the desk in some bank.

Trump's pal, Getty, crouches lithely beside the bullet-riddled bed of the second Toyota. Getty's girlfriend, or maybe his mom or even his grandmother, has stitched his gang-name across the back of his Chamber of Commerce camou-jacket. He's reassembling his assault-rifle. A pair of rags, a long brass rod, and a reeking tray of solvent hang over the edge of the truck bed.

Getty shoves a clip into the rifle. "Keep your butt down, boy!" he says. "You might could get shot."

"What's going on?" Sniffy asks.

"Strange helicopter," Trump says laconically.

"National Guard?"

"European, most likely. Looked like a Swiss flag on 'er; white cross on red. Right, Sniff?"

"Right, that's Switzerland," Sniffy says. He's got a reputation as the bookish type.

"Scoping out the city," Getty says, and looks unhappy.

As if talking about it has called it back, the air throbs with the beating of rotors and a copter slides into view, a hundred yards above the trees. Sniffy ducks through reflex, but then he sees it's a cargo-job—not one of the lethal National Guard battle-copters. He squints, recognizes the starred emblem of the European Community.

The cargo door slides open and the copter dumps a cloud of yellow leaflets. The leaflets are blasted down by the rotor's downdraft, then flutter toward the trees and street. The copter circles off, still dumping.

A thin rain of leaflets settles gently over the roadblock. Sniffy plucks one out of the air. The cheap paper features a grimy photocopy of a dumpy, balding man in thick glasses.

He reads:

REWARD * REWARD * REWARD

HAVE YOU SEEN THIS MAN?

SIDNEY J. HAVERCAMP, calendar age forty-two, blond hair, 160 centimeters tall, weight 84 kilograms. M.D., Ph.D. in biochemistry. Former associate, Burroughs

Wellcome Research Triangle Facility. The European Community Health Service urgently seeks Dr. Havercamp. His safe delivery to EC representatives will be rewarded by fifty ampules of Free Radical Endocrine Enhancer.

REWARD * REWARD * REWARD

"Hell," Getty mutters. "Now even the Euros are looking for Havercamp."

"Fifty ampules," Trump says. "A man could live a long, long time on fifty ampules."

"My ass," says Getty. "Hell, if you could get your hands on Sidney Havercamp, you could have all the FREE you wanted."

"Havercamp's dead," Sniffy says brightly. "Died a long time ago, everybody knows that."

"No he's not dead, man," Getty says seriously. "Havercamp's in Costa Rica. They say his dope posse owns that whole country."

"I heard the Feds have him under wraps," Trump says. "They keep him prisoner in one of the old NORAD sites."

Getty examines the leaflet again. "Fuckin' Euro faggots. 'One hundred and sixty centimeters.' Who the fuck knows what a centimeter is?"

"How tall does that make him, Sniff?" Trump asks.

Sniffy stuffs the leaflet in his jeans pocket. Trump is watching him in a way that makes Sniffy nervous. "Real tall," he says. "Six-five, six-six—a real beanpole . . . Look out guys—here comes a patrol!"

A caravan of four station wagons appears on the crest of the next hill, east on Wade. They're flying militia flags from tall, wobbling C.B. aerials. The glass in all the windows has been replaced with slitted sheet-iron. It's a patrol from the Library Defense League.

The caravan stops at the foot of the hill, considering the Chamber of Commerce outpost. A fat guy in helmet and flak jacket leaps out, collects a few scattered leaflets,

leaps back to safety again with a heavy slam of the door.
Then the cars turn south, down Gardner, rolling sluggishly back toward their own turf on the university campus.

The Chamber of Commerce men begin to breathe
normally again. "Yeah man, those Library boys," Trump
drawls, his eyes slitted. "They never have the guts for a
face-off."

"Yeah," Getty muses with nonchalant menace.
"Them intellectuals all wanna live forever."

It's true that the eggheads of the Library Defense
League usually avoid close combat. However, they've
cunningly staked out all of West Raleigh on accurate artillery grids. A battery of 105-millimeter cannon lurks on
the top floor of the D.H. Hill Tower, on the north edge of
campus. A definite possibility exists that the L.D.L. might
airmail a sudden barrage this way.

Getty washes his hands, greasy from the gun-
cleaning, with a gush of brown water from a five-gallon
plastic jug. He inspects his fingernails cautiously. They
were bad to start with, and the solvent hasn't done them
much good. His thumbnail is cracked.

Sniffy's nails are even worse, worn-down far below
the quick. His fingertips bulge with callused skin. His hair
is two blond inches of frizzy split-ends. It's not that he
cuts his hair short. Over the years, Sniffy's hair has simply
worn-out while still rooted in his skull, like the fur on an
old horsehair sofa.

As for Trump, he's wearing a valuable antique set of
Lee Press-On Nails.

A humid breeze rustles the oak trees, blowing one of
the leaflets against Trump's sneaker. He plucks it off, examines it. "Maybe these Euros plan to move in permanently. Try and take us over." He impales the flyer on the
Toyota's rusty aerial. The aerial pierces Sidney Havercamp's photocopied left eye.

"They better not," Getty says.

A car honks, distantly. The driver's hitting his horn

while still a block away, which is standard practice when approaching a militia roadblock. Trump tugs the black ski-mask over his face and swaggers out in the road, while Getty covers him with his M-16.

"Wish I had a gun," Sniffy says.

"I dunno, Sniff," Getty mutters. "That time with the nuns and the shotgun, y'all didn't handle it too good."

The van pulls up. It's the Kentucky Fried Chicken man, and his personal bodyguard. The Chamber of Commerce guys enjoy fried chicken as much as anybody, but Trump demands a toll payment anyway.

The chicken man digs into a bulging wallet full of militia passes. He's got them all. Library Defense League, Brown Berets, Raleigh Police Department, Christian Faith Militia, Bellevue Terrace Community Watch, Popular Front for the Liberation of Robeson County. Even the little splinter groups and dope posses who control only a block or two, like the Preacher's Crew and the John-Johns.

"That copter hit your end of town?" Trump asks.

"Yessir. Dumpin' leaflets all over. Thought I saw 'em try to land, over by the campus."

"Think they'll find old Havercamp?"

The chicken man laughs nervously, nods at his bodyguard. "Bobby here says Havercamp is the Antichrist. The one that made these bad things to happen."

"He's got one eye and ten horns," says Bobby.

"Ought to make him easy to spot," Trump says.

Bobby just stares at him. Bobby's a large black guy with part of his face missing. Car-bomb work. No wonder he thinks the world is coming to an end.

The chicken man finds a Chamber of Commerce pass—but it's expired. So he gives up, and hands Trump five old silver quarters. Trump gives him a new pass, and messily whacks it with a rubber stamp.

With this transaction safely over, Sniffy approaches the car. "Hey," he says, sticking his frizzy blond head through the open window, "you got any chicken livers?"

"What's it to you, kid?" says Bobby.

"I got twenty milligrams here, for some chicken livers."

That changes matters. The chicken man gives Sniffy a cardboard box of cold fried livers, in exchange for the homemade ampule.

The chicken men drive off, weaving cautiously down the potholed length of Wade Avenue, toward the next checkpoint. Trump looks at Sniffy, speculatively. "Seems like you always got a spare shot of FREE, Sniffy."

"And it's always really good-quality, too," grumbles Getty.

It's borne home to Sniffy how he's gotten careless in the last months, as if being on friendly terms with the Chamber of Commerce made him safe. Being a kid deflected a lot of suspicion, but the Swiss helicopter and those bales of leaflets are going to heat things up again.

"It's in the nose," Sniffy says, tapping it. "I may be just a kid, but I can tell quality chemistry, just by smelling it. If it weren't for me, us Commerce guys would get burned all the time on bad FREE." He straps the chicken-box to the back of his bike. "You guys want a chicken liver? Lotta good iron in a chicken liver. Real good for your bone-marrow."

"You sure know a lot about nutrition and that stuff, Sniff," Getty says.

A bead of sweat runs down Sniffy's ribs. He's too damn talkative for his own good. He picks up his baseball bat, measures the distance to the tray of solvent on the truck bed. Maybe he can knock the solvent into Getty's face, then whip the bat into Trump's gut before Trump can squeeze off a shot.

Maybe not, though.

They're not really on to him. He's imagining things. This is no time for panic. "Well boys, I got to move on," Sniffy says.

Turning his back on them, trying hard not to hurry, he mounts his bike and pedals off.

• • •

Out of sight of the roadblock, he sneaks across Wade and into L.D.L. territory. He knows he's running a risk, but he needs information more than he needs safety. He probably shouldn't have come back to Raleigh at all, but at least he does know the city from his years at the lab, and hiding out on the Carolina dirt farm was boring him to death. A guy can only eat so many cans of chili.

Besides, he's made out pretty well over the years by improvising, and he isn't ready to panic yet. Brains still count for something.

He pedals through the old neighborhoods. Years of moldering leaves choke the broken gutters. Kudzu smothers the porch rails of former shot-houses and gang-centers, now derelict and blackened by Molotovs. Doors, walls, and windowframes are lavishly bullet-pocked. Here and there, roofs have been knocked in by mortar-fire or rocket grenades.

It's surprising, though, how many Raleighites have survived the endless years of troubles. Like Sniffy, they've learned to become unobtrusive. The doors are reinforced now, barred and triple-bolted, backed by sheet-iron or concrete. Windows are shuttered, the glass taped against the prospect of sudden concussions.

A kind of demented routine has settled in. There are vegetable gardens, chicken coops, bomb shelters, private water tanks, basements, trenches, tunnels. Lately, the electric power's been on again, for two or three hours a day. And the water runs once a week.

Most of the locals have loyally stencilled their doors with L.D.L. insignia. A few houses feature North Carolina flag-decals, but not many, since the National Guard atrocities.

The east side of campus is quiet. On the corner by the Pullen Memorial Baptist Church, Sniffy sees an L.D.L. steerer pushing the library's dope to a dozen shot-hungry

Raleighites. As it happens, these customers are senior citizens, yanked back by the Free Radical Endocrine Enhancer from the brink of death by old age.

Those few oldsters who have survived the years of troubles have been taking shots longer than anyone else. The aged were the first of the population to get a steady supply, back in the days when there was still a national health-care policy, and a government to back it up. As they bargain skeptically in their cautious group, they appear blissfully, unnaturally spry. The life-infusing FREE shots have worked absolute wonders on them. Except for a few unavoidable details.

Sniffy's practiced eye spots the symptoms easily. A frizzy white-haired gal triumphantly displays sleek legs in tight jogging shorts, but her puffy blouse and windbreaker can't conceal a dowager's hump. Osteoporosis; that's a difficult syndrome.

A grinning smooth-faced geezer restlessly swings his heavy cane. Advanced degenerative arthritis; his knees are still bad.

The very old make interesting case-studies. At one time, back in his scientist days, Sniffy would have given his right arm to get them into a lab with a control group. But who wants to be in a control group? That's pretty much the whole problem, in a nutshell. No one wants to grow old. Get a steady supply of FREE when you're young, though, and you never do. In theory, it was a wonderful prospect. The practice hasn't quite panned out.

The problem's simple enough. If there's not enough dope to go around, it's gotta mean somebody's cheating. If there are shortages, if the price is too high, it's because somebody's stealing your share of FREE, stealing and shooting-up the years of your life! It's obvious when you think about it. Only a fool would trust those government crooks and hustlers, with their big connections. They expect you to grow old gracefully, because they don't have to. All those politicians and millionaires will dance on your grave a hundred years from now, and laugh at you for being such a sucker.

Unless you get them first, that is. If you want your share, you gotta make connections.

So everybody starts making connections. That puts a strain on things. As soon as the government falls, you really need connections, just to survive. Kinda funny how fast the logic of chaos hits. Kind of a modern miracle. Not exactly the miracle he'd had in mind, but then, he doesn't remember having had much of anything in mind, at the time.

The yellow leaflets are everywhere. Sniffy forces himself to ignore them. He rides fearlessly past the barbed-wire lawn of the L.D.L. shot-house, ignoring the snipers in the bell-tower, and waves cheerily to the guards in their sandbagged kiosk. The guards let him pass. They, too, recognize Sniffy's usefulness.

He pedals on down Pullen, then ditches his bike in the hedges, on the bank above the old football practice field. He crawls through the thick photinia and crosses the field of tents and shacks, where the Robeson County refugees live, to the hospital tent. He's looking for the hospital doctor, Cecily Russell. The refugee camp and Red Cross field hospital are there on L.D.L. sufferance. The L.D.L. would prefer to have Dr. Russell work only for them, but as long as she gives preference to L.D.L. casualties, they're willing to let her doctor some others. Cecily Russell is the closest thing to a welfare agency left.

At length Sniffy finds her in a corner of one of the tents. She's eating a skimpy breakfast of brown rice. Her white cotton smock is bloodied from surgery. "Cecily!" Sniffy says.

She looks up, frowns. "I keep telling you: call me Dr. Russell," she says testily. Her hair has gone lackluster from poor diet, and her glasses are held together with wire and surgical tape. When she was thirty-five, Sniffy recalls, she looked more attractive than she does now at twenty or so.

"Don't get uptight, Cecily."

"Go away, Sidney."

Sniffy looks around to see if anybody's heard. "Don't call me that."

"Now who's uptight?"

"I brought you some chicken livers," Sniffy says. "For you, or the kids here . . . you know . . . whatever." Sniffy sets the chicken box on the hospital's wooden picnic table, which has been stolen from a public park. He sits beside her on the bench, digs out a handful of cold livers, crams them into his mouth. "You need some iron, Cecily. Help that low red-corpuscle count. Enhancer bone-marrow depletion."

"Why do you do this stuff? Every time I figure I've got you pegged as a mercenary little creep, you do something nice."

"Maybe it's love."

"Uh-huh."

"I don't know why I do it, Cecily. Who cares about that stuff? Life's for the living. That's my philosophy."

"I guess that works pretty well if you're not dead."

"And we're not, are we. We're younger than we ever were."

"Right. I just wonder what kind of man wants to be twelve years old forever."

"This? This is purely practical. Supplies of FREE are erratic. The best insurance I have against a prolonged drought is to build up an age cushion. This way, even if I run out, it'll be years before I even hit puberty."

"Don't you miss puberty?"

Cecily is very big on guilt trips, but Sniffy is immune. "Not in any way that really matters."

Russell puts down her spoon and stares into her bowl. She picks out something. A weevil, maybe.

Sniffy pulls the leaflet from his pocket, slides it in front of her. "Listen, Cecily, what about this European helicopter? Pretty threatening to see them hunting for one of us. The old team and all. Once a thing like that gets started, who knows where it will end? They get a foot-hold here, they might just try to take over."

"Fine by me. Maybe they can impose some order on this chaos."

"What about our freedom? Don't you believe in the Stars and Stripes?"

"I believe in antibiotics and public health. And a few less automatic weapons would help."

"Now, now. Someday you'll thank me for this. When the troubles are over, and things settle down."

"When will that be? A hundred years?"

"Maybe," he shrugs. "Why should that bother us?"

"We'll both be dead, you little fool!"

Sniffy laughs. "Possibly. But not from old age, that's for sure."

"Go ahead, laugh, but you're in trouble." Dr. Russell shakes her head wearily, her eyes glazed with fatigue. "One of their helicopters is parked over in the brickyard right now."

"Do you know what this is all about?"

"They probably want to rip your lungs out for transplants. Or put you on trial."

"On trial for what?"

She looks at him with open loathing. "Why don't you leave me alone?"

Good old Cecily, the selfless humanitarian. He'd always been a big devotee of public benefactors. Especially when they had grant money. But what right did she have to be so stiff-necked? All this was just an episode—compared with the Ultimate Life-Enhancing Benefits of Modern Medicine's Astonishing Miracle Breakthrough.

"Cecily, we need to find out what's going on."

She ignores him. "You should head for the hills. I'll keep my mouth shut."

"Sure you will."

Russell looks at the leaflet. "Why should I help you anyway?"

"Because of the chicken livers. And because, if I didn't come here, who'd give you your shots?"

"I don't want any more of your shots!"

Sniffy pulls a vial from the pocket of his jeans. He palms it expertly, twists the top off, sniffs carefully. "Pure as gold," he whispers. "Crisp, dry, and smooth, with a distinctive varietal flavor."

"Go away," she says hopelessly.

"You know you can't keep up your pace of work without your shots. And if you get weak, or sick, or even just too tired, think how many here will die."

A light drug-hungry sweat beads the hollows of the doctor's temples. "Well, this isn't the place for it . . ."

Sniffy glances over his shoulder, down the length of the hospital tent. Victims of mortar and sniper fire sprawl on their khaki-colored cots, wrapped in bloodied gauze. "I could pop you a quick one, in the leg. But I need some new works first. My old ones are getting dull."

"You can't have any more of my needles."

"Heck, Cecily, who'll miss a hypodermic here? You're Red Cross, you can get plenty."

"No. They're for the sick and dying!"

"Hey, without a proper taste of FREE, everybody's dying, every minute. That's the human condition, right? Used to be, anyhow."

She gives in, and they slip into the screened-off surgery at the end of the tent. "You don't have to act like this," she hisses. "You're not really twelve, even if you look and feel like you are. You don't have to nag and pester me in this compulsive, juvenile way."

"Don't get Freudian on me," Sniffy says. "You're the one with the stone-obvious self-sacrificial death wish."

Dr. Russell bites her lip, turns her back on him. She bends a little, tugs her trousers down over one hip. Sniffy jabs neatly through the vial top, sucks the drug into the hypo with an analytical look. He gives her buttock a sharp proprietarial spank, and jabs the needle in. A quick squeeze, and out again.

"Damn," she says. "That thing *is* dull."

They sit again on the picnic bench. Sniffy, something of a connoisseur of the effects of FREE, watches with interest as color floods Cecily's sallow cheeks. She stretches, yawns, shivers, tries to hide a grin.

Uniformed men appear at the entrance of the tent. Europeans! Sniffy ducks and scrambles back to the surgery.

He watches warily around the edge of the surgery screen, as Russell rises to greet the intruders: two khaki-clad privates carrying elegant-looking French automatic rifles, and a sergeant in a peaked cap. The sergeant's smooth chin is shaved blue and looks about as hard as granite. One of the privates pulls a cart carrying white boxes of medical supplies, stencilled with red crosses.

"May I help you gentlemen?"

"Are you Dr. Cecily Russell, in charge of this camp?"

"Yes I am."

"Herr Spittzler of the European Red Cross sends you his greetings," the sergeant said. "We are on a mission of mercy and goodwill. We bring you these supplies as a gift."

"Any hypodermic needles?"

"Some."

"That's great. What can I do for you, then?"

"We need your aid, doctor, in our negotiations with all local militia groups. We hope to arrange a general cease-fire, and establish economic relations . . ." The sergeant glances at the picnic table. "I see that you have our leaflet. Can you aid us in our search for Dr. Havercamp?"

"He's probably dead."

"We doubt that. Our reports say he is a very clever man."

"I haven't seen Dr. Havercamp in years. Why are you looking for him?"

"Let us only say we want him. And, of course, he is a criminal."

Cecily shifts a bit from foot to foot. "The, uh, medical research he was engaged in—that wasn't illegal, you know."

"Not illegal, but criminally irresponsible."

"What are you going to do with him?"

The sergeant smiles. "We shoot him—with the moral bullet." He touches his index finger to the middle of his forehead. "Right between the eyes."

That's enough for Sniffy. Time to hit the road. No way to get past these soldiers, though. These are no sloppy militia amateurs, but wary-looking hard-bitten veteran military professionals, totally disciplined and dutiful and spooky, the kind of people he hasn't seen in ages.

Sniffy spies a scalpel on a stainless-steel cart, just past the screen. If he can filch it, he can slice his way out through the back of the tent.

He crouches down silently, leans out behind the shelter of the cart, tries a grab, misses. Damn. He waits. They're still talking. He tries again, touches the hilt of the scalpel . . .

Someone grabs his wrist and yanks him up. One of the soldiers.

"Who is this?" the sergeant demands.

Russell looks flustered. "That's my—my son. Chip," she says. "Chip, what were you doing, hiding back there?"

"Sorry, mom. I was just curious."

"Curiosity killed the cat, young man."

"Herr Spittzler did not tell us that you have a son," the sergeant says.

"How would he know?"

Time for the helpless kid routine. "You're not gonna shoot me, are you, mister?" Sniffy whimpers. He squirms in the grasp of the soldier.

"Release him," the sergeant says. The soldier lets go, takes a step back.

Sniffy tugs his T-shirt straight. "Thanks, sergeant. I was afraid you guys were Nazis or something."

The sergeant stares at Sniffy. "How old are you, young man?"

"Twelve."

"So you are born since Dr. Havercamp's great discovery? You don't remember the world before the change? How is it you learn about bad men like Nazis?"

"I learned in school."

"The schools are lately not working, I understand."

"Mom taught me."

"He's very bright," Russell says, without conviction.

The sergeant's eyes narrow. "I think he is very clever, this boy. I think he comes along with us to meet Herr Spittzler."

So much for misdirection. Sniffy flings himself to the ground with a howl of terror. Before their embarrassed shock can fade, Sniffy darts on hands and knees beneath the cot of a casualty. They can't get a shot off while he's in the midst of the sick. Ducking, leaping, sometimes trampling the patients, he evades the sergeant's attempt to block him, and dashes out the front of the tent.

Outside, he knows the place, they don't. In a minute and a half, weaving through tents and behind the stadium along the track, he's up the embankment and out. He retrieves his bike and his bat and speeds down the hill to Western Boulevard.

A fat lot of good a baseball bat will do him now. And now they know what he looks like! He really is going to have to get himself a gun.

Sniffy feels a little safer when he hits Chamber of Commerce territory. He's not an official member of the Commerce gang or anything, but General Rockefeller, their head, is his pal.

The L.D.L. is clearly awed by the Europeans, since they let them land in their turf. They've already struck some deal. If these Euros are trying to ingratiate them-

selves with the militia groups, that's all the more reason
for Sniffy to get to Rockefeller first.

The Chamber HQ is one of the biggest shot-houses in
Raleigh, maybe in the whole state of North Carolina. It's
a mansion on White Oak, a white antebellum sprawl with
a pillared porch like Tara, covered with sandbags. Twin
trenches cut the streets east and west of it, dug-in roadblocks, anchored by machine-gun nests. Ack-ack guns
lurk on the mansion's roof, to keep the copters off. A
half-track is parked on the lawn, under a pegged-out
tarpaulin.

The sight of all these guns makes the customers con-
fident. There's a big crowd of the shot-hungry here, shuffling in with a glazed impatience, then gliding out with
that loose-looking happy step that comes with a skinful
of FREE. Some are wealthy and have come in their cars,
but they parked blocks away; there's no way the wily
Commerce boys will let a car-bomb near their HQ. You
only have to have your ass blown up once, to get hip to
that trick.

A skinny tout in a Commerce jacket and sunglasses
assembles the customers in the shade of the porch. He
marches up and down the line, checking their faces for
the proper vibe of submission and dope-greed. As he
walks and peers, he chants at them: kind of an auction-
eer's spiel. "Open for bidness, folks, open and smokin'!
Got them Green-Top vials, fresh shipment from the
brothers in Chapel Hill! Buy y'self five, get one for play.
Ten silver quarters for a jugular hit!"

Sniffy crosses the lawn and clomps up the porch. He
doesn't see any yellow flyers lying around here, but that
doesn't much reassure him. He feels like someone's gonna
collar him any minute. It isn't fair.

Down the mansion's big entrance hall there's a barred
nook where the house's bag man sits. He's taking in
money, passing out vials, with the crisp fluid ease of
habit. Old biker's tattoos show, very faded, on the dewy

fresh skin of his arms. He has a frizzy crew-cut, a chubby face, and a holstered .45 in one sweaty armpit.

"Have that money ready folks," he calls, in a high, sweet voice. "Have them dimes and quarters counted and ready, or you lose y'all's place in line. Jabbin' parlor up-stairs to your left, we got a special today on jugular hits, a real M.D., folks! Got a real gentle hand. Ten silver quarters, and get that goodness straight to y'all's brain tissue!"

The Chamber of Commerce HQ possesses the modern miracle of air conditioning. The A.C. is a status symbol and the Chamber runs it whenever they can spare the generator fuel.

The mansion is packed to the walls with loot. It spills right into the halls, room doors jammed open with collapsing stacks of goodies. Crates of whiskey, vodka, tequila—the real stuff, not moonshine. A whole room crammed with video recorders. Another full of ten-speed bikes, wheels and frames neatly disassembled. Three piece men's suits, all styles and sizes, hung on shiny wheeled racks. Lots of mink and sable, with some sad moth damage; furs are hard to keep through a Carolina summer.

The Chamber has lost the habit of guarding their "valuables." Nowadays it's food that really counts: bags of rice and beans. You can smell them but not see them; they're snookered away.

Sniffy goes on back toward Rockefeller's office, where Lindsey, Rockefeller's secretary, holds court. Lindsey was once the wife of a Governor of North Carolina. She's maybe eighty-five, but looks about thirty, and wears enough jewelry to choke an old-fashioned Las Vegas showgirl. It's real gold and emeralds and diamonds. Or at least Lindsey thinks it's real. All the Commerce guys like her because she's so crazy, so they never tell her otherwise.

Today she's busy talking to three Chamber toughs. Everybody seems pretty excited, shuffling around whispering and peering back toward the General's office.

When Sniffy approaches, Lindsey jumps up, a big frozen grin on her face. It's enough to make even Sniffy flinch. "Sniffy, you charming boy, how are you? Haven't seen you for an age!"

"Lindsey, I need to talk to the General."

"I'm afraid he's busy," she says. "Hadn't you heard? We have some European visitors—Swiss I think. They're in there with him right now. And they have a TV camera! They want to do a documentary about us!" This explains Lindsey's demented energy. The thought of being on TV again has triggered some deep-buried media reflexes.

"I remember television," one of the toughs says.

"Think they got any hard cash on 'em?" another asks. "Maybe some of that European paper money."

"They probably got credit cards," the third says.

"I *remember* credit cards," the first guy says.

Sniffy hops up and down to get their attention. "I came to warn the General about these guys. I was just over at the Red Cross camp. These Euro bastards are hooked up with the Library gang—they want to put us out of business!"

Lindsey looks at him with fatuous credulity. "Maybe you better go back there, Sniffy."

So Sniffy pushes past the desk and through the General's office. The door is open and he walks right in.

Rockefeller's office has Persian rugs, walnut panelling and gold-stencilled leather chairs looted from the State Capitol. All the windows are securely bricked up. An open closet door shows more loot: a microcomputer, an open case of Canadian Club, boxes of light bulbs, tins of sardines. There's a lot of stuffed animal heads on the walls, big game trophies. Elk, bear, and moose, mostly. Too many, probably. There's about fifty of them.

Rockefeller wears a Giorgio Armani gray wool suit, a gold-threaded gambler's waistcoat, and silver-spurred python-skin cowboy boots. He's chewing meditatively on a Mars Bar, an item of great rarity and price. He's talking with two blond men in black baggy cotton pants and white shirts. They are unarmed. One of them holds a floppy sunhat on his lap; the other has a compact video-camera, and moves deftly around the room.

One of Rockefeller's lieutenants, Forbes, lounges by the door, in a baseball hat and flak-jacket. Rockefeller looks up as Sniffy enters. Rockefeller smiles broadly. Sniffy realizes at that moment that Rockefeller has read the leaflets.

The blond man sitting in the chair turns to inspect Sniffy. "Who is this?" He has an odd accent, like he studied his English in Britain.

"This here's Sniffy. Howdy, Sniff. Long time no see."

"At your service, General," Sniffy says. "You know you can count on me. But I wouldn't trust these guys."

"This is Herr Spittzler," the General says. "And Signor Andolini."

"I am pleased to meet you," Spittzler says, rising from the chair. He moves like he's got a pole stuck up his ass. "But you are wrong to mistrust our intentions. We are here to help you."

"Last we heard about the situation over the water, you guys needed help yourselves," Rockefeller says.

"Conditions in Europe are much improved," replies Spittzler. "We have developed a working system of Enhancer distribution. We are past the stage of social breakdown and chaos."

Sniffy takes a seat on the sofa against the wall, and keeps an eye on the door, in case he needs to beat a retreat. Not much use in hoping for that, though. It would take heavy artillery to fight your way out of this shothouse. He'll have to play this situation out to a finish, right here.

"Glad to hear it," Rockefeller says. "Y'all had it pretty bad, I hear."

"We lost two million in Switzerland alone. Fifty million in Europe overall. Most the first years of the crisis. The worst is past, now."

Rockefeller sobers. "That's a lot. Wonder how many America lost."

"We estimate ninety-five million," Spittzler says readily. "Maybe many more. Estimates are difficult, in the absence of a federal census or central authority."

"My God," Rockefeller muses, "ninety-five million!"

"We estimate the global population at only three billion, now. That means three billion people have died in the last fifteen years." Spittzler pauses. If he's not the cleanest person Sniffy has seen in the last ten years, he's a close runner-up. His blue eyes are calm and precise and even though he looks twenty-five Sniffy figures he's at least fifty. Then again, he probably looked just as overcontrolled when he was twenty-five for real. "May I ask you," Spittzler says, "your opinion of this terrible catastrophe?"

Rockefeller takes a meditative bite of his Mars Bar.

"Well," Sniffy breaks in, "that leaves the survivors some room, anyhow. I mean, people used to worry a lot about the tremendous strain on global resources. What with the vast increase in human lifespan, and all."

"Thanks to the social breakdown brought on by FREE—the plagues and starvation—the average lifespan today is less than twenty years."

"Y'all sure are big on statistics," Rockefeller says. "What's the point of all this?"

"The point is that we must heal the wounds to civilization," Spittzler says. "The European Community can now feed itself, with surplus for export. The United Nations has been re-established in Geneva. We have a plan for restoring world order and trade."

Rockefeller crumples his candy wrapper and tosses it at a wastebasket. "Well, the Raleigh Chamber of Commerce is all for world trade. I mean, we're the strongest banking and resource center in the Piedmont. And we're prepared to deal. Raleigh's the capital of North Carolina, a big strategic center. Once we take over this city, we're poised to move on Charlotte, Richmond, Charleston—up and down the whole Eastern seaboard. It's rich country, too. We got whatever you Europeans need: dope, tobacco, you name it! You help us, we help you!"

Rockefeller bends and hauls a large crate from beneath his massive office desk. He tugs it one-handed around the desk into the center of the room, ruffling the Persian carpet. Sniffy has seen this box before, but Rockefeller has always been pretty secretive about its contents. It's khaki-colored metal, the size of a deluxe microwave oven, with US military stencils. He opens it on a squeaking hinge. "This is a U.S. Army Model M3 50-Caliber Heavy Machine Gun," he announces, hauling the monster out by its perforated matte-black barrel. "Now this baby was a total design breakthrough! Real Yankee know-how, right? Ceramic barrel, foamed-metal stock and tripod, weighs half what the old Browning 50-Caliber did. The rate of fire kicks ass, there's no recoil to speak of, and the slugs can pierce battleship armor."

Rockefeller shakes his head mournfully. "They didn't make many of these, though. They were barely off the Pentagon production-line, when the shit hit the fan. Experimental model, really. Cost a fortune to make 'em. I've never even fired it; I was lucky to find one."

He grins at Spitzler, slaps an ammunition belt into the feed tray. The Swiss looks poker-faced. Andolini focuses his camera on the gun, and Rockefeller obligingly shows it off. "Bet you got nothing like this over there. Shit, everybody knows y'all in Europe were only good for making watches! But you can copy any American breakthrough, right? Better, if you got the krauts to manage the factories and the wops to work the line." He draws a breath. "So I tell you what. Y'all give me thirty of these, with ammo belts to match, and I'll give you the City of Raleigh. Simple as that!"

"Weapons are not an answer to this global crisis."

"They'll do till a better one comes along."

Spitzler nods calmly. "We have a better answer now," he says. "The moral bullet."

"Say what?"

Spittzler's voice takes on a schoolmarmish tone. "People want longer lives, from medicine—not a faster death from guns. The problem centers on a proper distribution of the medical resources. The moral bullet has given us a system that works, without violence and greed."

"People are never *satisfied*, Spittzler."

"Even if I grant you that everybody has the ape in them, they can still be socialized. They have the angel in them, too. The Endocrine Enhancer has freed us from human mortality; we humans must now act morally in a manner which matches our new potentials. Together with each dose of FREE, we distribute—the moral bullet. It is our own medical breakthrough, the proper complement to the rejuvenation drug. It is the Empathic Enhancer."

Sniffy's curiosity is piqued. "This is some kind of neuro-physiological agent? Not a real bullet?"

"No, not a bullet. It affects the limbic system. I am not a neurologist, and cannot explain its workings, but it vastly increases our compassion, our sympathy for our fellow human beings. It restores the person's capacity to act morally."

"Doesn't sound very moral to me," Rockefeller says. "Sounds like some kind of mind-altering drug. You say everybody in Europe is shooting up this stuff?"

"Everyone who takes the rejuvenation drug. Immortality cannot come without a price. Better the moral bullet than the physical one."

"That's *brainwashing*!" Sniffy says. "Maybe you got a bunch of sheep over there willing to give up freedom for security, but this is America!" Despite himself, Sniffy's getting drawn into the argument. The clash of ideas has always stimulated him.

"We are not entirely happy with the system, either," Spittzler says. "It is an improvement over chaos, but manufacturing and distributing both these drugs still strains our limited resources. We have a bolder plan yet: we will

alter the human genetic system so that the human body itself produces both FREE and the moral bullet, internally.
When human nature is permanently changed on the cellular level—then we can say that the angel has overwhelmed the ape. We will finally transcend this squalid
catastrophe, to enter a new order of being."

"That's pretty ambitious," Sniffy says.

"We are working very hard at it," Spittzler says.
"Unfortunately, progress is slow."

"Yeah, I bet," Sniffy says. "Cellular synthesis of endocrine enhancer would take a major design breakthrough. Not to mention that other gunk. . . . It would
take more than just hard work. It'd take genius."

"That is why we want Sidney Havercamp," Spittzler
says. "He is a genius. But he's also an amoral sociopath.
He is the one who created this tragedy. You give
Havercamp to us. We shoot him with the moral bullet,
and we put him to work in the World Health Organization's pharmaceutical labs in Zurich. Then we will do better than merely dole out the youth drug. We will
transform the world."

"I prefer the old-fashioned kind of bullets," Rockefeller says. "They're still a lot cheaper, plus a lot more
permanent."

Spittzler ignores him. "I can't imagine that Havercamp is using his abilities here," he continues. "It is a
waste of his intellect. Let us take him back, where he can
work again in the service of mankind, and atone for his
great crime."

Spittzler's voice is cool. It's the kind of infuriating
voice that used to drive Sniffy wild when he was in grad
school. His girlfriend, the ice maiden, Miss Moral Philosophy of 1996, had a voice like that. "Crime, huh?" Sniffy
says. "You'll thank Sidney Havercamp on your knees
when you're two hundred years old, buster."

Spittzler inspects him calmly. "It's the greatest crime
in history."

"History's over, man! We can outlive history now."

"Why are you defending Dr. Havercamp? It is your country that was ruined. We suffered in Europe, but we endure. We are coming back. Poor America today is nothing but a collection of bandit kingdoms, many of them no bigger than a few city blocks. Not even kingdoms—pitiful drug-gangs."

"Watch your mouth, pal!" Rockefeller says. "What makes you so great?"

"I don't wish to argue with you. All you need do, is look in the sad life in your own nation. The sight is almost unbearable. I fear you will all die in this endless anarchy; there will be no one left here for us to help, when we step in to gather up the pieces."

Rockefeller leans on his desk, fists clenched. "That's what this is really all about, isn't it? Well, if you think you can just step in here and take over, you faggot cuckoo-clock-winders are in for a surprise. Maybe we're down, but it doesn't take but one half-witted American fighting-man to whup a whole platoon of your candyass bleeding-heart soldiers. If it weren't for us Americans bailing you out, you'd be speaking Russian now, or German."

"I do speak German. Russian, too."

"It figures. Nazi superman bastards."

Sniffy likes the way this has turned. The cameraman is shuffling from foot to foot as if this is more documentary than he bargained for. Now for a little inflammatory rhetoric to nail it down. "Maybe you can con those egghead wimps at the Library Defense League," Sniffy sneers, "but the Chamber of Commerce is made of *real* men! Don't let these cheese-eaters push you around, General!"

At last Spittzler begins to look worried. "We are unarmed," he points out, raising his empty hands. "It is true that we are engaged in dialogue with other factions. But the moral bullet can bring peace here. It can save your world!"

"The stars and stripes and a continent of kicked European asses will save the world!" Rockefeller shouts. "Forbes, collar these two loudmouth foreigners and throw their butts in the cell."

"Yes sir!" Forbes says gratefully.

Spittzler stiffens. "That would be foolish. What do you hope to accomplish?"

"I'm taking you hostage, for ransom," Rockefeller announces. "It's the only way to get any real use out of you sanctimonious bastards. Moral bullet, my ass!"

Forbes advances. Spittzler, still holding up empty hands, places his palms gently over his eyes. Andolini squeezes the video camera.

A blistering flash of white lightning sheets through the room.

Sniffy can't see anything.

"I'm blind!" Rockefeller howls. "Goddammit, they've blinded me!"

There are long moments of frantic stumbling confusion and desperate cursing. At last a loud wooden thump. "I'm at the door, chief!" Forbes shouts. "They can't escape while I block this door!"

"That's great, Forbes. You're a smart sucker."

"Thanks, chief. I'm blind, though."

"Me, too," Sniffy says. Everything is a red fog, fading to black. He stumbles toward what he hopes is the center of the room, until he barks his shin against the box. He stoops, hauls out the machine gun. He fumbles with the feed-cover, feeling for the ammunition belt. The smooth cartridges are as big as his thumb. Luckily, the belt-feed is already engaged. He backs away, feeling a surge of power like a coke high, suffused with supreme confidence, an edgy energy. "Say, chief," Sniffy says, "you were right. This baby hardly weighs a thing. How do you fire it?"

"Wait a sec, Sniff," Rockefeller says. "We don't even know the bastards are really still here in the room with us."

"Oh, they're here, all right," Sniffy says. "I can hear 'em snickering."

"You've never been exactly a crack shot, Sniffy. You have any idea what that thing in your hands can really do?"

"Not really, no. But I just found the trigger." Sniffy steps forward, tripping for a moment on the ammunition belt. He jerks up on the barrel, raises his voice. "Okay, you two. Give up or be cheesecloth." He laughs. "Swiss cheesecloth!"

No answer.

"You know I mean it!"

Nothing.

"Chief?" Forbes says quietly. He's closer than Sniffy expected, and off to the left. Sniffy had been sure that Forbes was on his right. "I'm pretty sure I got this door blocked real good, but it may be the closet door, actually. I mean, maybe those two already snuck off."

"Yeah, or maybe they're gonna wrestle this machine-gun right out of my hands, and cut loose on us with it," Sniffy says. "That's why I wanted to grab it first, right?"

"Great thinking, Sidney," Rockefeller says. "You always were clever."

Sniffy thinks furiously. They could try to yell for reinforcements, but then Spittzler would almost surely try to grab the gun.

"They could kill us easy while we're blind, and then blast their way out," Sniffy says. "I mean, wouldn't you?"

"Yeah," Rockefeller admits. "You bet I would. Especially now that you've pointed that possibility out to them, pal."

For the first time, Sniffy begins to feel panic. His knees get a little shaky. "They might be sneaking up on me right now!" he says, swinging the gun muzzle wildly. "What do I do?"

"I didn't really want to live forever," Rockefeller says. "But I'm damned if *they* will. I say cut loose and the hell with it."

"I think you should hold your fire," Forbes says. "Just keep the best grip on it you can, and yell for help."

Maybe, Sniffy realizes, he isn't as good at this as he thought. Despite its advanced design, the machine gun is getting heavy. His shoulders ache. The pistol grip feels slick in his hand. He can hardly get his fingers around it; it's too big for a kid. He listens. Is that the sound of a footstep on the rug?

What the hey. "I'm gonna give our audience a chance to decide," he says. "If we *have* an audience. I'm gonna count to ten . . ."

THE UNTHINKABLE

Since the Strategic Arms Talks of the early 1970s, it had been the policy of the Soviets to keep to their own quarters as much as the negotiations permitted—in fear, the Americans surmised, of novel forms of technical eavesdropping.

Dr. Tsyganov's Baba Yaga hut now crouched warily on the meticulously groomed Swiss lawn. Dr. Elwood Doughty assembled a hand of cards and glanced out the hut's window. Protruding just above the sill was the great scaly knee of one of the hut's six giant chicken legs, a monstrous knobby member as big around as an urban water main. As Doughty watched, the chicken knee flexed restlessly, and the hut stirred around them, rising with a seasick lurch, then settling with a squeak of timbers and a rustle of close-packed thatch.

Tsyganov discarded, drew two cards from the deck, and examined them, his wily blue eyes shrouded in greasy wisps of long graying hair. He plucked his shabby beard with professionally black-rimmed nails.

Doughty, to his pleased surprise, had been dealt a straight flush in the suit of Wands. With a deft pinch, he dropped two ten-dollar bills from the top of the stack at his elbow.

Tsyganov examined his dwindling supply of hard currency with a look of Slavic fatalism. He grunted, scratched, then threw his cards face-up on the table. Death. The Tower. The deuce, trey, and five of Coins.

"Chess?" Tsyganov suggested, rising.

"Another time," said Doughty. Though, for security reasons, he lacked any official ranking in the chess world, Doughty was in fact quite an accomplished chess strategist, particularly strong in the end game. Back in the marathon sessions of '83, he and Tsyganov had dazzled their fellow arms wizards with an impromptu tournament lasting almost four months, while the team awaited (fruitlessly) any movement on the stalled verification accords. Doughty could not outmatch the truly gifted Tsyganov, but he had come to know and recognize the flow of his opponent's thought.

Mostly, though, Doughty had conceived a vague loathing for Tsyganov's prized personal chess set, which had been designed on a Reds versus Whites Russian Civil War theme. The little animate pawns uttered tiny, but rather dreadful, squeaks of anguish, when set upon by the commissar bishops and cossack knights.

"Another time?" murmured Tsyganov, opening a tiny cabinet and extracting a bottle of Stolichnaya vodka. Inside the fridge a small, overworked frost demon glowered in its trap of coils and blew a spiteful gasp of cold fog. "There will not be many more such opportunities for us, Elwood."

"Don't I know it." Doughty noted that the Russian's vodka bottle bore an export label printed in English. There had been a time when Doughty would have hesitated to accept a drink in a Russian's quarters. Treason in the cup. Subversion potions. Those times already seemed quaint.

"I mean this will be over. History, grinding on. This entire business—" Tsyganov waved his sinewy hand, as if including not merely Geneva, but a whole state of mind— "will become a mere historical episode."

"I'm ready for that," Doughty said stoutly. Vodka

splashed up the sides of his shot glass with a chill, oily threading. "I never much liked this life, Ivan."

"No?"

"I did it for duty."

"Ah." Tsyganov smiled. "Not for the travel privileges?"

"I'm going home," Doughty said. "Home for good. There's a place outside Fort Worth where I plan to raise cattle."

"Back to Texas?" Tsyganov seemed amused, touched. "The hard-line weapons theorist become a *farmer*, Elwood? You are a second Roman Cincinnatus!"

Doughty sipped vodka and examined the gold-flake socialist-realist icons hung on Tsyganov's rough timber walls. He thought of his own office, in the basement of the Pentagon. Relatively commodious, by basement standards. Comfortably carpeted. Mere yards from the world's weightiest centers of military power. Secretary of Defense. Joint Chiefs of Staff. Secretaries of the Army, Navy, Air Force. Director of Defense Research and Necromancy. The Lagoon, the Potomac, the Jefferson Memorial. The sight of pink dawn on the Capitol Dome after pulling an all-nighter. Would he miss the place? No. "Washington D.C. is no proper place to raise a kid."

"Ah." Tsyganov's peaked eyebrows twitched. "I heard that you married at last." He had, of course, read Doughty's dossier. "And your child, Elwood, he is strong and well?"

Doughty said nothing. It would be hard to keep the tone of pride from his voice. Instead, he opened his wallet of tanned basilisk skin and showed the Russian a portrait of his wife and infant son. Tsyganov brushed hair from his eyes and examined the portrait closely. "Ah," he said. "The boy much resembles you."

"Could be," Doughty said.

"Your wife," Tsyganov said politely, "has a very striking face."

"The former Jeane Siegel. Staffer for the Senate Foreign Relations Committee."

"I see. The defense intelligentsia?"

"She edited *Korea and the Theory of Limited War.* Considered one of the premier works on the topic."

"She must make a fine little mother." Tsyganov gulped his vodka, ripped into a crust of black rye bread. "My son is quite grown now. He writes for *Literaturnaya Gazeta.* Did you see his article on the Iraqi arms question? Some very serious developments lately concerning the Islamic jinni."

"I should have read it," Doughty said. "But I'm getting out of the game, Ivan. Out while the getting's good." The cold vodka was biting into him. He laughed briefly. "They're going to shut us down in the States. Pull our funding. Pare us back to the bone, and past the bone. 'Peace dividend.' We'll all fade away. Like MacArthur. Like Robert Oppenheimer."

" 'I am become Death, the Destroyer of Worlds,' " Tsyganov quoted.

"Yeah," Doughty mused. "That was too bad about poor old Oppy having to become Death."

Tsyganov examined his nails. "Will there be purges, do you think?"

"I beg your pardon?"

"I understand the citizens in Utah are suing your federal government. Over conduct of the arms tests, forty years ago . . ."

"Oh," Doughty said. "The two-headed sheep, and all that . . . There are still night-gaunts and banshees downwind of the old test sites. Up in the Rockies . . . Not a place to go during the full moon." He shuddered. "But 'purges'? No. That's not how it works for us."

"You should have seen the sheep around Chernobyl."

" 'Bitter wormwood,' " Doughty quoted.

"No act of duty avoids its punishment." Tsyganov opened a can of dark fish that smelled like spiced kippered herring. "And what of the Unthinkable, eh? What price have you paid for *that* business?"

Doughty's voice was level, quite serious. " 'We bear any burden in defense of freedom.' "

"Not the best of your American notions, perhaps." Tsyganov speared a chunk of fish from the can with a three-tined fork. "To deliberately contact an utterly alien entity from the abyss between universes ... an ultra-demonic demi-god whose very geometry is, as it were, an affront to sanity ... That Creature of nameless eons and inconceivable dimensions ..." Tsyganov patted his bearded lips with a napkin. "That hideous Radiance that bubbles and blasphemes at the center of all infinity—"

"You're being sentimental," Doughty said. "We must recall the historical circumstances in which the decision was made to develop the Azathoth Bomb. Giant Japanese Majins and Gojiras crashing through Asia. Vast squadrons of Nazi juggernauts blitzkrieging Europe ... And their undersea leviathans, preying on shipping ..."

"Have you ever seen a *modern* leviathan, Elwood?"

"Yes. I witnessed one ... feeding. At the base in San Diego." Doughty could recall it with an awful clarity— the great finned Navy monster, the barnacled pockets in its vast ribbed belly holding a slumbering cargo of hideous batwinged gaunts. On order from Washington, the minor demons would waken, slash their way free of the monster's belly, launch, and fly to their appointed targets with pitiless accuracy and the speed of a tempest. In their talons, they clutched triple-sealed spells that could open, for a few hideous microseconds, the portal between universes. And for an instant, the Radiance of Azathoth would gush through. And whatever that Color touched— wherever its unthinkable beam contacted earthly substance—the Earth would blister and bubble in cosmic torment. The very dust of the explosion would carry an unearthly taint.

"And have you seen them test the Bomb, Elwood?"

"Only underground. The atmospheric testing was rather before my time . . ."

"And what of the poisoned waste, Elwood? From behind the cyclopean walls of our scores of power plants . . ."

"We'll deal with that. Launch it into the abyss of space, if we must." Doughty hid his irritation with an effort. "What are you driving at?"

"I worry, my friend. I fear that we've gone too far. We have been responsible men, you and I. We have labored in the service of responsible leaders. Fifty long years have passed, and not once has the Unthinkable been unleashed in anger. But we have trifled with the Eternal in pursuit of mortal ends. What is our pitiful fifty years in the eons of the Elder Gods? Now, it seems, we will rid ourselves of our foolish applications of this dreadful knowledge. But will we ever be clean?"

"That's a challenge for the next generation. I've done what I can. I'm only mortal. I accept that."

"I do not think we can put it away. It is too close to us. We have lived in its shadow too long, and it has touched our souls."

"I'm through with it," Doughty insisted. "My duty is done. And I'm tired of the burden. I'm tired of trying to grasp issues, and imagine horrors, and feel fears and temptations, that are beyond the normal bounds of sane human contemplation. I've earned my retirement, Ivan. I have a right to a human life."

"The Unthinkable has touched you. Can you truly put that aside?"

"I'm a professional," Doughty said. "I've always taken the proper precautions. The best military exorcists have looked me over . . . I'm clean."

"Can you know that?"

"They're the best exorcists we have; I trust their professional judgement . . . If I find the shadow in my life again, I'll put it aside. I'll cut it away. Believe me, I know the feel and smell of the Unthinkable—it'll never find a

foothold in my life again . . ." A merry chiming came
from Doughty's right trouser pocket.

Tsyganov blinked, then went on. "But what if you
find it is simply too close to you?"

Doughty's pocket rang again. He stood up absently.
"You've known me for years, Ivan," he said, digging into
his pocket. "We may be mortal men, but we were always
prepared to take the necessary steps. We were prepared.
No matter what the costs."

Doughty whipped a large square of pentagram-
printed silk from his pocket, spread it with a flourish.

Tsyganov was startled. "What is that?"

"Portable telephone," Doughty said. "Newfangled
gadget—I always carry one now."

Tsyganov was scandalized. "You brought a telephone
into my private quarters?"

"Damn," Doughty said with genuine contrition.
"Forgive me, Ivan. I truly forgot I had this thing with me.
Look, I won't take the call here. I'll leave." He opened the
door, descended the wooden stair into grass and Swiss
sunlight.

Behind him, Tsyganov's hut rose on its monster
chicken legs, and stalked away—wobbling, it seemed to
Doughty, with a kind of offended dignity. In the hut's
retreating window, he glimpsed Tsyganov, peering out
half-hidden, unable to restrain his curiosity. Portable telephones. Another technical breakthrough of the inventive
West.

Doughty smoothed the ringing silk on the top of an
iron lawn table and muttered a Word of power. An image
rose sparking above the woven pentagram—the head and
shoulders of his wife.

He knew at once from her look that the news was
bad. "Jeane?" he said.

"It's Tommy," she said.

"What happened?"

"Oh," she said with brittle clarity, "nothing. Nothing

you'd see. But the lab tests are in. The exorcists—they say he's tainted."

The foundation blocks of Doughty's life cracked swiftly and soundlessly apart. "Tainted," he said blankly. "Yes ... I hear you, dear ..."

"They came to the house and examined him. They say he's monstrous."

Now anger seized him. "Monstrous. How can they say that? He's only a four-month-old kid! How the hell could they know he's monstrous? What the hell do they really know, anyway? Some crowd of ivory-tower witch doctors ..."

His wife was weeping openly now. "You know what they recommended, Elwood? You know what they want us to do?"

"We can't just—put him away," Doughty said. "He's our son." He paused, took a breath, looked about him. Smooth lawn, sunlight, trees. The world. The future. A bird flickered past him.

"Let's think about this," he said. "Let's think this through. Just how monstrous is he, exactly?"

WE SEE THINGS DIFFERENTLY

This was the *jahiliyah*—the land of ignorance. This was America. The Great Satan, the Arsenal of Imperialism, the Bankroller of Zionism, the Bastion of Neo-Colonialism. The home of Hollywood and blonde sluts in black nylon. The land of rocket-equipped F-15s that slashed across God's sky, in godless pride. The land of nuclear-powered global navies, with cannon that fired shells as large as cars.

They have forgotten that they used to shoot us, shell us, insult us, and equip our enemies. They have no memory, the Americans, and no history. Wind sweeps through them, and the past vanishes. They are like dead leaves.

I flew into Miami, on a winter afternoon. The jet banked over a tangle of empty highways, then a large dead section of the city—a ghetto perhaps. In our final approach we passed a coal-burning power plant, reflected in the canal. For a moment I mistook it for a mosque, its tall smokestacks slender as minarets. A Mosque for the American Dynamo.

I had trouble with my cameras at customs. The customs officer was a grimy-looking American white with hair the color of clay. He squinted at my passport. "That's an awful lot of film, Mr. Cuttab," he said.

"Qutb," I said, smiling. "Sayyid Qutb. Call me Charlie."

"Journalist, huh?" He looked unhappy. It seemed that I owed substantial import duties on my Japanese cameras, as well as my numerous rolls of Pakistani color film. He invited me into a small back office to discuss it. Money changed hands. I departed with my papers in order.

The airport was half-full: mostly prosperous Venezuelans and Cubans, with the haunted look of men pursuing sin. I caught a taxi outside, a tiny vehicle like a motorcycle wrapped in glass. The cabbie, an ancient black man, stowed my luggage in the cab's trailer.

Within the cab's cramped confines, we were soon unwilling intimates. The cabbie's breath smelled of sweetened alcohol. "You Iranian?" the cabbie asked.

"Arab."

"We respect Iranians around here, we really do," the cabbie insisted.

"So do we," I said. "We fought them on the Iraqi front for years."

"Yeah?" said the cabbie uncertainly. "Seems to me I heard about that. How'd that end up?"

"The Shi'ite holy cities were ceded to Iran. The Ba'athist regime is dead, and Iraq is now part of the Arab Caliphate." My words made no impression on him, and I had known it before I spoke. This is the land of ignorance. They know nothing about us, the Americans. After all this, and they still know nothing whatsoever.

"Well, who's got more money these days?" the cabbie asked. "Y'all, or the Iranians?"

"The Iranians have heavy industry," I said. "But we Arabs tip better."

The cabbie smiled. It is very easy to buy Americans. The mention of money brightens them like a shot of drugs. It is not just the poverty; they were always like this, even when they were rich. It is the effect of spiritual emptiness. A terrible grinding emptiness in the very guts of the West, which no amount of Coca-Cola seems able to fill.

We rolled down gloomy streets toward the hotel. Miami's streetlights were subsidized by commercial enterprises. It was another way of, as they say, shrugging the burden of essential services from the exhausted backs of the taxpayers. And onto the far sturdier shoulders of peddlers of aspirin, sticky sweetened drinks, and cosmetics. Their billboards gleamed bluely under harsh lights encased in bulletproof glass. It reminded me so strongly of Soviet agitprop that I had a sudden jarring sense of displacement, as if I were being sold Lenin and Engels and Marx in the handy jumbo size.

The cabbie, wondering perhaps about his tip, offered to exchange dollars for riyals at black-market rates. I declined politely, having already done this in Cairo. The lining of my coat was stuffed with crisp Reagan $1,000 bills. I also had several hundred in pocket change, and an extensive credit line at the Islamic Bank of Jerusalem. I foresaw no difficulties.

Outside the hotel, I gave the ancient driver a pair of fifties. Another very old man, of Hispanic descent, took my bags on a trolley. I registered under the gaze of a very old woman. Like all American women, she was dressed in a way intended to provoke lust. In the young, this technique works admirably, as proved by America's unhappy history of sexually transmitted plague. In the old, it provokes only sad disgust.

I smiled on the horrible old woman and paid in advance.

I was rewarded by a double-handful of glossy brochures promoting local casinos, strip-joints, and bars.

The room was adequate. This had once been a fine hotel. The air-conditioning was quiet and both hot and cold water worked well. A wide flat screen covering most of one wall offered dozens of channels of television.

My wristwatch buzzed quietly, its programmed dial indicating the direction of Mecca. I took the rug from my luggage and spread it before the window. I cleansed my face, my hands, my feet. Then I knelt before the darkening chaos of Miami, many stories below. I assumed the eight positions, sinking with gratitude into deep meditation. I forced away the stress of jet-lag, the innate tension and fear of a Believer among enemies.

Prayer completed, I changed my clothing, putting aside my dark Western business suit. I assumed denim jeans, a long-sleeved shirt, and a photographer's vest. I slipped my press card, my passport, my health cards into the vest's zippered pockets, and draped the cameras around myself. I then returned to the lobby downstairs, to await the arrival of the American rock star.

He came on schedule, even slightly early. There was only a small crowd, as the rock star's organization had sought confidentiality. A train of seven monstrous buses pulled into the hotel's lot, their whale-like sides gleaming with brushed aluminum. They bore Massachusetts license plates. I walked out on to the tarmac and began photographing.

All seven buses carried the rock star's favored insignia, the thirteen-starred blue field of the early American flag. The buses pulled up with military precision, forming a wagon-train fortress across a large section of the weedy, broken tarmac. Folding doors hissed open and a swarm of road crew piled out into the circle of buses.

Men and women alike wore baggy fatigues, covered with buttoned pockets and block-shaped streaks of urban camouflage: brick red, asphalt black, and concrete gray. Dark-blue shoulder patches showed the thirteen-starred circle. Working efficiently, without haste, they erected large satellite dishes on the roofs of two buses. The buses were soon linked together in formation, shaped barriers of woven wire securing the gaps between each nose and tail. The machines seemed to sit breathing, with the stoked-up, leviathan air of steam locomotives.

A dozen identically dressed crewmen broke from the buses and departed in a group for the hotel. Within their midst, shielded by their bodies, was the rock star, Tom Boston. The broken outlines of their camouflaged fatigues made them seem to blur into a single mass, like a herd of moving zebras. I followed them; they vanished quickly within the hotel. One crew woman tarried outside.

I approached her. She had been hauling a bulky piece of metal luggage on trolley wheels. It was a newspaper vending machine. She set it beside three other machines at the hotel's entrance. It was the Boston organization's propaganda paper, *Poor Richard's.*

I drew near. "Ah, the latest issue," I said. "May I have one?"

"It will cost five dollars," she said, in painstaking English. To my surprise, I recognized her as Boston's wife. "Valya Plisetskaya," I said with pleasure, and handed her a five-dollar nickel. "My name is Sayyid; my American friends call me Charlie."

She looked about her. A small crowd already gathered at the buses, kept at a distance by the Boston crew. Others clustered under the hotel's green-and-white awning.

"Who are you with?" she said.

"*Al-Ahram,* of Cairo. An Arabic newspaper."

"You're not a political?" she said.

I shook my head in amusement at this typical show of Russian paranoia. "Here's my press card." I showed her the tangle of Arabic. "I am here to cover Tom Boston. The Boston phenomenon."

She squinted. "Tom is big in Cairo these days? Muslims, yes? Down on rock and roll."

"We're not all ayatollahs," I said, smiling up at her. She was very tall. "Many still listen to Western pop music; they ignore the advice of their betters. They used to rock all night in Leningrad. Despite the Communist Party. Isn't that so?"

"You know about us Russians, do you, Charlie?" She handed me my paper, watching me with cool suspicion.

"No, I can't keep up," I said. "Like Lebanon in the old days. Too many factions." I followed her through the swinging glass doors of the hotel. Valentina Plisetskaya was a broad-cheeked Slav with glacial blue eyes and hair the color of corn tassels. She was a childless woman in her thirties, starved as thin as a girl. She played saxophone in Boston's band. She was a native of Moscow, but had survived its destruction. She had been on tour with her jazz band when the Afghan Martyrs' Front detonated their nuclear bomb.

I tagged after her. I was interested in the view of another foreigner. "What do you think of the Americans these days?" I asked her.

We waited beside the elevator.

"Are you recording?" she said.

"No! I'm a print journalist. I know you don't like tapes," I said.

"We like tapes fine," she said, staring down at me. "As long as they are ours." The elevator was sluggish. "You want to know what I think, Charlie? I think Americans are fucked. Not as bad as Soviets, but fucked anyway. What do you think?"

"Oh," I said. "American gloom-and-doom is an old story. At *Al-Ahram*, we are more interested in the signs of American resurgence. That's the big angle, now. That's why I'm here."

She looked at me with remote sarcasm. "Aren't you a little afraid they will beat the shit out of you? They're not happy, the Americans. Not sweet and easygoing like before."

I wanted to ask her how sweet the CIA had been when their bomb killed half the Iranian government in 1981. Instead, I shrugged. "There's no substitute for a man on the ground. That's what my editors say." The elevator shunted open. "May I come up with you?"

"I won't stop you." We stepped in. "But they won't let you in to see Tom."

"They will if you ask them to, Mrs. Boston."

"I'm called Plisetskaya," she said, fluffing her yellow hair. "See? No veil." It was the old story of the so-called "liberated" Western woman. They call the simple, modest clothing of Islam "bondage"—while they spend countless hours, and millions of dollars, painting themselves. They grow their nails into talons, cram their feet into high heels, strap their breasts and hips into spandex. All for the sake of male lust.

It baffles the imagination. Naturally I told her nothing of this, but only smiled. "I'm afraid I will be a pest," I said. "I have a room in this hotel. Some time I will see your husband. I must, my editors demand it."

The doors opened. We stepped into the hall of the fourteenth floor. Boston's entourage had taken over the entire floor. Men in fatigues and sunglasses guarded the hallway; one of them had a trained dog.

"Your paper is big, is it?" the woman said.

"Biggest in Cairo, millions of readers," I said. "We still read, in the Caliphate."

"State-controlled television," she muttered.

"Is that worse than corporations?" I asked. "I saw what CBS said about Tom Boston." She hesitated, and I continued to prod. "A 'Luddite fanatic,' am I right? A 'rock demagogue.' "

"Give me your room number." I did this. "I'll call," she said, striding away down the corridor. I almost expected the guards to salute her as she passed so regally, but they made no move, their eyes invisible behind the glasses. They looked old and rather tired, but with the alert relaxation of professionals. They had the look of former Secret Service bodyguards. Their city-colored fatigues were baggy enough to hide almost any amount of weaponry.

I returned to my room. I ordered Japanese food from room service, and ate it. Wine had been used in its cooking, but I am not a prude in these matters. It was now time for the day's last prayer, though my body, still attuned to Cairo, did not believe it.

My devotions were broken by a knocking at the door. I opened it. It was another of Boston's staff, a small black woman whose hair had been treated. It had a nylon sheen. It looked like the plastic hair on a child's doll. "You Charlie?"

"Yes."

"Valya says, you want to see the gig. See us set up. Got you a backstage pass."

"Thank you very much." I let her clip the plastic-coated pass to my vest. She looked past me into the room, and saw my prayer rug at the window. "What you doin' in there? Prayin'?"

"Yes."

"Weird," she said. "You coming or what?"

I followed my nameless benefactor to the elevator.

Down at ground level, the crowd had swollen. Two security guards stood outside the glass doors, refusing admittance to anyone without a room key. The girl ducked, and plowed through the crowd with sudden headlong force, like an American football player. I struggled in her wake, the gawkers, pickpockets and autograph hounds closing at my heels. The crowd was liberally sprinkled with the repulsive derelicts one sees so often in America: those without homes, without family, without charity.

I was surprised at the age of the people. For a rock-star's audience, one expects dizzy teenaged girls and the libidinous young street-toughs that pursue them. There were many of these, but more of another type: tired, footsore people with crow's-feet and graying hair. Men and women in their thirties and forties, with a shabby, crushed look. Unemployed, obviously, and with time on their hands to cluster around anything that resembled hope.

We walked without hurry to the fortress circle of buses. A rear guard of Boston's kept the onlookers at bay.

Two of the buses were already unlinked from the others and under full steam. I followed the black woman up perforated steps and into the bowels of one of the shining machines.

She called brief greetings to the others already inside. The air held the sharp reek of cleaning fluid. Neat elastic cords held down stacks of amplifiers, stencilled instrument cases, wheeled dollies of black rubber and crisp yellow pine. The thirteen-starred circle marked everything, stamped or spray-painted. A methane-burning steam generator sat at the back of the bus, next to a tall crashproof rack of high-pressure fuel tanks. We skirted the equipment and joined the others in a narrow row of second-hand airplane seats. We buckled ourselves in. I sat next to the Doll-Haired Girl.

The bus surged into motion. "It's very clean," I said. "I expected something a bit wilder on a rock and roll bus."

"Maybe in Egypt," she said, with the instinctive assumption that Egypt was in the Dark Ages. "We don't have the luxury to screw around. Not now."

I decided not to tell her that Egypt, as a nation-state, no longer existed. "American pop culture is a very big industry."

"Biggest we have left," she said. "And if you Muslims weren't so pimpy about it, maybe we could pull down a few riyals and get out of debt."

"We buy a great deal from America," I told her. "Grain and timber and minerals."

"That's Third-World stuff. We're not your farm." She looked at the spotless floor. "Look, our industries suck, everybody knows it. So we sell entertainment. Except where there's media barriers. And even then the fucking video pirates rip us off."

"We see things differently," I said. "America ruled the global media for decades. To us, it's cultural imperialism. We have many talented musicians in the Arab world. Have you ever heard them?"

"Can't afford it," she said crisply. "We spent all our money saving the Persian Gulf from commies."

"The Global Threat of Red Totalitarianism," said the heavyset man in the seat next to Doll-Hair. The others laughed grimly.

"Oh," I said. "Actually, it was Zionism that concerned us. When there was a Zionism."

"I can't believe the hate shit I see about America," said the heavy man. "You know how much money we gave away to people, just gave away, for nothing? Billions and billions. Peace Corps, development aid ... for decades. Any disaster anywhere, and we fall all over ourselves to give food, medicine ... Then the Russians go down and the whole world turns against us like we were monsters."

"Moscow," said another crewman, shaking his shaggy head.

"You know, there are still motherfuckers who think we Americans killed Moscow. They think we gave a Bomb to those Afghani terrorists."

"It had to come from somewhere," I said.

"No, man. We wouldn't do that to them. No, man, things were going great between us. Rock for Detente—I was at that gig."

We drove to Miami's Memorial Colosseum. It was an ambitious structure, left half-completed when the American banking system collapsed.

We entered double-doors at the back, wheeling the equipment along dusty corridors. The Colosseum's interior was skeletal; inside it was clammy and cavernous. A stage, a concrete floor. Bare steel arched high overhead, with crudely bracketed stage-lights. Large sections of that bizarre American parody of grass, "Astroturf," had been dragged before the stage. The itchy green fur was still lined with yard-marks from some forgotten stadium.

The crew worked with smooth precision, setting up amplifiers, spindly mike-stands, a huge high-tech drum kit with the clustered, shiny look of an oil refinery. Others checked lighting, flicking blue and yellow spots across the stage. At the public entrances, two crewmen from a second bus erected metal detectors for illicit cameras, recorders, or handguns. Especially handguns. Two attempts had already been made on Boston's life, one at the Chicago Freedom Festival, when Chicago's Mayor had been wounded at Boston's side.

For a moment, to understand it, I mounted the empty stage and stood before Boston's microphone. I imagined the crowd before me, ten thousand souls, twenty thousand eyes. Under that attention, I realized, every motion was amplified. To move my arm would be like moving ten thousand arms, my every word like the voice of thousands. I felt like a Nasser, a Qadaffi, a Saddam Hussein.

This was the nature of secular power. Industrial power. It was the West that invented it, that invented Hitler, the gutter orator turned trampler of nations, that invented Stalin, the man they called "Genghis Khan with a telephone." The media pop star, the politician. Was there any difference anymore? Not in America; it was all a question of seizing eyes, of seizing attention. Attention is wealth, in an age of mass media. Center stage is more important than armies.

The last unearthly moans and squeals of sound-check faded. The Miami crowd began to filter into the Colosseum. They looked livelier than the desperate searchers who had pursued Boston to his hotel. America was still a wealthy country, by most standards; the professional classes had kept much of their prosperity. There were the legions of lawyers, for instance, that secular priesthood that had done so much to drain America's once-vaunted enterprise. And their associated legions of state bureaucrats. They were instantly recognizable; the cut of their suits, their telltale pocket telephones proclaiming their status.

What were they looking for here? Had they never read Boston's propaganda paper, with its bitter condemnations of the wealthy? With its fierce attacks on the "legislative-litigative complex," its demands for purges and sweeping reforms?

Was it possible that they had failed to take him seriously?

I joined the crowd, mingling, listening to conversations. At the doors, Boston cadres were cutting ticket prices for those who showed voter registrations. Those who showed unemployment cards got in for even less.

The more prosperous Americans stood in little knots of besieged gentility, frightened of the others, yet curious, smiling. There was a liveliness in the destitute: brighter clothing, knotted kerchiefs at the elbows, cheap Korean boots of iridescent cloth. Many wore tricornered hats, some with a cockade of red, white, and blue, or the circle of thirteen stars.

This was the milieu of rock and roll, I realized; that was the secret. They had all grown up on it, these Americans, even the richer ones. To them, the sixty-year tradition of rock music seemed as ancient as the Pyramids. It had become a Jerusalem, a Mecca of American tribes.

The crowd milled, waiting, and Boston let them wait. At the back of the crowd, Boston crewmen did a brisk business in starred souvenir shirts, programs, and tapes. Heat and tension mounted, and people began to sweat. The stage remained dark.

I bought the souvenir items and studied them. They talked about cheap computers, a phone company owned by its workers, a free data-base, neighborhood co-operatives that could buy unmilled grain by the ton. ATTENTION MIAMI, read one brochure in letters of dripping red. It named the ten largest global corporations and meticulously listed every subsidiary doing business in Miami, with its address, its phone number, the percentage of income shipped to banks in Europe and Japan. Each list went on for pages. Nothing else. To Boston's audience, nothing else was necessary.

The house lights darkened. A frightening animal roar

rose from the crowd. A single spot lit Tom Boston, stenciling him against darkness.

"My fellow Americans," he said. A funereal hush followed. Boston smirked. "My f-f-f-fellow Americans." He had a clever microphone, digitized, a small synthesizer in itself. "My fellow Am-am-am-am-AMM!" His words vanished in a sudden wail of feedback. "My Am—my fellows—my am—my fellows—my am my, Miami, Miami, MIAMI!" Boston's warped voice, suddenly leaping out of all human context, became shattering, superhuman—the effect was bone-chilling. It passed all barriers, it seeped directly into the skin, the blood.

"Tom Jefferson Died Broke!" he shouted. It was the title of his first song. Stage lights flashed up and hell broke its gates. Was this a "song" at all, this strange, volcanic creation? There was a melody loose in it somewhere, pursued by Plisetskaya's saxophone, but the sheer volume and impact hurled it through the audience like a sheet of flame. I had never before heard anything so loud. What Cairo's renegade set called rock music paled to nothing beside this invisible hurricane.

At first it seemed raw noise. But that was only a kind of flooring, a merciless grinding foundation below the rising architectures of sound. Technology did it: that piercing, soaring, digitized, utter clarity, of perfect computer acoustics adjusting for every echo, a hundred times a second.

Boston played a glass harmonica: an instrument invented by the early American genius Benjamin Franklin. The harmonica was made of carefully tuned glass disks, rotating on a spindle, and played by streaking a wet fingertip across each moving edge.

It was the sound of crystal, seemingly sourceless, of tooth-aching purity.

The famous Western musician, Wolfgang Mozart, had composed for the Franklin harmonica in the days of its novelty. Legend said that its players went mad, their nerves shredded by its clarity of sound. It was a legend

Boston was careful to exploit. He played the machine sparingly, with the air of a magician, of a Solomon unbottling demons. I was glad of this, for the beauty of its sound stung the brain.

Boston threw aside his hat. Long coiled hair spilled free. Boston was what Americans called "black"; at least, he was often referred to as black, though no one seemed certain. He was no darker than myself. The beat rose up, a strong animal heaving. Boston stalked across the stage as if on strings, clutching his microphone. He began to sing.

The song concerned Thomas Jefferson, a famous American president of the eighteenth century. Jefferson was a political theorist who wrote revolutionary manifestos and favored a decentralist mode of government. The song, however, dealt with the relations of Jefferson and a black concubine in his household. He had several children by this woman, who were a source of great shame, due to the odd legal code of the period. Legally, they were his slaves, and it was only at the end of his life, when he was in great poverty, that Jefferson set them free.

It was a story whose pathos makes little sense to a Muslim. But Boston's audience, knowing themselves Jefferson's children, took it to heart.

The heat became stifling, as massed bodies swayed in rhythm. The next song began in a torrent of punishing noise. Frantic hysteria seized the crowd; their bodies spasmed with each beat, the shaman Boston seeming to scourge them. It was a fearsome song, called "The Whites of Their Eyes," after an American war-cry. He sang of a tactic of battle: to wait until the enemy comes close enough so that you can meet his eyes, frighten him with your conviction, and then shoot him point blank.

Three more songs followed, one of them slower, the others battering the audience like iron rods. Boston stalked like a madman, his clothing dark with sweat. My heart spasmed as heavy bass notes, filled with dark murderous power, surged through my ribs. I moved away

from the heat to the fringe of the crowd, feeling light-
headed and sick.

I had not expected this. I had expected a political
spokesman, but instead it seemed I was assaulted by the
very Voice of the West. The Voice of a society drunk with
raw power, maddened by the grinding roar of machines.
It filled me with terrified awe.

To think that, once, the West had held us in its
armored hands. It had treated Islam as it treated a natural
resource, its invincible armies tearing through the lands of
the Faithful like bulldozers. The West had chopped our
world up into colonies, and smiled upon us with its awful
schizophrenic perfidy. It told us to separate God and
State, to separate Mind and Body, to separate Reason and
Faith. It had torn us apart.

I stood shaking as the first set ended. The band vanished backstage, and a single figure approached the microphone. I recognized him as a famous American
television comedian, who had abandoned his own career
to join Boston.

The man began to joke and clown, his antics seeming
to soothe the crowd, which hooted with laughter. This in-
termission was a wise move on Boston's part, I thought.
The level of intensity, of pain, had become unbearable.

It struck me then how much Boston was like the
great Khomeini. Boston too had the persona of the Man
of Sorrows, the sufferer after justice, the ascetic among
corruption, the battler against odds. And the air of the
mystic, the adept, at least as far as such a thing was possible in America. I contemplated this, and deep fear
struck me once again.

I walked through the gates to the Colosseum's outer
hall, seeking air and room to think. Others had come out
too. They leaned against the walls, men and women, with
the look of wrung-out mops. Some smoked cigarettes,
others argued over brochures, others simply sat with pal-
sied grins.

Still others wept. These disturbed me most, for these

were the ones whose souls seemed stung and opened. Khomeini made men weep like that, tearing aside despair like a bandage from a burn. I walked among them, watching them, making mental notes.

I stopped by a woman in dark glasses and a trim business suit. She leaned within an alcove by a set of telephones, shaking, her face beneath the glasses slick with silent tears. Her cheekbones, the precision of her styled hair, struck a memory. I stood beside her, waiting, and recognition came.

"Hello," I said. "We have something in common, I think. You've been covering the Boston tour. For CBS."

She glanced at me once, and away. "I don't know you."

"You're Marjory Cale, the correspondent."

She drew in a breath. "You're mistaken."

" 'Luddite fanatic,' " I said lightly. " 'Rock demagogue.' "

"Go away," she said.

"Why not talk about it? I'd like to know your point of view."

"Go away, you nasty little man."

I returned to the crowd inside. The comedian was now reading at length from the American Bill of Rights, his voice thick with sarcasm. "Freedom of advertising," he said. "Freedom of global network television conglomerates. Right to a speedy and public trial, to be repeated until the richest lawyers win. A well-regulated militia being necessary, citizens will be issued orbital lasers and aircraft carriers . . ." No one was laughing.

The crowd was in an ugly mood when Boston reappeared. Even the well-dressed ones now seemed surly and militant, not recognizing themselves as the enemy. Like the Shah's soldiers who at last refused to fire, who threw themselves sobbing at Khomeini's feet.

"You all know this one," Boston said. With his wife, he raised a banner, one of the first flags of the American Revolution. It bore a coiled snake, a native American viper, with the legend: DON'T TREAD ON ME. A sinister, scaly rattling poured from the depths of a synthesizer, merging with the crowd's roar of recognition, and a sprung, loping rhythm broke loose. Boston edged back and forth at the stage's rim, his eyes fixed, his long neck swaying. He shook himself like a man saved from drowning and leaned into the microphone.

"We know you own us/ You step upon us/ We feel the onus/ But here's a bonus/ Today I see/ So enemy/ Don't tread on me/ Don't tread on me . . ." Simple words, fitting each beat with all the harsh precision of the English language. A chant of raw hostility. The crowd took it up. This was the hatred, the humiliation of a society brought low. Americans. Somewhere within them conviction still burned. The conviction they had always had: that they were the only real people on the planet. The chosen ones, the Light of the World, the Last Best Hope of Mankind, the Free and the Brave, the crown of creation. They would have killed for him. I knew, someday, they would.

I was called to Boston's suite at two o'clock that morning. I had shaved and showered, dashed on the hotel's complimentary cologne. I wanted to smell like an American.

Boston's guards frisked me, carefully and thoroughly, outside the elevator. I submitted with good grace.

Boston's suite was crowded. It had the air of an election victory. There were many politicians, sipping glasses of bubbling alcohol, laughing, shaking hands. Miami's Mayor was there, with half his city council. I recognized a young woman Senator, speaking urgently into her pocket phone, her large freckled breasts on display in an evening gown.

I mingled, listening. Men spoke of Boston's ability to raise funds, of the growing importance of his endorsement. More of Boston's guards stood in corners, arms folded, eyes hidden, their faces stony. A black man distributed lapel buttons with the face of Martin Luther King on a background of red and white stripes. The wall-sized television played a tape of the first Moon Landing. The sound had been turned off, and people all over the world, in the garb of the 1960's, mouthed silently at the camera, their eyes shining.

It was not until four o'clock that I finally met the star himself. The party had broken up by then, the politicians politely ushered out, their vows of undying loyalty met with discreet smiles. Boston was in a back bedroom with his wife and a pair of aides.

"Sayyid," he said, and shook my hand. In person he seemed smaller, older, his hybrid face, with stage makeup, beginning to peel.

"Dr. Boston," I said.

He laughed freely. "Sayyid, my friend. You'll ruin my street fucking credibility."

"I want to tell the story as I see it," I said.

"Then you'll have to tell me what you see," he said, and turned briefly to an aide, who had a laptop computer. Boston dictated in a low, staccato voice, not losing his place in our conversation, simply loosing a burst of thought. "Let us be frank. Before I showed an interest you were willing to sell the ship for scrap iron. This is not an era for supertankers. Your property is dead tech, smokestack-era garbage. Reconsider my offer." The secretary pounded keys. Boston looked at me again, returning the searchlight of his attention.

"You want to buy a supertanker?" I said.

"I wanted an aircraft carrier," he said, smiling. "They're all in mothballs, but the Feds frown on selling nuke powerplants to private citizens."

"We will make the tanker into a floating stadium," Plisetskaya put in. She sat slumped in a padded chair, wearing satin lounge pajamas. A half-filled ashtray on the chair's arm reeked of strong tobacco.

"Ever been inside a tanker?" Boston said. "Huge. Great acoustics." He sat suddenly on the sprawling bed and pulled off his snakeskin boots. "So, Sayyid. Tell me this story of yours."

"You graduated magna cum laude from Rutgers with a doctorate in political science," I said. "In five years."

"That doesn't count," Boston said, yawning behind his hand. "That was before rock and roll beat my brains out."

"You ran for state office in Massachusetts," I said. "You lost a close race. Two years later you were touring with your first band—Swamp Fox. You were an immediate success. You became involved in political fund-raising, recruiting your friends in the music industry. You started your own recording label, your own studios. You helped organize rock concerts in Russia, where you met your wife-to-be. Your romance was front-page news on both continents. Record sales soared."

"You left out the first time I got shot at," Boston said. "That's more interesting; Val and I are old hat by now."

He paused, then burst out at the second secretary. "I urge you once again not to go public. You will find yourself vulnerable to a buyout. I've told you that Evans is an agent of Marubeni. If he brings your precious plant down around your ears, don't come crying to me."

"February 1998," I said. "An anti-communist zealot fired on your bus."

"You're a big fan, Sayyid."

"Why are you afraid of multinationals?" I said. "That was the American preference, wasn't it? Global trade, global economics?"

"We screwed up," Boston said. "Things got out of hand."

"Out of American hands, you mean?"

"We used our companies as tools for development," Boston said, with the patience of a man instructing a child. "But then our lovely friends in South America refused to pay their debts. And our staunch allies in Europe and Japan signed the Geneva Economic Agreement and decided to crash the dollar. And our friends in the Arab countries decided not to be countries anymore, but one almighty Caliphate, and, just for good measure, they pulled all their oil money out of our banks and put it into Islamic ones. How could we compete? Islamic banks are holy banks, and our banks pay interest, which is a sin, I understand." He fluffed curls from his neck, his eyes glittering. "And all that time, we were already in hock to our fucking ears to pay for being the world's policeman."

"So the world betrayed your country," I said. "Why?"

He shook his head. "Isn't it obvious? Who needs St. George when the dragon is dead? Some Afghani fanatics scraped together enough plutonium for a Big One, and they blew the dragon's fucking head off. And the rest of the body is still convulsing, ten years later. We bled ourselves white competing against Russia, which was stupid, but we'd won. With two giants, the world trembles. One giant, and the midgets can drag it down. They took us out, that's all. They own us."

"It sounds very simple," I said.

He showed annoyance for the first time. "Valya says you've read our newspapers. I'm not telling you anything new. Should I lie about it? Look at the figures, for Christ's sake. The EEC and the Japanese use their companies for money pumps, they're sucking us dry, deliberately. You don't look stupid, Sayyid. You know very well what's happening to us, anyone in the Third World knows."

"You mentioned Christ," I said. "Do you believe in Him?"

Boston rocked back on his elbows and grinned. "Do you?"

"Of course. He is one of our Prophets. We call Him Isa."

Boston looked cautious. "I never stand between a man and his God." He paused. "We have a lot of respect for the Arabs, truly. What they've accomplished. Breaking free from the world economic system, returning to authentic local tradition ... You see the parallels."

"Yes," I said. I smiled sleepily, and covered my mouth as I yawned. "Jet lag. Your pardon, please. These are only questions my editors would want me to ask. If I were not an admirer, a fan as you say, I would not have this assignment."

He smiled and looked at his wife. Plisetskaya lit another cigarette and leaned back, looking skeptical. Boston grinned. "So the sparring's over, Charlie?"

"I have every record you've made," I said. "This is not a job for hatchets." I paused, weighing my words. "I still believe that our Caliph is a great man. I support the Islamic Resurgence. I am Muslim. But I think, like many others, that we have gone a bit too far in closing every window to the West. Rock and roll is a Third World music at heart. Don't you agree?"

"Sure," said Boston, closing his eyes. "Do you know the first words spoken in independent Zimbabwe? Right after they ran up the flag."

"No."

He spoke out blindly, savoring the words. "Ladies and gentlemen. Bob Marley. And the Wailers."

"You admire Bob Marley."

"Comes with the territory," Boston said, flipping a coil of hair.

"He had a black mother, a white father. And you?"

"Oh, both my parents were shameless mongrels like myself," Boston said. "I'm a second-generation nothing-in-particular. An American." He sat up, knotting his hands, looking tired. "You going to stay with the tour a while, Charlie?" He spoke to a secretary. "Get me a klee-nex." The woman rose.

"Till Philadelphia," I said. "Like Marjory Cale."

Plisetskaya blew smoke, frowning. "You spoke to that woman?"

"Of course. About the concert."

"What did the bitch say?" Boston asked lazily. His aide handed him tissues and cold cream. Boston dabbed the kleenex and smeared makeup from his face.

"She asked me what I thought. I said it was too loud," I said.

Plisetskaya laughed once, sharply. I smiled. "It was quite amusing. She said that you were in good form. She said that I should not be so tight-arsed."

" 'Tight-arsed'?" Boston said, raising his brows. Fine wrinkles had appeared beneath the greasepaint. "She said that?"

"She said we Muslims were afraid of modern life. Of new experience. Of course I told her that this wasn't true. Then she gave me this." I reached into one of the pockets of my vest and pulled out a flat packet of aluminum foil.

"Marjory Cale gave you cocaine?" Boston asked.

"Wyoming Flake," I said. "She said she has friends who grow it in the Rocky Mountains." I opened the packet, exposing a little mound of white powder. "I saw her use some. I think it will help my jet lag." I pulled my chair closer to the bedside phone-table. I shook the packet out, with much care, on the shining mahogany surface. The tiny crystals glittered. It was finely chopped.

I opened my wallet and removed a crisp thousand-dollar bill. The actor-president smiled benignly. "Would this be appropriate?"

"Tom does not do drugs," Plisetskaya said, too quickly.

"Ever do coke before?" Boston asked. He threw a wadded tissue to the floor.

"I hope I'm not offending you," I said. "This is Miami, isn't it? This is America." I began rolling the bill, clumsily.

"We are not impressed," Plisetskaya said sternly. She ground out her cigarette. "You are being a rube, Charlie. A hick from the NICs."

"There is a lot of it," I said, allowing doubt to creep into my voice. I reached into my pocket, then divided the pile in half with the sharp edge of a developed slide. I arranged the lines neatly. They were several centimeters long.

I sat back in the chair. "You think it's a bad idea? I

admit, this is new to me." I paused. "I have drunk wine several times, although the Koran forbids it."

One of the secretaries laughed. "Sorry," she said. "He drinks wine. That's cute."

I sat and watched temptation dig into Boston. Plisetskaya shook her head.

"Cale's cocaine," Boston mused. "Man."

We watched the lines together for several seconds, he and I. "I did not mean to be trouble," I said. "I can throw it away."

"Never mind Val," Boston said. "Russians chain-smoke." He slid across the bed.

I bent quickly and sniffed. I leaned back, touching my nose. The cocaine quickly numbed it. I handed the paper tube to Boston. It was done in a moment. We sat back, our eyes watering.

"Oh," I said, drug seeping through tissue. "Oh, this is excellent."

"It's good toot," Boston agreed. "Looks like you get an extended interview."

We talked through the rest of the night, he and I.

My story is almost over. From where I sit to write this, I can hear the sound of Boston's music, pouring from the crude speakers of a tape pirate in the bazaar. There is no doubt in my mind that Boston is a great man.

I accompanied the tour to Philadelphia. I spoke to Boston several times during the tour, though never again with the first fine rapport of the drug. We parted as friends, and I spoke well of him in my article for *Al-Ahram*. I did not hide what he was, I did not hide his threat. But I did not malign him. We see things differently. But he is a man, a child of God like all of us.

His music even saw brief popularity in Cairo, after the article. Children listen to it, and then turn to other things, as children will. They like the sound, they dance, but the words mean nothing to them. The thoughts, the feelings, are alien.

This is the *dar-al-harb*, the land of peace. We have peeled the hands of the West from our throat, we draw breath again, under God's sky. Our Caliph is a good man, and I am proud to serve him. He reigns, he does not rule. Learned men debate in the *Majlis*, not squabbling like politicians, but seeking truth in dignity. We have the world's respect.

We have earned it, for we paid the martyr's price. We Muslims are one in five in all the world, and as long as ignorance of God persists, there will always be the struggle, the *jihad*. It is a proud thing to be one of the Caliph's *Mujihadeen*. It is not that we value our lives lightly. But that we value God more.

Some call us backward, reactionary. I laughed at this when I carried the powder. It had the subtlest of poisons: a living virus. It is a tiny thing, bred in secret laboratories, and in itself it does no harm. But it spreads throughout the body, and it bleeds out a chemical, a faint but potent trace that carries the rot of cancer.

The West can do much with cancer these days, and a wealthy man like Boston can buy much treatment. They may cure the first attack, or the second. But within five years he will surely be dead.

People will mourn his loss. Perhaps they will put his image on a postage stamp, as they did for Bob Marley. Marley, who also died of systemic cancer; whether by the hand of God or man, only Allah knows.

I have taken the life of a great man; in trapping him I took my own life as well, but that means nothing. I am no one. I am not even Sayyid Qutb, the Martyr and theorist of Resurgence, though I took that great man's name as cover. I meant only respect, and believe I have not shamed his memory.

I do not plan to wait for the disease. The struggle continues in the Muslim lands of what was once the Soviet Union. There the Believers ride in Holy Jihad, freeing

their ancient lands from the talons of Marxist atheism.
Secretly, we send them carbines, rockets, mortars, and
nameless men. I shall be one of them; when I meet death,
my grave will be nameless also. But nothing is nameless
to God.

God is Great; men are mortal, and err. If I have done
wrong, let the Judge of Men decide. Before His Will, as
always, I submit.

HOLLYWOOD
KREMLIN

The ZIL-135 was vital to national security. Therefore, it was built only in Russia. It looked it, too.

The ZIL was a Red Army battlefield truck, with eight monster rubber-lugged wheels and a ten-ton canvas-topped flatbed. This particular ZIL, which had a busted suspension and four burned-out gears, sat in darkness beside a makeshift airstrip. The place stank of kerosene, diesel, tarmac, and the smoke of guttering runway flares. All of it wrapped in the cricket-shrieking night of rural Azerbaijan.

Azerbaijan was a southern Soviet province, with 8 million citizens and thirty-three thousand square miles. Azerbaijan bordered on all kinds of trouble: Iran, Turkey, the highly polluted Caspian Sea, and 3.5 million angry Soviet Armenians.

From within the ZIL's cramped little khaki-colored cab came the crisp beeping of a digital watch.

The driver yanked back the shoddy sleeve of his secondhand Red Army jacket and pressed a watch stud. A dial light glowed, showing thirty seconds from midnight. The driver grinned and mashed more little buttons with his blunt, precise fingers. The watch emitted a twittering Japanese folk tune.

The driver, hanging on to the ZIL's no-power, gut-busting steering wheel, leaned far out the open door and squinted at the horizon. A phantom silhouette slid across the southern stars—a plane without running lights, painted black for night flight.

The driver gulped from a Stolichnaya bottle and lit a Marlboro.

The flare of his Cricket lighter briefly threw his blurred yellow reflection against the ZIL's windshield. He was unshaven, pumpkin-faced, bristle-headed. His eyes were slitted, yet somehow malignantly radiant with preternatural survival instincts. The driver's name was Leggy Starlitz. The locals, who knew no better, called him "Lekhi Starlits."

Starlitz kicked the cab's rusty door open and climbed down the ZIL's iron rungs.

The black plane hit tarmac, bounced drunkenly down the potholed strip, and taxied up. It was a twin-engine Soviet military turboprop, an Ilyushin-14.

Starlitz beckoned at the spyplane with a pair of orange semaphore paddles. He waved it along brusquely. He was not a big fan of the Ilyushin-14.

The IL-14 was already obsolete in the high-tech Soviet Air Force. So the aging planes had been consigned to the puppet Air Force of the Democratic Republic of Afghanistan: the DRAAF. This plane had a big Afghan logo clumsily painted over its Soviet red star. The DRAAF logo was a smaller, fatter, maroon-colored star, ringed in an inviting target circle of red, green and black. It looked a lot like a Texaco sign.

Still, the IL-14 was the best spyplane that the DRAAF had to offer. It had fine range and speed; it could fly smuggling runs under the Iranian radar, all the way from Kabul to Soviet Azerbaijan.

Starlitz much preferred the DRAAF's antique "Badger" medium bombers. Badgers had good range and superb cargo capacity. You could haul anything in a Badger. Trucks, refugees, chemical feedstocks . . . the works.

It was too bad that the Badger was such a hog to fly. The smugglers had given the Badger up. For months they'd been embezzling tons of aviation kerosene from the Afghan Air Force fuel dumps. The thievery was becoming too obvious, even for the utterly corrupt Afghan military.

Starlitz guided the creeping, storm-colored plane into the makeshift airstrip's hangar. The hangar was a tin-roofed livestock barn, built to the colossal proportions of a Soviet collective farm. The morale of the collectivized peasants had been lousy, though, and all the cattle had starved to death during the Brezhnev era. Now the barn was free for new restructured uses: something with a lot more initiative, a lot more *up-to-date*.

The plane's engines died, their eighteen cylinders coughing into echoing silence. Starlitz heaved concrete parking blocks under the nosewheels. He propped a paint-stained wooden ladder against the cockpit.

The aircraft's bulletproof canopy creaked up and open. A pilot in an earflapped leather helmet leaned out on one elbow, an oxygen mask dangling from his neck.

"How's it going, ace?" Starlitz said in his foully accented dog-Russian.

"Where are the disembarkation stairs?" demanded the pilot. He was Captain Pulat R. Khoklov, a Soviet "adviser" to the DRAAF.

"Huh?" Starlitz said.

Khoklov frowned. "You know very well, Comrade Starlits. The device that rolls here on wheels, with the proper sturdy metal steps, for my descending."

"Oh. *That*," Starlitz said. "I dunno, man. I guess somebody sold it."

"Where is the rest of your ground crew?" said Captain Khoklov. The handsome young pilot's eyelids were reddened and his tapered fingertips were corpse-pale from Dexedrine. It had been a long flight. The IL-14 was a two-man plane, but Khoklov flew it alone.

Khoklov and his pals didn't trust the DRAAF's native pilots. In 1985 the Afghans had mutinied and torched twenty of their best MiG fighters on the ground at Shindand Air Base. Since that incident, most DRAAF missions had been flown by Russian pilots, "unofficially." Pakistani border violations, civilian bombings, a little gas work . . . the sort of mission where DRAAF cover came in handy.

Some DRAAF missions, though, were far more "unofficial" than others.

Starlitz grinned up at the pilot. "The ground crew's on strike, comrade," he said. "Politics. 'The nationalities problem.' You know how it is here in Azerbaijan."

Khoklov was scandalized. "They can't strike against *smugglers*! We're not the government! We are a criminal private-enterprise operation!"

"They *know* that, man," Starlitz said. "But they wanted to show solidarity. With their fellow Armenian Christians. Against the Moslem Azerbaijanis."

"You should not have let your Armenian workers go," Khoklov said. "They can't be allowed to run riot just as they please!"

"What the hey," Starlitz said. "Can't *make* 'em work."

"Of course you can," Khoklov said, surprised.

Starlitz shrugged. "Tell it to Gorbachev . . . Forget the stairs. Use the paint ladder, ace. Nobody's looking."

With reluctance, Khoklov abandoned his dignity. He shrugged out of his harness, set his mask and helmet aside, and clambered down.

Khoklov's DRAAF flight jacket was gaudy with mission patches. Beneath it he sported a civilian Afghan blouse of hand-embroidered paisley, and a white silk ascot. Walkman earphones bracketed his neck. The antique wailing of the Jefferson Airplane rang faintly from the Walkman's foam-padded speakers.

Khoklov stretched and twisted, his spine popping

loudly. He walked to the edge of the hangar and peered warily into the darkness, as if suspecting ambush from local unfriendlies. Nothing whatever happened. Khoklov sighed and shook himself. He tiptoed into darkness to relieve himself on the tarmac.

Starlitz coupled the plane's nosewheel to the drawbar of a small diesel tractor.

Khoklov returned. He looked at Starlitz gravely, his poet's face anemic in the hangar's naked overhead lights. "You remained here faithfully, all alone, Comrade Starlits?"

"Yeah."

"How unusual. You yourself are not Armenian?"

"I'm not religious," Starlitz said. He offered Khoklov a Marlboro.

Khoklov examined the cigarette's brand name, nodded, and accepted a light. "What *is* your ethnic nationality, Comrade Starlits? I have often wondered."

"I'm an Uzbek," Starlitz said.

Khoklov thought it over, breathing smoke through his nose. "An Uzbek," he said at last. "I suppose I could believe that, if I really tried."

"My mom was a Kirghiz," Starlitz said glibly. "What's in the plane this time, ace? Good cargo?"

"Excellent cargo," Khoklov said. "But you have no crew to unload it!"

"I can handle it all myself." Starlitz pointed overhead. "I rigged some pulleys. And I just tuned up the forklift. I can improvise, ace, no problem."

"But that isn't permitted," Khoklov said. "One individual can't replace a team, through some private whim of his own! The entire work team is at fault. They must all be disciplined. Otherwise there will be recurrences of this irresponsible behavior."

"Big deal," Starlitz said, setting to work. "The job gets done anyway. The system is functional, ace. So who cares?"

"With such an incorrect attitude from their team leader, no wonder things have come to grief here," Khoklov observed. "You had better work like a Hero of Labor, comrade. Otherwise it will delay my return to base." Khoklov scowled. "And that would be hard to explain."

"Can't have that," Starlitz said lazily. "You might get transferred to Siberia or something. Not much fun, ace."

"I've already been to Siberia, and there is plenty of fun," Khoklov said. "We scrambled every day against Yankee spyplanes ... And Korean airliners. If there's a difference." He shrugged.

Starlitz moved the ladder down the plane's fuselage, past a long, spiky row of embedded ELINT antennas. He propped the ladder beside a radome blister, climbed up, and opened the plane's bay.

The Ilyushin's electronic spygear had been partially stripped, replaced with tarped-down heaps and stacks of contraband. Starlitz bonked his head on the plane's low bulkhead. "Damn," he said. "I sure miss those Badgers."

"Be grateful we have aircraft at all!" Khoklov said. He climbed the ladder and peered in curiously. "Think how many mule-loads of treasure have flown in my plane tonight. Romantic secret caravans, creeping slowly over the Khyber Pass ... And this is just a fraction of the secret trade. Many mules die in the minefields."

"Toss me that pulley hook, ace." Starlitz swung out a strapped-up stack of Hitachi videocassette recorders.

Starlitz, with methodic efficiency, drove forklift-loads of loot from the hangar out to the truck. Korean "Gold Star" tape players. Compact discs of re-mixed jazz classics. Fifty-kilo bricks of fudge-soft black Afghani hashish. Ten crates of J&B Scotch. A box of foil-sealed lubricated condoms, items of avid and fabulous rarity. Two hundred red cartons of Dunhills, still in their cellophane. Black nylon panty hose.

And gold. Gold czarist rubles, the lifeblood of the

Soviet black economy. The original slim supply of nine-teenth-century imperial rubles couldn't meet the frenzied modern demand, so they were counterfeited especially for the Soviet market, by goldsmiths in Egypt, Lebanon and Pakistan. The rubles came sealed in long strips of trans-parent plastic, for use in money belts.

Khoklov was fidgeting. "We have re-created the *Ara-bian Nights*," he said, running a flat ribbon of plasticized bullion over his sleeve. He leaned against a dusty concrete feeding trough. "It is Ali Baba and the forty *shabash-niki* ... We meant to 'smash the last vestiges of feudal-ism.' We meant to 'defend the socialist revolution.' All we have really done is create a thieves' market worthy of leg-end! With ourselves as the eager customers."

Khoklov lit a fresh Dunhill from the stub of the last. "You should see Kabul today, Comrade Starlits. It's still a vile medieval dump, but every alleyway is full of whores and thieves, every breed of petty capitalist! They tug our sleeves and offer us smuggled Western luxuries we could never find at home. Even the mujihadeen bandits drop their Yankee rifles to sell us soap and aspirin. Now that we're leaving, no one thinks of anything but backdoor hustling. We are all desperate for one last tasty drink of Coca-Cola, before our Afghan adventure is over."

"You sound a little wired, ace," Starlitz said. "You could lend me a hand, you know. Might get the kinks out."

"Not my assignment," Khoklov sniffed. "You can take your share of all this, comrade. Be content."

"What with the trouble it took, you'd think this junk would have more class," Starlitz said. He slid down the ladder with a cardboard box.

"Ah!" said Khoklov. "So it's glamour you want, my grimy Uzbek friend? You have it there in your hands. A wonderful Hollywood movie! Give me that box."

Starlitz tossed it to him. Khoklov ripped it open. "I must take a few cassettes for my fellows at DRAAF. They

love this film. *Top Gun!* Yankee pilots kill Moslems in it.
They strafe with F-16s, in many excellent flying-combat
scenes!"

"Hollywood," Starlitz said. "A bunch of crap."

Khoklov shook his head carefully. "The Yankees will
have to kill the Moslems, now that we're giving it up!
Libya, that Persian Gulf business . . . It's only a matter of
time." Khoklov began stuffing videocassettes into his
flight jacket. He took a handgun from within the jacket
and set it on the edge of the trough.

"Cool!" Starlitz said, staring at it. "What model is
that?"

"It's a war trophy," Khoklov said. "A luck charm, is
all."

"Lemme look, ace."

Khoklov showed him the gun.

"Looks like a Czech 'Skorpion' 5.66 millimeter," Starlitz said. "Something really *weird* about it, though . . ."

"It's homemade," Khoklov said. "An Afghan village
blacksmith copied it. They are clever as monkeys with
their hands." He shook his head. "It's pig-iron, hand-
drilled . . . You can see where he engraved some little
flowers into the pistol butt."

"Wow!" Starlitz exulted. "How much?"

"It's not for sale, comrade."

Starlitz reached into a pocket of his tattered Levi's
and pulled out a fat roll of dollars, held with a twist of
wire. "Say when, ace." He began peeling off bills and
slapping them down: one hundred, two hundred . . .

"That's enough," Khoklov said after a moment. He
examined the bills carefully, his pale hands shaking a little. "These are real American dollars! Where did you get
all this?"

"Found it in a turnip patch," Starlitz said. He
crammed the wad carelessly back into his jeans, then
lifted the gun with reverence, and sniffed its barrel. "You
ever fire this thing?"

"No. But its first owner did. At the people's fraternal forces."

"Huh. It'd be better if it were mint. It's beautiful anyway, though." Starlitz twirled the pistol on one finger, grinning triumphantly. "Too bad there's no safety catch."

"The Afghans never bother with them."

"Neither do I," Starlitz said. He stuffed the gun in the back of his jeans.

There were odds and ends in the plane, and one big item left: a Whirlpool clothes washer in bright lemon-yellow enamel. Starlitz manhandled it into the back of the ZIL with the other loot, and carefully laced the truck's canvas, hiding everything from view.

"Well, that's about it," Starlitz said, dusting his callused hands. "Now we'll get you gassed up and out of here, ace."

"About time," Khoklov said. He dry-swallowed a pair of white tablets from a gunmetal pillbox. "Next time be sure your worthless crew of Armenian ethnics is fully prepared for my arrival."

Starlitz jammed a big tin funnel into the Ilyushin's starboard wing tank. Against the hangar wall were two long rows of oily jerry cans, full of aviation kerosene. Starlitz hoisted a can one-handed to his shoulder and began decanting fuel, humming to himself. It was a slow process. As the pills came on, impatience struck Khoklov. He lugged jerry cans two-handed to the port wing tank, waddling with the weight.

The first row of cans was emptied. Khoklov started on the second. He heaved at a can and stumbled backward. "This one is empty!" he said. He tried the next. "This one, too."

The entire second row of cans had been drained. Khoklov kicked the final can across the hangar with a hollow bonging. "We've been robbed!"

"Looks that way," Starlitz admitted.

"Your thieving Armenians!" Khoklov shouted. "They

have embezzled the fuel! For a few lousy black-market rubles, they have stranded me here! My God, I'm finished!"

"Coulda been worse," Starlitz offered. "They coulda filled the cans with water instead. Flying low and fast, you'da pranged for sure." He thought it over. "Or bailed out over Iran. That woulda been hairy, ace."

"But they've ruined me! Ruined the whole operation! How could they be such meatheads?"

"Beats me," Starlitz said. "Times are tough here; fuel's in short supply . . . But be cool. We'll find you some go-juice somehow. The Boss must have some. The Boss may be mean, and ruthless, and greedy, and totally corrupt, but he's not *stupid*, y'know. He's probably got kerosene hoarded just in case."

"He'd better!" Khoklov said.

"We'll go to the Estate and ask around," Starlitz told him. "I'll give you a lift in the truck."

Khoklov's panic faded. He tagged after Starlitz and climbed up into the cab of the ZIL. Starlitz steered the truck down the airstrip, mashing the runway flares into embers under the ZIL's giant wheels. He flicked on the ZIL's headlights and turned onto a dirt road.

"Such a big truck and such a nasty little cab," Khoklov griped. He killed what was left of the vodka. Then he stared moodily out the windshield, at tall weeds ghost-pale by the roadside. "This situation's an outrage. The whole nation has lost its bearings, if you ask me. Especially in the provinces. It's getting very bad here, isn't it?"

"Yeah, this used to be good cropland," Starlitz said.

"Never mind the mere physical landscape," Khoklov scoffed. "I mean *politically*, comrade. Even lousy black marketeers openly defy Party authority."

"The Party *is* the black marketeers, ace. It couldn't work any other way."

The headquarters of the local agricultural complex had an official name, something with a long Cyrillic acronym. To those who knew about the place, it was just the Estate. It was the country seat of the Party chairman of the Azerbaijani Soviet Socialist Republic. The chairman had a proper name, too, but no one used it. He was generally known as "the Boss."

Starlitz took the back entrance through the high, wire-topped walls. It was late, and he didn't want to wake the armed guards in their marble kiosks in the front. He thoughtfully parked the monster truck by the racehorse stables, where its booming diesel would not disturb the slumber of the staff.

Starlitz and Khoklov walked across a groomed lawn, slick with peacock droppings. Massive sprinklers, purloined from a farm project, clanked and hissed above the croquet grounds. Starlitz paused to tie his shoe under the giant concrete statue of Lenin. Khoklov chased some monster goldfish away in the fountain, and drank from his hands.

Starlitz yanked a bell-pull at one of the back doors. There was no response. Starlitz kicked the door heartily with his tattered Keds high-top sneaker. Lights came on inside, and a butler showed, in pants and undershirt.

This man was not officially a "butler," but a production-team brigade leader for the collective farm. The distinction didn't mean much. The butler's name was Yan "Cross-Eyes" Rakotov. Rakotov, who was corpulent and scarred, favored the two of them with his eerie gaze. "Now what?" he said.

"Need some kerosene," Starlitz said.

"How much?"

"Maybe five hundred liters?" Starlitz said.

Rakotov showed no surprise. "Would gasoline do?" he said. Khoklov shook his head. Rakotov thought about it. "How about pure alcohol? I think we have enough to fill an airplane. Ever since the Kremlin's sobriety campaign started, we've been bringing it in by the truckload."

Rakotov's wife showed up, squint-eyed and clutching

her houserobe. "You bastard drunks!" she hissed. "*Shabashniki!* Buying booze at this time of night! Go home and let good Communists sleep in peace!"

"Shut up, woman," Rakotov said. "Look, this is pilot here."

"Oh," said Mrs. Rakotov, startled. "Sorry, Comrade Pilot! Would you like some nice tea? Did you bring any nylons?"

"Life is hard," Rakotov muttered. "I know the Boss keeps kerosene, but I think it's stored in town. He's in town now, you know. Political problems."

"Too bad," Starlitz said.

"Yes, he left this morning. Took the limousine, the kitchen bus, the cooks, his personal staff, even the live baby lamb for his lunch. He said not to expect him back for at least a week." Rakotov straightened. "So you two can regard me as the Boss here, for the time being."

"My people expect *me* back by morning!" Khoklov shouted. "There's going to be big trouble when I fail to show at the Kabul air base!"

Rakotov's giddy eyes narrowed. "Really? Why's that?"

"A military plane is not like one of your rural buses, comrade! There's no excuse for a failure to show up! And if I return too late, they'll know I have landed somewhere, illegally! The whole business here will be exposed!"

"That would be a terrible tragedy for a great many people," Rakotov said slowly. He cleared his throat. "Say . . . I just remembered something. We have an underground fuel cistern, in the east wing. Why don't you come with me, Comrade Pilot? We can inspect it."

"Good idea!" Starlitz broke in. "There's some empty jerry cans in the truck. Me and the ace here will fetch 'em. We'll be right back." He grabbed Khoklov's sleeve.

Khoklov came reluctantly across the darkened lawn. "Can't you wake up some local peasants, and have them do this haulage labor? They ought to do *something*; God knows they're not growing any food here."

Starlitz lowered his voice. "Wise up, ace. The east wing is a *dungeon*, man, a big underground bunker."

"But . . ." Khoklov hesitated. "You really think . . . ? But I'm a Red Army officer!"

"So what? The Boss has already got a State Farm chief in there, a personnel director, a couple of busybody snoops from Internal Affairs . . . He bottles up anybody he likes, and there's no appeal, no recourse—the guy runs everything. He's a top Party Moslem, man, the closest thing to Genghis Khan." Starlitz urged Khoklov up into the truck. "Think it over from their angle, ace. If you just vanish here, DRAAF will think you've been killed on duty. Hit by ack-ack, down somewhere in rough terrain. Nothing to tie you to the Boss, or Azerbaijan, or the black market."

"They'd put me in a dungeon?"

"They can't let you run around loose here—you're AWOL, with no residence passport. And you're Russian, too—you could never pass for a local."

"My God!" Khoklov put his head in his hands. "I'm done for!"

Starlitz threw the truck into gear. "How long have you *been* in the military, man? Show some initiative, for Christ's sake."

"What are you doing?" Khoklov said.

"Winging it," Starlitz said, driving off. "After all, there's a lotta possibilities." He thumbed over his shoulder. "We got a truckload of very heavy capital back there." He shifted his denim-clad butt on the busted springs of the truck seat. "And pretty soon you'll be officially dead, ace. That's kind of a neat thing to be, actually . . ."

"What's the point of this? What can we possibly accomplish, all by ourselves, out here?"

"Well, lemme think out loud," Starlitz said cheerily, taking a corner with a squeal. "We do have half a load of fuel in your plane; that's something, at least . . . Kabul's definitely out of range, but you could make Turkey, easy. There's a big NATO base in Kars, just over the border from Tbilisi. Maybe you could land there. The West would love to have an Ilyushin-14. It'd be the biggest haul for 'em since Lieutenant Belenko flew his MiG-25 to Japan."

"That's *treason*!" Khoklov shouted.

"Yeah, it is," Starlitz said indifferently. "And that's one tough border, too ... Not like Iran, y'know. You might pull a Matthias Rust on the way out, if you're a real hot-dog terrain flyer. But there's no way you're gonna get your crate past NATO."

"Don't insult me by questioning my professional abilities!" Khoklov said. "I could do it, easily enough! But I am a loyal Soviet officer, not a traitor to my Motherland like Viktor Ivanovich Belenko."

"I hear old Viktor's living somewhere near Washington now," Starlitz said. "Got big cars, blondes, whiskey ... But if that's not for you, it's fine with me, ace ..." Starlitz grinned toothily.

"The criminal life must be rotting your brain," Khoklov said, crossing his arms. His chin sank slowly into the white silk of his ascot. "Besides, they wouldn't let me *fly*, would they? The Yankees would never let me fly their best aircraft. An F-16, say. A Lockheed SR-71." His voice was reverent.

"You'd be rich, though," Starlitz said. "You could buy, like ... a Cessna, all for yourself."

Khoklov laughed harshly. "A civilian subsonic. No, thank you."

"I know how ya feel," Starlitz admitted. "Well, ace, we gotta find you your fuel. We got a chance, at least, if we can find the Boss. I'm gonna roll this baby into town."

The private police force at the border of the collective farm did not stop them. They were used to heavily loaded trucks leaving at odd hours. Starlitz slung the ZIL onto the neatly paved road. Through no accident, this was the best-maintained road in Azerbaijan. At this hour it was almost deserted. Starlitz ratcheted his manual accelerator up to top speed.

The road was lined for miles with elegant shade trees, a transplanted species unsuited to the local climate. The dead trees' peeling trunks zipped by in the headlights, their bare twigs ripped by the ZIL's backwash. Planting the trees had been an attractive idea, carried out with complete incompetence. The Boss wouldn't mind, however. Abject failure always made him redouble his efforts.

Khoklov looked jittery. He was having second thoughts. "Why are you doing this, Starlits?" he shouted over the blasting roar of the engine. "Why are you taking such trouble for my sake? I don't understand your motives."

Starlitz felt for a cigarette, speeding along one-handed. "I'm the *ground crew*, man. I handle the planes. That's my *function*."

"But won't you get in trouble for these actions? You could have let Rakotov put me in the prison. Destroy all evidence, and so forth."

Starlitz was disgusted. "That's no use. That won't make the plane *fly*, man."

"Oh," Khoklov said.

"The system must be maintained, ace." Starlitz lit up with a flick of the Cricket, his eyes glazed with eerie ontological assurance. "It's . . . what there *is*. As long as it lasts." He blew smoke.

"Right," Khoklov said uneasily. He put on his Walkman headphones and searched in his jacket for a cassette. Soon the reedy buzz of The Doors percolated out past his translucent, close-cropped ears.

They drove into the capital of Nagorno-Karabakh, the most miserable province of the Azerbaijani Soviet Socialist Republic. The town had never fully recovered from the Civil War of the twenties, or the purges of the thirties, or even the Great Patriotic War of the forties. Collapse had become the status quo.

Most of the townsfolk were Armenians, an ethnic group whom everyone else within thousands of kilometers delighted in oppressing. Thanks to Stalin, a big lump of lost Armenians had been caught here in the middle of Azerbaijan, like a Christian prune in a Moslem fruitcake. And here they were still, with their cruddy, flyspecked stores and beat-up, dusty churches, and cracked streets blocked off for "repair" for years at a time.

Starlitz drove his truck down an alley, through towering, overcrowded apartment blocks built of substandard concrete. Discarded protest signs crunched under the ZIL's monster tires. The plaza still stank of tear gas; empty canisters of it lay around like Schlitz cans after a beer bust. There were sticky patches of blood, and odd greenish lumps that were the manure of police horses.

A large and hideous government building, in Stalinesque fifties gingerbread, had been stoned by the mob. Shattered glass lay before its gaping windows, glinting in the headlights.

Starlitz drove on warily. The crowd had pulled a big ferroconcrete statue from its pedestal in the center of the plaza. After its sudden descent down to earth, the statue's stone head had broken into disenchanting rubble. Chunks of its face had been stolen, presumably as souvenirs.

"Wonder who that was?" Starlitz said. "That statue, I mean."

"Some local ruffian, no doubt," Khoklov said. He shook his head. "At heart, the People are still loyal to the Soviet ideals of the Party. It is only the provincial distortions of the economy that have provoked this ugly event."

"Oh," said Starlitz. "Good. For a minute I figured there was some kinda real trouble here."

"You mean, like an ethnic, nationalist mass movement, demanding self-determination and a devolution of centralized state power?" Khoklov said. "No, comrade; a serious political analysis will show that's not the true case at all. I'm sure that a measured restructuring of state resources, and a cautious but thorough redressing of their economic grievances, will soon lead the Armenians back to the path of socialist cooperation."

"Nice to know somebody still reads *Pravda*," Starlitz said. He brightened. "Look, ace, we're in luck. Here come some cops!"

An open-topped jeep came tearing across the plaza, crammed with uniformed local police in riot helmets. Khoklov went pale and shrank down in his seat, but Starlitz stopped the ZIL and climbed out.

The jeep screeched up short. A militia sergeant jumped out and menaced Starlitz with a riot baton. "Your papers!"

"Never mind that crap," Starlitz told him. "Where have you been? We've been waiting."

"What?" the sergeant said.

"This is a special shipment for the Boss," Starlitz said, pointing at the truck. "Aren't you our police escort?"

"No! What are you doing here at this hour?"

"Isn't it obvious?" Starlitz said. "I can't drive a black-market truck in broad daylight, through streets full of thieving, rioting Armenians! There've been enough delays in this shipment already! If you're not our special escort, then where the hell are they?"

"Everyone's doing overtime," the cop said wearily. "Perhaps we somehow lost track of our Party Chairman's whims. We're trying to keep order here. There's been confusion."

"Hell," Starlitz said, kicking at a pried-up cobblestone. "I'm gonna catch it for this ... Look, stop whatever you're doing, and take us straight to the Boss, okay? I'll make it worth your while. Come round to the back of the truck. Nobody'll miss a little off the top."

The sergeant grinned slowly. He waved the other

cops into the back of the ZIL. After some gleeful argument, they decamped with a video recorder and six bottles of J&B Scotch.

"You're robbing me," Starlitz complained.

The jeep led the way. This was useful, as it got them past the nervous police checkpoints around the Boss's urban headquarters.

Officially, this place was a Workers' Palace of Culture, built years ago for a puppet trade union of textile workers. The textile workers now existed only on paper, as the Azerbaijani cotton crops had been disastrous for years. The Boss had put the building to his own uses, and improved it considerably, with lavish use of stolen state materials and impressed labor. The Boss's five-story city palace looked like a diseased wedding cake, brilliantly lit and painted in ghastly pastels.

Inside the courtyard the palace grounds were clustered with the black limousines of Party notables. The Boss's customary caravan of brushed-aluminum tour buses was parked on the lawn, next to a gaily frilled pavilion with picnic tables and fire-blackened shish-kebab pits. It was very late, and a meeting was in the final throes of dissolution. Vomiting Azerbaijani bigwigs tottered to their limos, assisted by mistresses and functionaries.

Starlitz parked the ZIL atop a fragrant row of oleander bushes.

"What's going on here?" Khoklov said, staring in disbelief. "Some kind of *festival*?"

"Yeah." Starlitz looked at Khoklov critically. "Straighten up that tie you're wearing, or whatever it is." Starlitz leaned from the window to peer into the ZIL's rearview mirror. He scrubbed grease from his face with his sleeve, then licked his hand and smeared at his hair. "We gotta pass for Beautiful People, okay?" he said. "Smoke those Marlboros like you get 'em every day, and make sure everybody sees you've got a Walkman."

The double doors of the palace were propped wide open. Starlitz and Khoklov swaggered in boldly. They followed music to a ground-floor workers' gymnasium, refitted to mimic a ballroom. A homemade mirror-ball wobbled on the ceiling before a lighted stage with heavy canvas draperies. Small tables lined the walls under chintzy fake gas lamps with forty-watt reddish bulbs.

The band had played its final set; they were packing up their *bazoukis* and a brace of slotted microphones the size of bread loaves. The velvet sound of a smuggled Mel Tormé tape came from the speakers. Most of the Party bigwigs were already gone; there were a dozen tired teenage Armenian hookers, dance girls, sitting in a line of folding chairs. At the sight of Khoklov's air force jacket, and Starlitz's bogus Red Army get-up, they started chattering and elbowing each other.

A sinuous woman with dark, high-piled hair approached them across the dance floor. She wore sequined velvet trousers, high-heeled pumps, and a fancy embroidered jacket. Starlitz straightened warily.

"Oh," the woman said, smiling with a flash of pointed teeth. "So it's you. What a pleasant surprise."

Starlitz tried an ingratiating grin. "Good evening, Tamara Akhmedovna."

"I thought you two were soldiers," Tamara said. She fingered the lapel of Starlitz's secondhand Red Army jacket. "You shouldn't wear clothes like this into town. People will talk."

"Who is this charming lady?" Khoklov said.

"This is the Boss's wife, ace," Starlitz muttered. " 'The Sultana.' "

"Please!" Tamara said, dimpling. "No *friend* of mine calls me that. A simple 'Madame Party Chairman' will do . . ." Tamara's kohl-lined, liquid eyes studied Khoklov with languorous attention. "Who is this mysterious young man, and why is he dressed like an airman?"

"Uh, we had a little trouble down by the airstrip,

Tamara ... Could we have a word outside, or something?"

Tamara's face went flinty for a moment. "Very well," she said. "Wait here, while I see that the artistes are properly compensated ..." She drifted away.

"Good God!" Khoklov whispered, grabbing Starlitz's elbow. "She's beautiful! What's she doing married to that old ogre?"

"Tamara's the biggest black-market hustler in Azerbaijan," Starlitz said, brushing Khoklov's hand away. "Her husband does everything illegal in Tamara's name. She's got a million Moslem relatives; they're all on the take. They smuggle everything, from diamonds to bananas. They carry big, sharp knives, too. So keep your pants on."

Tamara returned, having fee'd off the musicians and hookers. "May I suggest a stroll in the garden?" she said, arching her brows. "The Bukhara roses are in bloom."

"That's swell," Starlitz said. They went outside, away from the palace's lavish inner network of listening devices. Starlitz made introductions.

"So you're our brave pilot?" Tamara said. "How nice to meet you. If it weren't for you, Captain, I wouldn't have this Final Net hair spray." She touched her coiffure. "It holds up even when I no longer can."

"Your hair does look lovely," Khoklov said. "And you speak such excellent Russian, too. It's a delight to the ear."

"Listen, Tamara," Starlitz broke in. "We need five hundred kilos of aviation kerosene. Old Cross-Eyes, back at the farm, said the Boss might have some."

"My husband is sleeping," Tamara said. "He's had a very trying day. All this political turmoil. He deserves his rest, poor dear."

"I must get fuel somehow, and fly back to Kabul tonight," Khoklov said. "If I don't, the sacrifice of my career is perhaps a small matter. But I'm afraid it might cause you some inconvenience."

"I'm sure I understand," Tamara nodded. "You were right to come to me, Captain Khoklov. We can't have our Kabul shipments disrupted. We'll need proper lavish gifts, to curry favor with the generals, now that the army's coming."

"The army, huh?" Starlitz said.

"They're invading tomorrow, to beat some sense into these ungrateful Christians," Tamara said. "My husband just announced the news to the Azerbaijan Party regulars, at our little business meeting here tonight. Everyone's delighted about the military crackdown. I think our troubles are over!"

"Hey, that's exciting news," Starlitz said. "We still need the fuel, though."

"Let me think," Tamara said. She touched her chin with one lacquered forefinger. "Aha! The military supply train. It's already here in town, prepared for the troops' arrival. I'm sure they wouldn't miss a few liters from their tank cars."

"That's great," Starlitz said. "I know the way to the railhead. We'll take the truck."

"You didn't bring the ZIL, did you?" Tamara gazed at the olive-drab bulk atop the crushed oleander bushes. "Oh dear, you did, didn't you?"

"Had to improvise," Starlitz said.

"We borrowed that Red Army truck from nice old General Akbarov, you know. We promised him that we wouldn't flaunt it around carelessly. People might talk."

"It's a problem," Starlitz admitted. "It's full of goodies, too. Coupla tons."

"Three tons!" Khoklov declared. "The choicest wares and viands of the Khyber caravans, fit for a czarina!"

"Now, now," said Tamara, favoring him with a smile. "We're simple servants of the People, Captain, doing what we can to keep our homeland prosperous, under very trying conditions . . . It's a pity you didn't come earlier. Your cargo would have made nice Party favors."

Tamara made a quick decision. "I'll have the servants—I mean the *service personnel*—unload the truck, here at our City Palace. There's plenty of storage room in our basement. And we'll take one of my husband's buses down to the train station, to get your fuel. I'm sure it won't take long."

Starlitz widened his eyes. "Great! I always wanted to drive one of those special buses."

Starlitz and Khoklov stacked the empty jerry cans into the back of the bus, while Tamara made arrangements. Soon they were in the bus together, behind a vast windshield expanse of smoked glass. Starlitz seized the driver's seat and gleefully fired the engine. Khoklov sat in the passenger's side, behind a bulky radiotelephone set. Tamara sat cross-legged between them, on a flat vinyl couch, which led, behind her, to a vast plush-padded nest with cozy bunk beds, brocade curtains, and a kitchenette. The bus reeked pleasantly of hashish and shish-kebab.

Starlitz rolled it smoothly out of the compound. "Now, don't show off," Tamara chided. "I know you're a very good driver, but don't scratch my husband's nice machine, or he'll shout at me."

"Can't have that," Starlitz said, spinning the wheel one-handed. He grinned. "This is living, though, isn't it, ace? We can drive anywhere in the province, at any speed we like, and no one will dare to touch us! Everybody knows this bus belongs to the Party Chairman. What a great setup!"

"You're a rascal," Tamara said. "You shouldn't talk like that; people listen, you know. You'll have to forgive him, Comrade Captain."

"Please," Khoklov said. "Call me Pulat Romanevich."

Tamara gazed limpidly out the windshield as they rolled past a long concrete-block wall splattered with angry Armenian graffiti. "Come now," she said softly. "We scarcely know each other, Captain."

"I'm a lonely warrior far from home," Khoklov told her. "If I seem too bold, forgive me. Friendship comes quickly in wartime. It's how we pilots live, you see. A flyer never knows if he will greet the dawn."

"Oh yes," Tamara mused. "There is a war on, isn't there?"

"My next assignment will be bombing bandit camps over the Pakistani border," Khoklov said. " 'Unofficially,' of course."

"That's a tough one," Starlitz nodded. "Some of those refugees have guns."

"It's nothing," Khoklov scoffed. "In the Panjgur Valley, they fire *down* onto the planes, from high on their mountainsides. And you must fly low, because the bandits hide their huts in little crevices."

Khoklov showed Tamara a gold-rimmed mission patch. "I got this one for the Panjgur campaign. The bandits there stopped nine different ground assaults: tanks, artillery, infantry columns . . . Finally we air boys stepped in. Just flattened the place, you see; there was nothing left, so resistance stopped."

"What about this patch?" Tamara said, touching his sleeve.

"That was the siege of Herat," Khoklov said. "The bandits there were total fanatics! We had to carpet-bomb half the city before we could save it."

"I can see that you love to flirt with danger," Tamara said.

Slowly, Khoklov smiled. "I'm a career officer, with close ties to the KGB. I'm a political liaison with the Afghan Air Force. It's a very . . . *special* kind of game."

Tamara's eyes sparkled. "What was the most *dangerous* thing that ever happened to you?"

"Ah," Khoklov said, "that would be the time a Chinese heat-seeker hit my aft engine in the Wakhan Corridor . . . I almost nursed my bird back to Bagram Air Base, but I had to hit the silk in bandit territory. After

three days in the wilderness, a Spetsnaz ranger team
picked me up with their helicopter gunship . . ." Khoklov
suavely lit a Marlboro and gazed dramatically out the
window. "I wouldn't want you to think it's something
special, Tamara. For us, it's a job, that's all; our socialist
duty. Those Spetsnaz rangers, the elite black berets . . .
now, those sons of bitches are what I call brave men! I
owe them my life, you know."

Khoklov felt inside his pocket. "They were good
friends. One of them gave me this souvenir . . . oh hell,
you've got it now."

"Yeah," Starlitz said. "And I've been meaning to ask
you about that jacket you're wearing, Tamara Akhmedovna. It's really beautiful."

"This?" Tamara said, spreading her arms. "Just a little homemade nothing."

"That's actually a black Levi's jean jacket, imported
from the West, right?" Starlitz said. "Only, it's been lined
with virgin wool, it's got a tanned sheepskin collar, and
somebody—somebody really good with a needle—has
blind-stitched an embroidery picture of a combine har-
vester across the back."

"That's right," Tamara said, surprised. "Plus a little
group of cheerful peasants with their sickles. It was a
socialist-realist poster, you see, from one of the collectivi-
zation campaigns . . . My husband came up through the
Agriculture Bureau. It was a little gift to us from some
grateful villagers."

"Wow," Starlitz said, reaching into his pocket. "I'd
really like to have that. Can we do business?"

"I do business," Tamara said with dignity. "But I'm
also the wife of the Party Chairman. I don't have to sell
the clothes off my back!"

"Yeah, I know that, but . . ." Starlitz began. "How
about if—"

"Turn here," Tamara commanded.

They had reached the railway. The place was black as

pitch. "Oh dear," Tamara said. "I wish they'd do something about these power failures. I can't go walking out there in these heels."

"And I don't know the territory," Khoklov said quickly.

"Yeah, yeah, I get the point," Starlitz said. He opened the door reluctantly, saddened to leave the driver's seat. "Well, there's bound to be somebody out there I can hustle. I'll be back later for the jerry cans."

"Maybe there's a flashlight," Tamara said, sliding lithely into the back of the bus. "If I can find it, we'll come after you."

"I'll help her look," Khoklov said.

"Sure, sure," Starlitz said.

He walked off into darkness, pebbles crunching under his sneakers. The smells were promising: hot brake oil, raw whiffs of petrochemical stench. Starlitz pulled his Cricket lighter, twisted it, and flicked the switch. A six-inch butane jet flared up. Starlitz lit a Marlboro at arm's length, and found his way up a concrete ramp to the loading docks.

A series of yellow-stencilled tank cars had been parked on a siding. Quick flashes of the lighter guided him.

Starlitz felt his way to the tank car's gigantic manual faucet. It wouldn't budge. Starlitz took a few deep breaths, then crouched down and wrenched a railroad spike from a tie with his bare fingers. He whacked enthusiastically at the tap, with earsplitting clanks and thuds. No dice.

A red railroad lantern came swaying down the line. Starlitz ducked under a freight car, clutching his spike. As the guard crept past, Starlitz recognized him. He crept out and tapped the man's shoulder.

The guard whirled with a yelp. "Be cool," Starlitz said. "It's me, man."

"Comrade Starlits!" the guard said.

"I thought you were on strike, Vartan," Starlitz said, tossing his spike.

"I'm on strike from my *illegal* job, unloading the Boss's black-market airplanes," the Armenian said. He was still jittery; his eyes rolled a little under their corduroy cap brim. "But my *legal* job here, as a railroad guard, is too vital to neglect!"

"You mean you can't give up stealing from freight cars," Starlitz said.

"Well, yes," Vartan admitted. "But if I didn't steal freight, I couldn't stay in the black market." He shrugged unhappily.

"Get real," Starlitz said, dusting his hands. "Everyone's in the black market. That's the beauty of the system."

Vartan cleared his throat uneasily. "It wasn't my idea to strike, you know," he said. "It was Hovanessian's."

"He's the skinny kid in the crew, with the glasses, right? The smart one?"

"The stupid one," Vartan said. "Always talking 'openness' and 'restructuring.' Calls himself a 'dissident' and leads protests in the street. He's a big pain in the ass."

"Lemme guess," Starlitz said. "He's the one who had the bright idea to steal our kerosene from the hangar."

"That's right."

"And it's all in empty vodka bottles now, with rags stuffed on top of it. Hidden in basements and attics. Belonging to Hovanessian and his radical nationalist pals."

"It's no use hiding anything from you, Comrade Starlits," Vartan said. "Yes, Hovanessian wants to fight. Any weapon is useful, he said. Even the famous flaming cocktails of former Minister Molotov."

"Yeah?" Starlitz said. "He's gonna match his little busted bottles against these big Red Army tank cars?"

Vartan smirked. "None of us want to fight soldiers. We're all good Soviets; ask anybody! The son-of-a-bitch Moslem ragheads are the real problem."

"Think so, huh?"

"They breed like rats. They're taking over everything! A whole swarm of them moved into the house next door, right into a Christian neighborhood. It's intolerable!" Vartan glowed with righteous determination. "Besides, the Red Army won't hurt *us*. They're used to killing Moslems. They're on *our* side, really."

"There's gonna be a crackdown," Starlitz told him. "Or a big crack-up . . . I'm not sure yet, but I can smell it coming. The system here is gonna blow." His words hung on the empty air. Starlitz scratched his bristled head and smirked, with a scary parody of candor. "I know what I'm talking about," he muttered. "I got a definite *feel* for this kind of situation."

Vartan shuffled his feet, which were clad in boots soled with folded newspapers. "I'm sure you do, Comrade Starlits! Although your role in the Boss's operation is humble, all your Armenian subordinates greatly respect your insight and political perspicacity."

"Knock it off with that crap!" Starlitz said. He frowned. "Listen to me. When your real trouble comes, it's gonna be serious news, pal. Not at all like you think."

Vartan blinked unhappily. "Life is hard," he said at last. "I'm not asking for miracles, comrade. All I really want, is to see my neighbor's house burn down." Vartan spread his hands modestly. "It wouldn't take very much, would it? Just lob in a few flaming bottles, some dark night . . . It's worth a try."

"You ever try to burn a house down before?" Starlitz said. "You'll burn down your own house, man."

"I thought *my* Russian was bad," Vartan scoffed. "I didn't say *my* house; I said *his* house." Vartan drew a breath. "We Armenians have had it, that's all. I'm a regular guy; I'm no egghead dissident. But we're gonna settle some scores here, once and for all. The old-fashioned way."

Vartan kicked the tank car viciously. "So just forget

about our little theft from the Boss's air strip. Here's all the fuel you need, right here. I'll steal it for you; you can take all you want. Just take it away, and forget you saw me here."

"Better think it over," Starlitz said.

Vartan narrowed his eyes. "Look, you're no red-blooded Armenian either, Comrade Straw Boss. You're a Tadjik, right? Or an Uzbek or something . . ."

Vartan stopped suddenly, surprised. An odd subliminal chill had entered the air. There was a faint, sullen, almost inaudible rumble. The railway cars rocked and squeaked on their axles.

Starlitz, his eyes alert, was balanced on the balls of his feet. He rolled a little from side to side, his knees bent, his hands hanging loose and open. "D'you *feel* that, man?"

Vartan shook his head. "It was nothing . . . just the rail settling. Some of the ties are rotten."

Starlitz looked at him. "Have it your way," he said at last. "I'll be back soon with some jerry cans."

Starlitz trotted back to the bus. He climbed into the driver's seat and started the engine. "You guys okay?" Starlitz said. Subdued giggling came from the back of the bus, and the springy crunching of a bunk.

Starlitz sighed. "Either of you feel the earth move, just a while ago?"

"Don't make bad jokes," Tamara chided.

"Okay," Starlitz shrugged. "We're gonna roll now."

He drove the bus along the rail line until he found the proper siding. He parked the bus and started ferrying jerry cans.

Vartan had opened the tap with a pry bar. Kerosene was dribbling steadily. The rails beneath the tank were already dark and slick with it. "You're wasting fuel," Starlitz said.

"So what?" Vartan said. "This is a whole tank car."

"It's splashing over everything," Starlitz said.

"You think the *army's* gonna put it to better use?"

Starlitz ferried filled cans to the back of the bus. "That fuel really stinks," Khoklov complained. "I hope you're almost done, Starlits."

"Close," Starlitz said.

"Burn some more hashish," Tamara suggested. "That Afghani brick smells lovely."

"I lost the matches," Khoklov said. "Throw me your lighter, Starlits."

Starlitz tossed him the Cricket. Khoklov thumbed it and shrieked as the flame jetted out. "Christ! Cut in the after-burner," he said. Tamara laughed.

"Gimme some of that," Starlitz said. Khoklov appeared from the darkness, in his ribbed Christian Dior undershirt. He passed Starlitz a fist-sized clod of hash.

When Starlitz had filled the last can, he gave the hash to the Armenian. "It's for your trouble," he said. "Don't smoke it on the job, okay?"

"Stop worrying," Vartan said, pocketing it.

"Here's a lighter," Starlitz said. "Be real careful with it."

"You must think I'm an idiot," Vartan said. He was struggling with the broken tank-car tap. It had been stripped somehow; it refused to shut off.

Starlitz drove away. "Well, ace, I told you we'd manage," he said. "What do you say, Tamara Akhmedovna? Do we drop you off at the Palace of Culture, or do we head straight for the airstrip?"

"If you think I'll let you drive this bus all by yourself, you must be more stoned than I am," Tamara said. "Open some windows, darling. That kerosene reeks."

"It's kind of a mess back there at the railhead," Starlitz said. "Had to smash and grab. Not too subtle."

"Drive fast, then, and drive to the farm," Tamara said. "Anyway, I'm not through consoling this Soviet hero yet." She laughed giddily. "Whoa! What a shiver! I think those pills are coming on . . . What did you call those?"

"Dexedrine," Khoklov said. "For combat alertness."

"And you say the *air force* gives you these?" Tamara said. "My! I think I *know* some people in the air force. They've been keeping secrets."

"Oh, not us air boys," Khoklov said. "We're as clear and simple as the day is long."

"Everyone has secrets," Tamara protested gaily. "Even the chauffeur. Tell Captain Khoklov some of your secrets, Lekhi Starlits!"

"Gimme a break," Starlitz said.

"You know where we found this man?" Tamara said. "In prison. The Soviet border guards had caught him trying to sneak into Iran!"

"Holy mother," Khoklov said, interested. "*Why?*"

"Smuggling gig," Starlitz said reluctantly. "Had some business friends there . . . trying to smuggle rock and roll into the country. The mullahs shoot people for possession of rock. Makes music worth a lot."

"Oh, I love rock and roll!" Khoklov enthused. "Especially Yankee music from the sixties. It really speaks to my groovy soul, when I'm strafing a village . . . What kind of rock music was it, exactly?"

"I dunno, man. Stuff I got cheap. Cowsills, Carpenters, Bobby Goldsboro . . ."

"I never heard of those," Khoklov said, crestfallen.

"Ask him about his money," Tamara prodded. "He always has a roll of hundred-dollar bills. Even in prison he had it! You can strip him naked and burn his clothes, and next day he just reaches into his pocket, and there it is again!"

"You're stoned," Khoklov protested. "If he can do that, why didn't you just shoot him?"

"We wanted to at first, but he's too useful," Tamara said. "He's the best mechanic we've ever had here in Azerbaijan. It's a weird ability he has—he can fix anything! We just give him some wires and screws, and maybe some oil and a jack-knife, and even rusty old wrecks start running again. Sometimes he just *stands next* to a machine, and *frowns* at it, and it gets better right away! Isn't that so, Lekhi?"

"It's no big deal," Starlitz muttered. "She's putting you on, ace."

"I know that," Khoklov said indulgently. "She talks just like Scheherazade. It's charming."

"No, it's true!" Tamara said. "That's exactly how he is! I'm not kidding, you know." There was a leaden silence. Tamara laughed gaily. "But it doesn't matter, really. I don't care if you believe me or not! We don't care *how* strange he is, as long as he belongs to us."

It was almost dawn when they reached the airstrip. They fueled the plane as quickly as they could. Even Tamara helped.

Khoklov helped Starlitz move the paint ladder to the cockpit. "I'll have to tell them I had engine trouble, and was forced to fly very slowly. To stay aloft so long, and still return safely to base—I think I just performed a superhuman feat of aviation!" Khoklov chuckled and elbowed Starlitz in the ribs. "Just like one of your so-called miracles, eh, Comrade Starlits? It's amazing what nontechnical people will believe."

"Sure," Starlitz muttered. "Whatever works, man."

Khoklov climbed up into the cockpit. "I'll die happy now, Tamara," he shouted. "Save a place for me in one of those black-market cemetery plots." He slid the cockpit shut.

Starlitz started the tractor and expertly backed the Ilyushin-14 out of its hangar and onto the runway. He decoupled and drove back to the hangar.

Tamara stood at the hangar gate, her arms folded, watching the spyplane climb. "Russians are so morbid," she said. "He's a very sweet boy, for KGB, but I don't trust him in our business. He's got Death written all over him." She shivered, and buttoned her jacket. "Besides, he might brag about me ... Get rid of him for me, Lekhi, there's a dear. Tell my husband that Captain Khoklov has a bad attitude. We'll find ourselves a different pilot. Someone who hasn't killed more people than I can count."

"Okay," Starlitz said.

"Why doesn't daylight come?" Tamara said. "Those pills of his are making me really nervous. Am I talking too much? This is a spooky hour, isn't it? Predawn. 'Predawn attack,' that's what they always say in the newspapers. 'Predawn arrest.' Policemen love this time of day."

"You're wired," Starlitz told her. "Let's get in the bus. I'll drive you back to town."

"All right. That might be best." They got back inside the bus. Starlitz threw it into gear and hit the gas.

They drove off. Out in a stubbled field, a large flock of crows was skirling about in confusion, cawing. They seemed reluctant to light on the earth.

Tamara fidgeted. She stuck her hands into the pockets of her jacket. Surprised, she pulled one out. It was full of foil-wrapped condoms.

"Oh look," she said. "He left me these. What a sweet gesture."

"That's a great jacket," Starlitz said.

"It's mine," she said irritably. "*Mine*, understand? I don't own much, you know. I just manage things, because of my husband's office. There's no security for us. Only power. And our power could all go, couldn't it? There've been purges before. So I don't want to bargain with the clothes on my back. Like I was some kind of labor-camp *zek*."

"I've got dollars," Starlitz wheedled.

She frowned. "Look, my jacket wouldn't even *fit* you. You must be crazy."

"I want it anyway," Starlitz said. "I'll be generous. Come on."

"You're very weird," Tamara said suddenly. "You're from America, aren't you?"

Starlitz grinned broadly. "Don't be silly."

"Only Americans throw dollars around for no sane reason."

"Easy come, easy go," Starlitz shrugged. "C'mon, Tamara, let's do business."

"Are you CIA—is that it? If you are, why don't you go spy on Shevardnadze, or something? Go to Moscow and bother real Russians."

"Shevardnadze's a Georgian," Starlitz said. "Anyway, I like it right here. The local situation's really interesting. I want to see what happens when it comes apart."

"You *must* be an American, because you're making me feel really *paranoid*!" Tamara shouted. "I have an awful feeling something really bad is about to happen! I'm going to call my husband on this radio. I need to know what's going on! I don't care what you are, but just shut up and keep driving! That's an order!"

She tried to raise the palace. There was no answer.

"Try the military band," Starlitz suggested.

The military wavelengths were crackling with traffic.

"Sounds like some of those 'predawn raids' you were talking about," Starlitz said, interested. "They're a little behind schedule, I guess." The sun was just rising. Starlitz killed the headlights. The bus topped a hill.

A long line of civilian cars was approaching the Estate.

Tamara dropped the microphone in horror. "Look at those cars!" she said, staring through the tinted windshield. "Only one kind of stupid cop drives around disguised in those stupid brown sedans! It's the DCMSP!"

"Which cops are those, exactly?" Starlitz asked.

"Department to Combat the Misappropriation of Socialist Property," Tamara said. "They've never dared to come near here before . . . They're the income people, the accountants, the nastiest little cops there are. Once they get their teeth in you, it's all over!"

Starlitz drove past the convoy. The brown cars, with

their packed, burr-headed Russian accountants, sped on without a pause.

"They're not trying to stop this bus," he said. "They didn't recognize it."

"They're not from Azerbaijan. We bribed all the locals. They're outside people," Tamara said. "These cops are Gorbachev's!" She slammed her fist against the window. "He's betrayed us! Stabbed us in the back! That hypocrite bastard! Where does his wife get those fancy furs and shoes, I wonder!"

"Earned 'em with her salary as an art historian," Starlitz said.

Tamara wiped bitterly at her kohl-smeared eyes. "It's so unfair! All we wanted was a decent life here! Those stupid Russians: they have a system that would make a donkey laugh, and now they want to *purify* it! God, I hate them!"

"What do you wanna do now?" Starlitz said. "Go back and stand 'em off on your doorstep?"

"No," she said grimly. "We'll have to bend to the almighty wind from Moscow. We'll wait, though, and we'll be back, as soon as they give up trying. It won't take long. The new god will fail."

"Okay, good," Starlitz said. "In the meantime, I'll just keep driving. I love this bus. It's great."

"Gorbachev won't dare try us publicly," Tamara said, gnawing one nail. "I'll bet they simply retire my husband. Maybe even *promote* him. Some post that's safe and completely meaningless. Like Environment, or Consumer Affairs."

"Yeah," Starlitz said. "This is the new era, right? They won't shoot Party bosses. Makes the Politburo nervous."

"That's right," Tamara said.

"But it's gonna be tough on your underlings. The people with no big-time strings to pull."

Tamara arched her brows. "Oh well . . . most of

them are lousy Armenians anyway. Born thieves . . . we were always careful to hire Armenians whenever we could."

Starlitz nodded. "Well, I held up my end of the system," he said. "Got the plane launched. Got the job done. The rest of it's not my lookout." He pulled over to the side of the road with a gentle hiss of airbrakes. "Looks like we part company here. So long, Tamara. It's been real."

She stared at him. "This is my bus!"

"Not any more. Sorry."

She was stunned for a moment. Then her face went bleak. "You can't get away with this, you know. The police will stop you. There will be roadblocks."

"It's gonna be *chaos*," Starlitz said. "The cops will have their hands full, or I miss my guess. But the cops won't stop the chairman's bus—old habits don't die that quick. So I'll just wing it. Improvise." Starlitz rubbed his stubbled chin. "I'll dress up as a paramedic, I guess. Get a Red Cross armband. Nobody stops rescue workers, not when there's really big trouble."

"I'm not leaving my bus!" Tamara said, grabbing the armrest. "You can't do this to me!"

Starlitz reached behind his back and produced the Afghan pistol. "Just a technicality," he said, not bothering to point it at her. "Open the door and get out, okay?"

Tamara got out. She stood at the muddy side of the road in her high heels. The bus drove off.

Seconds ticked by.

A brutal tide of shock coursed through the landscape. Trees whipped at the air; the earth rippled. Tamara was knocked from her feet. She clutched at the roadside as a deep, subterranean rumble seeped up through her hands and knees.

The bus stopped dead, fishtailing. She saw it sway and rattle on its shocks, until the tremor slowed, and, finally, came to a grinding end.

Then the bus turned and raced back toward her. Tamara got to her feet, trembling, wiping mechanically at the mud on her hands.

Starlitz pulled over. He opened the door and leaned out. "I forgot the jacket," he said.

ARE YOU
FOR 86?

Leggy Starlitz emerged from behind cool smoked glass to the raucous screeching of seagulls. Hot summer sun glinted fiercely off the Pacific. The harbor smelled of tar, and of poorly processed animal fats from an urban sewage-treatment outlet.

"Hell of a place for a dope deal," Starlitz observed.

Mr. Judy hopped lithely out of the van. Mr. Judy was a petite blonde with long pale schoolgirl braids; the top of her well-scrubbed scalp, which smelled strongly of peppermint and wintergreen, barely came to Starlitz's shoulder. Starlitz nevertheless took a cautious half-step out of her way.

Vanna, in khaki shorts and a Hawaiian blouse, leaned placidly against the white hull of the van, which bore the large chromed logo of an extinct televangelist satellite-TV empire. She dug into a brown paper bag of trail mix and began munching.

"It's broad daylight, too," Starlitz grumbled. He plucked sunglasses from a velcro pocket of his cameraman's vest, and jammed the shades onto his face. He scanned the harbor's parking lot with paranoiac care. Not much there: a couple of yellow taxis, three big-wheeled yuppie pickups with Oregon plates, a family station wagon. "What the hell kind of connection is this guy?"

"The Wolverine's got a very good rep," Mr. Judy said. She wore a white college jersey, and baggy black pants with drawstrings at the waist and ankles. Tarred gravel crunched under the cloth soles of her size-four kung-fu shoes as she examined a Mexican cruise ship through a dainty pair of Nikon binoculars.

Half a dozen sun-wrinkled, tottering oldsters, accompanied by wheeled luggage trolleys, were making their way down the pier to dry land and the customs shed.

Starlitz snorted skeptically. "This place is nowhere! If Wolverine's a no-show, are you gonna let me call the Polynesians?"

"No way," Mr. Judy told him.

Vanna nodded. She shook the last powdery nuggets of trail mix into her pale, long-fingered palm, ate them, then folded the paper bag neatly and stuck it in the top of her hiking boot.

"C'mon," Starlitz protested. "We can do whatever we want out here, now that we're on the road. Let's do it the smart way, for once. Nobody's looking."

Mr. Judy shook her head. "The New Caledonians are into *armed struggle*, they want *guns*. The commune doesn't *deal* guns."

"But the Polynesians have much better product," Starlitz insisted. "It's not Mexican homebrew crap like Wolverine's, this is actual no-kidding RU-486 right out of legitimate French drug-labs. Got the genuine industrial logos on the ampules and everything."

Mr. Judy lowered her Nikons in exasperation. "So what? We're not making commercials about the stuff. Hell, we're not even trying to clear a profit."

"Yeah, yeah, politically correct," Starlitz said irritably. "Well, the French are testing *dirty nuke explosives* in the South Pacific, in case you haven't been reading your Greenpeace agitprop lately. And the Caledonian rebel front stole a bunch of French RU-486 and want to *give* these pills to us. They're an insurgent Third-World colonial ethnic minority. Hell, all they want is a few lousy Vietnam-era M-16s and some ammo. You can't *get* more politically correct than a deal like that."

"Look, I've *seen* your Polynesians, and they're a clique of patriarchal terrorists," Mr. Judy said. "Let 'em put a woman on their central committee, then maybe I'll get impressed."

Starlitz grunted.

Mr. Judy sniffed in disdain. "You're just pissed-off because we wouldn't move that arsenal you bought in Las Vegas."

Vanna broke in. "You oughta be glad we're letting you keep *guns* on our property, Leggy."

"Yeah, Vanna, thanks a lot for nothing."

Vanna chided him with a shake of her shaggy brown head. "At least you know that your, uhm . . . your *armament* . . ." She searched for words. "It's all really safe with us. Right? Okay?"

Starlitz shrugged.

"Have a nice cold guava fizz," Vanna offered sweetly. "There's still two left under the ice in the cooler."

Starlitz said nothing. He sat on the chromed bumper and deliberately lit a ginseng cigarette.

"I wonder how a heavy operator like Wolverine ended up with all these retirees," Mr. Judy said, lowering her binocs. "You think the parabolic mike can pick up any conversation from on board?"

"Not at this range," Starlitz said.

"How about the scanner? Ship-to-shore radio?"

"Worth a try," Starlitz said, brightening. He slid into the driver's seat and began fiddling with a Korean-made broadband scanner, rigged under the dashboard.

An elderly woman with a luggage trolley descended the pier to the edge of the parking lot. She took off a large woven-straw sun-hat and waved it above her head. *"Yoo-hoo!"*

Vanna and Mr. Judy traded looks.

"Yoo-hoo! You girls, you with the van!"

"Mother of God," Mr. Judy muttered. She flung her braids back, climbed into the passenger seat. "We gotta roll, Leggy!"

Starlitz looked up sharply from the scanner's elliptical green readouts and square yellow buttons. "You drive," he said. He worked his way back, between the cryptic ranks of electronic equipment lining both walls of the van, then crouched warily behind the driver's seat. He yanked a semi-automatic pistol from within his vest, and slid a round into the chamber.

Mr. Judy drove carefully across the gravel and pulled up beside the woman from the cruise ship. The stranger had blue hair, orthopedic hose, a flowered sundress. Her trolley sported a baby-blue Samsonite case, a handbag, and a menagerie of Mexican stuffed animals: neon-green and fuchsia poodles, a pair of giant toddler-sized stuffed pandas.

Mr. Judy rolled the tinted window down. "Yes ma'am?" she said politely.

"Can you take me to a hotel?" the woman said. She lowered her voice. "I need—*a room of my own*."

"We can take you to the lighthouse," Mr. Judy countersigned.

"Wonderful!" the woman said, nodding. "So very nice to make this rendezvous . . . Well, it's all here, ladies." She waved triumphantly at her trolley.

"You're 'Wolverine'?" Vanna said.

"Yes I am. Sort of." Wolverine smiled. "You see, three of the women in my study-group have children attending Michigan University . . ."

"Maybe we better pat her down anyway, Jude," Starlitz said. "She's got room for a couple of frag grenades in that handbag."

Wolverine lifted a pair of horn-rimmed bifocals on a neck chain and peered through the driver's window.

She seemed surprised to see Starlitz. "Hello, young man."

"*Que tal?*" Starlitz said in resignation, putting his pistol away.

"*Muy bien, señor, y usted?*"

"Get her luggage, Leggy," Mr. Judy said. "Vanna, you better let Sister Wolverine sit in the passenger seat."

Vanna got out and helped Wolverine into the front of the van. Starlitz, his mouth set in a line of grim distaste, hurled the stuffed animals into the back.

"Be careful," Wolverine protested, "those are for my grandchildren! The pills are in the middle, hidden in the stuffing."

Vanna deftly ripped a seam open and burrowed into the puffed-polyester guts of a panda. She pulled out a shining wad of contraband and gazed at it with interest. "Where'd you find Saran Wrap in Cancún?"

"Oh, I always carry Saran Wrap, dear," said Wolverine, fastening her shoulder harness. "That, and nylon net."

"Lemme drive," Starlitz demanded, at the door. Mr. Judy nodded and crept lithely into the back, where she sat cross-legged on the rubber-matted aisle between the bolted-down racks of equipment. Vanna slammed the van's back door from the inside, locked it, and sat on Wolverine's Samsonite suitcase.

Starlitz threw the van into gear. "Where you wanna go?" he said.

"Bus station, please," Wolverine said.

"Great. No problem." Starlitz began humming. He loved driving.

Mr. Judy broke the sutures on a lime-green poodle and removed another neatly wrapped bundle of abortifacient pills. "Great work, Wolverine. You been doing this long?"

"Not long enough to get caught," Wolverine said. She removed her bifocals, and patted her powdered chin and forehead with a neatly folded linen handkerchief. " 'Wolverine' will be somebody else, next time. Don't expect to see *me* again, thank you very much."

"We appreciate your brave action, sister," Mr. Judy said formally. "Please convey our very best regards to your study-group." She rose to her knees and extended her hand. Wolverine turned clumsily in her seat and shook Mr. Judy's hand warmly.

"This certainly is an odd vehicle," Wolverine said, peering at the blinking lights and racks of switches. "You're not really Christian evangelists, are you?"

"Oh no, we're Goddess pagans," Mr. Judy declared, carefully disemboweling another poodle. "Our associate Leggy here bought this van at an auction. After Six Flags Over Jesus went bust in the rape scandal. We just use it for cover."

"It rather worried me," Wolverine confessed. "My friends told me to watch out carefully for any church groups. They might be right-to-lifers." She glanced warily at Starlitz. "They also said that if I met any tough-looking male hippies, they were probably drug enforcement people."

"Not me," Starlitz demurred. "All D.E.A. guys have pony-tails and earrings."

"What do you do with all these machines? Are those computers?"

"It's telephone equipment," Mr. Judy said cheerfully. "You may have heard of us—I mean, besides our health-and-reproductive services. People call us the Pheminist Phone Phreaks."

"No," Wolverine said thoughtfully, "I hadn't heard."

"We're do-it-yourself telephone operators. My hacker handle is 'Mr. Judy,' and this is 'Vanna.' "

"How do you do?" Wolverine said. "So you young ladies really know how to operate all this machinery? That certainly is impressive."

"Oh, it's real simple," Mr. Judy assured her. "This is

our fax machine ... That big noisy thing is the battery power unit. This one, with the fake mahogany console, is our voice-mail system ... And this one, the off-white gizmo with the peach trim, runs our satellite dish."

"It's the *uplink*," Starlitz said, deeply pained. "*Don't* call it 'the gizmo with peach trim.' "

"And these are home computers with modem phone-links," Mr. Judy said, ignoring him. "This one is running our underground bulletin board service. We run a 900 dial-up service with this one: it has the voice generator, and a big hard worm."

"Hard *disk*. WORM *drive*," Starlitz groaned.

"You know what a *bridge* is?" Vanna said. "That's a conference call, when sisters from out-of-state can all relate together." She smiled sweetly. "And you bill it to, like, a really big stupid corporation. Or a U.S. Army base!"

Mr. Judy nodded vigorously. "We do a lot of that! Maybe you'd like to join us on a phone-conference, sometime soon."

"Isn't that *illegal*?" Wolverine asked.

"We think of it as 'long-distance liberation,' " Mr. Judy said.

"We certainly do use plenty of long-distance phone service in my group," Wolverine said, intrigued. "Mostly we charge it to the foundation's SPRINT card, though ..."

"You're nonprofit? 501(c)(3)?"

Wolverine nodded.

"That's really good activist tactics, getting foundation backing," Mr. Judy said politely. "But we can hack all the SPRINT codes you want, right off our Commodore."

"Really?"

"It's easy, if you're not afraid to experiment," Vanna said brightly. "I mean, they're just phones. Phones can't hurt you."

"And this is a cellular power-booster," Mr. Judy said, affectionately patting an oblong box of putty-colored high-

impact plastic. "It's wonderful! The phone companies install them in places like tunnels, where you can't get good
phone reception from your carphone. But if you know
where to find one of these for yourself, then you can lib-
erate it, and re-wire it. So now, this is our own little portable cellular phone-station. It patches right into the phone
network, but it doesn't show up on their computers at all,
so there's never any bills!"

"How do you afford all these things?" Wolverine
asked.

"Oh, that's the best part," Mr. Judy said, "the whole
operation pays for itself! I'll show you. Just listen to this!"

Mr. Judy typed briefly on the keyboard of a Commodore, pausing as Starlitz forded a pothole. Then she hit a
return key, and twisted an audio dial. A fist-sized audio
speaker, trailing a flat rainbow-striped cord, emitted a
twittering screech. Then a hesitant male voice, lightly
scratched with static, filled the van.

". . . just don't like men anymore," the voice complained.

"Why don't you *think* they *like* you?" a silky, breathy
voice responded. "Does it have something to do with the
money?"

"It's not the money, I tell you," the man whined. "It's
AIDS. Men are poisonous now." His voice shook. "It's all
so different nowadays."

"*Why* is it all so different?"

"It's because cum is poisonous. That's the real truth,
isn't it?" The man was bitter suddenly, demanding. "You
can die just from touching cum! I mean, every chick I ever
knew in my life was kind of scared of that stuff . . . But
now it's a hundred times worse."

"*I'm* not afraid of you," the voice soothed. "You can
tell me *anything*."

"Well, that's what's so different about you," the man
told the voice unconvincingly. "But goddamn Linda—
remember I was telling you about Linda? She acted like it
was *napalm* or something . . ."

Mr. Judy turned the dial down. "This guy's a customer of ours; he's talking on one of our 900 lines, and he's paying a buck per minute on his credit card."

Vanna examined another console. "It's a VISA card. On a savings-and-loan from Colorado. Equifax checkout says it's good."

"You're running phone pornography?" Wolverine said, appalled.

"Of course not," Mr. Judy said. "You can't really call it 'pornography' if there's no oppression-of-women involved. Our 900 service is entirely cruelty- and exploitation-free!"

Wolverine was skeptical. "What about that woman who's talking on the phone, though? You can't tell me she's not being exploited."

"That's the amazing beauty of it!" Mr. Judy declared. "There's no real woman there at all! That voice is just a kind of Artificial Intelligence thing! It's not 'talking' at all, really—it's just *generating speech*, using Marilyn Monroe's voice mixed with Karen Carpenter's. It's all just digital, like on a CD."

"What?" said Wolverine. "I don't understand."

Mr. Judy patted her console; the top was out of it, revealing a miniature urban high-rise of accelerator cards and plug-in modules. "This computer's got a voice-recognition card. The software just picks words at random out of the customer's own sick, pathetic rant! Whenever he stops for breath, it feeds a question back to him, using his own vocabulary. I mean, if he talks about shaved hamsters—or whatever his kink is—then *it* talks about shaved hamsters. The system knows how to construct sentences in English, but it doesn't have to *understand* a single thing he says! All it does is *claim* to understand him."

"Every two or three minutes it stops and says really nice things to him off the hard disk," Vanna said helpfully. "Kind of a flattery subroutine."

"And he doesn't *realize* that?"

"Nobody's ever complained so far," Vanna said. "We get men calling in steady, week after week!"

"When it comes to men and sex, being *human* has never *been* part of the transaction," Mr. Judy said. "If you just give men *exactly* what they want, they *never miss the rest*. It's really true!"

Wolverine was troubled. "You must get a lot of really sick people."

"Well, sure," Mr. Judy said. "Actually, we hardly ever bother to listen-in to the calls anymore ... But if he's really disgusting, like a child-porn guy or something, we just rip-off his card-number and post it on an underground bulletin board. A week later this guy gets taken to the cleaners by hacker kids all over America."

"How on earth did you start this project?" Wolverine said.

"Well," Mr. Judy said, "phreaking long-distance is an old trick. We've been doing that since '84. But we didn't get into the heavy digital stuff until 1989." She hesitated. "As it happens, this van itself belongs to Leggy here."

Starlitz was watching his rear-view mirror. "Well, the van," he mumbled absently, "I got a lot of software with the van ... this box of Commodore floppies tucked in the back, somebody's back-ups, with addresses and phone numbers ... About a million suckers who'd pledged money to Six Flags Over Jesus. Man, you can't *ask* for a softer bunch of marks and rubes than *that*." He turned off the highway suddenly.

"Pretty soon we're gonna branch out!" Mr. Judy said. "Our group is onto something really hot here. We're gonna run a gay-rights BBS—a dating service—voice-mail classified ads—why, by '95 we'll be doing dial-up Goddess videos on fiber-to-the-curb!"

"Problem, Jude," Starlitz announced.

Mr. Judy's face fell. "What is it?"

"The blue Toyota," Starlitz said. "It picked us up outside the harbor. Been right on our ass ever since."

"Cops?"

"They've got CB, but I don't see any microwave," Starlitz said.

Vanna's blue eyes went wide. "Anti-choice people!"

"Lose 'em," Mr. Judy commanded.

Starlitz floored it. The van's suspension scrunched angrily as they pitched headlong down the road. Wolverine, clinging to her plastic handhold above the passenger door, reached up to steady her dentures. "I'm afraid!" she said. "Will they hurt us?"

Starlitz grunted.

"I can't take this! I'm sorry! I'd rather be arrested!" Wolverine cried.

"They're not cops, they don't *do* arrests," Starlitz said. He crossed three lines of traffic against the light and hit an access ramp. Both Vanna and Mr. Judy were flung headlong across their rubber mats on the floor. The van's jounced machinery settled with a violent clatter.

The speaker emitted a crackle and a loud dial-tone.

"God damn it, Leggy," Mr. Judy shouted, "okay, forget 'losing' them!"

Starlitz ignored her, checking the mirror, then scanning the highway mechanically. "I lost 'em, all right. For a while, anyhow."

"Who *were* those people?" Wolverine wailed.

"Pro-life fanatics . . ." Mr. Judy grunted. "Christian cultist weirdos . . ." She clutched a slotted metal column for support as Starlitz weaved violently into the fast lane. "I sure hope it's not 'Sword of the Unborn.' They hit a clinic in Alabama once with a shoulder-launched rocket."

"Hang on," Starlitz said. He braked, fishtailed ninety degrees, then struck out headlong across a grassy meridian. They crossed in the teeth of oncoming traffic, off the gravelled shoulder, then up and down through a shallow ditch. The van took a curb hard, became briefly airborne, crossed a street, and skidded with miraculous ease through the crowded lot of a convenience grocery.

Starlitz veered left, onto the striped tarmac of a tree-clustered strip mall.

Starlitz drove swiftly to the back of the mall and parked illegally in the delivery-access slot of a florist's shop. "This baby's kinda hard to hide," he said, setting the emergency brake. "Now that they're onto us, we gotta get the hell out of this town."

"He's right. I think we'd better drop you off here, Wolverine," Mr. Judy said. "If that's okay with you."

Vanna unlocked the van's back door and flung herself out, yanking Wolverine's Samsonite case behind her with a thud and a clatter.

"Yes, that's quite all right, dear," Wolverine said dazedly. She touched a lump on the top of her scalp, and examined the trace of blood on her fingertips. She winced, then stuffed the Mexican straw sun-hat over her head.

With brutal haste, Mr. Judy palpated the stuffed animals for any remaining contraband. She flung them headlong from the van into Vanna's waiting arms.

Wolverine opened the passenger door and climbed down, with arthritic awkwardness. The tires stank direly of scorched rubber. "I'm sure that I can call a taxi here, young man," she told Starlitz, hanging to the door like a drunk from a lamp-post. "Never you mind about little me . . ."

Starlitz was fiddling with his broadband scanner-set, below the dash. He looked up sharply. "Right. You clean now?"

"What?" Wolverine said.

"Are you *holding*?"

"I beg your pardon?"

Starlitz gritted his teeth. "Do you have any *illegal drugs*? On your person? Right now?"

"Oh. No. I gave them all to you!"

"Great. Then stick right by the payphones till your taxi comes. If anyone gives you any kind of shit, scream like hell and dial 9–1–1."

"All right," Wolverine said bravely. "I understand. Anything else?"

"Yeah. Shut the door," Starlitz said. Wolverine closed the door gently. "And lose that fuckin' ugly hat," Starlitz muttered.

Vanna heaved the leaky stuffed toys into Wolverine's arms, kissed her cheek briefly and awkwardly, then ran to the back of the van. "Split!" she yelled. Starlitz threw it into reverse and the rear doors banged shut.

Wolverine waved dazedly as she stood beside the florist's dumpster.

"I'm gonna take 26 West," Starlitz announced.

"You're kidding," Mr. Judy said, clambering into the front passenger seat. She tugged her harness tight as they pulled out of the mall's parking lot. "That's miles out of our way! Why?"

Starlitz shrugged. "Mystical Zen intuition."

Mr. Judy frowned at him, rubbing a bruise on her thigh. "Look, don't even start on me with that crap, Leggy."

A distant trucker's voice drawled from the scanner. *"So then I tell him, look, Alar is downright good for kids, it kills pinworms for one thing . . ."* Starlitz punched the radio back onto channel-scan.

Mr. Judy bent to turn down the hiss.

"Leave it," Starlitz said. "ELINT traffic intercept. Standard evasive tactics."

"Look, Starlitz," Mr. Judy said, "were you ever in the U.S. Army?"

"No . . ."

"Then don't *talk* like you were in the goddamn Army. Say something normal. Say something like 'maybe we can overhear what they say.' " Mr. Judy fetched a pad of Post-It notes and a pencil-stub from the glove compartment.

"I think our fax just blew a chip," Vanna announced mournfully from the back. "All its little red lights are blinking."

"Small wonder! Mr. Zen Intuition here was driving like a fucking maniac," Mr. Judy said. She groaned. "Remind me to wrap some padding on those goddamned metal uprights. I feel like I've been nunchucked."

An excited voice burst scratchily from the scanner. *"Where is Big Fish? Repeat, where is Big Fish? What was their last heading? Ten-six, Salvation!"*

"This is Salvation," a second voice replied. *"Calm the heck down, for pete's sake! We've got the description now. We'll pick 'em up on 101 South if we have to. Over."*

"Bingo," Mr. Judy exulted. "Citizen's Band channel 13." She made a quick note on her Post-It pad.

Starlitz rubbed his stubbled chin. "Good thing we avoided Highway 101."

"Don't be smug, Leggy."

The CB spoke up again. *"This is Isaiah, everybody. On Tenth and, uh, Sherbrooke, okay? I don't think they could have possibly come this far, over."*

"Heck no they couldn't," Salvation said angrily. *"What in blazes are you doing over into Sector B? Get back to Sector A, over."*

"Ezekiel here," said another voice. *"We're in A, but we surmise they must have parked somewhere. That sounds reasonable, doesn't it? Uhm, over . . ."*

"No air chatter, over," Salvation commanded. His signal was fading.

" 'Salvation,' 'Ezekiel,' and 'Isaiah,' " Vanna said. "Wow, their handles really suck!"

"I know, I know," Mr. Judy said. "Mother of God, the bastards are swarming like locusts. I can't understand this!"

Starlitz sighed patiently. "Look, Jude. There's nothing to understand, okay? Somebody must have finked. That little coven of yours has got an informer."

"No way!" Vanna said.

"Yes way. One of your favorite backwoods mantra-chanters is a pro-life plant, okay? They knew we were coming here. Maybe they didn't know everything, but they sure knew enough to stake us out."

Mr. Judy clenched her small, gnarled fists and stared out the windshield, biting her lip. "Maybe it was Wolverine's people that leaked! Ever think of that?"

"If it were Wolverine, they'd have hit us at the docks," Starlitz said. "You're being a sap, Jude. Your problem is, you don't think there's any pro-life woman smart enough to run a scam on the sisters. Come on, get real! It doesn't take a genius to wear chi-pants and tattoo a yin-yang on your tit."

Mr. Judy tugged at the front of her jersey. "Thanks a lot. Creep."

Starlitz shrugged. "The underground-right are as smart as you are, *easy*. They know everything they *wanna* know about the 'Liberal Humanist Movement.' Hell, they've all got subscriptions to *Utne Reader*."

"So what do *you* think we should do?"

Starlitz grinned. "This gig of yours is blown, so let's forget it. Brand-new deal, okay? Let's card us a big rental-car and call the New Caledonians."

"No way," Mr. Judy said. "No way we're losing this van! Besides, I draw the line at credit-card theft. Unless the victim is Republican."

"And no way we're calling any Polynesians, anyway," Vanna said.

Starlitz dug in his vest for a cigarette, lit it, and blew ochre smoke across the windshield. "I'll trade you," he said at last. "You tell me where the kid is. You can borrow my van for a while, and I'll rent a V-8 and do the Utah run all by myself."

"Fat chance!" Mr. Judy shouted. "Last time we trusted you with our stash, we didn't see you for three fucking years!"

"And we're not telling you anything more about the kid until this is all over," Vanna said firmly.

Starlitz snorted smoke. "You think *I* got any use for

a wimpy abortion drug? Hell, RU-486 isn't even *illegal* in most other countries. Lemme deliver it—heck, I'll even get you a receipt. And when I'm back, we all go meet the kid. Just like we agreed before. If that goes okay, I might even throw in the van later. Deal?"

"No deal," Mr. Judy said.

"Think about it. It's really a lot easier."

Mr. Judy silently peeled the Post-It and slapped it on the scanner.

"Don't you make trouble for us, Leggy," Vanna spoke up. "You don't know anything! You don't know who we're meeting. You don't know the passwords. You don't know the time or the place." Vanna took a breath. "You don't even know which one of us is the kid's real mother."

"You act like that's *my* fault," Starlitz said. "That's not the way I remember it." He grinned, a curl of ginseng smoke escaping his back molars. "Anyway, I can guess."

"No you can't!" Vanna said heatedly. "Don't you dare guess!"

"Forget it," Mr. Judy said. "We shouldn't even talk about the kid. We shouldn't have mentioned the kid. We won't talk about the kid anymore. Not till the trip's over and we've done the deal just like we agreed back at the commune."

"Fine," Starlitz sneered. "That's real handy. For you, anyway."

Mr. Judy cracked her knuckles. "Okay, call me stupid. Call me reckless. I admit that, okay? And if me and Vanna hadn't both been *incredibly* stupid *and* reckless around you three years ago, pal, there wouldn't even *be* any kid now."

Starlitz said nothing.

Mr. Judy sniffed. "What happened that time—between the three of us—we never talk about it, I know that . . . And for God's sake, after this, let's not ever talk about it again." She lowered her voice. "But privately—

that thing we did—with the tequila and the benwa balls and the big rubber hammock—yeah, I remember it just as well as you do, and I blame myself for that. Completely. I take that entire karmic burden upon myself. I absorb all guilt trips, I take upon myself complete moral account-ability. Okay, Leggy? I'm responsible, you're not responsi-ble. You happy now?"

"Sure thing," Starlitz said sullenly, grinding out his cigarette.

They drove on then, in ominous silence, for two full hours: through Portland and up the Columbia River Val-ley. Vanna finally broke the ice again by passing out tofu-loaf, Ginseng Rush, and rice cakes.

"We've lost 'em good," Mr. Judy decided.

"Maybe," Starlitz said. There had been no traffic on Channel 13, except the usual truck farmers, speedballers and lot lizards. "But the situation's changed some now . . . Why don't you phone your friends back at the commune? Tell 'em to dig up my arsenal and Fed-Ex us three Mac-10s to Pocatello. With plenty of ammo."

Mr. Judy frowned. "So we can risk dope *and* federal weapons charges? Forget it! We said no guns, remember? I don't think you even ought to have that goddamn pis-tol."

"Sure," Starlitz sneered, "so when they pull up right next to us at sixty miles per, and cut loose on us with a repeating combat-shotgun . . ." Vanna flinched. "Yeah," Starlitz continued, "Judy here is gonna do a Chuck Norris out the window and side-kick 'em right through their windshield!" He patted his holstered gun. "Fuckin' black belts . . . I've seen acidheads with more sense!"

"And I've seen you with a loaded Ingram!" Vanna re-torted. "I'd rather face a hundred right-to-lifers."

"Oh stop it," Mr. Judy said. "You're both making trouble for nothing. We lost 'em, remember? They're probably still hunting us on 101 South. We got a big lead now." She munched her last rice cake. "If we had any

sense, we'd take a couple hours and completely change
this van's appearance. Vanna's pretty good with graphics.
We can buy paint at an auto store and re-do our van like
a diaper service. Something a lot less macho than white
pearlized paint with two big chrome TV logos."

"It's not *your* van," Starlitz said angrily. "It's *my* van,
and you're not putting any crappy paint on it. Anyway,
we've *got* to look like a TV van. What if somebody looks
in the window and sees all this equipment? You can't get
more suspicious and obvious than a van full of monitors
that's painted like some wimpy diaper service. Everybody'll
think we're the goddamned FBI."

"Okay, okay, have it your way," Mr. Judy shrugged.
She put on a pair of black drugstore Polaroids. "We'll just
take it easy. Keep a low profile. We'll make it fine."

They spent the night in a lot in a campground near a
state park on the Oregon-Idaho border. The lots were a
bargain for the TV van, for its demand for electrical
power was enormous, and rental campgrounds offered
cheap hookups. Judy and Vanna slept outside in a hemi-
spherical, bright pink alpine tent. Starlitz slept inside the
van.

Next morning they were enjoying three bowls of
muesli when an open-faced young man in a lumberjack
shirt and overalls meandered up, carrying a rubber-
antennaed cellular phone.

"Good morning," he said.

"Hi," Mr. Judy said, pausing in mid-spoon.

"Spend a pleasant night?"

"Why don't you guys install proper telephone hookups here?" Mr. Judy demanded. "We need copper-cable.
You know, twisted-pair."

"Oh I'm sorry, I don't run this campground," the
young man apologized, propping one booted foot on the
edge of their wooden picnic table. "You see, I just happen
to live in this area." He cleared his throat. "I thought we
might counsel together about your activities."

"Huh?" Vanna said.

"I got an alarm posted on my Christian BBS last night," the young man told them. "Got up at five a.m., and spent the whole morning lookin' for you and this van." He pointed with his thumb. "You're the people who import abortion pills." He looked at them soberly. "Word's out about you all over our network."

Mr. Judy put down her muesli spoon with an unsteady hand. "You've made a mistake."

"Don't worry, I won't hurt you," the young man said. "I'm just a regular guy. My name's Charles. That's my car right over there." Charles pointed to a rust-spotted station-wagon with Idaho plates. "My wife's in there—Monica—and our little kid Jimmy." He turned and waved. Monica, in the driver's seat, waved back. She wore sunglasses and a head-kerchief. She looked very anxious.

Jimmy was asleep in the back in a toddler's safety-seat. Apparently getting up early had been too much for the tyke.

"Our group is strictly nonviolent," Charles said.

"Gosh, that's swell," Starlitz said, relaxing visibly. He splashed a little more bottled goat-milk into his muesli.

"Violence against the unborn is wrong," Charles said steadily. "It's not a 'choice,' it's a *child*. You're spreading a Frankenstein technology that lets women poison and murder their own unborn children. And they can do it in complete stealth."

"You mean in complete privacy," Vanna said.

Mr. Judy knocked her cheap plastic bowl aside and leapt to her feet. "Don't even talk to him, Vanna! Leggy, start the van, let's get out of here!"

Starlitz looked up in annoyance from his half-finished cereal. "Are you kidding? There's only one of him. I'm not through eating yet. Kick his ass!"

Mr. Judy glanced from side to side, warily. She glared at Charles, then hitched up her pants and settled into a menacing kung-fu crouch. "Go away! We don't want you here."

"It's my moral duty to bear witness to evil," Charles told her mildly, showing her his open hands. "I'm not armed, and I mean you no harm. If you feel you must hit me, then I can't prevent you. But you're very wrong to answer words with blows."

Birds sang in the pines above the campground.

"He's right," Vanna said in a small voice.

" 'He who diggeth a pit will fall in it,' " Charles quoted.

"Okay, okay," Mr. Judy muttered. "I'm not going to hit you."

"She who lives by the sword will die by it."

Mr. Judy frowned darkly. "Don't *push* me, asshole!"

"I know what you're doing, even if you yourselves are too corrupt to recognize it," Charles continued eagerly. "You're trying to legitimize the mass poisoning of the unborn generation." Charles seemed encouraged by their confusion, and waved his arms eloquently. "Your contempt for the sanctity of human life legitimizes murder! Today, you're killing kids. Tomorrow, you'll be renting wombs. Pretty soon you'll be selling fetal tissue on the open market!"

"Hey, we're not capitalists," Vanna protested.

Charles was on a roll. "First comes abortion, then euthanasia! The suicide machines . . . The so-called right-to-die—it's really the *right-to-kill*, isn't it? Pretty soon you'll be quietly poisoning not just unborn kids and old sick people, but everybody else who's inconvenient to you! That's just how the Holocaust started—with so-called euthanasia!"

"We're not the Nazis in this situation," Mr. Judy grated. "*You're* the Nazis."

"We're pro-life. You're making life cheap. You're the pro-death secular forces!"

"Hey, don't call us 'secular,' " Vanna said, wounded. "We're Goddess pagans."

Starlitz was steadily munching his cereal.

"I think you should give me all those pills," Charles said quietly. "It's no use going on with this scheme of yours, now that we know, and you know that we know. Be reasonable. Just give all the pills to me, and I'll burn them all. You can go back home quietly. Nobody will bother you. Don't you have any sense of shame?"

Mr. Judy grated her teeth. "Look, buster. In a second, I'm gonna lose my temper and break your fucking arm. I'd sure as hell rather die by the sword than by the coat-hanger."

"Sure, resort to repressive thuggish violence," Charles shrugged. "But I promise you this: you won't thrive by your crimes. We are everywhere!"

"Goddamn you, that's *our* slogan!" Mr. Judy shouted.

Starlitz washed his muesli bowl under a rusty water-faucet, and belched. "Well, that's that. Let's get goin'." He opened the door of the van.

"We know darned well what you're up to!" Charles cried, as Vanna and Judy fled hastily into the van. "We're going to videotape you, and photograph you, and speak about you in public!" Starlitz fired up the van and pumped the engine. "We're gonna make dossiers about you and put you on our computer mailing lists!" Charles shouted, raising one calloused hand in solemn impreca-tion. "We'll call your Congressman and complain about you! We'll start civil suits and take out injunctions!"

Starlitz drove away.

"We'll call you at your home!" Charles bellowed, hands cupped at his lips. "And call your offices! All day and all night, hundreds of us! With automatic dialers! For years and years!" His voice faded in a final shout. *"We'll call your parents!"*

"Mother of God," Mr. Judy said, shaken, buckling herself into the passenger seat. "That was *horrible*! What are we going to do about that guy?"

"No problem," Starlitz said, setting the scanner for

cellular-phone frequencies. "I mean, *my* parents died in a tornado in a Florida trailer park." He shrugged. "And besides, I never show up on videotape."

Mr. Judy frowned suspiciously. "What do you mean?"

"It's just this, uhm, thing that happens," Starlitz said, shrugging. "I mean videos just never work when they're pointed at me. Either the battery's dead, or the tape jams, or the player blows a chip and just starts blinking twelve-o'clock, or the tape splits so there's nothing but scratches and blur . . . I just don't show up on videotape. Ever."

Mr. Judy took a deep breath. "Leggy, that's got to be just about the wildest, stupidest—"

"Hush!" Starlitz said. Charles' voice was emerging from the scanner.

"*I told you they wouldn't hurt me,*" he said.

"*Well, we're not gonna follow them,*" said a woman's voice—his wife Monica, presumably. "*It's too dangerous. I'm sure they have guns in that van.*" She lowered her voice. "*Charlie, were they lesbians?*"

"*Well, I dunno about the guy they had with them,*" Charles replied, "*but yeah, those girls were sexual deviants all right. It's just like Salvation told us. Really makes your blood run cold!*" He paused. "*Is the car fax still working? Better dial him a report right away!*"

"Typical," Mr. Judy said. "We ought to go back there and slash his tires!"

"Let's just get out of here," Vanna sighed.

"I don't have to take any gay-bashing lip out of that Norman Rockwell hayseed."

"If you beat him up, they'll know we're listening to the cellular band," Vanna pointed out wisely.

"Well, your pal Charlie was right about one thing," Starlitz said cheerfully. "This whole scam of yours is totally fucked now! Time to lose the van and pick up some action with the Polynesians."

"We're going to Salt Lake City, Leggy." Mr. Judy's face was set stonily. "We'll get there if we have to drive all day and all night. We'll make the delivery, dammit. Now it's a matter of political principle."

They met their first roadblock in Gooding County, Idaho. A dozen placard-waving militants burst from the back of two pickups and threw a cardboard box of caltrops across Highway 84. Starlitz, suspecting land mines or blasting-caps, slowed drastically.

The sides of the van were hammered with blood-balloons, and glass Christmas-tree ornaments filled with skunk-stinking butyl mercaptan and rotten-egg hydrogen sulfide. An especially brave militant with a set of grappling hooks was yanked from his feet and road-burned for ten yards.

The trucks did not pursue them. Starlitz stopped at a carwash in Shoshone Falls. After the stomach-turning stink-liquids had been rinsed off with high-pressure soap, he yanked seven caltrops from the van's tires. The caltrops were homemade devices—golf-balls, with half-a-dozen six-inch nails driven through them, the whole thing cunningly spray-painted black to match highway tarmac.

"Good thing I bought these solid-rubber tires and ditched those fancy-ass Michelins," Starlitz said with satisfaction.

"Yeah," Vanna said. Mr. Judy said nothing. She'd given Starlitz a hard time about the tires earlier.

"Shoulda saved money on that fancy fiber-optics kit, and gone for the Plexiglas windows, instead," Starlitz opined. "The bulletproof option. Just like I said." Mr. Judy, who'd done the lion's share of the scrubbing, went to the ladies' and threw up.

• • •

They took 93 south of Twin Falls and across the border to Wells, Nevada. The switch to a smaller highway
seemed to stymie their pursuers, but only temporarily. At
80 West just east of Oasis they found the desert highway
entirely blocked. A church bus full of protestors in
death's-head masks had physically blocked the road with
their black-cloaked bodies. As the van drew nearer, they
began chaining themselves together, somewhat hampered
by their placards and scythes.

Starlitz rolled down the driver's-side window, took
his hands off the steering-wheel and stuck them both out
the window, visibly. Then he hit the accelerator.

The blockaders scattered wildly as the van bore down
upon them. The van whacked, bumped, and crunched
over chains, scythes, and placards as shrieks of rage and
horror dopplered past the open window.

"I think you hit one of them, Leggy," Vanna gasped.

"Nah," Starlitz said. "Probably one of those dead-
baby dummies."

"They wouldn't be carrying *real* babies with them,
would they?" Vanna said.

"In this heat?" Starlitz said.

The bus pursued them at high speed all the way to
Wendover, but it grew dark, and they entered some light
traffic. Starlitz turned the van's lights off, and pulled into
an access road to the Bonneville Salt Flats. The bus, de-
ceived, roared past them in pursuit of someone else.

They spent the night outside the military chain-link
around an Air Force test-range, then drove into Salt Lake
City in the morning.

It was Sunday, the Sabbath. Utah's capital was utterly se-
pulchral. The streets were as blank and deserted as so
many bowling lanes.

The van felt pitifully conspicuous as they drove past
blank storefronts and shuttered windows. At length they

hid the van on the sheltered grounds of a planetarium and stuffed all the contraband into Mr. Judy's backpack.

They then hiked uphill to the Utah State Capitol. The great stone edifice was open to the public. There was not a soul inside it. No police, no tourists—no one at all. The only company the three of them had were the Ikegami charged-couple-device security minicams, which were bolted well above the line-of-sight on eight-inch swivel pedestals.

"We're early," Mr. Judy said. "Our contact hasn't shown yet." She shrugged. "Might as well have a good look at the place."

"I like this building," Starlitz announced, gazing around raptly. "This contact of yours must be okay. Setting up a dope-deal here in Boy Scout Central was a 'way gutsy move." He closely examined a Howard Chandler Christy reproduction of the Signing of the US Constitution. The gilt-framed tableau of the Founding Fathers had been formally presented to the State of Utah by the Walt Disney Corporation.

The capitol's rotunda was a sky-blue dome with a massive dangling chandelier. It featured funky-looking 30s frescos with the unmistakable look of state-supported social-realism. "Advent of Irrigation by Pioneers." "Driving the Golden Spike." "General Connor Inaugurates Mining."

"Listen to this," Mr. Judy marveled. "It's a statement by the bureaucrat that commissioned this stuff. *This is the greatest opportunity that the artists of this or any other country have ever had to show their mettle.* He actually says that—'mettle'! *It is a call to them to make good and prove that they have something worth while to say.* Yeah, unlike you, you evil little redneck philistine! *It is an opportunity to sell themselves to the country and I know they will answer the challenge.*" Suddenly she flushed.

"Take it easy," Starlitz muttered.

" '*Sell themselves to the country,*' " Mr. Judy said

venomously. "Mother of God ... sometimes you forget just how bad it really is in the good ol' USA."

Farther down the hall they discovered an extremely campy figurine of an astronaut on a black plastic pedestal. The pedestal was made of O-ring material from Utah-produced Morton Thiokol solid-rocket boosters.

Every other nook or cranny seemed to feature a lurking statue of some fat-cat local businessman: a "world-renowned mining engineer"—a "pioneer in the development of supermarkets."

"Wow, look who built this place!" Mr. Judy said, gazing at a bronze plaque. "It was the Utah state governor who had Joe Hill shot by a firing squad! Man, that sure explains a lot ..."

"This place is creepin' me out," Vanna said, hugging herself. "Let's go outside and wait on the lawn ..."

"No, this place is great!" Starlitz objected. "Six Flags Over Jesus was decorated just like this ... Let's go down in the basement!"

The basement featured a gigantic hand-embroidered silk tapestry: with the purple slope of Mount Fuji, a couple of wooden sailboats and a big cheesy spray of cherry blossoms. It had been presented to the People of Utah by the Japanese American Citizens League—"For Better Americans in a Greater America"—on July 21, 1940.

"Five months before Pearl Harbor," Mr. Judy said, aghast.

"Musta been mighty reassuring," Starlitz said slowly. He wandered off.

Mr. Judy stared at the eldritch relic with mingled pity and horror. "I wonder how many of these poor people ended up in relocation camps."

Vanna silently wiped her eyes on the tail of her shirt.

Starlitz stopped at the end of the hall and looked around the corner to his right. Suddenly he broke into a run.

They found him with his nose pressed to the glass framework around "The Mormon Meteor"—"designed, built and driven by 'Ab' Jenkins on the Bonneville Salt Flats." The 1930s racer, which had topped two hundred miles per hour in its day, sported a 750 hp Curtis Conqueror engine. Streamlined to the point of phallicism, the racer was fire-engine red and twenty-two feet long—except for the huge yellow Flash Gordon fin behind the tiny riveted one-man cockpit.

The two women left Starlitz alone a while, respecting his obsession.

Eventually Mr. Judy came to join him.

"Ab Jenkins," Starlitz breathed aloud. " 'The only man who has raced an automobile 24 continuous hours without leaving the driver's seat.' "

Mr. Judy laughed. "Big deal, Leggy. You think this stupid boy-toy's impressive?" She waved at a set of glass-fronted exhibits. "That cheap-ass tourist art is ten times as weird. And the souvenir shop's got a sign that says *All shoplifters will be cheerfully beaten to a pulp!*"

"I wonder if it's got any fuel in it," Starlitz said dreamily. "The Firestones still look good—you suppose the points are clean?"

Mr. Judy's smile faded. "C'mon, Leggy. Snap out of it."

He turned to her, his eyeballs gone dark as slate. "You don't get it, do you? You can't even see it when it's right in front of you. This is *it*, Jude. The rest of the crap here is just so much cheesy bullshit, you could see stuff like that in Romania, but *this*"—he slapped the glass—"this is *America*, goddamn it!" He took a deep breath. "And I want it."

"Well, you can't *have* the 'Mormon Meteor.' "

"The hell," he said. "Look at this glass case. One good swift kick would break it. The cops would never expect anybody to boost this car. And if the engine would turn over, you could drive it right out the capitol door!" Starlitz ran both hands over his filthy hair and shivered. "Sunday night in Mormonville—there's not a soul in the fuckin' streets! And the Meteor does 200 miles an hour!

By dawn we could have it safely buried under a dune in White Sands, come back whenever we need it . . ."

"But we *don't* need it," Mr. Judy said. "We'll *never* need this!"

He folded his arms. "You didn't know you needed the van, either. And I brought you the van, didn't I?"

"This thing isn't like the van. The van is useful in the liberation struggle."

Starlitz was scandalized. "Christ, you don't know *anything* about machinery. The way you talk about it, you'd think technology was for what people *need*!" He took a deep breath. "Look, Jude, trust me on this. This fucker is voodoo. It's a canopic jar, it's the Pharaoh's guts! It's the Holy Tabernacle, okay? We steal this baby, and the whole goddamn karmic keystone falls out of this place . . ."

Judy frowned. "Knock it off with the New Age crap, Legs. From you, it sounds really stupid."

They suddenly heard the echoing chang and whine of electric guitars, a thudding concussion of drums. Somewhere, someone in the Capitol was rocking out.

They hurried back upstairs. As they drew nearer they could hear the high-pitched wail of alien lyrics, cut with a panting electric clarinet and a whomping bassline.

Four young Japanese women with broad-brimmed felt hats and snarled dreadlocks were slouching against the wall of the Utah State Capitol rotunda, clustered around a monster Sony boom box. The women wore short stiff paisley skirts, tattered net stockings, a great deal of eye-makeup, and elaborate, near-psychedelic pearl-buttoned cowboy shirts. They were nodding, foot-tapping, chainsmoking and tapping ashes into a Nikon lens-cap.

Mr. Judy gave them the password. The Japanese women smiled brightly, without bothering to get up. One of them turned off their howling tape, and made introductions. Their names were Sachiho, Ako, Sayoko and

Hukie. They were an all-girl heavy-metal rockband from Tokyo called "90s Girl"—*Nineties Gyaru*.

Sachiho, the 90s Girl among the foursome with the most tenacious grasp on English, tried to get the skinny across to Vanna and Judy. The latest DC from 90s Girl had topped out at 200,000 units, which was major commercial action in Tokyo pop circles, but peanuts compared to the legendary American pop market. 90s Girl, who nourished a blazing determination to become the *o-goruden bando*—great golden band—of Nipponese hard-rock, were determined to break the US through dogged club-touring. A college-circuit alternative radio network based in Georgia had reluctantly agreed to get them some American gigs.

The band members of 90s Girl had already spent plenty of vacation-time slumming in Manhattan, skin-diving in Guam, and skiing in Utah, so they figured they had the Yankee scene aced. Any serious commercial analysis of the American rock scene made it obvious that most of the wannabe acts in America were supporting themselves with narcotics trafficking. This was the real nature of the American rock'n'roll competitive advantage.

The Tokyo-based management of 90s Girl had therefore made a careful market-study of American drug-consumption patterns and concluded that RU-486 was the hot and coming commodity. RU-486 was non-addictive, didn't show up on the user, and it was not yet controlled by Yankee mafia, Jamaican dope-posses, or heavily armed Colombians. The profit potential was bright, the consumers relatively non-violent, and the penalties for distribution still confused.

90s Girl planned to sell the capsules through a network of metal-chick cult-fans in Arizona, Texas, Georgia, Florida, and North Carolina, with a final big blow-out in Brooklyn if they had any dope left when they finished their tour.

"This management of yours," Mr. Judy said. "The

people doing all this market analysis. They're not men, are they?"

"Oh no," said Sachiho. "Never, never."

"Great." Mr. Judy handed over her backpack. 90s Girl began stuffing dope into their camera cases.

Footsteps approached.

The assorted smugglers glanced around wildly for an escape route. There was none. The pro-life forces had deployed themselves with cunning skill. Enemies blocked each of the rotunda exits, in groups of six.

Their leader muscled his way to the fore. "Caught you red-handed!" he announced gleefully in the sullen silence. "You'll hand that contraband over now, if you please."

"Forget it," Mr. Judy said.

"You're not leaving this building with that wicked poison in your possession," the leader assured her. "We won't allow it."

Mr. Judy glared at him. "What're you gonna do, Mr. Nonviolence? Preach us to death?"

"That won't be necessary," he said grimly, veins protruding on the sides of his throat. "If you resist us violently, then we'll mace you with pepper-spray. We'll superglue your bodies to the floor of the Capitol, and leave you there soaked in bottled blood, with placards around your necks, fully describing your awful crimes." Two of the nonviolent thugs began vigorously shaking aerosol cans.

"You Salvation?" Starlitz asked. He slipped his hand inside his photographer's vest.

"Some people call me that," the leader said. He was tall and clear-eyed and clean-shaven. He had a large nose and close-set eyes and wore a blue denim shirt and brown sans-a-belt slacks. He looked completely undistinguished. He looked like the kind of guy who might own a bowling alley. The only remarkable quality about Salvation was that he clearly meant every word he said.

"You might as well forget about that gun, sir," he

said. "You can't massacre all of us, and we're not afraid to die in the service of humanity. And in any case, we're videotaping this entire encounter. If you murder us, you'll surely pay a terrible price." He clapped his hand on the shoulder of a companion with a videocam.

The guy with the minicam spoke up in an anxious whisper, which the odd acoustics of the rotunda carried perfectly. *"Uh, Salvation . . . something's gone wrong with the camera . . ."*

"How'd you know we were here?" Mr. Judy demanded.

"We're monitoring the Capitol's security cameras," Salvation said triumphantly, gesturing at an overhead surveillance unit. "You're not the only people in the world who can hack computers, you know!" He took a deep breath. "You're not the only people who can sing *We Shall Overcome*. You're not the only ones who can raise consciousness, and hold sit-ins, and block streets!" He laughed harshly. "You thought you were the Revolution. You thought you were the New Age. Well, ladies, *we are the change*. We're the Revolution now!"

Suddenly, and without warning, a great buzzing voice echoed down the hall behind him. *"Up against the wall!"* It was the cry of a police bullhorn.

A squad of heavily armed Secret Service agents burst headlong into the rotunda, in a flying wedge. Salvation's little knot of pro-lifers scattered and fell like bowling pins.

At the sight of the charging federal agents, Vanna, Mr. Judy, and Starlitz each sat down immediately, almost reflexively, tucking their laced hands behind their heads. The four members of 90s Girl sat up a little straighter, and watched bemused.

The feds surged through the rotunda like red-dogging linebackers. The pro-lifers blocking the other exits panicked and started to flee headlong, but were tackled and fell thrashing.

A redheaded woman in jeans and a blue-and-yellow

Secret Service windbreaker danced into the rotunda, and lifted her bullhorn again. "The building's surrounded by federal agents!" she bellowed electronically. "I advise you dumb bastards to surrender peacefully!"

Her yell tore through the echoing rotunda like God shouting through a tin drum. The pro-lifers, stunned, went limp and nonresisting. She lowered her bullhorn and smiled at the sight of them, then nudged a nearby agent. "Read 'em their Miranda rights, Ehrlichman."

The fed, methodically bending over groups of his captured prey, began reading aloud from a laminated index card. The pro-lifers grunted in anguish as they were seized with cunning Secret Service judo-holds, then trussed like turkeys with whip-thin lengths of plastic handcuff.

The woman with the bullhorn approached the assorted smugglers, stopping by their Sony boom box. "Jane O'Houlihan, Utah Attorney General's office," she announced crisply, exhibiting a brass badge.

Mr. Judy looked up brightly. "How do you do, Ms. O'Houlihan? I think you'd better take it easy on these Japanese nationals. They're tourists, and don't have anything to do with this."

"How fuckin' stupid do you think I am?" O'Houlihan said. She sighed aloud. "You're sure lucky these pro-life dorks are wanted on a Kansas warrant for aggravated vandalism. Otherwise you and me would all be goin' downtown."

"You don't need to do that," Vanna told her timidly, wide-eyed.

O'Houlihan glared at them. "I'd bust you clowns in a hot second, only it would complicate my prosecution to bring you jerks into the picture . . . Besides, these dipshits just hacked a State Police video installation. They screwed it up, too, the cameras have been malfin' like crazy all morning . . . That's a Section 1030 federal computer-intrusion offense! They're gonna break rocks!"

"It's certainly good to know that a sister is fully in

charge of this situation," Mr. Judy said, tentatively lifting her hands from the nape of her neck. "These right-wing vigilantes are a menace to all women's civil rights."

"Sister me no sisterhood," O'Houlihan said, deftly prodding Mr. Judy with one Adidas-clad foot. "I didn't see you worthless New Age libbies lifting one damn finger to help me when I was busting check-forgers in the county attorney's office."

"We don't even live around here," Vanna protested. "We're from Ore—I mean, we're from another state."

"Yeah? Well, welcome to Utah, the Beehive State. Next time stay the fuck out of my jurisdiction."

A Secret Service agent clomped over. His sleeveless Kevlar flak jacket now hung loose, its Velcro tabs dangling. He looked very tough indeed. He looked as if he could bite bricks in half. "Any problem here, Janie?"

O'Houlihan smiled at him winningly. "None at all, Bob. These are just small-time losers . . . Besides, there seems to be an international angle." Sachiho, Ako, Hukie and Sayoko looked up impassively, their mascaraed eyes gone blank with sullen global-teenager Bohemianism.

"International, huh?" Bob muttered, gazing at the girl-group as if they'd just arrived via saucer from Venus. "That would let the Bureau in . . ." Bob adjusted his Ray-Bans. "Okay, Janie, if you say so, I guess they walk. But be sure and upload their dossiers to Washington."

"Will do!" O'Houlihan beamed.

Bob was reluctant. "You're damned sure they didn't try to get into any police systems?"

"They're not that smart," O'Houlihan told him. Bob nodded and returned to his cohorts, who were hauling handcuffed pro-lifers, by their armpits, face first down the echoing corridors. The arrestees wailed in anguish and struggled fitfully as their shoulders began to dislocate.

O'Houlihan raised the bullhorn to her lips. "Take it easy on 'em, boys! Remember, one of them is a secret federal informant." O'Houlihan lowered the bullhorn and grinned wickedly.

"We don't raid police systems," Mr. Judy assured her. "We wouldn't ever, ever raid federal computers."

"I *know* you don't," O'Houlihan said, with a chilly I-know-all cop's smile. "But if you little hippie bitches don't knock it off with the toll-fraud scams, you're gonna do time." She examined her polished nails. "If I ever meet you again, you're gonna regret it. Now get lost before I change my mind."

The seven contraceptive conspirators immediately fled the building. The unlucky pro-life agitators, now beginning to argue violently among themselves, were being flung headlong into a series of white Chevy vans.

"Whew," Vanna said. "That could have been us!"

"I think that's *supposed* to be us," Mr. Judy said, confused. "I mean, it always was us *before* . . . I guess that's what they get for trying to *be* us."

"Boy, that cop Jane sure is . . ." Vanna drew a breath . . . "*attractive.*"

Mr. Judy cast her a sharp and jealous look. "Come on! She's the heat!"

"So what?" Vanna shot back, wounded. "I can't help it if she happens to be 'way hot."

"Great," Mr. Judy said sourly. "Well, we'd better blow this nowhere burg before your girlfriend puts a tail on us."

"What about the Mormon Meteor?" Starlitz demanded.

"Have you gone completely insane?" Mr. Judy said. "The place is swarming with feds!"

"Not anymore," Starlitz said. "This is the perfect time to boost it. They'll blame it on Salvation's crowd!"

Sachiho, who had been listening with interest, spoke up suddenly. "It's cool car," she remarked. "Gnarly American car to buy for trade balance. I like it excellent! Let's rent it and make cool video like ZZ Top."

"*Great* fuckin' idea!" Starlitz said.

"We have a perfectly good van that's a lot more use," Mr. Judy said.

Sachiho looked utterly blank. "*Wakarimasen* . . . I think we Nineties Girl have to go rehearse now." She did a little serpentine side-step. "Good-bye to you forever, okay? Don't call us, we'll call you." She quipped something in Japanese to the others. They began laughing merrily and bounced off down the stairs.

"Now that's attitude," Starlitz said admiringly, watching them go. "Those gals have got some real dress sense, too."

"But we're done here now, Leggy," Vanna said. "I thought you couldn't wait to go see the kid."

Starlitz grunted.

Mr. Judy took Vanna by the wrist. "I've got to level with you about that issue, Leggy."

Starlitz stopped gazing in admiration and looked up. "Yeah?"

"There isn't any kid."

Starlitz said nothing. His face clouded.

"Look, Leggy, think about it. We're abortionists. We know what to do about unwanted pregnancies. There never was a kid. We made up the kid after you came back from Europe."

"No kid, huh," Starlitz said. "You burned me."

Mr. Judy nodded somberly.

"It was all a scam, huh? Just some big scheme you came up with to lead me around with." He laughed sharply. "Jesus, I can't believe you thought that would work."

"Sorry, Leggy. It seemed like a good idea at the time. Don't hold it against us."

Starlitz laughed. "You did it just because I got absent-minded that time, and didn't bring you back your dope. I got a little distracted, so you shaft me! Well, to hell with you! Good-bye forever, suckers."

Suddenly Starlitz ran downhill, headlong, after the retreating Japanese. "Hey!" he bellowed. "Girls! Nineties Girls! *Matte ite kudasai! Roadie-san wa arimasu ka?*"

Vanna and Judy watched as Starlitz vanished with the Japanese behind a line of trees.

"Why'd you lie to him like that?" Vanna said. "That was terrible."

Mr. Judy pulled a jingling set of keys from her pocket. " 'Cause we need that van of his, that's why. Let's drive it off back to Oregon while we've got the chance."

"He'll get mad," Vanna said. "And he knows where we live. He'll come back for all his stuff."

"Sure, we'll see him again all right," Mr. Judy said. "In four years or something. He'll never miss the stuff, or us, in the meantime. When he sees something he really wants, he doesn't have any more sense than a blood-crazed weasel."

"You're not being very fair," Vanna said.

"That's just the way he is ... We can't depend on him for anything. We don't *dare* depend on him. He can't think politically." Mr. Judy took a deep breath. "And even if he *could* think politically, he's basically motivated by the interests of the macho-imperialist oppressor class."

"I was thinking *mechanically*," Vanna said. "We had a really rough ride through the desert, and we just lost our only mechanic. I sure hope that van starts."

"Of course it's gonna start!" Mr. Judy said, annoyed. "You think we did all those years of work, and organizing, and consciousness-raising, and took all those risks, just to end up here in the world capital of reactionary family-values bullshit, with our engine grinding uselessly, unable to move one inch off dead center? That's ridiculous."

Vanna said nothing. Contemplating the possibility had made her go a little pale.

"We're gonna drive it off easy as pie," Mr. Judy insisted. "And we'll change the paint first thing. We'll lose that dumb-ass televangelist logo, and paint it up as something really cool and happening. Like a portable notary service, or a digital bookmobile."

Vanna bit her lip. "I'm still worried ... The kid's gonna want to know all about her father someday. She'll *demand* to know. Don't you think so?"

"No, I don't," Mr. Judy said, with complete conviction. "She'll never even have to ask."

DORI BANGS

True facts, mostly: Lester Bangs was born in California in 1948. He published his first article in 1969. It came over the transom at *Rolling Stone*. It was a frenzied review of the MC5's "Kick Out the Jams."

Without much meaning to, Lester Bangs slowly changed from a Romilar-guzzling college kid into a "professional rock critic." There wasn't much precedent for this job in 1969, so Lester kinda had to make it up as he went along. Kind of *smell* his way into the role, as it were. But Lester had a fine set of cultural antennae. For instance, Lester invented the tag "punk rock." This is posterity's primary debt to the Bangs oeuvre.

Lester's not as famous now as he used to be, because he's been dead for some time, but in the '70s Lester wrote a million record reviews, for *Creem* and the *Village Voice* and *NME* and *Who Put the Bomp*. He liked to crouch over his old manual typewriter, and slam out wild Beat-influenced copy, while the Velvet Underground or the Stooges were on the box. This made life a hideous trial for the neighborhood, but in Lester's opinion the neighborhood pretty much had it coming. *Epater les bourgeois*, man!

Lester was a party animal. It was a professional obligation, actually. Lester was great fun to hang with, be-

cause he usually had a jagged speed-edge, which made
him smart and bold and rude and crazy. Lester was a one-
man band, until he got drunk. Nutmeg, Romilar, bella-
donna, crank, those substances Lester could handle. But
booze seemed to crack him open, and an unexpected
black dreck of rage and pain would come dripping out,
like oil from a broken crankcase.

Toward the end—but Lester had no notion that the
end was nigh. He'd given up the booze, more or less. Even
a single beer often triggered frenzies of self-contempt.
Lester was thirty-three, and sick of being groovy; he was
restless, and the stuff he'd been writing lately no longer
meshed with the surroundings that had made him what he
was. Lester told his friends that he was gonna leave New
York and go to Mexico and work on a deep, serious novel,
about deep, serious issues, man. The real thing, this time.
He was really gonna pin it down, get into the guts of Western Culture, what it really was, how it really felt.

But then, in April '82, Lester happened to catch the
flu. Lester was living alone at the time, his mom, the Je-
hovah's Witness, having died recently. He had no one to
make him chicken soup, and the flu really took him
down. Tricky stuff, flu; it has a way of getting on top of
you.

Lester ate some Darvon, but instead of giving him
that buzzed-out float it usually did, the pills made him
feel foggy and dull and desperate. He was too sick to
leave his room, or hassle with doctors or ambulances, so
instead he just did more Darvon. And his heart stopped.

There was nobody there to do anything about it, so
he lay there for a while, until eventually a friend showed
up, and found him.

More true fax, pretty much: Dori Seda was born in 1951.
She was a cartoonist, of the "underground" variety. Dori

wasn't ever famous, certainly not in Lester's league, but then she didn't beat her chest and bend every ear in the effort to make herself a Living Legend, either. She had a lot of friends in San Francisco, anyway.

Dori did a "comic book" once, called *Lonely Nights*. An unusual "comic book" for those who haven't followed the "funnies" trade lately, as *Lonely Nights* was not particularly "funny," unless you really get a hoot from deeply revealing tales of frustrated personal relationships. Dori also did a lot of work for *WEIRDO* magazine, which emanated from the artistic circles of R. Crumb, he of "Keep On Truckin'" and "Fritz the Cat" fame.

R. Crumb once said: "Comics are words and pictures. You can do anything with words and pictures!" As a manifesto, it was a typically American declaration, and it was a truth that Dori held to be self-evident.

Dori wanted to be a True Artist in her own real-gone little '80s-esque medium. Comix, or "graphic narrative" if you want a snazzier cognomen for it, was a breaking thing, and she had to feel her way into it. You can see the struggle in her "comics"'—always relentlessly autobiographical—Dori hanging around the "Cafè La Bohme" trying to trade food stamps for cigs; Dori living in drafty warehouses in the Shabby Hippie Section of San Francisco, sketching under the skylight and squabbling with her roommate's boyfriend; Dori trying to scrape up money to have her dog treated for mange.

Dori's comics are littered with dead cig-butts and toppled wine-bottles. She was, in a classic nutshell, Wild, Zany and Self-Destructive. In 1988 Dori was in a car-wreck which cracked her pelvis and collarbone. She was laid-up, bored, and in pain. To kill time, she drank and smoked and took painkillers.

She caught the flu. She had friends who loved her, but nobody realized how badly off she was; probably she didn't know herself. She just went down hard, and couldn't get up alone. On February 26 her heart stopped. She was thirty-six.

So enough "true facts." Now for some comforting lies.

As it happens, even while a malignant cloud of flu virus was lying in wait for the warm hospitable lungs of Lester Bangs, the Fate, Atropos, she who weaves the things that are to be, accidentally dropped a stitch. Knit one? Purl two? What the hell does it matter, anyway? It's just human lives, right?

So, Lester, instead of inhaling a cloud of invisible contagion from the exhalations of a passing junkie, is almost hit by a Yellow Cab. This mishap on the way back from the deli shocks Lester out of his dogmatic slumbers. High time, Lester concludes, to get out of this burg and down to sunny old Mexico. He's gonna tackle his great American novel: *All My Friends Are Hermits*.

So true. None of Lester's groovy friends go out much anymore. Always ahead of their time, Lester's Bohemian cadre are no longer rock and roll animals. They still wear black leather jackets, they still stay up all night, they still hate Ronald Reagan with fantastic virulence; but they never leave home. They pursue an unnamed lifestyle that sociologist Faith Popcorn (and how can you doubt anyone with a name like *Faith Popcorn*)—will describe years later as "cocooning."

Lester has eight zillion rock, blues and jazz albums, crammed into his grubby NYC apartment. Books are piled feet deep on every available surface: Wm. Burroughs, Hunter Thompson, Celine, Kerouac, Huysmans, Foucault, and dozens of unsold copies of *Blondie*, Lester's book-length band-bio.

More albums and singles come in the mail every day. People used to send Lester records in the forlorn hope that he would review them. But now it's simply a tradition. Lester has transformed himself into a countercultural info-sump. People send him vinyl just because he's *Lester Bangs*, man!

Still jittery from his thrilling brush with death, Lester looks over this lifetime of loot with a surge of Sartrean nausea. He resists the urge to raid the fridge for his last desperate can of Blatz Beer. Instead, Lester snorts some speed, and calls an airline to plan his Mexican *wanderjahr*. After screaming in confusion at the hopeless stupid bitch of a receptionist, he gets a ticket to San Francisco, best he can do on short notice. He packs in a frenzy and splits.

Next morning finds Lester exhausted and wired and on the wrong side of the continent. He's brought nothing with him but an Army duffel-bag with his Olympia portable, some typing paper, shirts, assorted vials of dope, and a paperback copy of *Moby Dick*, which he's always meant to get around to re-reading.

Lester takes a cab out of the airport. He tells the cabbie to drive nowhere, feeling a vague compulsion to soak up the local vibe. San Francisco reminds him of his *Rolling Stone* days, back before Wenner fired him for being nasty to rock-stars. Fuck Wenner, he thinks. Fuck this city that was almost Avalon for a few months in '67 and has been on greased skids to Hell ever since.

The hilly half-familiar streets creep and wriggle with memories, avatars, talismans. Decadence, man, a no-kidding *death of affect*. It all ties in for Lester, in a bilious mental stew: snuff movies, discos, the cold-blooded whine of synthesizers, Pet Rocks, S&M, mindfuck self-improvement cults, Winning Through Intimidation, every aspect of the invisible war slowly eating the soul of the world.

After an hour he stops the cab at random. He needs coffee, white sugar, human beings, maybe a cheese Danish. Lester glimpses himself in the cab's window as he turns to pay: a chunky jobless thirty-three-year-old in a biker jacket, speed-pale dissipated New York face, Fu Manchu mustache looking pasted-on. Running to fat, running for shelter—no excuses, Bangs! Lester hands the driver a big tip. Chew on that, pal—you just drove the next Oswald Spengler.

Lester staggers into the café. It's crowded and stinks of patchouli and clove. He sees two chainsmoking punkettes hanging out at a Formica table. CBGB's types, but with California suntans. The kind of women, Lester thinks, who sit cross-legged on the floor and won't fuck you but are perfectly willing to describe in detail their highly complex postexistential *weltanschauung*. Tall and skinny and crazy-looking and bad news. Exactly his type, really. Lester sits down at their table and gives them his big rubber grin.

"Been having fun?" Lester says.

They look at him like he's crazy, which he is, but he wangles their names out: "Dori" and "Krystine." Dori's wearing fishnet stockings, cowboy boots, a strapless second-hand bodice-hugger covered with peeling pink feathers. Her long brown hair's streaked blonde. Krystine's got a black knit tank-top and a leather skirt and a skull-tattoo on her stomach.

Dori and Krystine have never heard of "Lester Bangs." They don't read much. They're *artists*. They do cartoons. Underground comix. Lester's mildly interested. Manifestations of the trash aesthetic always strongly appeal to him. It seems so American, the *good* America that is: the righteous wild America of rootless European refuse picking up discarded pop-junk and making it shine like the Koh-i-noor. To make "comic books" into *Art*—what a hopeless fucking effort, worse than rock and roll and you don't even get heavy bread for it. Lester says as much, to see what they'll do.

Krystine wanders off for a refill. Dori, who is mildly weirded-out by this tubby red-eyed stranger with his loud

come-on, gives Lester her double-barreled brush-off.
Which consists of opening up this Windex-clear vision
into the Vent of Hell that is her daily life. Dori lights another Camel from the butt of the last, smiles at Lester
with her big gappy front teeth and says brightly:

"You like *dogs*, Lester? I have this dog, and he has
eczema and disgusting open sores all over his body, and
he smells *really* bad . . . I can't get friends to come over
because he likes to shove his nose right into their, you
know, *crotch* . . . and go *Snort! Snort!*"

"I want to scream with wild dog joy in the smoking
pit of a charnel house," Lester says.

Dori stares at him. "Did you make that up?"

"Yeah," Lester says. "Where were you when Elvis
died?"

"You taking a survey on it?" Dori says.

"No, I just wondered," Lester says. "There was talk
of having his corpse dug up, and the stomach analyzed.
For dope, y'know. Can you *imagine* that? I mean, the
thrill of sticking your hand and forearm into Elvis's rotted
guts and slopping around in the stomach lining and liver
and kidneys and coming up out of dead Elvis's innards
triumphantly clutching some crumbs off a few Percodans
and Desoxyns and 'ludes . . . and then this is the *real*
thrill, Dori: you pop these crumbled-up bits of pills into
your *own mouth* and bolt 'em down and get high on
drugs that not only has Elvis Presley, the King, gotten
high on, not the same brand mind you but the same *pills*,
all slimy with little bits of his innards, so you've actually
gotten to *eat* the King of Rock and Roll!"

"*Who* did you say you were?" Dori says. "A rock
journalist? I thought you were putting me on. 'Lester
Bangs,' that's a fucking weird name!"

Dori and Krystine have been up all night, dancing to
the heroin headbanger vibes of Darby Crash and the
Germs. Lester watches through hooded eyes: this Dori is
a woman over thirty, but she's got this wacky airhead

routine down smooth, the Big Shiny Fun of the American Pop Bohemia. "Fuck you for believing I'm this shallow." Beneath the skin of her Attitude he can sense a bracing skeleton of pure desperation. There is hollow fear and sadness in the marrow of her bones. He's been writing about a topic just like this lately.

They talk a while, about the city mostly, about their variant scenes. Sparring, but he's interested. Dori yawns with pretended disinterest and gets up to leave. Lester notes that Dori is taller than he is. It doesn't bother him. He gets her phone number.

Lester crashes in a Holiday Inn. Next day he leaves town. He spends a week in a flophouse in Tijuana with his Great American Novel, which sucks. Despondent and terrified, he writes himself little cheering notes: "Burroughs was almost fifty when he wrote *Nova Express*! Hey boy, you only thirty-three! Burnt-out! Washed-up! Finished! A bit of flotsam! And in that flotsam your salvation! In that one grain of wood. In that one bit of that irrelevance. If you can bring yourself to describe it . . ."

It's no good. He's fucked. He knows he is, too, he's been reading over his scrapbooks lately, those clippings of yellowing newsprint, thinking: it was all a box, man! *El Cajon!* You'd think: wow, a groovy youth-rebel Rock Writer, he can talk about *anything*, can't he? Sex, dope, violence, Mazola parties with teenage Indonesian groupies, Nancy Reagan publicly fucked by a herd of clapped-out bull walruses . . . but when you actually READ a bunch of Lester Bangs Rock Reviews in a row, the whole shebang has a delicate hermetic whiff, like so many eighteenth-century sonnets. It is to dance in chains; it is to see the whole world through a little chromed window of Silva-Thin 'shades . . .

Lester Bangs is nothing if not a consummate romantic. He is, after all, a man who *really no kidding believes* that Rock and Roll Could Change the World, and when he writes something which isn't an impromptu free lesson

on what's wrong with Western Culture and how it can't
survive without grabbing itself by the backbrain and turning itself inside-out, he feels like he's wasted a day. Now
Lester, fretfully abandoning his typewriter to stalk and
kill flophouse roaches, comes to realize that HE will have
to turn himself inside out. Grow, or die. Grow into something but he has no idea what. He feels beaten.

So Lester gets drunk. Starts with Tecate, works his
way up to tequila. He wakes up with a savage hangover.
Life seems hideous and utterly meaningless. He abandons
himself to senseless impulse. Or, in alternate terms, Lester
allows himself to follow the numinous artistic promptings
of his holy intuition. He returns to San Francisco and
calls Dori Seda.

Dori, in the meantime, has learned from friends that
there is indeed a rock journalist named "Lester Bangs"
who's actually kind of *famous*. He once appeared on
stage with the J. Geils Band "playing" his typewriter.
He's kind of a big deal, which probably accounts for his
being kind of an asshole. On a dare, Dori calls Lester
Bangs in New York, gets his answering machine, and recognizes the voice. It was him, all right. Through some
cosmic freak, she met Lester Bangs and he tried to pick
her up! No dice, though. More Lonely Nights, Dori!

Then Lester calls. He's back in town again. Dori's so
flustered she ends up being nicer to him on the phone
than she means to be.

She goes out with him. To rock clubs. Lester never
has to pay; he just mutters at people, and they let him in
and find him a table. Strangers rush up to gladhand
Lester and jostle around the table and pay court. Lester
finds the music mostly boring, and it's no pretense; he actually *is* bored, he's heard it all. He sits there sipping club
sodas and handing out these little chips of witty guru insight to these sleaze-ass Hollywood guys and bighaired
coke-whores in black Spandex. Like it was his *job*.

Dori can't believe he's going to all this trouble just to

jump her bones. It's not like he can't get women, or like
their own relationship is all that tremendously scintillat-
ing. Lester's whole set-up is alien. But it *is* kind of interesting, and doesn't demand much. All Dori has to do is
dress in her sluttiest Goodwill get-up, and be This Chick
With Lester. Dori likes being invisible, and watching people when they don't know she's looking. She can see in
their eyes that Lester's people wonder Who The Hell Is
She? Dori finds this really funny, and makes sketches of
his creepiest acquaintances on cocktail napkins. At night
she puts them in her sketchbooks and writes dialogue bal-
loons. It's all really good material.

Lester's also very funny, in a way. He's smart, not just
hustler-clever but scary-crazy smart, like he's sometimes
profound without knowing it or even *wanting* it. But
when he thinks he's being most amusing, is when he's actually the most incredibly depressing. It bothers her that
he doesn't drink around her; it's a bad sign. He knows almost nothing about art or drawing, he dresses like a jerk,
he dances like a trained bear. And she's fallen in love with
him and she knows he's going to break her goddamned
heart.

Lester has put his novel aside for the moment. Nothing new there; he's been working on it, in hopeless
spasms, for ten years. But now juggling this affair takes
all he's got.

Lester is terrified that this amazing woman is going to
go to pieces on him. He's seen enough of her work now
to recognize that she's possessed of some kind of genuine
demented genius. He can smell it; the vibe pours off her
like Everglades swamp-reek. Even in her frowsy houserobe and bunny slippers, hair a mess, no make-up, half-
asleep, he can see something there like Dresden china,
something fragile and precious. And the world seems like
a maelstrom of jungle hate, sinking into entropy or gear-
ing up for Armageddon, and what the hell can anybody
do? How can he be happy with her and not be punished

for it? How long can they break the rules before the Nova Police show?

But nothing horrible happens to them. They just go on living.

Then Lester blunders into a virulent cloud of Hollywood money. He's written a stupid and utterly commercial screenplay about the laff-a-minute fictional antics of a heavy-metal band, and without warning he gets eighty thousand dollars for it.

He's never had so much money in one piece before. He has, he realizes with dawning horror, sold out.

To mark the occasion Lester buys some freebase, six grams of crystal meth, and rents a big white Cadillac. He fast-talks Dori into joining him for a supernaturally cool Kerouac adventure into the Savage Heart of America, and they get in the car laughing like hyenas and take off for parts unknown.

Four days later they're in Kansas City. Lester's lying in the backseat in a jittery Hank Williams half-doze and Dori is driving. They have nothing to say, as they've been arguing viciously ever since Albuquerque.

Dori, white-knuckled, sinuses scorched with crank, loses it behind the wheel. Lester's slammed from the backseat and wakes up to find Dori knocked out and drizzling blood from a scalp wound. The Caddy's wrapped messily in the buckled ruins of a sidewalk mailbox.

Lester holds the resultant nightmare together for about two hours, which is long enough to flag down help and get Dori into a Kansas City trauma room.

He sits there, watching over her, convinced he's lost it, blown it; it's over, she'll hate him forever now. My God, she could have died! As soon as she comes to, he'll have to face her. The thought of this makes something buckle inside him. He flees the hospital in headlong panic.

He ends up in a sleazy little rock dive downtown where he jumps onto a table and picks a fight with the bouncer. After he's knocked down for the third time, he gets up screaming for the manager, how he's going to *ruin that motherfucker!* and the club's owner shows up, tired and red-faced and sweating. The owner, whose own tragedy must go mostly unexpressed here, is a fat white-haired cigar-chewing third-rater who attempted, and failed, to model his life on Elvis's Colonel Parker. He hates kids, he hates rock and roll, he hates the aggravation of smart-ass doped-up hippies screaming threats and pimping off the hard work of businessmen just trying to make a living.

He has Lester hauled to his office backstage and tells him all this. Toward the end, the owner's confused, almost plaintive, because he's never seen anyone as utterly, obviously, and desperately fucked-up as Lester Bangs, but who can still be coherent about it and use phrases like "rendered to the factor of machinehood" while mopping blood from his punched nose.

And Lester, trembling and red-eyed, tells him: fuck you Jack, I could run this jerkoff place, I could do everything you do blind drunk, and make this place a fucking *legend in American culture*, you booshwah sonofabitch.

Yeah punk if you had the money, the owner says.

I've *got* the money! Let's see your papers, you evil cracker bastard! In a few minutes Lester is the owner-to-be on a handshake and an earnest check.

Next day he brings Dori roses from the hospital shop downstairs. He sits next to the bed; they compare bruises, and Lester explains to her that he has just blown his fortune. They are now tied down and beaten in the cornshucking heart of America. There is only one possible action left to complete this situation.

Three days later they are married in Kansas City by a justice of the peace.

Needless to say marriage does not solve any of their problems. It's a minor big deal for a while, gets mentioned in rock-mag gossip columns; they get some tele-

grams from friends, and Dori's mom seems pretty glad
about it. They even get a nice note from Julie Burchill, the
Marxist Amazon from *New Musical Express* who has
quit the game to write for fashion mags, and her husband
Tony Parsons the proverbial "hip young gunslinger" who
now writes weird potboiler novels about racetrack gangsters. Tony & Julie seem to be making some kind of go of
it. Kinda inspirational.

For a while Dori calls herself Dori Seda-Bangs, like
her good friend Aline Komisky-Crumb, but after a while
she figures what's the use? and just calls herself Dori
Bangs which sounds pretty weird enough on its own.

Lester can't say he's really *happy* or anything, but he's
sure *busy*. He renames the club "Waxy's Travel Lounge"
for some reason known only to himself. The club loses
money quickly and consistently. After the first month
Lester stops playing Lou Reed's *Metal Machine Music* before sets, and that helps attendance some, but Waxy's is
still a club which books a lot of tiny weird college-circuit
acts that Albert Average just doesn't get yet. Pretty soon
they're broke again and living off Lester's reviews.

They'd be even worse off, except Dori does a series of
promo posters for Waxy's that are so amazing they draw
people in, even after they've been burned again and again
on weird-ass bands only Lester can listen to.

After a couple of years they're still together, only they
have shrieking crockery-throwing fights and once, when
he's been drinking, Lester wrenches her arm so badly
Dori's truly afraid it's broken. It isn't, luckily, but it's sure
no great kick being Mrs. Lester Bangs. Dori was always
afraid of this: that what he does is *work* and what she
does is *cute*. How many Great Women Artists are there
anyway, and what happened to 'em? They went into
patching the wounded ego and picking up the dropped
socks of Mr. Wonderful, that's what. No big mystery
about it.

And besides, she's thirty-six and still barely scraping

a living. She pedals her beat-up bike through the awful Kansas weather and sees these yuppies come by with these smarmy grins: hey, we don't *have* to invent our lives, our lives are *invented for us* and boy, does that ever save a lot of soul-searching.

But still somehow they blunder along; they have the occasional good break. Like when Lester turns over the club on Wednesdays to some black kids for (ecch!) "disco nite" and it turns out to be the beginning of a little Kansas City rap-scratch scene which actually makes the club some money. And "Polyrock," a band Lester hates at first but later champions to global megastardom, cuts a live album in Waxy's.

And Dori gets a contract to do one of those twenty-second animated logos for MTV, and really gets into it. It's fun, so she starts doing video animation work for (fairly) big bucks and even gets a Macintosh II from a video-hack admirer in Silicon Valley. Dori had always loathed, feared and despised *computers* but this thing is *different*. This is a kind of art that *nobody's ever done before* and has to be invented from leftovers, sweat, and thin air! It's wide open and 'way rad!

Lester's novel doesn't get anywhere, but he does write a book called *A Reasonable Guide to Horrible Noise* which becomes a hip coffeetable cult item with an admiring introduction by a trendy French semiotician. Among other things, this book introduces the term "chipster" which describes a kind of person who, well, didn't really *exist* before Lester described them but once he'd pointed 'em out it was *obvious to everybody*.

But they're still not *happy*. They both have a hard time taking the "marital fidelity" notion with anything like seriousness. They have a vicious fight once, over who gave who herpes, and Dori splits for six months and goes back to California. Where she looks up her old girlfriends and finds the survivors married with kids, and her old boyfriends are even seedier and more pathetic than Lester.

What the hell, it's not happiness but it's something. She goes back to Lester. He's gratifyingly humble and appreciative for almost six weeks.

Waxy's does in fact become a cultural legend of sorts, but they don't pay you for that; and anyway it's hell to own a bar while attending sessions of Alcoholics Anonymous. So Lester gives in, and sells the club. He and Dori buy a house, which turns out to be far more hassle than it's worth, and then they go to Paris for a while, where they argue bitterly and squander all their remaining money.

When they come back Lester gets, of all the awful things, an academic gig. For a Kansas state college. Lester teaches Rock and Popular Culture. In the '70s there'd have been no room for such a hopeless skidrow weirdo in a, like, Serious Academic Environment, but it's the late '90s by now, and Lester has outlived the era of outlawhood. Because who are we kidding? Rock and Roll is a satellite-driven worldwide information-industry which is worth billions and *billions*, and if they don't study *major industries* then what the hell are the taxpayers funding colleges for?

Self-destruction is awfully tiring. After a while, they just give it up. They've lost the energy to flame-out, and it hurts too much; besides, it's less trouble just to live. They eat balanced meals, go to bed early, and attend faculty parties where Lester argues violently about the parking privileges.

Just after the turn of the century, Lester finally gets his novel published, but it seems quaint and dated, and gets panned and quickly remaindered. It would be nice to say that Lester's book was discovered years later as a Klassic of Litratchur but the truth is that Lester's no novelist; what he is, is a cultural mutant, and what he has in the way of insight and energy has been eaten up. Subsumed by the Beast, man. What he thought and said made some kind of difference, but nowhere near as big a difference as he'd dreamed.

In the year 2015, Lester dies of a heart attack while shoveling snow off his lawn. Dori has him cremated, in one of those plasma-flash cremators that are all the mode in the 21st-cent. undertaking business. There's a nice respectful retrospective on Lester in the *New York Times Review of Books*, but the truth is Lester's pretty much a forgotten man; a colorful footnote for cultural historians who can see the twentieth century with the unflattering advantage of hindsight.

A year after Lester's death they demolish the remnants of Waxy's Travel Lounge to make room for a giant high-rise. Dori goes out to see the ruins. As she wanders amid the shockingly staid and unromantic rubble, there's another of those slips in the fabric of Fate, and Dori is approached by a Vision.

Thomas Hardy used to call it the Immanent Will and in China it might have been the Tao, but we late 20th-cent. postmoderns would probably call it something soothingly pseudoscientific like the "genetic imperative." Dori, being Dori, recognizes this glowing androgynous figure as The Child They Never Had.

"Don't worry, Mrs. Bangs," the Child tells her, "I might have died young of some ghastly disease, or grown up to shoot the President and break your heart, and anyhow you two woulda been no prize as parents." Dori can see herself and Lester in this Child, there's a definite nacreous gleam in its right eye that's Lester's, and the sharp quiet left eye is hers; but behind the eyes where there should be a living breathing human being there's *nothing*, just a kind of chill galactic twinkling.

"And don't feel guilty for outliving him either," the Child tells her, "because you're going to have what we laughingly call a natural death, which means you're going to die in the company of strangers hooked up to tubes when you're old and helpless."

"But did it *mean* anything?" Dori says.

"If you mean were you Immortal Artists leaving indelible graffiti in the concrete sidewalk of Time, no. You never walked the Earth as Gods, you were just people. But it's better to have a real life than no life." The Child shrugs. "You weren't all that happy together, but you *did* suit each other, and if you'd married other people instead, there would have been *four* people unhappy. So here's your consolation: you helped each other."

"So?" Dori says.

"So that's enough. Just to shelter each other, and help each other up. Everything else is gravy. Someday, no matter what, you go down forever. Art can't make you immortal. Art can't Change the World. Art can't even heal your soul. All it can do is maybe ease the pain a bit or make you feel more awake. And that's enough. It only matters as much as it matters, which is zilch to an ice-cold interstellar Cosmic Principle like yours truly. But if you try to live by my standards it will only kill you faster. By your own standards, you did pretty good, really."

"Well okay then," Dori says.

After this purportedly earth-shattering mystical encounter, her life simply went on, day following day, just like always. Dori gave up computer-art; it was too hairy trying to keep up with the hotshot high-tech cutting edge, and kind of undignified, when you came right down to it. Better to leave that to hungry kids. She was idle for a while, feeling quiet inside, but finally she took up watercolors. For a while Dori played the Crazy Old Lady Artist and was kind of a mainstay of the Kansas regionalist art scene. Granted, Dori was no Georgia O'Keeffe, but she was working, and living, and she touched a few people's lives.

Or, at least, Dori surely would have touched those people, if she'd been there to do it. But of course she wasn't, and didn't. Dori Seda never met Lester Bangs. Two simple real-life acts of human caring, at the proper moment, might have saved them both; but when those moments came, they had no one, not even each other. And so they went down into darkness, like skaters, breaking through the hard bright shiny surface of our true-facts world.

Today I made this white paper dream to cover the holes they left.

ABOUT THE AUTHOR

Bruce Sterling was born in 1954 in Brownsville, Texas. His grandfather was a rancher, his father an engineer. Sterling, purportedly a novelist by trade, actually spends most of his time aimlessly messing with computers, modems, and fax machines. He and his wife Nancy have a daughter Amy, born in 1987. They live in Austin.

Sterling sold his first science fiction story in 1976. His solo novels include *Involution Ocean* (1977), *The Artificial Kid* (1980), *Schismatrix* (1985), and *Islands in the Net* (1988). In 1986 he edited *Mirrorshades: the Cyberpunk Anthology*. His first collection of short stories was *Crystal Express* (1989). In 1990 he and William Gibson published their collaborative novel *The Difference Engine*.

1992 saw the appearance of Sterling's first nonfiction book, *The Hacker Crackdown: Law and Disorder on the Electronic Frontier*, a work of investigative journalism exploring issues in computer-crime and civil liberties. Sterling maintains a long-term interest in electronic user rights and free-expression; his Internet address is: bruces @ well.sf.ca.us. Other nonfiction work by Sterling has appeared in *The New York Times*, *Newsday*, *Whole Earth Review*, *Details*, *Mondo 2000*, *bOING bOING*, and *Wired*.

He has also written SF criticism for *Science Fiction Eye* and *Monad*, and regular columns for *Interzone* and *The Magazine of Fantasy and Science Fiction*. He has been a member of the Science Fiction and Fantasy Writers of America ever since Salman Rushdie was condemned by religious fanatics.

Turn the page for a special preview of
HEAVY WEATHER
by Bruce Sterling

Bruce Sterling's long-awaited new novel is set forty years from now, with Earth's climate drastically changed by the greenhouse effect. Tornadoes of almost unimaginable force roam the open spaces of Texas like huge, howling predators. And on their trail are the Storm Troupers: a ragtag band of computer experts, atmospheric scientists and outright revolutionaries who live to hack heavy weather—to document it and spread the information as far as the digital networks will stretch. Here is a special preview of *Heavy Weather*'s opening scene, set in a black-market medical clinic in the near future.

HEAVY WEATHER, available now in hardcover wherever Bantam Books are sold.

Smart machines lurked about the suite, their power lights in the shuttered dimness like the small red eyes of bats. The machines crouched in niches in white walls of Mexican stucco: an ionizer, a television, a smoke alarm, a squad of motion sensors. A vaporizer hissed and bubbled gently in the corner, emitting a potent reek of oil, ginseng, and eucalyptus.

Alex lay propped on silk-cased pillows, his feet and knees denting the starched cotton sheets. His flesh felt like wet clay, something greased and damp and utterly inert. Since morning he had been huffing at the black neoprene mask of his bedside inhaler, and now his fingertips, gone pale as wax and lightly trembling, seemed to be melting into the mask. Alex thought briefly of hanging the mask from its stainless-steel hook at the bedside medical rack. He rejected the idea. It was too much of a hassle to have the tasty mask out of reach.

The pain in his lungs and throat had not really gone away. Such a miracle was perhaps too much to ask, even of a Mexican black-market medical clinic. Nevertheless, after two weeks of treatment in the *clínica*, his pain had assumed a new subtlety. The scorched inflammation had dwindled to an interestingly novel feeling, something thin and rather theoretical.

The suite was as chilly as a fishbowl and Alex felt as cozy and as torpid as a carp. He lay collapsed in semidarkness, eyes blinking grainily, as a deeper texture of his illness languorously revealed itself. Beneath his starched sheets, Alex began to feel warm. Then light-headed. Then slightly nauseous, a customary progression of symptoms. He felt the dark rush build within his chest.

Then it poured through him. He felt his spine melting. He seemed to percolate into the mattress.

These spells had been coming more often lately, and with more power behind them. On the other hand, their dark currents were taking Alex into some interesting places. Alex, not breathing, swam along pleasantly under the rim of unconsciousness for a long moment.

Then, without his will, breath came again. His mind broke delirium's surface. When his eyes reopened, the suite around him seemed intensely surreal. Crawling walls of white stucco, swirling white stucco ceiling, thick wormy carpet of chemical aqua blue. Bulbous pottery lamps squatted unlit on elaborate wicker tables. The chest of drawers, and the bureau, the wooden bedframe, were all marked with the same creepy conspiracy of aqua-blue octagons. . . . Iron-hinged wooden shutters guarded the putty-sealed windows. A dying tropical houseplant, the gaunt rubber-leafed monster that had become his most faithful companion here, stood in its terra-cotta pot, gently poisoned by the constant darkness, and the medicated vaporous damp. . . .

A sharp buzz sounded alongside his bed. Alex twisted his matted head on the pillow. The machine buzzed again. Then, yet again.

Alex realized with vague surprise that the machine was a telephone. He had never received any calls on the telephone in his suite. He did not even know that he had one. The elderly, humble machine had been sitting there among its fellow machines, much overshadowed.

Alex examined the phone's antique, poorly designed push-button interface for a long groggy moment. The phone buzzed again, insistently. He dropped the inhaler mask and leaned across the bed, with a twist, and a rustle, and a pop, and a groan. He pressed the tiny button denominated *ESPKR*.

"*Hola,*" he puffed. His gummy larynx crackled and shrieked, bringing sudden tears to his eyes.

"*¿Quien es?*" the phone replied.

"Nobody," Alex rasped in English. "Get lost." He wiped at one eye and glared at the phone. He had no idea how to hang up.

"Alex!" the phone said in English. "Is that you?"

Alex blinked. Blood was rushing through his numbed flesh. Beneath the sheet, his calves and toes began to tingle resentfully.

"I want to speak to Alex Unger!" the phone insisted sharply. "*¿Dónde está?*"

"Who is this?" Alex said.

"It's Jane! Juanita Unger, your sister!"

"Janey?" Alex said, stunned. "Gosh, is this Christmas? I'm sorry, Janey. . . ."

"What!" the phone shouted. "It's *May the ninth*! Jesus, you sound really trashed!"

"Hey . . ." Alex said weakly. He'd never known his sister to phone him up, except at Christmas. There was an ominous silence. Alex blearily studied the cryptic buttons on the speakerphone. *RDIAL, FLAS, PROGMA.* No clue how to hang up. The open phone line sat there eavesdropping on him, a torment demanding response. "I'm okay," he protested at last. "How're you, Janey?"

"Do you even know what *year* this is?" the phone demanded. "Or where you *are*?"

"Umm . . . Sure . . ." Vague guilty panic penetrated his medicated haze. Getting along with his older sister had never been Alex's strong suit even in the best of times, and now he felt far too weak and dazed to defend himself. "Janey, I'm not up for this right now. . . . Lemme call you back. . . ."

"Don't you dare hang up on me, you little weasel!" the phone shrieked. "What the hell are they doing to you in there? Do you have any idea what these *bills* look like?"

"They're helping me here," Alex said. "I'm in treatment. . . . Go away."

"They're a bunch of con-artist quacks! They'll take you for every cent you have! And then kill you! And bury you in some goddamned toxic waste dump on the border!"

Juanita's shrill assaultive words swarmed through his head like hornets. Alex slumped back into his pillow heap and gazed at the slowly turning ceiling fan, trying to gather his strength. "How'd you find me here?"

"It wasn't easy, that's for sure!"

Alex grunted. "Good . . ."

"And getting this phone line was no picnic either!"

Alex drew a slow deep breath, relaxed, exhaled. Something viscous gurgled nastily, deep within him.

"Goddamn it, Alex! You just can't do this! I spent three weeks tracking you down! Even Dad's people couldn't track you down this time."

"Well, yeah," Alex muttered. "That's why I did it that way."

When his sister spoke again, her voice was full of grim resolve. "Get packed, Alejandro. You're getting out of there."

"Don't bother me. Let me be."

"I'm your *sister*! Dad's written you off—don't you get that yet? You're grown up now, and you've hurt him too many times. I'm the only one left who cares."

"Don't be so stupid," Alex croaked wearily. "Take it easy."

"I know where you are. And I'm coming to get you. And anybody who tries to stop me—you included—is gonna regret it a lot!"

"You can't do anything," Alex told her. "I signed all the clinic papers . . . they've got lawyers." He cleared his throat, with a long rasping ache. Returning to full alertness was far from pleasant; variant parts of his carcass—upper spine, ankles, sinuses, diaphragm—registered sharp aching protests and a deep reluctance to function. "I want to sleep," he said. "I came here to rest."

"You can't kid me, Alejandro! If you want to drop

dead, then go ahead! But don't blow family money on that pack of thieves."

"You're always so goddamned stubborn," Alex said. "You've gone and woke me up now, and I feel like hell!" He sat up straight. "It's my money, and it's my life! I'll do whatever I want with it! Go back to art school." He reached across the bed, grabbed the phone lead, and yanked it free, snapping its plastic clip.

Alex picked the dead phone up, examined it, then stuffed it securely under the pillows. His throat hurt. He reached back to the bedside table, dipped his fingers into a tray of hammered Mexican silver, and came up with a narcotic lozenge. He unwrapped it and crunched it sweetly between his molars.

Sleep was far away now. His mind was working again, and required numbing. Alex slid out of the bed onto his hands and knees and searched around on the thick, plush, ugly carpet. His head swam and pounded with the effort. Alex persisted, being used to this.

The TV's remote control, with the foxlike cunning of all important inanimate objects, had gone to earth in a collapsing heap of Mexican true-crime *fotonovelas*. Alex noted that his bed's iron springs, after three weeks of constant humidity, were gently but thoroughly going to rust.

Alex rose to his knees, clutching his prize, and slid with arthritic languor beneath the sheets again. He caught his breath, blew his nose, neatly placed two cold drops of medicated saline against the surface of each eyeball, then began combing the clinic's cable service with minimal twitches of his thumb. Weepy Mexican melodramas. A word-game show. Kids chasing robot dinosaurs in some massive underground mall. The ever-present Thai pop music.

And some English-language happytalk news. Spanish happytalk news. Japanese happytalk news. Alex, born in 2010, had watched the news grow steadily more glossy and cheerful for all of his twenty-one years. As a mere tot, he'd witnessed hundreds of hours of raw bloodstained footage: plagues, mass death, desperate riot, ghastly military wreckage, all against a panicky backdrop of ominous and unrelenting environmental decline. All that stuff was still out there, just as every aspect of modern reality had its mirrored shadow in the Net somewhere, but nowadays you had to hunt hard to find it, and the people discussing it didn't seem to have much in the way of budgets. Somewhere along the line, the entire global village had slipped into neurotic denial.

Today, as an adult, Alex found the glass pipelines of the Net chockablock with jet-set glamour weddings and cute dog stories. Perky heroines and square-jawed heroes were still, somehow, getting rich quick. Starlets won lotteries and lottery winners became starlets. Little children, with their heads sealed in virtuality helmets, mimed delighted surprise as they waved their tiny gloved hands at enormous hallucinations. Alex had never been that big a fan of current events anyway, but he had now come to feel that the world's cheerful shiny-toothed bullshitters were the primal source of all true evil.

Alex collided and stuck in a Mexican docudrama about UFOs; they were known as *los OVNIS* in Spanish, and on 9 de mayo, 2031, a large fraction of the Latin American populace seemed afflicted with spectacular attacks of *ovnimanía*. Long minutes of Alex's life seeped idly away as the screen pumped images at him: monster fireballs by night, puffball-headed dwarfs in jumpsuits of silver lamé, and a video prophecy from some interstellar Virgen de Guadalupe with her own Internet address and a toll-free phone number . . . .

The day nurse tapped at the door and bustled in. The day nurse was named Concepción. She was a hefty, no-nonsense, fortyish individual with a taste for liposuction, face-lifts, and breast augmentation.

"*¿Ya le hicieron la prueba de la sangre?*" she said.

Alex turned off the television. "The blood test? Yeah, I had one this morning."

"*¿Le duele todavía el pecho como anoche?*"

"Pretty bad last night," Alex admitted. "Lots better, though, since I started using the mask."

"*Un catarro atroz, complicado con una alergia,*" Concepción sympathized.

"No problem with pain, at least," Alex said. "I'm getting the best of treatment."

Concepción sighed and gestured him up. *"Todavía no acabamos, muchacho, le falta la enema de los pulmones."*

"A *lung* enema?" Alex said, puzzled.

"Sí."

"Today? Right now? *¿Ahora?*"

She nodded.

"Do I have to?"

Concepción looked stern. *"¡El doctor Mirabi le recetó! Fue muy claro. 'Cuidado con una pulmonía.' El nuevo tipo de pulmonía es peor que el SIDA, han muerto ya centenares de personas."*

"Okay, okay," Alex said. "Sure, no problem. I'm doing lots better lately, though. I don't even need the chair."

Concepción nodded and helped him out of bed, shoving her solid shoulder under his armpit. The two of them made it out the door of the suite and a good ten meters down the carpeted hall before Alex's knees buckled. The wheelchair, a machine of limited but highly specialized intelligence, was right behind Alex as he stumbled. He gave up the struggle gracefully and sat within the chrome-and-leather machine.

Concepción left Alex in the treatment room to wait for Dr. Mirabi. Alex was quite sure that Dr. Mirabi was doing nothing of consequence. Having Alex wait alone in a closed room was simply medical etiquette, a way to establish whose time was more important. Though Dr. Mirabi's employees were kept on the hustle—especially the hardworking retail pharmacists—Dr. Mirabi himself hardly seemed oppressed by his duties. As far as Alex could deduce from the staff schedules, there were only four long-term patients in the whole *clínica*. Alex was pretty sure that most of the *clínica's* income came from yanquis on day trips down from Laredo. Before he himself had checked in last April, he'd seen a line of Americans halfway down the block, eagerly picking up Mexican megadosage nostrums for the new ultraresistant strains of TB.

Dr. Mirabi's treatment room was long and rectangular and full of tall canvas-shrouded machinery. Like every place else in the *clínica*, it was air-conditioned to a deathly chill, and smelled of sharp and potent disinfectant. Alex wished that he had thought to snag a *fotonovela* on the way out of his room. Alex pretended distaste for the *novelas'* clumsy and violence-soaked porn, but their comically distorted gutter-level Spanish was of a lot of philological interest.

Concepción opened the door and stepped in. Behind her, Dr. Mirabi arrived, his ever-present notepad in hand. Despite his vaguely Islamic surname, Alex suspected strongly that Dr. Mirabi was, in fact, Hungarian.

Dr. Mirabi tapped the glass face of his notepad with a neat black stylus and examined the result. "Well, Alex," he said briskly in accented English, "we seem to have defeated that dirty streptococcus once for all."

"That's right," Alex said. "Haven't had a night sweat in ages."

"That's quite a good step, quite good," Dr. Mirabi encouraged. "Of course, that infection was only the crisis symptom of your syndrome. The next stage of your cure"—he examined the notepad—"is the chronic mucus congestion! We must deal with that chronic mucus, Alex. It might have been protective mucus at first, but now is your metabolic burden. Once the chronic mucus is gone, and the tubercles are entirely cleansed—cleaned . . ." He paused. "Is it 'cleaned,' or 'cleansed'?"

"Either one works," Alex said.

"Thank you," the doctor said. "Once the chronic mucus is scrubbed away from the lung surfaces, then we can treat the membranes directly. There is membrane damage in your lungs, of course, deep cellular damage, but we cannot get to the damaged surfaces until the mucus is removed." He looked at Alex seriously, over his glasses. "Your chronic mucus is full of many contaminations, you know! Years of bad gases and particles you have inhaled. Environmental pollutions, allergic pollens, smoke particles, virus and bacteria. They have all adhered to the chronic mucus. When your lungs are scrubbed clean with the enema, the lungs will be as the lungs of a newborn child!" He smiled.

Alex nodded silently.

"It won't be pleasant at first, but afterward you will feel quite lovely."

"Do you have to knock me out again?" Alex said.

"No, Alex. It's important that you breathe properly during the procedure. The detergent has to reach the very bottom of the lungs. You understand?" He paused, tapping his notepad. "Are you a good swimmer, Alex?"

"No," Alex said.

"Then you know that sensation when you swallow water down the wrong pipe," said the doctor, nodding triumphantly. "That choking reflex. You see, Alex, the reason Mother Nature makes you choke on water, is because there is no proper oxygen in water for your lungs. The enema liquid, though, which will be filling your lungs, is not water, Alex. It is a dense silicone fluid. It carries much oxygen dissolved inside it, plenty of oxygen." Dr. Mirabi chuckled. "If you lie still without breathing, you can live half a hour on the oxygen in a single lungful of enema fluid! It has so much oxygen that at first you will feel hyperventilated."

"I have to inhale this stuff somehow, is that it?"

"Not quite. It's too dense to be inhaled. In any case, we don't want it to enter your sinuses." He frowned. "We have to decant the fluid into your lungs, gently."

"I see."

"We fit a thin tube through your mouth and down past the epiglottis. The end of the tube will have a local anesthetic, so you should not feel the pain in the epiglottis very long. . . . You must remain quite still during the procedure, try to relax fully, and breathe only on my order."

Alex nodded.

"The sensations are very unusual, but they are not dangerous. You must make up your mind to accept the procedure. If you choke up the fluid, then we have to begin again."

"Doctor," Alex said, "you don't have to go on persuading me. I'm not afraid. You can trust me. I don't stop. I never stop. If I stopped at things, I wouldn't be here now, would I?"

"There will be some discomfort."

"That's not new. I'm not afraid of that, either."

"Very well, Alex." Dr. Mirabi patted Alex's shoulder.

"Then we will begin. Take your place on the manipulation table, please."

Concepción helped Alex to lie on the jointed leather table. She touched her foot to a floor pedal. A worm gear whined beneath the floor. The table bent at Alex's hips and rose beneath his back, to a sharp angle. Alex coughed twice.

Dr. Mirabi drew on a pair of translucent gloves, deftly unwrapped one of his canvas-bound machines, and busied himself at the switches. He opened a cabinet, retrieved a pair of matched, bright yellow aerosol tanks, and inserted both tanks into sockets at the top of the machine. He attached clear plastic tubing to the taps on the tanks and opened both the taps, with brief pneumatic hisses. The machine hummed and sizzled a bit and gave off a hot waft of electrical resistance.

"We will set the liquid to blood heat," Dr. Mirabi explained. "That way there is no thermal shock to the tubercles. Also heat will dissolve the chronic mucus more effectively. Efficiently? Is it 'efficiently' or 'effectively'?"

"They're synonyms," Alex said. "Do you think I might throw up? These are my favorite pajamas."

Concepción stripped the pajamas off, then wrapped him briskly in a paper medical gown. She strapped him against the table with a pair of fabric belts. Dr. Mirabi approached him with the soft plastic nozzle of the insert, smeared with a pink paste. "Open widely, don't taste the anesthetic," he warned. Alex nevertheless got a generous smear of the paste against the root of his tongue, which immediately went as numb as a severed beef tongue on a butcher's block.

The nozzle slid its way down a narrow road of pain along his throat. Alex felt the fleshy valve within his chest leap and flap as the tube touched and penetrated. Then the numbness struck, and a great core of meat behind his heart simply lost sensation, went into nothingness, like a core mechanically punched from an apple.

His eyes filled with tears. He heard more than saw, Dr. Mirabi touching taps. Then the heat came.

He'd never known that blood was so hot. The fluid was hotter than blood, and much, much heavier, like fizzing, creamy, molten lead. He could see the fluid moving into him through the tube. It was chemical-colored, aqua blue. "Breathe!" Dr. Mirabi shouted.

Alex heaved for air. A bizarre reverberating belch tore free from the back of his throat, something like the cry of a monster bullfrog. For an instant he tried to laugh; his diaphragm heaved futilely at the liquid weight within him, and went still.

"El niño tiene un bulto en la garganta," said Concepción, conversationally. She placed her latex-gloved hand against his forehead. *"Muy doloroso."*

"Poco a poco," Dr. Mirabi said, gesturing. The worm gear rustled beneath the table and Alex rose in place, liquid shifting within him with the gut-bulging inertia of a nine-course meal. Air popped in bursts from his clamped lips and a hot gummy froth rose against his upper palate.

"Good," said Dr. Mirabi. "Breathe!"

Alex tried again, his eyes bulging. His spine popped audibly and he felt another pair of great loathsome bubbles come up, stinking ancient bubbles like something from the bottom of LaBrea.

Then suddenly the oxygen hit his brain. An orgasmic blush ran up his neck, his cheeks. For a supreme moment he forgot what it was to be sick. He felt lovely. He felt free. He felt without constraint. He felt pretty sure that he was about to die.

He tried to speak, to babble something—gratitude perhaps, or last words, or an eager yell for more—but there was only silence. His lungs were like two casts of plaster and bone-meal, each filled to brimming with hot liquid rubber. His muscles heaved against the taut liquid bags like two fists clenching two tennis balls, and his ears roared, and things went black. Suddenly he could hear his heart straining to beat, *thud-thud, thud-thud*, each concussive shock of the ventricles passing through his liquid-filled lungs with booming subaqueous clarity.

And then the beat stopped too.

ON THE EVENING of May 10, Jane Unger made a reconnaissance of her target, on the pretext of buying heroin. She spent half an hour in line outside the clinic with desolate, wheezing Yankees from over the border. The customers lined outside the clinic were the seediest, creepiest, most desperate people she'd ever seen who were not actual criminals. Jane was familiar with the look of actual criminals, because the vast network of former Texas prisons had been emptied of felons and retrofitted as medical quarantine centers and emergency weather shelters. The former inhabitants of the Texas gulag, the actual criminals, were confined by software nowadays. Convicted criminals, in their tamper-proof parole cuffs, couldn't make it down to Nuevo Laredo, because they'd be marooned on the far side of the Rio Grande by their government tracking software. Nobody in the clinic line wore a parole cuff. But they were clearly the kind of people who had many good friends wearing them.

All of the American customers, without exception, wore sinister breathing masks. Presumably to avoid contracting an infection. Or to avoid spreading an infection that they already had. Or probably just to conceal their identities while they bought drugs.

The older customers wore plain ribbed breathing masks in antiseptic medical white. The younger folks were into elaborate knobby strap-ons with vivid designer colors.

The line of Americans snaked along steadily, helped by the presence of a pair of Mexican cops, who kept the local street hustlers off the backs of the paying clientele. Jane patiently made her way up the clinic steps, through the double doors, and to the barred and bulletproof glass of the pharmacy windows.

There Jane discovered that the clinic didn't sell any "brown Mexican heroin." Apparently they had no "heroin" at all in stock, there being little demand for this legendary substance among people with respiratory illnesses.

Jane slid a private-currency card through the slit beneath the window. The pharmacist swiped Jane's card through a reader, studied the results on the network link, and began to show real interest. Jane was politely abstracted from the line and introduced to the pharmacist's superior, who escorted her up to his office. There he showed her a vial of a more modern analgesic, a designer endorphin a thousand times more potent than morphine. Jane turned down his offer of a free trial injection.

When Jane haltingly brought up the subject of bribery, the supervisor's face clouded. He called a big private-security thug, and Jane was shown out the clinic's back entrance, and told not to return.

Keep It Simple, Stupid. The famous KISS acronym had always been Jane's favorite design principle. If you need access, keep it simple. Bribing the staff of the clinic sounded like the simplest solution to her problem. But it wasn't.

At least one of the staff seemed happy enough to take her bribe money. Over a long-distance phone line from Texas, Jane had managed to subvert the clinic's receptionist. The receptionist was delighted to take Jane's electronic funds in exchange for ten minutes' free run on the clinic's internal phone system.

And accessing the clinic's floor plans had been pretty simple too; they'd turned out to be Mexican public records. It had been useful, too, to sneak into the building under the simple pretext of a drug buy. That had confirmed Jane's ideas of the clinic's internal layout.

Nothing about Alex was ever simple, though. Having talked to her brother on the phone, Jane now knew that Alex, who should have been her ally inside the enemy gates, was, as usual, worse than useless.

Carol and Greg—Jane's favorite confidants within the Storm Troupe—had urged her to stay as simple as possible. Forget any romantic ninja break-and-enter muscle stuff. That kind of stunt hardly ever worked, even when the U.S. Army tried it. It was smarter just to show up in Nuevo Laredo in person, whip out a nicely untraceable electronic debit card, and tell the night guard that it was Alejandro Unger out the door, or *No hay dinero.* Chances were that the guard would spring Alex in exchange for, say, three months' salary, local rates. Everybody could pretend later that the kid had escaped the building under his own power. That scheme was nice and straightforward. It was pretty hard to prosecute criminally.

And if it ended up in a complete collapse and debacle and embarrassment, then it would look a lot better, later.

By stark contrast, breaking into a Mexican black-market clinic and kidnapping a patient was the sort of overly complex maneuver that almost never looked better later.

There'd been a time in Jane Unger's life when she'd cared a lot about "later." But that time was gone, and "later" had lost all its charm. She had traveled twelve hundred kilometers in a day, and now she was on foot, alone, in a dark alley at night in a foreign country, preparing to assault a hospital single-handed. And unless they caught her on the spot, she was pretty sure that she was going to get away with it.

This was an area of Nuevo Laredo the locals aptly called "Salsipuedes," or "Leave-if-you-can." Besides Alex's slick but modest clinic, it had two other thriving private hospitals stuffed with gullible gringos, as well as a monster public hospital, a big septic killing zone very poorly managed by the remains of the Mexican government. Jane watched a beat-up robot truck rumble past, marked with a peeling red cross. Then she watched her hands trembling. Her unpainted fingertips were ivory pale and full of nervous jitter. Just like the jitter she had before a storm chase. Jane was glad to see that jitter, the fear and the energy racing along her nerves. She knew that the jitter would melt off like dry ice once the action started. She had learned that about herself in the past year. It was a good thing to know.

Jane made a final check of her equipment. Glue gun, jigsaw, penlight, cellular phone, ceramic crowbar—all hooked and holstered to her webbing belt, hidden inside her baggy paper refugee suit. Equipment check was a calming ritual. She zipped the paper suit up to the neck, over her denim shorts and cotton T-shirt. She strapped on a plain white antiseptic mask.

Then she cut off the clinic's electrical power.

Thermite sizzled briefly on the power pole overhead, and half the city block went dark. Jane swore briefly inside her mask. Clearly there had been some changes made lately in the Nuevo Laredo municipal power grid. Jane Unger's first terrorist structure hit had turned out to be less than surgical.

"Not my fault," she muttered. Mexican power engineers were always hacking around; and people stole city power, too, all kinds of illegal network linkups around here. . . . They called the hookups *diablitos*, "little devils," another pretty apt name, considering that the world was well on its way to hell. . . . Anyway, it wouldn't kill them to repair one little outage.

Greg's thermite bomb had really worked. Every other week or so, Greg would drop macho hints about his military background doing structure hits. Jane had never quite believed him, before this.

Jane tied a pair of paper decontamination covers over her trail boots. She cinched and knotted the boot covers tightly at the ankles, then ghosted across the blacked-out street, puddles gleaming damply underfoot. She stepped up three stone stairs, entered the now pitch-black alcove at the clinic's rear exit, and checked the street behind her. No cars, no people, no visible witnesses. . . . Jane pulled a translucent rain hood over her head, cinched and knotted it. Then she peeled open a paper pack and pulled on a pair of tough plastic surgical gloves.

She slapped the steel doorframe with the flat of her hand.

The clinic's door opened with a shudder.

Jane had structure-hit the door earlier, on her way out of the clinic. She'd distracted her security escort for two vital seconds and craftily jammed the exit's elaborate keypad lock with a quick, secret gush of glue. Jane had palmed the aerosol glue can, a tiny thing not much bigger than a shotgun cartridge. Glue spray was one of Carol's favorite tricks, something Carol had taught her. Carol could do things with glue spray that were halfway to witchcraft.

Despite the power outage, the door's keypad lock was still alive on its battery backup—but the door mistakenly thought it was working. Smart machines were smart enough to make some really dumb blunders.

Only once in a great while does a writer come along who defies comparison—a writer so original he redefines the way we look at the world. Neal Stephenson is such a writer and *Snow Crash* is such a novel, weaving virtual reality, Sumerian myth, and just about everything in between with a cool, hip cybersensibility to bring us the gigathriller of the information age.

SNOW CRASH

NEAL STEPHENSON

"A cross between *Neuromancer* and Thomas Pinchon's *Vineland*. This is no mere hyperbole."
—*San Francisco Bay Guardian*

"Fast-forward free-style mall mythology for the 21st century."—*Wiliam Gibson*

"Brilliantly realized...Stephenson turns out to be an engaging guide to an onrushing tomorrow."
—*New York Times Book Review*